From the reviews for *T*

www.penguin.co.uk

Also by Nick Bradley

The Cat and The City

FOUR SEASONS IN JAPAN

NICK BRADLEY

PENGUIN BOOKS

TRANSWORLD PUBLISHERS
Penguin Random House, One Embassy Gardens,
8 Viaduct Gardens, London SW11 7BW
www.penguin.co.uk

Transworld is part of the Penguin Random House group of companies
whose addresses can be found at global.penguinrandomhouse.com

First published in Great Britain in 2023 by Doubleday
an imprint of Transworld Publishers
Penguin paperback edition published 2024

A CIP catalogue record for this book is available from the British Library.

ISBN 9781804991688

Typeset in Dante MT Pro by Jouve (UK), Milton Keynes.
Printed and bound in Great Britain by Clays Ltd, Elcograf S.p.A.

The authorized representative in the EEA is Penguin Random House Ireland,
Morrison Chambers, 32 Nassau Street, Dublin D02 YH68.

Penguin Random House is committed to a sustainable future
for our business, our readers and our planet. This book is made
from Forest Stewardship Council® certified paper.

For
E. H. Bradley
and Pansy

雨ニモマケズ

宮沢賢治　（昭和6年）

雨ニモマケズ　風ニモマケズ

雪ニモ夏ノ暑サニモマケヌ丈夫ナカラダヲモチ

欲ハナク　決シテ瞋ラズ　イツモシズカニワラッテイル

一日ニ玄米四合ト　味噌ト少シノ野菜ヲタベ

アラユルコトヲ　ジブンヲカンジョウニ入レズニ

ヨクミキキシワカリ　ソシテワスレズ

野原ノ松ノ林ノ蔭ノ　小サナ萱ブキノ小屋ニイテ

東ニ病気ノコドモアレバ　行ッテ看病シテヤリ

西ニツカレタ母アレバ　行ッテソノ稲ノ束ヲ負イ

南ニ死ニソウナ人アレバ　行ッテコワガラナクテモイイトイイ

北ニケンカヤソショウガアレバツマラナイカラヤメロトイイ

ヒデリノトキハナミダヲナガシ

サムサノナツハオロオロアルキ

ミンナニデクノボ一トヨバレ

ホメラレモセズ　クニモサレズ

ソウイウモノニ　ワタシハナリタイ

Without Losing to the Rain

by Miyazawa Kenji (1931)
Translation by Nick Bradley

Without losing to the rain   without losing to the wind
Neither beaten by snow   nor summer's heat
Keep a strong body   absent of desire
Neither angry nor resentful   always smiling calmly
Four cups of brown rice   miso and a few vegetables each day
Observe all things   impartially and selflessly
Look, listen, understand deeply   never forget lessons learnt
Dwell in a humble thatched house   in the shade of forest pines
To the east if there is a sick child   go nurse them to health
To the west a weary mother   go help her harvest rice
To the south a person dying   go tell them there's no need to fear
To the north a fight or squabble   go tell them to make peace
In times of drought shed tears   wander at a loss in cold summer
Called a nobody by all   without praise or being noticed
That's the kind of person   I wish to be

Flo: Spring

'So what's going on with you these days, Flo-chan?' Kyoko took a sip from her beer and placed it back on the table, next to a bowl of edamame shells.

'Yeah, what's up?' said Makoto, tapping ash on a plate of chicken bones before taking another drag on his cigarette. 'You've seemed down recently.'

Flo gripped her glass of oolong tea and laughed awkwardly. 'Down? I'm fine!'

Kyoko, Makoto and Flo were sitting around a low table in a Shinjuku izakaya famous for its imported beers. They'd come here together directly from their office. Flo had initially refused the invitation, citing a combination of exhaustion and not wanting to be amongst the crowds of cherry blossom viewers – it was peak hanami season. But then Kyoko had grabbed her by the arm and escorted her firmly towards the office door, like a security guard removing a troublemaker from the premises.

'You're coming with us,' she said, ignoring Flo's weak protests. 'Whether you like it or not.'

Now that she was here, Flo had to admit it felt good to be somewhere other than work, home, or on her laptop in the neighbourhood café – the only three places she'd been spending time the past few months. Initially Kyoko and Makoto had suggested going to Ueno Park to sit out beneath the blossoms, and when Flo had begun a diatribe on how she thought sakura was overrated compared to the autumn leaves, Kyoko had interrupted her and insisted they go to their favourite izakaya instead. The small Japanese-style pub was sparsely decorated, with tatami reed matting floors and rustic wooden low tables. The air was thick with Makoto's cigarette

3

smoke, despite the restaurant's tables being thinner with customers this evening.

'You just don't seem yourself recently,' said Kyoko, a frown forming on her forehead. 'You never come out with us any more. You don't respond to my texts. Even the calligraphy teacher keeps asking why you don't come to class. I had to lie to Chie-sensei and tell her you'd been sick.'

Flo didn't say anything. She put her glass of oolong tea down and watched Makoto blow out a cloud of smoke in the direction of the table next to them. The two girls eating there scowled at him, but he remained oblivious.

Kyoko was dressed in her usual immaculate office clothes: pink Polo sweater and cream trousers, hair tied back in a neat ponytail and make-up perfectly understated, as ever. Flo always felt a little jealous of how effortless Kyoko looked, incredibly beautiful, without even trying. In contrast, Flo's office clothes were shabby and old, definitely not the kind of clothes a Japanese employee could get away with wearing. Loose slacks and a collared shirt were about as smart as she could muster. Makoto looked like every other salaryman in Tokyo, the only unique addition being a classy maroon tie Kyoko had picked out for him in Ginza last month. He'd loosened the tie a little already.

'I'm sorry if I'm being too direct,' Kyoko said, her voice softening a little. Flo couldn't help but smile at this – Kyoko was always direct! It was one of the things Flo appreciated about her. 'I just worried that . . . I don't know. That you didn't want to be friends any more.'

'No!' Flo said, immediately alarmed. 'Of course not!'

Kyoko was one of her closest friends in Tokyo. Flo wouldn't say she was her 'best' friend – 'best' implied a degree of intimacy that she didn't have with anyone in the city. Except for Yuki. When Flo and Kyoko had first started hanging out together outside of work, going to calligraphy lessons in Chiba, Flo had even been hopeful of – you know – something more with her. But thankfully, before Flo could do anything to embarrass herself, she'd discovered that Kyoko was seeing a guy she was really into. Luckily, that guy was

Makoto, an affable co-worker whom Flo already knew and liked, and Flo was more than happy to hang out with the pair of them, never feeling like a third wheel.

Until several weeks ago, Wednesday night dinner had been a ritual for the three, especially since Flo had cut down on the number of days she came into the office. Flo was in the enviable position of finishing her working week on a Wednesday, using Thursday, Friday and Saturday to work on her literary translation projects. But Flo hadn't been out with them in ages. When was the last time all three had hung out? A month ago? Two?

'Even Makoto has noticed you're different,' said Kyoko quickly, switching from Japanese to English in an effort to cut him out of the conversation. 'And he's usually clueless about women.'

Makoto strained his ears to listen to Kyoko's superior English, and just about caught what she was saying. Kyoko snickered at his efforts.

'It's true,' he said in English, humbly yet with a certain awkwardness.

Poor Makoto. He was sitting next to Kyoko, both of them on the other side of the table from Flo. He was about to tap the ash out on the plate of chicken bones again, but Kyoko slapped him on the wrist gently. He bowed his head slightly, and reached for the ashtray she was sliding his way.

'Come on, Flo-chan,' said Kyoko kindly, switching back to Japanese. 'You can tell us.'

Flo bit her lip. She glanced down at her phone – no new messages.

Flo was, in general, open and honest, but she'd always kept her personal life private, even with these two. Above all, she didn't feel like she could talk to them about Yuki. Would Kyoko and Makoto be surprised that Flo dated women? Probably not – nothing they had ever said or done indicated otherwise – but Flo had never mentioned it to them, deeming it her own business, and now they'd known each other so long she had no idea how to even begin raising the subject. It was as though she'd built a giant wall around herself, an impenetrable barrier, and the possibility of breaking it all down to let anyone in felt absolutely terrifying. It felt much safer – more secure – to be closed off. So no, she'd never talked to them about Yuki. Not about how they'd met, nor about Yuki moving in with her, and especially not about Yuki's plan to move to New York in a month and work in a bookshop while attending an English language school. Flo's relationship with Yuki, more than anything, was what was causing her stress these days.

So no, Flo couldn't talk about any of that. Instead, she did what anyone else would do: she used this as an opportunity to talk about other anxieties she was experiencing in her life. Ones that were just as pressing, but easier to discuss in public.

'Just . . .' she began.

'Yes?' Makoto nodded.

'Go on,' said Kyoko, unable to hide her eagerness.

'Well, I've been having some doubts recently.'

'What kind of doubts?' asked Kyoko instantly.

Flo's shoulders dipped, and she looked down at the table, unable to maintain eye contact with either of them.

'It's going to sound melodramatic.' She paused. 'But . . . I'm just not sure what I'm doing with my life.'

Kyoko and Makoto both sat quietly, waiting for her to keep going. Makoto stubbed out his cigarette. Flo continued.

'I mean – I don't know if I get any pleasure from – you know – what I'm doing any more.'

'Oh, Flo-chan.' Creases appeared on Kyoko's perfect face as a deep look of concern rose to the surface. 'Is the office job getting in the way of your translation work? Because if it is, we can cut down your hours again. We can—'

'No,' said Flo, shaking her head. 'It's not that.'

'You miss Portland?' asked Makoto. 'You miss your family?'

'Well . . .' Flo stuttered and stumbled over her words. 'I do miss my mom, yes. Of course. And sometimes I miss Portland. But that's not what's bothering me.'

'Tell us!' Kyoko and Makoto both leant forward at the exact same time. It was hard for Flo not to feel like she was being interrogated, but she couldn't hold it against them. They were her friends, and that's what friends did, wasn't it? They cared about each other. How inconsiderate she'd been, blowing them off for so long.

Flo pulled up the sleeves of the sweater she was wearing and rested her bare arms on the edge of the table. 'It's just . . . I'm not sure if I get any joy from reading any more.' She stopped, feeling stupid once the words were out there. Kyoko and Makoto looked puzzled, but she carried on. 'I mean, I always thought that literature and translation were the most important things in my life. I worked so hard to translate that book, and get it published—'

'It's a wonderful book,' Kyoko interrupted, 'and you did an amazing job. You're an incredible translator . . .' Makoto gently nudged her, before lighting another cigarette. 'Sorry,' said Kyoko, leaning back slightly. 'Please, go on.'

'No, it's okay,' Flo said. Flo was never good with Kyoko's praise. Or praise from anyone, for that matter. How hollow words sounded! But again, that was something she should never share. 'I'm happy with the work I did, but now I feel – well – kind of empty. I don't want to sound ungrateful, but . . . God, I feel like such a whiny whinger right now. Oh woe is me!' Flo shook her head before taking another sip of her tea. What a pity party she'd thrown for herself! She should've just kept her mouth shut instead of burdening them like this.

'You don't sound like that, Flo-chan,' said Kyoko quietly. 'Not at all. Any problem is a problem, no matter how big or small.'

'I think I understand how you feel,' said Makoto, nodding thoughtfully.

Kyoko narrowed her eyes at Makoto. 'What do you mean?'

Makoto sucked his teeth in mock irritation. 'Flo's achieved her dream.'

'What do you know about her dreams?' asked Kyoko, rolling her eyes.

'Well, not specifically *her* dreams. But I do know a thing or two about dreams in general.' He took a deep drag on his cigarette and blew another huge cloud of smoke at the girls on the other table, who this time fanned the air in front of their noses and grimaced.

But Makoto carried on, in his own little world. 'It's a dangerous thing sometimes, achieving your dream.'

'Who the hell do you think you are?' Kyoko scoffed and shook her head. 'Sitting there, smoking and trying to make deep philosophical pronouncements. You're acting like you're some kind of Hollywood movie star. Don't interrupt! Flo-chan was in the middle of explaining how she felt, and there you go, yabbering on about dreams as if you know exactly what she's talking about. Be quiet. Listen.'

Makoto shook his head. 'But I think I know what she means—'

'Let her finish!'

'How about letting *me* finish?!'

Flo couldn't help but laugh a little at their pretend bickering. She knew they were doing it in jest for her benefit – like a manzai comedy duo – to cheer her up and raise her spirits. She leant forwards, raising her hand. 'Please don't argue. I just mean . . . I think Makoto's kind of right. What do you do *after* you've achieved your biggest dream? What do you do next?'

Makoto lit another cigarette and sat back, folding his arms smugly. 'I thought that's what you meant.' He gave another quick look at Kyoko, who was wobbling her head, mimicking Makoto's words. He ignored her, looking at Flo again and carrying on. 'It's like these guys who enter Street Fighter II competitions.'

'*How?*' demanded Kyoko, sounding genuinely exasperated this time. '*How* is it like that?'

'Let me finish!' he said, losing his cool a little.

'Everything with you is about Street Fighter II,' grumbled Kyoko. 'You relate everything to that game. You're not even that good at it. I whip your butt every time.'

'Shhh!'

Flo laughed again, as Makoto and Kyoko tried to keep straight faces.

'What I'm trying to say,' said Makoto, 'is that after you achieve one dream, you make another . . . maybe . . .' He trailed off lamely.

Kyoko sighed. 'We had to listen to you just now. All of that . . . for what?'

Makoto tilted his head. 'Maybe it sounded more profound and helpful in my mind, before I said it.'

'Maybe you should listen more and talk less.' Kyoko scowled at Makoto, then grinned at Flo, who smiled back – it was cheering her up slightly, but there was still more to say.

'I just keep reading these books that don't inspire me.'

Kyoko nodded.

Flo continued. 'I need to find the right one to translate, but it doesn't seem to come.'

Makoto stubbed out his cigarette, and breathed smoke out through his nostrils.

'It'll come, Flo-chan,' he said, looking at Kyoko as he spoke. 'The right one will come along at the right time. You just have to be patient.'

⁂

Flo rode the train home later that evening after parting ways with Kyoko and Makoto inside the gates at Shinjuku Station. Kyoko had gripped her arm tenderly as they said goodbye, while Makoto smiled and waved before they both walked along the busy concourse to their platform. In general, Flo tried her best to avoid the last train at night, ever since she'd been in a jam-packed carriage when someone had thrown up. Not an experience she was keen to repeat.

Sitting now, Flo checked her phone mindlessly again, but there were no messages. She scrolled through social media, but there were no notifications. Instead, there were just photos of things that vaguely held her interest – reminding her that she was not on holiday right now, that she hadn't eaten out at a fancy restaurant in a long time, that she didn't have a baby, that she wasn't married, and that with Yuki leaving next month she was soon to be very alone, unless she went too. Her most recent post was from a couple of months ago, something about a review of the book she'd translated in a minor publication. Recently, she'd been losing the will to even promote her own work. Not that there was that much of her own work these days, anyway.

She started writing out a translation-themed tweet on her phone – she'd been continually adding to an old thread for some time, about her favourite Japanese words:

木漏れ日 (komorebi) – sunlight filtering through the trees

But everyone knew that word now, didn't they? She had seen it on numerous blog posts with titles like *Top 10 Untranslatable Words!* Ironically, all ten words listed were promptly translated in the article. She deleted the komorebi tweet and tried another:

諸行無常 (shogyo mujo) – the impermanence of worldly things

She allowed herself a wry smile before deleting this tweet too.

As the train trundled slowly along the tracks of the Yamanote Line, she watched the towering grey glass buildings and the garish billboards of central Tokyo flick past the window against the night sky. When was it she'd started taking the city for granted? People back home in Oregon wouldn't believe what she saw every day, but Flo had become so accustomed to the Tokyo cityscape that it was now mundane to her. Slightly boring. What a terrible thought to have. Tokyo. Boring. Not even the hanami festivities excited her any more – she'd told Kyoko as much.

Was she sick of Japan? Should she move to New York with Yuki?

Next month – that was Yuki's departure date. Sooner rather than later, Flo was going to have to make her decision.

She looked about the carriage, casting around for something to take her mind off the anxieties running through her head. Even thinking about work was preferable, though of course Flo's workload had been relatively easy for months.

Ever since Flo had become a part-time contractor for her company, she'd essentially been able to pick her own schedule. In her capacity as line manager, Kyoko had been extremely kind and lenient with Flo in terms of her working hours and responsibilities. But strangely, when she'd cut down on her office time, she started to miss working amongst all the people there. Everyone at work had been extremely supportive of her foray into the world of literary translation – her colleagues seemed happy, and wanted her to succeed.

They'd even held a mini book launch for Flo when her first translation had come out – the collected sci-fi stories of one of her favourite writers, Nishi Furuni. Kyoko and Makoto had organized the launch for her as a surprise. They'd put it on in a private area of the izakaya they'd been in earlier, and had copies of the book there for her to sign.

Even the two sons of the deceased author had turned up together to congratulate her. What a pair they'd been! The elder brother, Ohashi, wore a purple bandana and a formal kimono, and happily signed autographs from random fans in the audience. He'd been a famous rakugo storyteller in the past, and after a battle with alcoholism and homelessness was once again making a comeback in the rakugo theatres of Shinjuku. He sipped on a cup of hot tea all evening, while his younger brother, Taro, nursed a glass of beer. They'd asked Flo to read a short section from a story in the collection called 'Copy Cat' – Flo read her English translation, and Ohashi read from the same section in Japanese. He read first, and Flo had been in awe at his incredible storytelling skill, how he'd drastically changed his voice for different characters, his comic timing and the neat gestures he employed to bring the performance to life. She'd looked over at Taro while his older brother was reading, and noticed a tear in his eye, and an expression of joyful pride that had almost assuaged her own nerves.

But more than anything, Flo experienced an overwhelming anxiety. She'd put on a brave, happy face for everyone there, but the truth was, deep inside she felt horribly sick. Sick of herself, namely. She'd been posting online for weeks, frantically inviting people, but now they'd all come, there was a tremendous pressure not to let them down, to make it all worthwhile.

Her own reading paled in comparison to Ohashi the professional entertainer. Her voice sounded weird and pompous as she read aloud, and she was left anxious and awkward with everybody's eyes fixed on her, stumbling over basic English words. She read a sentence she'd always found extremely funny, and even dared to look up from the page to make eye contact, but to her horror no one was smiling – her hesitant delivery had made the humour fall completely flat. She'd even noticed a typo on the first page of the story, the day before when she'd been rehearsing. A typo! After all that editing! She'd corrected it in pen, but ended up clumsily stuttering on the corrected section anyhow. Of course, all were kind and supportive, applauding once she'd finished, but she couldn't shake the feeling that she'd failed. There was something about her that was terribly disappointing – embarrassing, even – that she felt everyone was too polite to acknowledge. But maybe that's what they were all thinking, in secret.

Sitting on the train now, Flo kept replaying the night in her mind.

It seemed so long ago.

Would she ever translate another book again? She'd thought getting published would make her happy – and it had, there was no denying it. She was tremendously proud of all the work she'd done on that book. And yet, it had introduced a feeling of stress and insecurity into her life that hadn't existed before. In some ways, she was more insecure now as a published translator – less confident than when she was working towards that dream.

Makoto had hit the nail on the head earlier.

It's a dangerous thing sometimes, achieving your dream.

Anyone else would have been elated to be in Flo's situation – she was certain of it. Clearly, there was something severely messed up about her as a person.

Flo stretched and yawned, shuddering slightly at the intensity of her thoughts. Round and round they went, in their exhausting never-ending loops. She got out her phone again and opened the TrashReads app. Despite every instinct in her body screaming *Don't do it, don't look*, she did it anyway: she looked up the title of the book she'd translated.

There it was – listed with a 3.3-star rating. Not bad. Not great. If it were a restaurant rating on Google, you probably wouldn't eat there, though. She would've liked it to be higher. But when she saw her name listed as the translator, pride bubbled up inside her. There it was, in black and white. The actual evidence: she was a literary translator.

She hadn't looked at the user reviews in a long time. Her finger hovered over the MOST RECENT link. She hesitated, thinking briefly about how she'd been burnt in the past, but tonight she desperately needed reassurance. She needed to feel encouragement. She tapped.

Her face fell as she read.

SEXIST RACIST GARBAGE

What the fuck did I just read???? So this 'collection' of sci-fi stories is like all collections of short stories. Some were ok, some were complete junk. I was reading this, being like OMG, so boring, but then when I got to the fifth story, I just couldn't hold it in any longer. WHAT THE HELL??? This writer Nishi Furuni (who I'd never heard about before in my life) wrote these garbage stories, and they weren't translated for years (probably for a good reason), anyway, the fifth story was just too much and I DNF'd midway through. HE WROTE ABOUT A PLANET POPULATED ENTIRELY WITH FEMALE SEX ROBOTS??? HOW FUCKING MISOGYNISTIC CAN YOU GET???? I picked up this book because I saw it was a JAPANESE WRITER on the cover, and I wanted to read stuff, like, duh . . . set in Japan LOL. I did not buy this book to read about a planet of female sex robots – if I wanted to read misogynistic male fantasies, I could've picked a book by any of the many straight, white, middle class American males that history has given us. I did not expect this from a writer of color. I had to actually sit down and process this for a bit. Also, all of the non-Japanese women in this book are blonde-haired and blue-eyed, which is completely racist. Anyways, it might just be the translation, but I'd give this one a miss. DNF

Flo's heart sank as she read the review. She'd known this was going to happen. And yet she'd gone ahead and done it anyway.

But the thing that hurt most – what really got to her – was that the person who wrote the review (as much as Flo wanted to gouge their eyes out for reducing such hard work down to an online review with GIFs, on both hers and Nishi Furuni's part) was unfortunately slightly right.

The fifth story in the collection, 'Planet Pleasure', was definitely on the edge of controversy. But Flo had argued with her editor to keep it in the collection. Nishi Furuni had depicted the planet as a dystopia, rather than a utopia, but you had to finish reading right to the end of the short story to get this message. In actuality, the story was an interrogation of sexual mores and Japan's historical laissez-faire attitude to sex work. It was a story that was supposed to spark debate in Japan, to make people empathize with sex workers, and the Japanese readership of the time would've picked up on this instantly.

But the last line of the review – *it might just be the translation* – stung especially.

Perhaps this was Flo's fault – she had lost something of the original in her translation.

It was her fault that this reader hadn't connected with the stories.

These thoughts made her feel particularly wretched, because she loved Nishi Furuni's work, and just wanted to share it with a larger audience. She closed the TrashReads app and vowed once more never to open it up again. Bleakness was overwhelming her.

She took a book from her backpack instead: *Tokyo Tennis Club*. A Japanese editor friend had sent it to her, to consider working on as her next project, but the story wasn't holding her attention. There was little within she could connect to. A high school romance about a guy and a girl who play tennis. She'd read a million stories like it before, and there was nothing new within its pages. It was formulaic content, like writing by numbers. Her eyes skipped over large chunks of the book without taking anything in, and she had to force herself to turn back several pages to go over parts she'd been daydreaming through.

She closed the book and looked up at the interior of the train carriage. This particular car was adorned with a glut of adverts for a brand new live-action blockbuster movie, adapted from a manga/anime series made with CGI. All the characters had spiky weird-coloured hair and looked a little silly. Her eyes tracked their way around the carriage.

The man in the seat opposite Flo was slumped on his side, snoring.

Good for him! Sleeping people on the subway never bothered Flo; she saved her resentment for other, more egregious behaviour. She admired the man's audacity to get drunk enough in public to fall asleep on the seat as if he were at home tucked up in his own futon. It was an action she herself would never contemplate, but it was mildly liberating to see others living so freely. This particular man was in his late twenties, and looked like any other run-of-the-mill salaryman. He'd probably come from a work party, having been forced to drink too much by his older colleagues.

Flo smiled and opened the book again, trying to force herself to follow the story, until a flurry of activity opposite tore her out of the book and back into her body. The man was leaping out of his seat, jumping up to get off the train before the doors shut on him. Flo breathed a sigh of relief on his behalf as he slipped through just as they closed. She was about to go back to reading, but then she saw it – lying on the seat where he'd been.

A small paperback with a simple black and white cover.

Flo cast her eyes around the carriage – completely empty, no witnesses to the crime. She couldn't stop herself.

She picked it up and put it in her backpack. Her stop was next.

▲▲

Who needs friends when you have books?

It was not the first time in her life Flo Dunthorpe had pondered this question. And now, as she opened the door of her compact Tokyo apartment, the familiar thought was once again swimming through her mind. In some ways, she'd made a life out of this maxim. Her apartment was crammed full of books, both in English and in Japanese, and her shelves were stuffed to bursting; there were even piles on the floor by her bed.

But then again, looking at the shelves, now there were also absences – spaces where books had obviously been removed and not replaced. Flo looked at the gaps, and could still clearly remember the spines of what had been there before. Flo would soon have to sort through the ones on the floor and shelve them now there was space. Another job to do. She also had the bigger decision to make – should she box them up (as Yuki had done with hers) and send them on to New York by sea? Or just leave everything as it was?

Flo paused at the genkan entranceway. It was only a few days previously that Yuki had packed up her books, and all the rest of her stuff. Flo had been unable to help her pack, and they'd had an argument when Flo had reneged on her promise to ship their books all together in the same batch.

'I just don't understand, Flo,' said Yuki, sighing heavily. 'If you're coming with me, why don't you send them on with mine? It's cheaper.'

Flo had ummed and ahhed, deflected and deferred. She needed these books now, for her job, she said. She couldn't part with the reference books – they were essential for her translation work. And she couldn't get rid of the piles she had waiting to read, for fear that her next translation project might be in that very pile. What was so bad about sending hers on later? So what if she would have to wait for them to arrive in New York? That would be fine, wouldn't it? Maybe she could just keep them in storage in Japan. They'd be coming back eventually, wouldn't they?

'It's fine,' said Yuki, interrupting gently. 'But it makes me think you don't want to come.'

'Of course I want to come!' Flo tried to make her voice sound bright as she said this. But Yuki wasn't an idiot. She could surely tell.

The argument that ensued prompted Yuki to announce that she would stay with some friends for now. They both needed the space to cool off, and she would like to spend some time with her college friends before she left. That's where Yuki was now, and where she'd presumably be until her departure date next month.

Flo was brought back to the present by a little mew, and the familiar sound of Lily's paws padding across the tatami. At least Yuki had left the cat with Flo during their cooling-off period.

'Tadaima,' Flo said to the cat in Japanese, as she stepped out of her shoes and into the apartment. She seated herself at her desk and covered her knees with a purple throw.

Lily leapt lightly on to Flo's lap, and began paddling her claws against the blanket. As the cat kneaded the material, Flo admired the round black patch of fur on her chest. Lily was long-haired and white all over, apart from this one curious spot. Lily loved the sensation of this particular purple throw, and when Flo was lying flat on her back would stand on Flo's tummy and gently knead away with her tiny claws. Flo began to stroke Lily's soft white fur, giving her scratches under the chin. The cat let out purrs of pleasure, and promptly began suckling on the blanket.

'Are you hungry, Lily-chan?' Flo still spoke to the cat in Japanese. It was a habit she'd got into since she and Yuki had first taken Lily in. Yuki spoke pretty good English, but they'd decided that a Tokyo street cat wouldn't understand English, and so Flo continued to speak to Lily in Japanese. 'You want supper?'

Flo got up to feed the cat, who skidded across the kitchen floor as she bounded towards her bowl. Flo stood in the tiny kitchenette, zoning out as she watched Lily chowing down on her food. She showered, dressed in her pyjamas, and settled into a comfy floor seat to finish reading *Tokyo Tennis Club*. The book had picked up a little, but still hadn't grabbed her fully. She was nearing the end, and pretty sure she didn't want to take on the job of translating it. Lily padded over and curled up on the tatami next to her, purring as Flo stroked her with her free hand.

Her phone vibrated. A message from Yuki.

Hey. Still on for tomorrow? We can have a walk along the river in Nakameguro and see the cherry blossoms? We have a lot to discuss xxx

Flo put the phone back on the low table, lacking the energy to respond.

They had to meet, but she had no idea what she wanted to say.

⁂

The next day, Flo woke early and put on her favourite dress for the occasion. It was the same one she'd worn to their first date. It put her in mind of when they'd first met, when Flo had nervously asked for Yuki's contact details in the bookstore Yuki worked in, after they'd had a long chat about their favourite books that had extended on and on until Yuki's manager had scowled at them both. At that time, neither had known the other's intentions. The same could be said of today's meeting.

Flo rode the train with the crowds on their way to enjoy han-ami parties. She looked at her phone, desperate to distract herself from the stress of the impending meeting, but it only made her more anxious. If only she'd brought a book with her. She'd finished *Tokyo Tennis Club* the night before, and in her rush to meet Yuki, she hadn't packed another. She rustled through her backpack looking for her notebooks at least. And that's when she saw it. The book the guy had left on the train the evening before.

She studied the cover, turning it over in her hands.

「水の音」
ヒビキ

Sound of Water
by Hibiki

The cogs in Flo's brain began whirring. The title – *Sound of Water* – must be an allusion to the famous haiku by Matsuo Basho. She opened it to the title page. She was right – the epigraph of the book had the full haiku inside:

古池や　蛙飛びこむ　水の音

An old pond and / a frog jumps in / sound of water.

She studied the cover. It was beautiful, but didn't give much away – plain white, with simple black lettering for the title and author name, and then beneath, just the concentric circles of ripples in water drawn in black ink. She'd never heard of the writer, Hibiki. Turning the book over in her hands, she ran her fingers over the gorgeous texture of the paper cover. She looked at the inner flaps – no blurbs. No author photo. Who was the publisher?

She examined the spine.

千光社 Senkosha. She'd never heard of it before. The kanji for the 'Senko' part meant 'one thousand lights', and the 'sha' just meant 'company'. She loved it. The colophon above it looked like the kanji 己 onore – an old word that meant 'you'. It was also incorporated into the romanized name for the publisher, with the kanji operating as a backwards 'S': 己enkosha. Very clever.

She turned to the first page and was about to begin reading, but the announcer called out over the loudspeaker:

'Nakameguro. Nakameguro. The next stop is Nakameguro.'

She returned the book to her backpack.

She would read it later.

▲▲

At the station, Yuki was already waiting for her outside the ticket gates, wearing jeans and a thin light blue sweater. Flo suddenly felt a little abashed that she'd got so dressed up.

'Hey,' said Yuki.

'Hey,' replied Flo, barely able to make eye contact. Neither of them made any motion to embrace each other. They never kissed in public, but the lack of even a hug now made Flo feel like dying. She'd known the relationship had been on the rocks for the past few weeks – a dead fish flopping on the bank, gasping for air – but never had it felt more brutally apparent than now.

They walked silently along the river, watching all the other couples and groups admiring the blossoms. Everyone they passed appeared happy, taking photos of each other, clasping cans of beer and bento lunchboxes. Flo wondered if she looked as miserable as Yuki did. Her insides felt completely black, as though they'd been scribbled over with thick felt marker.

They eventually paused on one of the bridges, staring out into the distance. Neither of them had talked the whole time.

As usual, it was Yuki who spoke first. 'So.'

'So,' said Flo.

'Are we not going to discuss it?'

Flo pinched the skin of her palms as hard as she could.

'You're not coming,' said Yuki. She didn't even phrase it as a question.

'I never said that!'

'You didn't have to. I can tell.' Yuki finally turned to face Flo and gave a weak smile. 'Look, Flo. Let's not drag this out. Or make it any harder than you're already making it.'

Flo's heart pounded. 'You're the one who's leaving.'

'Stop, Flo.' Yuki gave a pained look, and raised her hand to her forehead. 'We've been over this. It's not anyone's fault. But it's obvious you don't want to come.'

Flo tried to interject again, but couldn't find the words.

'I'm sorry if I did anything to pressure you,' said Yuki. 'I always told you, Flo: you should do what you want – what's best for you.'

'But I want to come. I do!'

'You say these things, Flo, but then your actions say something completely different.' Yuki's voice was sharp. 'You haven't bought a ticket. You haven't packed anything. I mean, you haven't even told anyone at your job that you're leaving! You say all the time *it's fine, I'm excited* – but you never tell me what you're actually feeling. I'm constantly guessing. I'm supposed to be the closed-off Japanese one. You're supposed to be the open and easy American who talks about her feelings. It's exhausting, Flo.' She took a deep breath. 'You exhaust me.'

Flo turned away from Yuki. She stared over the bridge at the river below, tears prickling behind her eyes.

Yuki ran a hand through her hair. 'Look . . . Either come, or don't. The choice is yours. But I've made mine, and I'm going.'

They'd only been dating two years, but Flo had always loved that about Yuki: her iron-hard confidence. Her drive. Whatever Yuki said she was going to do, she did. She never doubted herself, ever. Not like Flo.

'I'd love for you to come,' said Yuki. 'That's never changed. But I don't want you to come like . . . like this.' Yuki paused, before barrelling onwards. 'You've not been the same since my manuscript was rejected. It wasn't your fault, Flo. I've moved on, but it seems like you still blame yourself. You've been passionless with your work ever since. Think about what *you* want.' She hesitated. 'What do you want, Flo?'

Now Flo's nails were digging deep into her wrists. If only they could dig deeper. The mention of Yuki's rejected manuscript they'd both worked so hard on stung. 'I want to come with you,' she whispered. 'Yuki . . . I do.'

Yuki didn't respond. A chilling bleakness gripped Flo. She found herself unable to tear her gaze from the dark waters below. She just kept staring at it: the river flowing under the bridge.

'Flo?'

She didn't move.

'Flo, say something.'

She couldn't speak. The wall was back, closing her in. There was no way Yuki would even be able to peek through the cracks now.

'Flo . . .' Yuki sighed impatiently. 'You know it's very childish when you do this.'

Flo's eyes were locked on the water. Those long, slow ripples.

Flo had always done this, shutting down for fear of saying the wrong thing, or misunderstanding her own emotions. She was silent, unable to form words.

'Okay, Flo. Fine. If you're going to be that way, that's your decision. I'm going to head home. I've got loads to do over the next few weeks, and if you're not even going to talk to me, what's the point?' Yuki let out another frustrated sigh. 'If you want to talk, you know how to get hold of me. Flo? Flo? Okay, Flo. Again . . . it's your choice.' Another hesitation, but only momentary this time. 'Goodbye.'

Without looking, Flo knew she'd gone.

But she couldn't take her eyes from the water.

Sound of Water

by Hibiki

Translated from the Japanese
by Flo Dunthorpe

水 蛙 古　An old pond and
の 飛 池
音 び や　A frog leaps in,
　 込
　 む　Sound of water

– Matsuo Basho

Spring

春

Ayako had a strict daily routine from which she did not like to deviate.

Each morning, she awoke with the sun, ate a simple breakfast of rice, miso soup, pickles, and a small piece of fish grilled on her gas-powered stove. After folding her futon neatly and stowing it away in the cupboard, she would dress in one of her many kimono, carefully choosing a pattern appropriate for the season. Then she would kneel on the tatami in front of her household shrine, praying to two black and white photos that rested peacefully side by side: one depicted her husband, and the other, her son. Although the photos had been taken far apart in time, both men looked roughly the same age in each.

Both had passed away too soon.

Sliding open her front door, she then walked the backstreets and small alleyways of Onomichi, only limping slightly, from her traditionally built house on the side of the mountain all the way to the little coffee shop she ran by herself in the centre of the shotengai covered market in front of the train station. She left the house early, before the crowds of businessmen milled around with their suits, briefcases and umbrellas on their way to catch trains into Hiroshima; before the schoolchildren swarmed along the paths and roads, some on bikes and some on foot; even before the housewives headed out to the markets to buy fish, vegetables and meat for their evening meals.

Ayako loved the town at this time of day.

One of Ayako's many small pleasures in life was to walk the same route each morning, but to try to notice a different thing each day. She would pass the same fellow early risers without fail, and would always smile, nod and greet each one of them in turn. Everyone in town knew Ayako, and she knew most people by face. She wouldn't have said it herself, but the fact of the matter was that she was a well-known figure in Onomichi. Occasionally, on her morning walk to the coffee shop, she might come across a tourist from Tokyo, Osaka or some such place and she would bow her head and greet them the same as she would any local.

Although, it was not particularly the people who caught Ayako's attention on her morning walks – she had her fill of people during the day working at her coffee shop – rather, it was the changing scenes of the town itself that fascinated her.

The journey was a private time to clear her head and to observe the natural world. And, without fail, she liked to pause at the same point each day, high up on the side of the mountain, on a concrete walkway with an iron handrail overlooking the town below. Here she'd stop awhile, resting her slender remaining fingers (and the short stumps of the fingers she'd lost) on the metal railings, to take in the view of houses nestled in by the coastline. She'd study the houses with their light blue tiled roofs, tightly packed together like fish scales between the mountain and the coast. And then her gaze would wander upwards, deeper into the scene, looking out across the Seto Inland Sea at the myriad of islands floating on the horizon. Boats and ferries chugged slowly back and forth across the blue calm, but with the seasons, and the changing day, a new detail would attract her eye and bring a sense of joy to her life.

In spring, the cherry blossoms caught the morning light as the sun sparkled and twinkled off the peaceful sea. In summer, she wiped sweat from her brow with a small hand towel as the cicadas sung around her in all directions. In autumn, her eyes were drawn to the colourful leaves that daubed the trees covering the mountainsides. In winter, she wrapped her heavier kimono tighter around herself, her breath visible in the morning chill as she studied the snow-capped mountains floating on the horizon in the distant islands of Shikoku.

Sometimes, as she viewed those snow-capped mountains in the distance, she heard the low sound of the mountain calling, trying to coax her from her peaceful daily routine, but she ignored that sound, despite its strong pull, and carried on making her way to work.

Drawing up the rusty shutter of her coffee shop, Ayako would then begin a litany of small tasks, such as cutting up vegetables and meat to throw into a big pot on a stove in the kitchen to make today's curry, and mopping down the floors once more. Ayako worked alone, and had no need for an assistant; her thoughts were her main companion. But a different matter was running through her head on this particular spring morning.

Will he like it here?

Ayako tried her best to push this concern from her mind. She still had to prepare the curry and other small snacks for today's customers – the tsukemono pickles, the onigiri rice balls and other tasty morsels, which altered each day, depending on the available ingredients in line with the changing seasons. She looked at the old grandfather clock in the corner, its *tick tock* accompanying the sound of her knife chopping onions.

His train arrives tomorrow.

Ayako dumped the chopped onions into the pan, picked up the knife again, clutching it deftly in her left hand – despite her missing fingers – and raised the back of her right hand to her forehead. She was perspiring only a little.

Will he be all right by himself on the train from Tokyo?

'Enough!' she said out loud, clattering down the knife before washing her hands and drying them on a towel.

She sat down at a table, took out a brush pen and a blank piece of paper and began writing out today's menu in her beautiful flowing script. After she'd done so, she felt calmer – the action of writing had this effect on her – and she took the written paper menu to the nearby convenience store and made black and white photocopies on their machine.

It would be fine; he was her grandson after all.

'What's wrong with you today, Aya-chan?'

Ayako turned her head to look at Sato-san. As ever, he was the first customer of the day – sitting at the counter, nursing a cup of coffee. Sato had his coffee strong and black. His appearance was in complete contrast to the blackness of his coffee: a shock of long white hair fell neatly around his kind face; his full lips always smiling, framed by a neat and well-trimmed white beard. He held the cup just below his lips, about to drink, but flicked his eyes upwards, clearly noticing Ayako's irritated expression through the rising steam.

'Nothing's wrong,' she muttered, looking back down at the counter.

She continued to take clumps of white rice from a bowl, shaping them into the triangular onigiri which she then filled with umeboshi plums before wrapping them with nori seaweed. These she gave to customers free of charge throughout the day.

Sato shrugged, and took a tentative sip of his coffee. He winced as the steaming-hot drink burnt his tongue.

Ayako chuckled. 'Nekojita! You really do have a cat's tongue, don't you?'

'Every *single* time I burn my tongue,' he said, placing the cup back down on its saucer and shaking his head. 'Every *single* time.'

They both laughed, and Ayako's shoulders shook as she dipped her hands in salted water in between making each rice ball, setting them all down neatly on a plate, ready to wrap in clingfilm. Sato's cheeks flushed red as he watched Ayako laughing; his face gave away the pleasure he derived from making her laugh.

'This one's yours.' She took out one in particular and set it aside from the others.

Sato remained silent, but bowed his head a touch. He sat back on his stool, crossing his arms over his fashionable white collared shirt, his thick black-rimmed reading glasses protruding from the top pocket. He looked through the window at the Inland Sea stretching out before them.

'Well, something's up,' he said, half to himself and half to Ayako. 'I can tell.'

Ayako sighed, and paused from making the onigiri.

'It's just—' she began.

But then came the soft jingle of the bell attached to the door.

'Irasshaimase!' Ayako called out instinctively.

'Hello, Ayako!' came the cheerful voice of Jun, and then his smiling wife Emi appeared following just behind him. Ayako nodded to Sato, who returned the nod briefly before turning in his seat to greet both Jun and Emi.

'Ohayo, Sato-san!' said Emi.

'Ohayo! Good morning to the both of you.'

Without asking, Ayako instantly began to make a coffee with milk and one sugar for Jun, and a black tea without milk for Emi.

Jun and Emi sat down at the wooden counter, immediately next to Sato, who politely moved his leather satchel from the stool so that Emi could sit in the middle. At once, faced with the youthful couple in their twenties, the sombre air dispersed, and now Sato had a huge grin on his face, and even Ayako looked less stern than usual.

Emi wore a fedora, a pair of light blue jeans and a striped blue and white top. Jun wore a scruffy plaid shirt covered in paint and pre-ripped jeans. Ayako often wondered whether Jun needed a new pair of trousers. Sato had explained to her before that it was the fashion these days to have ripped trousers, to which Ayako scowled and said, 'So they buy them like that? Ripped already? Utter madness.' She shook her head. 'If I was Emi, I'd sew them up for him while he was sleeping. Absolute madness.' At which Sato had guffawed with laughter.

'So how are the renovations going?' asked Sato, turning on his stool to face Jun and Emi.

Jun took a sip from his coffee and placed it back down on the counter. 'Good. So far.'

'We're making progress,' said Emi, nodding enthusiastically to Sato.

Sato ran a hand through his short beard. 'Well, as I've said before, if there's anything I can do to help, please do let me know.'

'Sato-san, you're too kind.' Young Jun placed both hands on the counter and bowed to Sato. 'The one thing I ask is that you keep recommending me good music to listen to while we work.'

Sato waved his hand in front of his face, dismissing the compliment with embarrassment. Although a sliver of pride was visible in the upturned corners of his mouth.

Ayako pulled a face. She was not a fan of Sato's music; it was a little too weird for her tastes – she preferred jazz and classical. Not this rock and roll or electronic stuff Sato peddled in his shop. She addressed Emi directly. 'And remind me, how many guests will you be able to host? When you're up and running, that is.'

'Well, the old building we're converting isn't the biggest.' Emi nodded, and counted off on her fingers. 'But we have a dormitory room, for individual travellers. That's five bunk beds.' She smiled eagerly at Ayako. 'And then we have two rooms for couples.'

Jun joined in. 'And we also have a communal space for travellers to sit and get drinks.' He paused. 'The kitchen is pretty limited in terms of space, so we won't be able to offer food, but we're hoping to be able to supply hot and cold drinks.' He looked at Ayako directly, bowing his head in deference. 'Uh, we're actually hoping we can advertise local restaurants at the hostel to perhaps recommend good cafés and izakaya for guests to visit while they're in the area, uh, uh, that is . . . if . . . well . . .' He trailed off under Ayako's withering and sceptical gaze.

Ayako was wary of having too many *new* customers.

'And,' added Emi, attempting to change the subject, 'we have bike racks for travellers.'

Sato nodded knowingly. 'Ah, so you're hoping to draw in tourists who are cycling the Shimanami Kaido bridge, eh?' He sipped his tepid coffee, continuing to nod. 'Good idea. Good idea.'

●

Just after Jun and Emi left the coffee shop to get started on another taxing day of renovation work, Sato also started to make a move. It was almost time for him to open up his CD shop.

'I hope they do well with their hostel,' said Sato, shouldering the strap of his old leather satchel. 'It's good to have young people in the town.'

Ayako began to clear away the cups from the counter. 'Makes a change from all the other youngsters, who run off to that Tokyo.' Ayako rolled her eyes at the last word in the universal manner of all provincials who cannot understand the pull of a big city. 'I hope their business gets off the ground – especially with a little one on the way.'

Sato swivelled his head around slowly like an owl. 'Emi's pregnant?' He raised an eyebrow. 'She wasn't showing, was she? Who did you hear from?'

'I didn't.' Ayako shook her head, smirking. 'Men are so unobservant.'

'So, how could you tell?'

'Oh come on. It was obvious – couldn't you see the glow in her cheeks?'

'She's always glowing.'

'Not like that.'

'Hmm.' Sato scratched his beard. 'Doesn't seem like much evidence to go on.'

'This,' said Ayako, picking up Emi's untouched cup of steaming black tea.

'She didn't drink her tea. So what?'

'Sato, you really have no idea about women, do you?' She mock scowled at him.

Was this Ayako's strange form of coquettishness? Sato could never tell.

'Well.' He pulled at his collar uncomfortably, face flushed.

'When a woman is pregnant, she gets aversions to certain foods and drinks, smells and tastes. Emi always drank her tea down before – never a drop left in her cup. It's not like her to not touch it at all. I was watching the whole time out of the corner of my eye – she was pulling little faces – she couldn't even stand the smell of it.' Ayako poured the tea down the sink. 'There's your *evidence*.' She wobbled her head and made a funny voice on the last word.

'Aya-chan.' Sato clicked his teeth. 'Nothing gets past you, does it?'

'No, it does not.' She scowled again, this time for real.

'I'm off now.' Sato took his cream blazer from the coat stand and slung it over his arm. It was too hot to be wearing a blazer, so he'd be carrying it like that for most of the day. 'See you later.'

He moved to the door, and was almost through it, the bell on the door tinkling, when Ayako called out to him.

'Sato-san! Wait.'

He stopped and turned around to see Ayako hurrying around the counter with something clutched in her hand.

'Your onigiri,' she said, offering it politely with two hands outstretched.

He bowed to her. 'Ah! Thank you, Aya-chan.'

'And don't go spreading the news of Emi's pregnancy, do you hear me?' said Ayako, wagging a finger. 'She might not want anyone to know just yet.'

Sato tapped his nose, placed the onigiri in his satchel, turned on his heels and strode off down the long shotengai, his Nike trainers in striking contrast to his smart cotton shirt and trousers. Ayako watched him walk away, before bowing to the owner of the knife shop on the other side of the street.

She went back inside to wash up the cups and dishes and prepare herself for the lunch rush.

●

Lunch was busy and unpredictable in the café. Business, or busyness, depended on the weather, but also if the tourists were out in force or not. Onomichi, unlike Kyoto, did not get the same numbers of foreign tourists milling around, snapping photos of temples and shrines. But it did get a lot of domestic tourists doing much the same, albeit in Onomichi's quieter, small-scale way. Kyoto, after all, was a *big* city – a former capital.

There was the constant but quiet stream of fans of the director Ozu, coming to see one of the settings for his famous film *Tokyo Story*. Equally, there were the dedicated fans of the writer Shiga Naoya, who set part of his novel *A Dark Night's Passing* in Onomichi. Ayako would often have to field questions from a variety of otaku, with differing obsessions (film, literature, manga, cycling, etc.), but all of them with Onomichi in common. She was deft at drawing makeshift maps of how to get to the house where this poet lived, or this famous writer stayed. For a time, she'd even photocopied some of these maps, so she could pass them on to tourists, but it seemed fewer and fewer young people even knew who Ozu was, let alone made the pilgrimage all the way to Onomichi just to see the place. All the while, the dignified town silently rusted and crumbled. But that was part of its charm.

Sometimes, on certain warm spring days when the blossoms were out, there would be a sudden influx of visitors. At those times, people would be queueing outside the Onomichi ramen shops, and Ayako would even find herself turning customers away – unable to cope with the crowds, either in terms of service, or the amount of food she had on offer that day.

Budding entrepreneurs would have been alarmed at Ayako's business practice. But she was not in this for the money. Ayako had enough by way of savings to get by in the rural town, with its low cost of living. But for her, the café was a daily routine; it was a place for her to meet her friends; it was something to do – to keep the mind and body occupied during the day, so she could sleep better at night. It was a spiritual practice – the inevitable small chores that kept her busy – these were things that stopped her thinking about larger, existential questions. Her favourite days were the ones when she had fewer customers – when she wasn't rushed off her feet. On some days, she'd have time to take small breaks, read a book, listen to jazz and have a cup of coffee herself in between the morning and lunchtime rushes.

Or on a normal day when just the locals visited the café, she'd have a decent chinwag about what was going on in the town. Ayako didn't spread gossip herself, but she liked to listen to the stories other people told. The thing she found most interesting was how one person's story would differ so wildly from another's – even when concerning the exact same event. She was sharp. Nothing got by her.

In another life, Ayako might have been a forensic scientist or a homicide detective, interviewing suspects, or rolling the body over at the scene and trying to work out what happened from the clues.

But society had never allowed her that.

●

Ayako usually closed the shop at around 4.30 p.m. She then locked up, pulling down the clanking metal shutter, which echoed around the shotengai. Heading home, she took the longest route back to her house.

Whether rain or snow, sun or wind, nothing stopped Ayako from walking to the top of the mountain. She took the same route each day – the long, winding paths that led up the mountainside, cutting past the Temple of One Thousand Lights, all the way to the summit. From the top, she would look out across the town and the surrounding mountains, admiring the view. On wet and windy days, she might wear a tonbi overcoat on top of her kimono and carry an umbrella. On hot, sunny days, she'd wear a sun hat and carry a fan in her obi sash.

After taking in the view she made her way back down, often passing through what was locally referred to as 'Neko no Hosomichi' – Cat Alley. Once there, she would take out tins of tuna from her bag and pieces of crabstick to feed the cats.

While feeding the cats, she would stroke and pet them each individually. The brave ones would lie on their backs on the grey cobblestoned path, allowing her to rub their tummies. She had nicknames for each of them, but her absolute favourite was a black cat with one eye and a little round tuft of white on his chest who she'd named Coltrane, after her favourite jazz musician. It was a good day in Ayako's mind if Coltrane turned up for a stroke and a fuss.

That day, Ayako was squatting down, stroking another cat, when he hopped up on to a low stone wall. She noticed him out of the corner of her eye, and cracked a smile.

'Coltrane,' she said, turning her head slowly towards him. 'Supper?'

He licked his lips and stared at her with his big green eye.

She waved a crabstick at him, and his eye bulged.

He hopped down nimbly from the wall and padded towards the piece of crabstick Ayako proffered. Sniffing it tentatively, he then took a bite and began chewing. Ayako let him have the stick and started to stroke him gently.

Whenever she stroked Coltrane, her mind fixated on her missing digits. She had the strange sensation that they were still there. It was a little confusing. She felt his thick, beautiful fur beneath her fingers, and if she looked away, she began to get the inclination that her missing fingers were still there – that they'd magically grown back. It wasn't until she looked down, and saw the stubs, that she came back to her body, with her missing toes and fingers. But if she looked away and kept stroking, it was almost as if they were there again.

Coltrane had finished the crabstick and was licking his lips again. As ever, she took inspiration from the cat – he had lost an eye, but was getting on with things just fine. Ayako gave him a scratch under the chin and dug out another crabstick for him. (She kept some extra stashed away, just in case he turned up late.)

'Well . . . Coltrane,' she said, running her hand through his fur absent-mindedly, 'he arrives tomorrow.'

Coltrane chewed on the last piece, and looked at Ayako expectantly for more.

'I don't know what it'll mean for me.' She sighed. 'But he's coming.'

Coltrane mewed his curiously high-pitched whine.

'All gone,' she said, showing her empty hands spread out. 'None left.'

Coltrane eyed her up and down, a little dubiously.

'You've eaten them all.' She stood up, and Coltrane began to rub up against her legs as she stared off into the distance. 'All gone, my darling.'

Having fed and stroked the cats, Ayako made her way back down the mountain a little, to her old wooden house, and she spent the rest of the evening reading a book and listening to music quietly on her small CD stereo system.

Ayako didn't go out much for fun. She would occasionally visit an izakaya with some of the café regulars, Sato, Station Master Ono and his wife Michiko, or Jun and Emi for dinner. But only after they'd begged her to the point that she couldn't refuse any longer. Ayako didn't drink excessively, although she liked a couple of glasses of umeshu plum wine when she got together with others. But most nights she spent at home, by herself. She rarely stayed up too late, as her early starts made her feel dozy in the evenings.

But that night, she struggled to fall asleep. Despite getting ready for bed and turning out the lights at the usual time, she kept fretting about her grandson's arrival. She tossed and turned in her futon. Unable to sleep, she switched on the light again and got up. She went out into the corridor and slid open the door of the other bedroom. She'd purchased a new futon set from the department store and had the delivery men bring it all over for her. The cupboards in this room had been empty for a long time, but she'd ensured there was fresh linen and towels for his stay. She looked at the calligraphic scroll hanging on the wall.

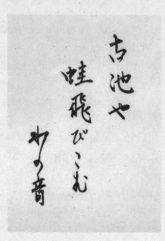

Would he be happy here? Would he be comfortable?

Ayako sighed.

There wasn't much she could do about it if he wasn't, but she wanted perfection.

Unattainable perfection.

She turned off the light in the spare bedroom, got herself a glass of water and opened the screen doors that led into the small garden. She sat down on the veranda, admiring her favourite Japanese maple tree bathed in soft moonlight. Her eyes wandered the rest of the garden, making notes of small jobs that needed doing soon. Looking up at the sky, she saw the stars and the moon shining brightly down on the town.

She drank her glass of water slowly.

It was a perfect spring evening, neither too hot nor too cold. Just right. Yet, for Ayako spring was the hardest season – a time of change, a time of loss and rebirth. As perfect as the weather was, Ayako hated spring. She didn't particularly care for the delirious blossom-induced mood everyone entered as soon as the sakura bloomed. Ayako preferred it when things were normal – when they were stable. It seemed sad to have such beautiful blossoms only for a fleeting moment, and then have them taken away instantly. One minute they were here, the next they were gone. Like so many things in her life.

Spring was when her son, Kenji, had taken his own life. Pain spread through her chest at the thought. Things could be different, with her grandson. She would do better.

Finally, after an hour sitting out, a heavy physical drowsiness gripped her, and she closed the sliding door, placed her empty glass in the sink and got back under the covers of her futon. Her eyelids drooped, but her mind still spun with an awful sense of foreboding. She drifted slowly off into a troubled night of sleep, strange dreams piling up one after another in her head – running from monsters, dropping and smashing cups and saucers in the café, chasing after Coltrane as he ran out into a street with heavy traffic – it was a night of awkward nightmares, and she was glad when morning finally came.

'Come on, Kyo. It's not forever, is it?'

Kyo looked at the shiny tiled floor, unable to return the intense gaze of his mother.

They were standing on the concourse in Tokyo Station, just outside the ticket gates to the Shinkansen bullet train. Kyo had only a light backpack slung over his left shoulder – the bulk of his baggage having been sent on ahead by Black Cat delivery services the day before.

'I still don't understand *why*,' he muttered, unable to look up from the floor.

'You know *why*, Kyo,' said his mother sharply. 'And we've been over this before.'

The station was fairly crowded, and there were people flying about in all directions, switching to local trains that ferried them throughout the city. But the bullet train was a gateway to the rest of Japan and its provincial folk. Kyo cast his eyes around, still avoiding his mother's gaze, and in his mind began filing people into two categories: Tokyoites and Out-of-towners.

The salarymen from other cities with their crumpled suits were easy enough to spot, with small wheelie suitcases and strange, almost frightened looks in their eyes. Their faces, unlike those of Kyo and his mother, showed an unease with the crush of the city and the masses of people swarming around them. The clothes the country bumpkins wore weren't the newest, and they weren't from the classier shops. They also wore naff sun hats and caps. Functional, but not fashionable. Clean, but not the cream.

In contrast to them, Kyo's mother was dressed in a sharp business suit, with a crisp white shirt underneath, her nails were painted and polished, and her long black hair was washed and conditioned to perfection. Kyo himself wore smart casual shorts, and a band t-shirt he'd bought last week at a gig – his hair was cropped in the current trend for young men in the capital.

And to think, Kyo would be going to live amongst the Out-of-towners. He shuddered at the thought.

'Look . . .' said his mother, softer than before. 'I really have to get going or I'll be late for work. I have patients back to back today.'

Kyo nodded glumly, resigned to his fate.

'But here.' Kyo's mother pulled out a thick envelope from her suit pocket and handed it to him. She'd written out his full name and Grandmother's address on it. 'There's enough for the bullet train, and the rest I want you to give to your grandmother when you arrive. It's to cover her costs in hosting you, so if you need anything else, just let me know and I can wire money to you. Okay?'

Kyo finally lifted his eyes to meet his mother's. She looked tired. Tired, but focused and professional. Ready to take on the day. Kyo couldn't help but smile when he saw her face, and the corners of her mouth twitched uncontrollably, too.

He took the package from her. 'Thank you, Mother.'

'Don't thank me.' She waved her hand dismissively. 'Thank your grandmother.'

'But . . .' Kyo hesitated. 'I barely know her.'

Kyo's mother sighed. 'Well, this is your chance to get to know her, right?'

'Right,' said Kyo, tucking the envelope of money into the side pocket of his backpack.

'Kyo,' said Mother with a look of irritation, 'put it away somewhere safer. It'll fall out there.'

Kyo dutifully opened the backpack and put the envelope away in the main compartment, clipping the straps shut. All the while his mother watched, nodding her head. After he slung the pack over his shoulder again, and Mother was reassured everything was safe, she looked at her watch.

'Right. I'd better get going. And you'd better go buy your ticket. There's a Shinkansen leaving in fifteen minutes which will take you all the way to Fukuyama. Then you just switch to the local train and it's less than thirty minutes on that. Just a few stops. She's expecting you this afternoon. Okay?'

'Okay.'

'Sure you'll be all right?' Mother eyed him up one last time, her eyes twinkling with moisture. Kyo nodded, and gave her a weak smile.

'Take care,' she said softly, wiping her eyes. 'And I'll see you soon. It's not forever. Okay?'

Kyo nodded, swallowing a lump in his throat. 'Okay.'

○

Kyo looked up the price of the bullet train at the ticket machine. He took out the envelope of cash his mother had given him, and leafed through the ten-thousand-yen bills, totting up the amount in his mind.

Then he got out his phone and booted up a train timetable app, studying it carefully.

If he rode local trains instead of the bullet train, it would only take two days to get there. He could stop overnight in Osaka at a net café, or find a family restaurant open all night and just sleep at the booth nursing a cup of coffee, or even just kip outside, somewhere out of sight. It'd take an extra day to arrive, but it would save a lot of money. Part of his mind told him he would get to appreciate the scenery more from the train window, and yet, underneath this sunny disposition, a deeper part of his psyche pulled him strongly towards the dark waters of the canal in Osaka.

He nodded, mind made up.

Slipping his phone back into the pocket of his shorts, Kyo walked away from the Shinkansen gates, looking for the local train to board. Riding the escalator up to the platform, he bought an onigiri and a can of iced coffee from the lady working at the kiosk, then spotted his train, which was due to depart in two minutes. He grabbed a seat, put on his headphones, and was pleased with himself for this excellent idea.

He also decided it was pointless to tell either Mother or Grandmother about his change of plan. Mother wouldn't see his messages while she was in clinic, and Grandmother didn't have a mobile phone, let alone a smartphone with LINE to message her on, so there was no way to contact her ahead of time. But it would be fine – he'd just be a day or two late, that was all. Maybe he could even spend a couple of days in Osaka – take in the sights. Why was he even rushing to Onomichi? And so what if he arrived late? It would be a nice surprise. As the train pulled away slowly from the platform, Kyo prepared himself for an adventure.

He'd drifted off, and when he opened his eyes, the girl was still there.

She'd caught Kyo's eye as soon as she'd sat down opposite him on the train at Yokohama. She'd also looked directly at Kyo, and he'd had to avert his gaze in embarrassment. Instead, he'd taken out his sketchbook. He was listening to the old Walkman he'd inherited from his father, a mix tape he'd made at home turning away on the spools inside. Most people found it weird when they saw him listening to a vintage Walkman, as the majority had MP3 players, iPods, or listened to music on their smartphones. But Kyo appreciated the Walkman. It was reliable.

It was not that Kyo completely disapproved of smartphones – he would've been a very strange nineteen-year-old had that been the case – but he was avoiding his right now, because it was getting harder and harder to see his friends posting photos of their new lives at university, while he was stuck in a limbo of his own making.

His mind flitted to the few and sparse conversations he'd had with his mother recently. The stress and strain of those already infrequent interactions, littered now with her concerns about his future and security. The idea that his failure to get into medical school was somehow paving the path to his imminent destruction. He hated disappointing his mother. From the beginning it had always been just her and him against the world; what little happiness she had in life seemed to come through his minor successes. When he thought of her face the night he'd got his results, he was filled with an overwhelming guilt and shame – he had caused her distress.

His failure had.

He tried to bury these thoughts, he had to.

Instead, Kyo passed the time by looking at the people around him, studying them carefully and trying to work out who they were, where they were from, where they were going, what they did. He looked for their strongest characteristics, the things that made them special. He'd sit with his sketchbook open, and just idly draw what he saw. It was easy while everyone was so absorbed in their phones to draw caricatures of his fellow passengers. Eyeballs being sucked into screens, devices growing mouths, hungrily devouring the faces of their owners.

Looking out of the window, he'd watched and sketched as the metallic grey high-rises of Tokyo slowly shrunk into the paddy fields, becoming peppered with mountains. He'd been sitting there quietly pencilling a man with a nose shaped like an aubergine when suddenly the vast shape of Mount Fuji had floated outside through the window. Kyo took off his headphones to the sounds of awe-filled gasps as everyone on the train turned their heads and pointed. That day, the sky was a clear blue, and visibility was perfect. The mountain was there, with soft white wispy clouds kissing its summit.

Kyo began to sketch the outline of the mountain before it disappeared from view. He then worked on the detail from memory, drawing in the line of snow and the surrounding clouds. He began to illustrate a small frog character of his own creation, slowly climbing the mountain. His sketchbook was filled with drawings of this same frog, and often people would ask him why he drew this particular character everywhere. He'd usually dismiss the question with a brief, 'Cos I like him.'

But this was not the whole truth. The truth was that, along with his Walkman, he'd only received a few items from Father before he died. One of which was a wood carving of a toy frog, currently residing in Kyo's backpack. Mother informed Kyo that it had been carved from a piece of Japanese maple wood by his father. But to Kyo, it represented more – a link to the father he had never known. Kyo slept with the frog at his bedside. He'd done so ever since he could remember.

Kyo's early memories of growing up were with just his mother looking after him, persevering as a single parent, while also holding down her full-time job as a doctor.

When he was younger, amusing himself during the day, he'd take the frog to his desk in his bedroom and play with it – putting him in different situations, imagining the frog was his father – still able to communicate from the next life. Sometimes the frog was a detective, wearing a hat and overcoat, solving murders. At times Frog was a firefighter, putting out blazing buildings with water from an old pond. Other times Frog was a ronin – a masterless samurai – travelling the countryside, aiding the poor and weak. And sometimes Frog was just Father, giving him advice, or reassuring words when he could hear Mother crying in the next room late at night. Frog could be whatever persona of his father Kyo wanted him to be, he could change, he could be special. Not like the fathers of his friends, who were always the same. Frog was a hero, battling against anything the world threw at him.

When he'd first started at elementary school, his mother hadn't allowed Kyo to take Frog with him, despite his insistence. Rightly so, because it's exactly the kind of thing he would've been bullied for at a Tokyo elementary school. Kyo remembered well his mother lecturing him before school started, about how he had to fit in, how he must not stand out, or be weird. How he had to get along with people – school was about making friends and learning to be a functioning member of society. At the end of each day, he would go to juku cram school, like so many other pupils, to actually learn the things needed to pass exams. But school itself was about learning social skills.

And Kyo took her advice – as he always did. His mother was an incredibly intelligent woman. He was good at fitting in, and he did his best to be like his classmates.

But the absence of Frog from his school life left him feeling empty.

So Kyo began to sketch little doodles of Frog in the back of his notebooks. He'd do these from memory, and would draw speech bubbles, and have Frog saying things, or wearing different costumes. He began, also, to draw a younger version of Frog, and this younger Frog, Kyo saw as himself. Sometimes he would draw the pair performing brave feats together, dressed in similar garb. The new younger Frog he named Sidekick Frog.

When his classmates saw the Frog doodles, they didn't think it strange or weird – quite the opposite. Boys pronounced the Samurai Frog he'd drawn 'kakkoii' (cool), and asked him to draw one for them in their notebooks. Equally, girls dubbed Detective Frog 'kawaii' (cute), and would demand Kyo replicate the character for them on the covers of their diaries. All through elementary, middle and high school, Kyo had the reputation of being a great cartoonist, and he was often called upon to draw scenes and characters on the blackboard by his classmates.

Now, on the train, Kyo added the finishing touches to his Frog Climbing Mount Fuji sketch – drawing in a walking stick, and a wide-brimmed hat on Frog, to give him the appearance of an ancient travelling haiku poet like Matsuo Basho. Underneath, he wrote the word 'PERSISTENCE'.

He looked up from his drawing.

The girl was smiling. At him.

Kyo felt his face flush, and looked back down at his sketchbook. He flicked back a few pages nonchalantly, ignoring the girl. And as he riffled nervously through the pages, he came to a big double-page sketch of Sidekick Frog dressed as a high school student, checking his exam results on the wall, with the other students crowded around pieces of paper pinned to the noticeboard. Frog's expression was downcast – distraught – and underneath the sketch, Kyo had written 'FAILURE' in fierce letters.

He shut the sketchbook and looked out of the window.

O

Kyo was a daydreamer. Now, on the train, he took in the world around him, and drew intently in his open notebook perched on his lap, depicting snatches of incidents from his long and solitary journey.

This is what he drew:

Sidekick Frog, dressed in shorts and a polo shirt, sitting alone in the car, the whole train wobbling on the rattling tracks of the slow local line. The emptiness of the train carriage. Sidekick Frog, leaping, manically hopping from one train to another. Sidekick Frog staring out of the windows – eyes bulging – passing innumerable small stations – the names a blur. Clouds . . . floating soft white clouds that spread out serenely across the azure sky. Clouds reflected in the waters of the paddy fields. Father Frog, reclining lazily on a cloud, floating on it like a magic carpet over the bright blue tiled roofs of traditionally built houses, with their porcelain flying fish, one at each end of the roof. The scenes of sky moved gently across the train's windowpane. All of this becoming different shades of black pencil mark on the whiteness of the page.

He had a lot of ideas, hundreds of them, but never acted on them. One of his absolute favourite things to do was to stare out of any given window examining what he saw in a half-hearted way. The objects in front of him were there, but they also weren't, at the same time. What appeared before Kyo was more like an *augmented* reality. When he saw the real mountains, a giant Godzilla would spring up from behind and crash down on the forest, ripping up tree trunks with its claws, breathing fire on the rest of the forest and surrounding the world in chaos and terror.

Or perhaps the pencil he was working with would grow a mouth and eyes, and would begin to talk to him.

'Hello, Kyo! How are you?' It would smile and wave at him with a funny expression.

Real objects around him began to take on lives of their own, and the boredom of reality was quickly assuaged by any kind of nonsensical idea he had come up with in his head. He would stare at objects for extended periods of time, thinking.

What if . . . ? What if . . . ?

Kyo sat on the train like this now, wondering at everything he could see, and all of the extra details his mind could add. Sometimes he doodled these ideas down in his notebook, and the act of drawing made him extremely calm. Shading and working away were actions he enjoyed deeply, and his most cherished dream in life was to become a manga artist.

But Kyo had a big problem. As good as he was at rendering real objects into a cartoon world, as much as he enjoyed drawing, as great as he was at coming up with characters, what he struggled with was finishing a story.

He would sit down and tell himself, 'Right! I'm going to draw and write a short manga story. It will have a beginning, a middle and an end!'

He would roll up his sleeves, take up his pencil and paper, sit there, and stare at the blankness of the page.

And the white page would stare back at him. He'd look out of the window . . .

'But first . . .' he'd say to himself.

And then he'd be off on another one of his daydreams.

○

One of the major problems with Kyo's plan to travel by local train, other than the long periods of time sitting down on less comfortable seats, was the interruption. Each local train would hit its terminus, and he'd have to get out with the other passengers and wait on the platform for another train which would take him further along on his route. Sometimes he'd get lucky, and the next train would be waiting for him to dash across to the other side of the platform. In these situations, everyone would be rushing across to make sure they got a seat for the next leg of the journey.

But, as he moved into the provinces, Kyo noticed people became more considerate about letting each other find a seat. He couldn't decide if they were kind or just foolish.

Each time Kyo changed trains, he noticed the same girl getting into the same carriage with him. And Kyo did his best not to stare, but something about the girl made him want to look at her more. Her eyes were so large and intelligent. She was reading a novel. On one leg of the journey he managed to get a glimpse of the author: Natsume Soseki. But he could not see the title. He desperately wanted to see what it was, but each time he looked, it was obscured by one of her slender fingers.

She'd looked up from the book directly at Kyo and smiled.

He'd shot his eyes back to his sketchbook, going back to shading a velociraptor attacking Frog, pretending he had always been doing so.

○

'What are you drawing?'

Kyo jumped, and almost dropped his pencil. He looked up to see the girl now sitting right opposite him in the four-seat section he'd thought he was occupying by himself. The rest of the carriage was empty, and, being absorbed in his drawing, he hadn't noticed the girl sit down right in front of him. He closed the sketchbook as casually as possible.

'Nothing,' he replied quickly. 'What are you reading?'

'Nothing,' she said mockingly, cocking her head, her eyes twinkling.

'I saw it's by Soseki,' said Kyo. 'But I couldn't see the title. Is it any good?'

'I'm still only a few chapters in.' She leant back in her seat and studied Kyo's face intently. 'It's about a young man starting at university in Tokyo. Some woman tries to seduce him on the train.'

Kyo blushed. The girl continued talking.

'I've seen you on these trains since Yokohama. You're in for the long haul, too, eh? Where you headed?'

'Hiroshima,' Kyo said without thinking. It was a vague answer which was neither a lie nor the whole truth. She could interpret the answer as Hiroshima City or Hiroshima Prefecture, whichever suited her. Kyo raised an eyebrow, turning the question on her. 'You?'

'Onomichi,' she said sunnily. Kyo winced. 'What are you doing in Hiroshima? University student?'

Kyo's face flushed again, and he stammered, unable to lie. 'Well . . . not exactly—'

'Are you still in high school?' she asked suddenly.

'No.' Kyo shook his head. 'I just graduated.'

'Okay, so why are you headed to Hiroshima? New job? Family?'

Kyo realized that she was asking him a lot of questions, and he hadn't got much information from her in return. She was putting him on the spot. Nevertheless, he answered politely.

'Not a new job.' Kyo shook his head. 'It's kind of a long story . . .' He trailed off.

She smiled at him, pointed out of the window at the scenery steadily scrolling past. 'We have time, don't we?'

Kyo sighed. 'Well, it's kind of embarrassing, but—'

'Embarrassing?' She laughed, sitting forward in her seat. 'This sounds interesting. Go on.'

'So, I'm a ronin-sei.'

'Ahhh.' She nodded, hitting her palm with her fist in realization. 'So you failed your university entrance exams, huh? A masterless samurai student.'

'Yup.'

'And you're going to Hiroshima to enrol in a yobiko university entrance cram school?'

'Er, yup.' Kyo looked out the window at the houses flicking by, one by one.

'That's not embarrassing,' she said. 'There are far worse things in life than that.'

She sighed, and they were quiet for a time. Kyo sipped his coffee. She eyed up the can.

'Can I have a sip?' she asked.

'Sure,' he said, handing her the can gingerly.

'Thanks.' She took the can from him, sipping on it as if they'd known each other for years, and then handed it back.

'Can I ask a question?' said Kyo, taking the can from her nervously.

'Sure. Was that it?' she said, giggling. The typical answer to such a timid question.

'No, uh, it's just . . .' he said, struggling to muster the courage.

'Come on, spit it out.' She screwed up her face. '*Do you have a boyfriend?*'

'No!' Kyo's bashful face transformed into one of shock, while the girl laughed.

'You're not interested?' She slapped him on the knee. 'Damn.'

'No, what I wanted to ask was—' Kyo collected himself. 'Well, why are you headed to Onomichi?'

'University,' she said quickly. 'I'm at Hiroshima University, but I live in Onomichi. Even longer story to that, and I don't want to go into it. Now, let me ask *you* questions, because that's more fun.'

For who, though? thought Kyo.

'What are you trying to get into university to study?' she asked; then before he could answer another question she blurted out, 'Art?'

'No,' Kyo said, shaking his head. 'It's—'

'Wait! Don't tell me! Let me guess!'

'Okay.'

'Japanese literature?'

'Nope.'

'Engineering?'

'Nope.'

'Hmmm . . .' She narrowed her eyes and studied his face for a while, then she clapped her hands together, pointing one finger straight at him. 'Got it. Medicine?'

'Ping pong.' Kyo nodded.

'I knew I'd get it.'

'Well done.'

'What's my prize?'

'This pencil.' Kyo offered her the pencil he'd been drawing with.

'Really?' She smirked. 'But it seems like it has a better home with you. I cannot accept this pencil.' She bowed her head in jest, pushing the pencil away.

'Please take it,' said Kyo, holding it out for her, bowing deeply. 'May it serve you well.'

'My humble thanks,' she said, formally receiving the pencil with a low bow in return. 'I shall treasure it, and when you become a famous manga artist, I shall tell everyone I received this pencil from you.'

Kyo snorted. 'Well, that's not gonna happen.'

'It might.' She raised an eyebrow. 'I saw your drawings – they're really good. That's why I thought you were going to study art. I'm kinda surprised you want to do medicine when you have a talent like that.' She shrugged. 'But what do I know?'

Kyo looked out of the window, an awkwardness descending over the pair of them. He didn't know what to say, so he said nothing. She broke the silence again.

'Where are you stopping over for the night?' she asked. For a moment, Kyo detected a tentative tone in her voice, but he shook the thought away quickly.

'Osaka,' said Kyo.

'Me too!' Her eyes lit up. 'We can be travel buddies.'

'Sure,' said Kyo, not exactly knowing what that entailed.

'Ayumi,' she said, extending her hand like a non-Japanese.

'Kyo.' He reached out and returned the handshake, worried that his palms were sweaty.

They chatted about all sorts, from manga, to music, to films, for the rest of the journey to Osaka, and Kyo barely noticed the time whizzing by. He became so absorbed in the conversation he didn't check his phone.

Or notice any of the many notifications it was getting inside his backpack.

○

When they arrived in Osaka and got off the train, it was already evening, and the night sky spread out above them. Kyo had not visited Osaka by himself before but was comfortable with the speed and pace of the place – he was back in a city again after all.

Kyo and Ayumi left through the ticket gates, and as they did, he felt a tightness in his chest. He had to say goodbye to her, but he wasn't sure whether he wanted to or not. When they came to a quiet spot outside the ticket gates, he stopped, and they both turned to face one another.

'So,' said Ayumi.

'So . . .' said Kyo.

She had a small wheelie suitcase with her, which he'd helped her carry off the train and down the stairs. Now she wheeled it by herself.

'So, I have to put this in a locker,' she said slowly. 'And then, maybe would you like to grab a bite to eat together?'

'Sure,' said Kyo, feeling the tightness in his chest release.

'Great! You wait here,' she said, heading off to stash her bag in a locker.

He was enjoying her company.

○

It was only much later, after they'd finished eating ramen, that it got awkward.

They'd continued to chat about mutual interests, debating the merits of Fukuoka's tonkotsu ramen, which the girl was a fervent champion of, versus Sapporo's miso ramen, which Kyo proposed as the best bowl he'd ever had, on one of the few holidays of his life. They'd then discussed the importance of al dente noodles – this, they both agreed on strongly. Halfway through eating, the girl had interrupted.

'I fancy a beer. Do you want one?'

Kyo looked around nervously. 'But I'm only nineteen.'

'Shhh!' She put her finger to her lips. 'Not so loud, idiot.'

Without waiting for a response from Kyo, she called out, 'Sumimasen!' to the cook and ordered two beers for the both of them.

Kyo took his icy glass, clinked it against Ayumi's and joined her in a hearty 'Kanpai!' She drained half in one go, making an 'Ahhhh!' sound after she swallowed. Meanwhile Kyo sipped slowly on his – not wanting to get drunk.

The girl had one more beer before Kyo could even finish his first.

He insisted on paying for the girl's ramen and beers, and she thanked him profusely, suggesting that she get the next round.

They moved on to a small bar, and were halfway through their drinks when the girl interrupted Kyo again, while he was delivering a short monologue on why *Akira* was overrated.

'Look, where are you staying tonight?' she demanded.

Kyo spluttered, caught off guard and unable to form a sentence. 'I dunno . . .'

'Listen,' she said, raising a finger. 'Do you want to stay somewhere together?'

'. . .' Kyo didn't know how to respond.

'Look, nothing like that is going to happen.' She swayed slightly as she spoke, and the way she said it made Kyo's heart sink. 'It'll just save us some money. Travel buddies. What do you say?'

Kyo looked down at the beer he was still drinking. She'd finished hers already.

'I'm not sure . . .'

'Come on, I don't bite, you know,' she said.

But Kyo had other plans. He wanted to go to a certain bridge in Dotonbori. He'd been planning on visiting this spot the whole time, but how would he bring someone he'd just met on a train to such a personal place in his life? A place where his past, present and future had been decided in his father's one selfish act. How would he even begin to explain why it was so important to him? He barely knew this girl, and couldn't bring himself to go into details.

'Look, I'm going to the ladies,' she said, standing up, leaning over and speaking quietly in his ear. 'Get us a couple more beers, okay? Don't worry so much about everything.'

She left Kyo staring down at his glass of fizzing beer, alone.

He waited for a minute. Unable to decide, yet knowing he had to. After a couple of minutes, he took out the envelope of money from his backpack, placed more than enough cash for the drinks next to her empty glass, bowed to the bartender, and walked straight out of the bar, out into the Mido-Suji night of downtown Osaka, disappearing immediately in the crowded streets.

Coward, said the voice in his head. *Failure.*

He most certainly was.

All he had to do was explain the situation to the girl. It would've only taken five minutes. Then he wouldn't have abandoned her like that, wordlessly.

He couldn't open up to her, because he was a coward.

A coward, and a failure.

A dropout. A masterless samurai student.

A disappointment to his busy mother, and his dead war photographer father.

Kyo wandered the bustling nightlife streets of Osaka's Minami district, watching friends sitting in bars, singing, laughing and enjoying themselves. The two beers he'd had earlier left him feeling morose and empty, not joyful like the rest of the drinkers who were out late.

He went to a family restaurant and sat inside reading a comic book – Urasawa Naoki's *20th Century Boys* – which he'd picked up from a second-hand shop, still open late into the night. The conveniences of city life would be hard to leave behind. He would miss this sense of vibrancy.

Being honest with himself, he'd taken the slow train because he didn't want to go to Onomichi. He didn't want to stay with his grandmother in the countryside. He hated the fact that all his friends were starting new lives at university, while he was trapped in a world of resitting failed exams. He slumped in the family restaurant, nursing cup after cup of sugary, milky coffee, reading manga and sketching ideas in his notebook when he could muster the energy. He thought back over abandoning Ayumi at the bar, without saying anything, and cringed. Mostly he rested his head in his hands and slept.

Before dawn broke, he left the café and strolled through the empty streets, past a few drunkards who'd fallen asleep on the road, past the puddles of sick left behind from the night before. He made his way to Dotonbori, where the canal passed under Ebisu Bridge. The famous Glico Running Man flashed on the side of the building, but now there were no tourists snapping selfies in front of it, the streets were deserted. He'd seen tons of photos of the place online, and had rehearsed this moment in his head many times before. The sun was rising slowly as Kyo leant out over the edge of the low bridge, his pensive reflection below looking back up at him from the surface of the water.

The same patch of water from which the police had pulled his father's bloated body all those years ago. Cool, calm, dark waters. It looked inviting, the way it ebbed and flowed, currents rippling in small waves. He had finally come to the place where his father had ended his own life. Kyo had envisaged this a million times up until this point. And now he was here.

He took out the little wooden frog from his backpack, and placed it on the edge of the bridge. He listened.

But all he could hear was the soft sound of water.

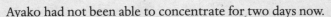

Ayako had not been able to concentrate for two days now.

Even at the café, she struggled to hear what customers were saying to her. At home, the phone, which she usually kept on a bookcase under a cloth cover, had been out in the centre of the living room on the low table since the night before, when she'd first rung Kyo's mother to let her know that Kyo had not yet arrived.

She had waited at Onomichi train station for two whole hours before finally deciding he wasn't coming. The trains rumbled back and forth, clattering on their tracks, and each time, before one rolled by, the bell of the crossing signal would *ding ding* away, making Ayako wonder if this would perhaps be Kyo's train. She sat in the foyer of the small station on one of the benches, passengers drifting to and fro past her, scouring faces for Kyo, but to no avail. There were two exits to the station – this main one on the sea side, and another on the mountain side of the tracks, which was much smaller and tended only to be used by locals who were heading north. Most people, especially those new to the town, would get off at this south exit. Ayako was pretty sure of that. Nevertheless, she still popped her head up nervously now and again to see if anyone was leaving through the north exit on the other side of the tracks.

Station Master Ono was working behind the ticket gate that day. He was a pleasant fellow, knew Ayako well, and had noticed her bobbing her head around looking for someone, so he came over to chat in a break between trains.

'Waiting for anyone in particular, Ayako-san?' he asked, stopping in front of the bench Ayako was seated on. 'You've been sitting here for quite a while, haven't you?' He put his hands on his hips, comfortable with his beer belly peeking out over the top of his smart uniform trousers. His spectacles were slowly sliding down his nose.

'Ono-san.' Ayako bowed her head to him. 'I'm waiting for my grandson, who's coming from Tokyo. He was supposed to arrive on a train quite some time ago.'

'Well, that is strange,' he said, pushing his spectacles back up his nose and blinking.

'Have there been any delays? Or accidents?' asked Ayako.

'Absolutely none today – we are running like clockwork.'

Ayako shifted nervously.

'But look,' said Station Master Ono. 'There's no need for you to wait here. If you tell me how old he is, and what he looks like, I'll keep my eye out for any tickets from Tokyo that look like him, and if I spot him, I can call you at home, or at the café. How does that sound?'

'Ono-san,' said Ayako, bowing her head again, this time in embarrassment. 'Please, it's too much to ask.'

'Not at all!' Ono waved his hand dismissively.

Ayako skipped her daily walk to the top of the mountain and went straight home. She'd got the phone out immediately, looked up Kyo's mother's mobile phone number in her diary and called her.

'Moshi moshi?' came her daughter-in-law's voice over the crackling line.

'Setchan?'

'Mother?'

Ayako still addressed Kyo's mother as Setchan, and Kyo's mother made sure to address Ayako as Mother. They didn't talk often these days, but whenever they did it felt right to use these terms.

'Setchan, I'm terribly sorry to bother you, and it's probably nothing, but Kyo-kun was not on the train I was expecting him on.'

'Strange . . .' Setsuko paused. 'That is strange, Mother, because I left him at the Shinkansen gates in Tokyo Station this morning with plenty of time to get his ticket and board his train. He should've arrived hours ago.'

'Yes,' said Ayako, nodding her head despite being on the phone. 'That's what I thought, too. I wrote down the times of the trains you'd given me, and even if there was a delay, or he missed a connection, or stopped for a bite to eat, well, he should've arrived long ago.'

'Okay, Mother.' Setsuko clicked her teeth. 'I'm terribly sorry. I'll have to contact Kyo on LINE, and then I will call you back when I hear from him. Sorry, but I'm very busy today.'

'What's a line?'

'It's a smartphone application, Mother,' Setsuko explained patiently. 'It lets you send text messages to people.'

'I see,' said Ayako. She had no idea what her daughter-in-law was talking about, but was too anxious about Kyo to pursue it. 'Would you give me Kyo's mobile telephone number, just in case? I can call him from my telephone.'

'Of course! I feel silly for not giving it to you before.'

Setsuko read out Kyo's number while Ayako jotted it down in her diary.

'But, Mother, I think it still best if I message him on LINE and then call you,' said Setsuko briskly. 'Because if he is on the train, he won't be able to take a direct call from you, will he?'

'Very true.' Ayako nodded again, pleased that her grandson had manners enough not to take phone calls on a train.

They rang off, and Ayako left the house phone out on the table. Occasionally that evening, she would try phoning the number Setsuko had given her for Kyo, but it just went straight through to voicemail. Each time Ayako listened to Kyo's recorded voice it made her shiver – sounding so similar to her son, Kenji, speaking to her from beyond the grave. Setsuko called Ayako back at 9 p.m. to tell her that she had still not heard a word from Kyo, but to please not worry about him, that he would be all right. She was sure of it.

That night, she again spent fitfully. Unable to sleep, she got up from her futon many times to sit and stare at the telephone on the table. When she did fall asleep, she had anxious nightmares that Coltrane the one-eyed black cat was mewing and yowling, scratching at her front door, because she had neglected to feed him the evening before.

Dawn could not come soon enough.

While she was having breakfast that morning the phone rang, and Ayako snatched up the receiver as quickly as she could.

'Yesh?' she spoke through a mouthful of fish, swallowing quickly.

'Mother, please don't worry,' said Setsuko's voice calmly over the phone. 'I've heard from Kyo. He sent me a LINE message this morning. For some reason that idiot boy decided to take the slow train. He's stayed the night in Osaka, and will take the local train to Onomichi. He said he should arrive mid-afternoon today. He says he's very sorry for making you worry. But, Mother, please do scold him when he arrives. And then tell him to phone me, so I can scold him some more.'

'Thank you for letting me know,' said Ayako, feeling a slight relief.

They chatted briefly, Setsuko apologizing profusely to Ayako for the trouble her child had caused, and for not having time to talk – she was in between patients. Ayako dismissed the apologies and told Setsuko to please not worry. His luggage had arrived by Black Cat delivery that morning, and was waiting in his room.

Ayako hung up the phone, but she could not shake her anxiety.

Osaka.

Why had he stopped in Osaka, of all places?

Ayako began to prepare herself for the day, stopping once more in front of the two black and white photos resting on her Butsudan family altar, and she prayed for longer that day.

One prayer to her husband. One to her son.

Both prayers for her grandson.

O

Kyo sat on the train as it pulled through a black tunnel, emerging into the white light of the bright spring day. He was relieved he had not seen the girl on the train he took from Osaka that morning.

He had his artist's sketchbook in his hands. On the cover was the kanji for his name written neatly, black pen marks on a blank white sticker he'd pasted to the front.

He usually had to write it out, or explain it to anyone asking how his name was written. He would tell them that it was written using the character for the word 'echo' – like the brand of whisky – which was not pronounced as 'kyo', but as 'hibiki'. The kanji character had enthralled him ever since a young age. The top part 郷 meant 'village' and the bottom part 音 meant 'sound'. When he was a young child learning to write his own name, he'd pictured the scene of an empty village, with a single bell ringing out throughout the houses, echoing off the walls and through the empty streets. And this story, this scene, played out in his mind and helped him to remember how to write the character.

Entering Hiroshima Prefecture, and nearing his final stop of Onomichi, with the mountains on his right, the Seto Inland Sea appeared to his left – countless islands floating in the distance. The blue sea . . . now a white space on the canvas . . . no way to depict the blueness of the ocean in black and white. But with deft pencil strokes the serenity of the cool waters shone through in the gaps on the page. It existed. Twice. And was that a kaiju sea monster peeking its head out from the cool, serene waters . . . ?

The train was empty. Kyo sat in a four-seater section, with his feet up on the seat in front of him. He'd taken off his sandals before putting his feet on the seat, but that didn't stop the conductor checking this with a nervous look each time he walked past. Kyo studied the conductor's face carefully – beady eyes, dishevelled shirt, crooked tie and hooked nose – he too became a cartoon caricature in Kyo's sketchbook – a huge black crow with exaggerated features dressed in a uniform, intently studying the soles of Sidekick Frog's out-stretched feet on the seat. Bulbous toes splayed wide.

Kyo did this to prevent himself from thinking about what was going to happen when he arrived in Onomichi. He had to admit he was worried about the frantic LINE messages from Mother and the alarming number of missed calls on his phone, some from an unknown number.

He immersed himself in his sketches, his comic books and his music so he wouldn't have to analyse anything happening to him in his life – leaving Tokyo behind – or how he'd felt that morning in Osaka, staring down off the side of Ebisu Bridge, into the darkness of the water.

●

'Sure you're all right, Ayako?' asked Sato nervously. 'You're not yourself this morning.'

Ayako shot Sato a frown, which made him sit back on his stool slightly and raise his hands. If there had been other customers around, he probably would've got an earful. But right now, because Jun and Emi had left for work, it was just the two of them in the café.

Ayako softened her expression and breathed a heavy sigh.

'Come on,' said Sato, with more courage this time. 'Something's up. You can tell me.'

Ayako was finishing making herself a cup of coffee, and she slid it over the counter on its saucer, came around to the other side and sat down on the stool next to Sato. *Kind of Blue* by Miles Davis was playing over the stereo, and the streets outside were quiet now – all the children tucked away neatly behind the desks of their various schools. Occasionally a 'Good morning' would echo out in the covered market street outside the shop, or a boat would drift lazily past the window of the café, but Sato and Ayako had the place to themselves for now.

'It's nothing much, Sato-san.' Ayako blew on her hot coffee.

'Well, even the smallest thing can get under your skin.'

'It's just, well . . .' Ayako frowned. 'I haven't been sleeping so well the past couple of nights.'

'Hmmm . . .' Sato furrowed his brow, too. 'That's not like you, Aya-chan.'

She took a sip of her coffee.

'Well, I suppose you were going to find out about this sooner or later – and to be honest, it should've been sooner rather than later – but, well.' She made a growling sound in her throat before continuing. 'I'm having my grandson to stay with me from Tokyo.'

'Oh!' Sato's face lit up. 'That's wonderful!'

Ayako shot him a sideways glance. 'Is it?' She shook her head, before carrying on. 'He was supposed to arrive yesterday, but for some reason that numbskull travelled on local trains instead of the bullet train, and ended up taking a day extra.'

'Oh, come on.' Sato chuckled. 'That's not so bad, is it? I did much worse when I was a lad. How old is he?'

'Nineteen.' Ayako put her cup down on its saucer. 'But that's not the point, Sato-san. Of course I was worried about him when he didn't arrive on time. But, well, the thing that bothers me is that he stopped over in Osaka.'

Sato's smile fell, and he crossed his arms.

'That is a little—'

'If it had been Kyoto, Kobe or Himeji or anywhere else, I would've thought nothing of it.'

'Hmm, hmm.' Sato made noises of agreement as Ayako spoke.

'But there's just something worrying about his stopping over in Osaka, considering what happened to Kenji there.'

'I see.' Sato nodded. 'But, Aya-chan, it might just be a coincidence, you know?'

'Oh, I know that!' She swatted a hand dismissively at Sato. 'But that still doesn't make me feel any better about the whole thing, does it?'

Sato merely nodded, knowing there was nothing he could say right now to help.

'I'm going to crucify that boy when he gets here,' said Ayako.

'Oh, Aya-chan.' Sato laughed. 'Go easy on him, will you? We were all young once. We all make mistakes.'

'He's got to learn, Sato-san.' Ayako began to stand up and tidy away her cup and saucer. 'There are consequences for everything in life.'

○

Onomichi Castle came into focus as Kyo opened his eyes. He must have drifted off. The castle appeared to be floating high above him amongst the clouds. At first, he thought he was still dreaming, but then he saw the mountain it was perched atop of.

'The next stop is Onomichi. Onomichi. Doors on the right-hand side will open,' came the Crow Conductor's crackly voice over the tannoy. 'Onomichi. Next stop, Onomichi. Be careful when alighting the train and please don't forget any of your belongings. Thank you for riding JR West, and we hope to see you again soon.'

Kyo grabbed his backpack quickly, yawning and stretching as he stood and waited for the train to come to a halt.

The doors slid open, and he stepped lightly off the train.

It was the middle of the afternoon, and only a handful of people got off at the same time as him – even fewer were waiting on the platform to board the almost-empty train bound for Hiroshima.

Kyo made his way slowly out of the station, letting others go through the barriers ahead of him. There was a man on the gates who was manually taking tickets from passengers, bowing and thanking each one in turn.

Unbelievable. In Tokyo there was no way anyone could do that kind of job. And anyway, most people had Suica cards which they just tapped on the IC panels to go through the automated barriers. Even people with paper tickets fed them into the machines and passed through the same way. No need for this poor sod with a beer belly and glasses to be taking tickets from people and thanking them each individually. He looked a bit like a tanuki racoon dog with his huge glasses slipping down his nose and that big belly poking out over his belt.

What was this backwater place he'd come to?

As Kyo handed his ticket to the station worker and passed through the gate, he looked up in surprise as the man addressed him directly.

''Ey, mister . . . scuse me, sir?' said the Tanuki, peering through his glasses at Kyo, after studying his ticket.

'Yes?' Kyo paused awkwardly outside the gate; the man's Hiroshima dialect was thick and his accent strong, making it difficult for Kyo to decode what he'd said.

'S'awfully ruder me ter ahsk, loik, but did'ya come frum Tokyo?'

A shock went through Kyo's body. Why was this man asking him a question like that? His accent was almost incomprehensible.

'Umm, no?' responded Kyo, technically not lying, because he'd come from Osaka that morning.

'Ya'sure?' The man eyed him up inquisitively through his glasses, which were slipping down his nose again.

Kyo felt a hot flash of rage. Who the hell did this tanuki think he was, to question a passenger like this? Was Kyo under police investigation?

'I came from Osaka this morning,' said Kyo, a little defiantly.

'Osaka, eh?' The man nodded. 'Strange, cos ya ticket says Tokyo onnit, andya don't 'ave an Osaka accent . . . F'I'ad ter placeya, I'd sayya sounded more like a Tokyo man ter me . . .' Tanuki must've noticed Kyo's face turning a burning crimson as he spoke because he suddenly changed tack. 'But whadda I know, eh?' He laughed to himself.

'Is there any particular reason you're asking me such personal questions?' Kyo folded his arms, speaking in his politest register.

The ticket collector realized he'd made Kyo angry, and straightened his posture, switching to standard Japanese.

'I'm terribly sorry, sir, for my rudeness.' He bowed low.

'That's all right,' said Kyo, feeling guilty for being prickly.

'Please forgive me, sir,' the man continued. 'It's just that one of my friends is expecting her grandson, visiting from Tokyo, and I said I'd keep an eye out for him. You sort of matched the description she gave, but please accept my humble apologies.' He bowed even lower this time, almost scraping his nose on the ticket gate.

'That's okay,' said Kyo, feeling awful now for losing his temper. 'Don't worry about it.'

Kyo turned on his heels and walked quickly away from the exchange. He heard the ticket man mumbling to himself again in dialect.

Kyo shivered.

Would he ever get used to the way they spoke down here?

●

'Hello?' Ayako picked up the café's phone on the second ring.

'Ayako-san?' came the crackling voice of what sounded like Station Master Ono over the line.

'Ono-san?'

'Yes, it's me. How did you guess?'

'Any news?'

'He arrived. At least, I'm pretty sure it was him.'

'Are you sure?'

Ono paused, and sighed deeply. 'Umm, I could see the family resemblance, Ayako, if you know what I mean . . .' He trailed off awkwardly.

Ayako's heart beat faster, and she breathed a sigh of relief.

'Did you speak to him?'

'I did, although he seemed a bit taken aback by my questions. He's quite the well-spoken young Tokyo gentleman, isn't he? I felt awfully uncouth, speaking to him in our dialect. Said he came from Osaka, thank you very much, and not Tokyo – but I could tell from the way he spoke he's a Tokyoite.'

'Ah, it's got to be him. He stopped over in Osaka last night.'

'That'll be where the confusion came in. Must've thought I was asking where he came from this morning. My fault for asking the wrong questions.'

'Did you see where he went?'

'He kind of wandered out the front of the station, stopped at the water's edge for a bit, then made his way towards the shotengai covered market. I wouldn't be surprised if he was on his way to the café.'

'Thank you so much, Ono-san. I very much appreciate it.'

'Most welcome. Don't mention it.'

Ayako hung up the phone, and felt better. It had to be him.

But she still couldn't focus on what she was doing. Now, instead of waiting for the phone to ring, she glanced at the door every few seconds. She ignored the idle chatter of her final few lunch customers, and instead kept listening for the tinkling ring of the bell on the door.

○

The first impression that struck Kyo about the town was how dead it was. Hardly any people.

And the ones he could see were so old they may as well be dead.

Boring. So boring. The only sounds he could hear were the *dings* and chimes of the train station. He moved away from the ticket barriers, slowly and laboriously stepping over a stretch of grass towards the sea. He came to the shore-front and looked out across the waters. Was this really the sea lazily lapping against the concrete? It looked more like a lake. Kyo had been on seaside daytrips with his mother from Tokyo to places like Kamakura, Chigasaki, Enoshima, and there he'd seen the waves crashing dramatically against rocks, sending white spray into the air.

But now, looking out across the Seto Inland Sea, it didn't move. It just sat there, still. Boats drifted back and forth across the small estuary, and on the other side of the water he saw the docks with 'MUKAISHIMA DOCKYARD' written on the buildings in huge letters. How original. The ancient yokels must've named the island literally – Mukaishima – 'that island over there'. It now looked industrial, rusted and run-down. Most of this town seemed to be rusting, decaying, or just generally falling apart.

How was he going to live here?

He shook his head, and strode off towards the shotengai.

On his way, he came across a bronze statue of a woman wearing a kimono, crouched down low next to an old wicker suitcase with an umbrella propped on it. Kyo read the plaque: Hayashi Fumiko.

What the hell was that supposed to be?

So naff. So boring. So uncool.

He walked past shuttered shops. Elderly people with tired postures waddled past him now and again. Their backs bent – spines almost at ninety degrees to their legs – they walked with assistance from pushcarts, their heads facing down at the ground. Still, when Kyo passed by, they somehow noticed his presence, and would sing out with a friendly 'Konnichiwa!'

Kyo reluctantly returned the greeting.

Did everyone talk to each other all the time in this town?

Kyo walked for a little while, and rapidly found himself emerging from the covered market street and approaching a residential area. Already? But he'd only been walking for a few minutes, and he'd made it from one side to the other. Was the town really that small?

He stopped at a vending machine and bought a can of coffee, cracking it open and squatting down to check his phone. His mother's LINE messages gave strict instructions to go directly to Grandmother's café, rather than her house. An awful dread swilled around his stomach with the coffee. He was going to get chewed out.

He knew it.

He fired up a couple of social media apps one after the other and scrolled through photos his classmates had posted: of their new university dorms, their matriculation ceremonies, the new cities they were living in, the impressive university buildings they now attended, the friends they were making. When he saw a photo of his ex-girlfriend, Yuriko, wearing a formal kimono for the entrance ceremony of her course in medicine at a prestigious Tokyo university, he paused. Of course, Yuriko would have to show off by wearing a kimono, unlike her classmates. His thumb hovered over the image and he felt a stabbing jealousy in his abdomen.

Kyo sighed.

He clicked the three dots above her picture, and selected 'Mute' from the pop-up menu.

His battery was about to die. He had to move on.

Kyo finished his coffee and looked at his watch – 4 p.m. – already much later than he said he'd be. He made his way back down the covered market to his grandmother's café.

He walked as slowly as he could, but eventually reached the door.

'CAFÉ EVER REST' said the sign in large letters. It had a mountain painted on it.

Kyo sighed once more, and pushed the door open gently.

A bell jingled softly above his head.

☯

'Irasshaimase!'

Ayako called out the standard shopkeeper's greeting without looking up. Despite the fact she'd been eyeing up the door since Ono's call from the station, when the bell did ring, she robotically called out the greeting without raising her eyes.

'Grandmother?' came a sheepish voice from the doorway.

Ayako looked up, and saw him.

She dropped the cup she was holding in her hand, and it smashed on the floor.

She raised both hands to her face momentarily, in shock.

There he was.

A young boy of nineteen, with the same eyes, the same chin, the same mouth.

His hair was cut in a newer style, but there he was.

'Please let me help you clean that up, Grandmother,' he said.

And when he spoke, Ayako came back to herself. This boy speaking perfect standard Japanese, with a slight Tokyo affectation, was not her Kenji. Kenji had spoken Hiroshima dialect.

Kenji was long gone now.

This was Kenji's son.

Her grandson.

And she was supposed to be angry with him.

'Leave it,' she snapped at the boy as he tried to help her clean up the broken shards of the cup. 'Just sit down there and keep quiet. You've caused enough trouble.'

Kyo handed the broken pieces he'd already picked up to Ayako, and sat down at the table she'd pointed at. All of the customers had left before he'd arrived, and Ayako had been clearing away and closing up the café. As she picked up the pieces, her anger simmered like a pot of curry on the boil. She'd let her emotions exhibit themselves – she'd shown that she was worried, that she cared deep down. She'd even smashed one of her lovely china cups, which would have to be replaced. She'd been manipulated into caring, and this made her feel all the angrier.

Well, she would remain silent while she finished her chores.

Kyo watched his grandmother as she tidied away.

He'd seen a flash in her eyes when she'd caught sight of him for the first time. Was it relief? Love? Something had flickered across her face, but it had disappeared as quickly as it had appeared. Now all he saw was her stony expression as she slammed around the shop putting cups, plates and bowls away, occasionally moving him out of the way to sweep up. And deep down inside himself, he felt a rising sense of guilt and shame for making her worry.

She left the café wordlessly, and Kyo followed behind. They walked the streets in silence; although each time they passed people they would all greet Ayako, and she would respond politely, ignoring their intrigued expressions as they looked at Kyo questioningly. Ayako had no intention of filling anyone in, and she kept walking a few paces in front of him. As they were walking up the hill to her house, she finally broke the silence.

'Absolutely irresponsible,' she said suddenly. 'You didn't call. You didn't let anyone know.'

Kyo walked glumly alongside her.

'When you make a promise, you're supposed to keep it,' she said, stopping to stroke a black cat with one eye who was perched on a Honda Super Cub motorbike; she continued to berate Kyo as she fussed the cat. 'I've never heard of such stupidity. You had your poor mother worried sick. Not me, I don't give a toffee what happens to you. But did you ever stop and think about your poor mother's feelings? No. Because you're selfish. You're a selfish, irresponsible boy.'

Kyo remained silent, listening to her rage away. Eventually she would have to subside.

They came to an ancient stone wall with a door in the middle. She continued to rant and rave, pushing down on its huge rusty iron handle. The hinges squealed as she leant her entire body weight against the door, swinging it open. They passed through into an enclosed garden, which surrounded and enveloped a beautiful traditionally built wooden house with shiny new ceramic tiles on its roof.

They stepped through the genkan entranceway, into the cool interior. She finally looked him in the eyes and demanded, 'Well, what have you got to say for yourself?'

He paused and bowed low. 'I'm sorry, Grandmother. I'll never do it again.'

'Too right you won't,' she shot back quickly, jabbing a finger at his chest. '*Go ni haitte wa go ni shitagae – When entering the village, abide by the village rules.*' So, she liked to speak in proverbs. 'We shan't be having any more of that nonsense while you're living with me. Got it?'

'Yes, Grandmother.'

'Good. Now ring your mother.'

'Yes, Grandmother. I just have to charge my phone.'

'Charge your phone? Don't be foolish – use the house phone!'

'I need to check my messages on my phone, to see if Mother has sent me a message on LINE.'

'Useless.' Ayako shook her head. 'Do as you will, but you'd better be speaking to her within the next five minutes, or there will be trouble in this house.'

Kyo stepped into the small tatami room he would now call his own.

He put his bag down on the floor, briefly noticing a hanging scroll in the corner.

It was while he was rooting in his bag for his phone charger that he discovered the envelope of money was missing.

四

They didn't talk much for the rest of spring.

Ayako kept to her own routine, mostly ignoring the boy. As long as he attended his classes at the cram school, she didn't have anything to say to him. After not only his tardy arrival, but also the debacle with the lost envelope of money that had followed, she'd made the decision to give him a good old case of the silent treatment. Of course, she'd heard him crying in his room softly on his first night at her house, and it had upset her – she wasn't heartless. But it wouldn't do to go in there and show him any sympathy. No, better to let him suffer a bit for now. Meanwhile, she would take action and fix the situation. The next day she'd gone early to see Ono-san at the train station, to thank him for calling, and then mentioned in passing the lost envelope. He'd swung by the café later that day with it. As expected, it had been found on the train by a passenger and handed in at Hiroshima Station. A colleague of his had sent it back down the line with a conductor. Ayako had given Station Master Ono his coffee and a plate of curry on the house, by way of thanks.

The foolish boy had put it in a side pocket of his backpack at some point during his journey, and it had fallen out. It was lucky Setsuko had the sense to write the fool's name and Ayako's Onomichi address on the envelope. Given that touch, Ayako assumed Kyo's mother had dealt with situations like this before.

Although she pitied the boy, she didn't want to ease off on him just yet. He had to learn that he'd messed up. Life was cruel at times, and this was a lesson Ayako wanted to teach him – if you break a promise, turn up late and lose an envelope of money, you can't expect the world to thank you for it, can you?

And anyway, he'd knuckled down to his schoolwork since – which was no bad thing.

○

Kyo, for his part, was truly miserable.

He missed Tokyo. He missed his friends. He missed a sense of life that was lacking from the town. The streets were dead and empty, and there were hardly any people his own age living there – just the extremely old, and the extremely young. No one in between. He greeted the elderly on the streets, but there was a wall of age between them. Equally, when he saw the school students out and about in their various uniforms, he no longer had common ground with them. It was true that he'd only recently graduated from high school, but the rift seemed like a chasm since he'd left behind that milieu. He could no longer call himself a high school student – it was no longer a part of his identity. Yet neither could he call himself a real member of society – a shakaijin – or a university student. He'd heard there was a university in Onomichi, but it must have been a particularly small one, or located in a different part of the town to where he lived, because he never saw any university students. Hiroshima University was the biggest one nearby, with its main campus situated in the town of Saijo. Either way, he did not belong to that social stratum – he was a masterless samurai student: a ronin-sei.

Each day he attended his own classes at the cram school with the other ronin-sei, and his days became a mundane routine, shaken awake by his grandmother early each morning.

Breakfast already sitting on the table.

The first day he'd made the mistake of asking questions.

'Grandma?'

'What?'

'Do you have any cereal?'

'*Cereal?* What are you on about?'

'Well, it's just Mother usually lets me have cereal, or toast for breakfast—'

'*Toast?!*'

'Yes . . . It's just, you know . . . rice, miso soup and fish aren't really my . . .'

He looked up and saw her expression, and thought better of continuing with his sentence.

'Eat.'

Grandmother would kick him out of the door at the same time she left the house, and they would walk into town together. In fact, she had literally kicked him in the backside one morning when he was being too slow. The first couple of days he'd had trouble falling asleep in a new place, and when he finally did drift off in the early hours, he'd then slept through his alarm. She had physically dragged him out of bed with her strong arms, her grip like iron despite her missing fingers. She would march him all the way to the entrance of the cram school and send him in early where he would sit with a teacher alone for an hour, waiting for the other students to turn up. Grandmother knew this young teacher and had requested that Kyo be allowed to sit and study silently beforehand. The other students eyed Kyo suspiciously as they arrived, wondering why he was there ahead of time, by himself.

Everyone in the cram school had a similar outlook to Kyo: a built-in chagrin. They had all failed terribly, and this was their final chance to achieve the grades they needed to get into medical school. Everyone in the room was an enemy – a competitor for a place at a university – and no one even tried to make friends. The teachers also knew this, and it made their jobs all the easier. None of the students talked back or played around. They had zero to joke about or see the funny side of. It was a private institution – if they messed around or got bad grades, that was it: they were out.

And so Kyo began to fall into a routine alongside his grandmother. Trying not to get in her way or incur her wrath. She was frightening when angered.

Nights had been a problem – unlike in Tokyo, where if he couldn't sleep he would slip out of the apartment quietly and walk the streets. Back there he could find a manga café, go to a games centre, or stop in at a convenience store and get a snack. But here in Ono-michi, at night it was deathly quiet, and all he could hear was the soft sound of boats on the water. The convenience stores were still open, but they were few and far between. Kyo had not been brave enough to try slipping out of the house while his grandmother was sleeping, and had not yet had the opportunity to explore the small night district where there were a few bars open. But even these closed early compared to Tokyo, and he was still technically too young to drink. At first, he'd stayed up late at night, quietly drawing at the desk in his room, listening to music on his Walkman, but this had caused problems in the mornings when his grandmother booted him out of bed.

Over time, his schedule began to match hers.

He would go straight to the café after cram school in the after-noons, and Ayako would nod silently to him as he came in. There was a table in the corner, on which she placed a RESERVED sign especially for him, and it was there that Kyo would sit and study. If any of the customers tried to ask Ayako about him, she shook her head and looked away, and that would bring an end to the matter.

Kyo focused on his books for the most part, but he did begin to notice the same people coming in regularly – who they were, what they did, what they ordered. Each day, he sat silently at the table studying, and once he finished, he would take out his sketchbook and a pen and begin to draw the various customers, but surrepti-tiously, so as not to be caught by his grandmother. One old man in particular caught his eye – Sato-san – who swivelled his head a bit like a snowy owl, so Kyo turned him into one. He drew his grand-mother in the same style as he drew his father – a frog. While he sketched, he listened to the customers speaking Hiroshima dialect, and gradually found his ears melding to their intonations. It wasn't massively different from standard Japanese, just shorter and rougher. They favoured an informal register, and didn't often use the masu/desu forms. While he couldn't speak like them, he had begun to understand them better. He made a note of the differences between standard Japanese and Hiroshima dialect in his notebook:

The (rough) male pronoun *I*: **ore** became **washi**
The female pronoun *I*: **atashi** became **uchi**
The verb *to be*: **iru** became **oru**
The verb *to reach*: **todoku** became **tau**
The adjective *difficult*: **muzukashii** became **itashii**
The adjective *easy*: **kantan** became **miyasui**
The adjective *annoying* or *bothersome*: **mendokusai** became
   taigii*
The adjective *warm*: **atatakai** became **nukui**
The noun *bruise*: **aza** became **aoji**
*they liked to say this one <u>a lot</u>

At the end of the day, Grandmother cleared away and closed up the café.

Then they both went for a walk.

●

The path to the Temple of One Thousand Lights was a steep one, and at first the boy had found it difficult to keep up with Ayako. He'd get out of breath quickly, and would have to stop and catch some air. Ayako found herself having to slow her own pace drastically, so as not to leave him behind. He would be sweating by the time they even made it halfway, and so Ayako adjusted the route to suit his fitness level better. She avoided the steep but most direct route she usually took, instead opting for one that wound slowly around the mountain, through the narrow streets between the ancient wooden houses – some of them lying derelict and empty now. Ayako found this route a little maudlin, for she could remember the days before, and who had lived in these houses (and how they'd passed). But to the boy, they were just piles of rotting wood. This path took a bit longer but would gradually build his fitness level. She was certain that within a week or two, he'd be able to go the steeper route.

It was not the highest mountain – Ayako would even refer to it as a hill, rather than a mountain – but it was sheer in parts, she could concede that much. The first time they'd been making their way up to the top, the boy had bent over out of breath and said in between gasps, 'Grandmother . . . couldn't we ride the cable car instead? I think I saw a sign for one on the shotengai . . .'

Ayako shook her head and wagged a finger at him.

'That's the problem with you young people today.'

The boy panted hard, sweat stains forming under his armpits.

Ayako continued. 'You want the view, but you're not willing to put in the legwork.'

'But . . . well . . .' He looked up at her, and wiped sweat from his brow. 'From what I've seen . . . it's mostly old people using the cable car, isn't it, Grandmother?'

'Pffft.' Ayako swatted the air dismissively. 'Are you one of them already?'

The boy didn't have anything to say to that.

'And don't get smart with me.' Ayako resumed her brisk stride.

'Yes, Grandmother.' She could hear him keeping step behind.

'You're on thin enough ice as it is.' She couldn't help crack a smile, but hid this from him.

When they'd made it to the top for the first time, the cherry blossoms were still out in full bloom. Ayako had taken a small amount of pleasure at seeing the surprise on his face. As they'd made their way slowly through the park under the blossoms, she'd noticed his expression gradually changing from one of mild boredom to obvious marvel. He'd taken out his phone camera thing and started to take photos. Ayako allowed this, but couldn't help thinking of her son as a young man, snapping away photos blithely on his old Nikon SLR. She could see now on Kyo's face that identical youthful innocence she'd seen in her son when he was taking photos – the total absorption in a creative endeavour. In time, she would see it often, especially when Kyo was drawing. He got so involved with his artwork he didn't notice her watching; she even caught sight of a rough caricature of Sato-san as an owl, and it was so good she'd almost burst out laughing. But Kyo and Kenji looked so alike, it was uncanny. The memory of her son practising calligraphy at that same low table in his room drifted through her mind. Now, when Kyo drew, it felt like she was watching a ghost, and it unnerved her.

As happened every year, the residents of the town would make their way to Senkoji Park at the top of the mountain and lay out blue sheets to sit down on and hold their hanami flower-viewing parties. A lot of these folk would come out in the evening after work – for as long as the blossoms were out – and they'd sit and enjoy one another's company. It was even busier at weekends when families and groups would spend the whole day in the park, eating, drinking and talking beneath the sakura. Small yatai food stalls sprung up overnight, selling local Hiroshima favourites like layered pancake okonomiyaki and fried oysters, but also nationwide standards such as grilled corn and yakisoba fried noodles.

'Grandmother?' came the boy's voice from beside her.

'What?' She shot him a sideways glance.

'Can I get some food from the yatai?'

'You'll ruin your appetite,' she said immediately, without even considering the matter.

☯

As they were walking silently through the park amongst the revellers, there came a shout from their left.

'Aya-chan?'

They both turned to see a small group enjoying hanami.

It was Sato who had called, but he was seated on a blue mat with Jun and Emi, Station Master Ono and his wife, Michiko.

Ayako let out a sigh, and considered pretending not to notice. It was not that she didn't like the group of people – quite the opposite. But she didn't have time for idle chitchat. She and Kyo had to get home for supper, and extended conversations with people who were drinking and loafing were not what the boy needed in his life right now. Quiet discipline and strict regimen. Stability, not frivolity.

Kyo smiled back at the group. He'd seen the couple Jun and Emi in the café when he was studying, and had noted that they looked only a few years older than him. They'd always both smiled pleasantly at Kyo, and if it weren't for Ayako's presence, they probably would have had several conversations by now.

The group were all waving at Ayako and Kyo, calling them over, so they had no choice but to go and say hello. They walked slowly, side by side, towards the seated group.

'We're not staying,' said Ayako under her breath to Kyo.

Kyo sighed, which did not go unnoticed.

'Hullo, you two,' said Sato as they approached the blue mat. 'Where are you off to?'

'We're just out for a walk,' replied Kyo.

Ayako shot him a withering look.

'So you're the famous Tokyo grandson, eh?' said Jun, bowing. 'Nice to meet you. Please treat us kindly.'

Kyo returned the bow and the formality. 'Please treat me kindly.'

Station Master Ono was grinning sheepishly at Kyo, who noticed him immediately.

The Tanuki!

'We've met already,' he said with a twinkle in his eye, either from the saké he was drinking, or as a result of their previous interaction. 'But it's good to see you again. Hope you're enjoying your stay.'

The woman by his side elbowed him in the ribs. 'Aren't you going to introduce me?'

'Can't you do that yourself?' he said, rubbing his side and grimacing.

'My name is Michiko,' she said, shaking her head at Ono. 'And I'm married to this lump. Pleased to meet you, Kyo-san. I hope you're enjoying your stay in this little town. I'm sure it's a step down from the bright lights of Tokyo, but if there's anything we can do to make your stay more bearable, just let us know.'

She smiled pleasantly at Kyo, and somehow from the way she spoke he knew she wasn't from Onomichi. Her accent was still Hiroshima dialect but slightly different from the others. When piecing her full name together, he also noticed a pun.

'Pardon me for saying this,' he said cautiously. 'But . . .'

All eyes in the group were now fixed on him. He was on the spot, doubly so because Ayako's seething presence made him feel like he shouldn't have spoken out of turn, other than to introduce himself.

'. . . and please don't think I'm rude for saying this, but . . . If your first name is Michiko, doesn't that mean your full name is Ono Michiko – which sounds like *child of Onomichi* . . . ?' Kyo trailed off lamely at the end, feeling stupid for talking at length. While they all spoke informal dialect to one another, he couldn't shake his standard Japanese, and he sounded pompous and affected because of it. Like he wasn't reciprocating their friendliness.

Ono looked down at the ground in embarrassment to avoid the glare from his wife.

'You're quite right, Kyo,' she said, looking back at Kyo warmly, then pouted at Ono. 'And had I known that this fool was travelling up from Onomichi scouring Hiroshima City for a girl named Michiko each weekend to marry – just so he could have his own stupid little joke to snigger at with his friends each time it came up – I never would've married the man.'

'Come on, darling,' said Ono to his wife. 'It's not the only reason I married you.'

Ono looked to the men, Sato and Jun, for support, cracking a smile. 'But it's a good joke, right?'

'It's definitely an elaborate one,' said Sato, chuckling.

Kyo smiled, warming to the group as they all laughed – even Michiko broke her pout and smiled.

'But why don't you both sit down and join us?' asked Sato, making space next to him for them both on the crinkling blue tarp while gesturing to the bento and drinks they had in the middle. 'Plenty of food and drink.'

Kyo stepped forward, and instantly felt Ayako's grip on his shoulder.

'Thank you, Sato-san. That's incredibly kind of you to offer,' she said coldly, yet politely. 'But Kyo and I must be getting home. Apologies, but not this time.'

Kyo's heart sank. Young Jun looked at him with some sympathy, holding a plate of yakisoba in one hand and an Asahi beer can in the other. Kyo's mouth was watering at the sight of a plastic tray containing okonomiyaki. He couldn't take his eyes from it.

Sato followed his gaze. 'Well, here.' He reached for the container and offered it to Kyo. 'Please take this for your evening meal, Kyo-kun.'

Kyo was mid-bow, and almost had his fingers on the container before Ayako's hand once again interceded.

'Thank you, Sato-san, but we couldn't possibly take your food.' She turned to Kyo and snapped at him. 'It's very kind of Sato-san to offer. You should thank him.'

'Thank you, Sato-san,' said Kyo. 'But I couldn't possibly take it. Please enjoy your food.'

Sato put the okonomiyaki down again and shrugged. 'Oh well.'

'Enjoy yourselves,' said Ayako, bowing and pulling Kyo away. 'I'll see you all soon at the café.'

They continued on their way, leaving the merry party behind them.

'Did Tanuki . . . sorry, Ono, really go to Hiroshima to find someone called Michiko?' asked Kyo hesitantly.

Ayako turned her head and laughed. 'Of course not! They made up that story to make you relax and feel better, after you said something stupid.'

Kyo blushed. Ayako tittered.

'And his name is Station Master Ono to you. Not Tanuki. Also, I told you not to talk.'

'Sorry, Grandmother, but,' Kyo ventured, 'you told me we weren't staying long. You didn't say I couldn't talk.'

Ayako ignored this.

They walked silently all the way to the observation tower at the crest of the hill. Ayako's walks would often end up here, and they would climb to the top of the lookout point, and stand at the barrier staring out across the sea, at the mountains in the distance.

But today, despite the enchanting spring view, waves of disappointment began seeping through Kyo's muscles. A blackness filled his entire body. His shoulders drooped visibly. Ayako noticed out of the corner of her eye.

'There will be plenty of times for celebration in your life,' she said quietly, all the while surveying the scenery. 'But you haven't earned the right to celebrate. Not yet.'

Kyo nodded glumly, and Ayako's chest panged with guilt.

Was she being too hard on the boy?

She paused, and ran some sentences through her head, almost hearing herself say them:

You're doing well, Kyo-kun. Keep working hard. Make your mother proud.

But she only let the words echo through her head, bouncing around inside her body, some softly vibrating on the tip of her tongue. They remained unsaid.

Instead, what she said was, 'Come on. Let's go.'

On the way down the mountain, they liked to stop off at Neko no Hosomichi, the alleyway filled with cats. On their first walk, Kyo had wondered what they were doing, pausing to hang out with a bunch of feral street cats, but when he saw Ayako remove the tins of tuna and packs of crabsticks from a bag she carried each day, he realized this was a ritual for her. Day by day, Kyo noticed that Ayako's evening moods seemed contingent on whether or not a certain one-eyed black tomcat made an appearance. If the cat was there, Ayako was a shade more agreeable.

That day, after having left the group enjoying hanami up at Senkoji Park, Kyo was relieved to see that the black tom was already there, waiting to be fed with all the other cats. He had climbed up on top of a dilapidated tiled wall, and was looking down at them both, licking his lips and yawning. Kyo allowed his tense muscles to relax.

'Ah! He's come,' said Ayako to herself cheerfully. 'Good.'

She dutifully fed the other cats first, and clicked her tongue and cooed to the black cat to come down to eat. He eventually leapt down, and Ayako ignored all the others and focused her entire attention upon him.

Kyo watched patiently, seated on another piece of low wall. The other cats gobbled down the tuna and crabsticks that Ayako had laid out for them. He discreetly snapped photos on his phone of Ayako stroking the black cat, worried that if she noticed, she'd get angry.

The sun had not yet set, and there was just light enough to see clearly, although the sky above them had turned a shade of deep purple, and the streets were deserted. They could hear the continuous low chatter coming from the top of the mountain, hanami parties in full flow. Down below, ships floated gently across the narrow sound of water that separated the mainland from Mukaishima. On the other side of the water, the cranes of the dockyards were lit up one by one in beautiful blue, yellow, green and orange lights.

Ayako stroked the black cat, and Kyo snuck a look at her hands with their missing fingers.

He wondered if one day he might have the courage to ask how she'd lost them. He'd asked Mother once, but she'd pretended she hadn't heard him. The whole family seemed to love secrets.

'Who's a good boy, Coltrane?' she cooed. 'Who's a precious puss?'

Kyo's ears perked up. 'You call him Coltrane?'

'I do,' said Ayako without looking up. 'Because that's his name.'

'Who named him?'

'I did. What's it to you?'

'Oh, nothing . . . just . . . well, is he named after John Coltrane, the jazz saxophonist?'

'Might be. Why?'

'Didn't he have two eyes?'

'He did. And so what?'

'Well . . . I hate to say this, but . . .'

'What?' She looked up at him. 'Spit it out.'

'Well, isn't it kind of racist to name him Coltrane . . . you know . . . just because he's black?'

Ayako looked taken aback for a second, scowled, and continued stroking the cat.

'What a stupid question. Better you hadn't asked it at all.'

Kyo sat silently, feeling a slight sense of victory at having hit home with his question, but also a creeping regret. Maybe he shouldn't have said that.

'If you must know, I named him Coltrane not because of his colour, nor anything to do with his missing eye, but because of the way he moves. It's magical. If you paid attention to these kinds of things you'd understand.'

'The way he moves?'

'Yes.' She took a deep breath, then continued. 'When I saw Coltrane the cat for the first time, prowling the streets, I heard John Coltrane's music in my head. Instantly.' She paused for a second, shaking her head, then talking to the cat again. 'Who's he calling racist? What a numbskull boy, eh?'

An awkward silence descended. Coltrane wolfed down his tuna and started on his crabsticks.

'Sorry, Grandmother.' Kyo picked at his fingernails nervously. 'I've never listened to his music.'

Ayako snorted. She regularly played it in her café and in the evenings – the boy clearly hadn't been paying attention.

Coltrane, having finished his food, sauntered away slowly. Ayako stood and watched him leave, then turned to Kyo. 'Come on. Let's go.'

●

Back at the house, they followed their usual early evening routine.

Kyo sat at the low table desk in his room and listened to his Walkman. He took out his phone, opened up his camera roll and looked at the photo he'd taken of Ayako feeding Coltrane earlier. He zoomed in on the cat, and began sketching a dark outline in his notebook.

Ayako sat in the living room reading a novel. She was reading *Kappa* by Akutagawa Ryunosuke. She'd read it many times before, and usually found it an easy novella to dip in and out of. But today she found herself incapable of focusing on the pages, her eyes slipping down the lines without absorbing the story in front of her. She looked at the clock. Perhaps an early bath would clear her mind.

The house was an old one, and so didn't have a proper bathroom. It had a kitchen sink for washing faces and brushing teeth, an outdoor toilet, but no tub. Each evening, Ayako and Kyo would walk together to the local sento bathhouse, and take a dip before bedtime. When they got back, she would immediately make him put away the dishes she'd washed up earlier.

Her head clouded and unable to concentrate, she decided that the sooner she took a bath, the better. She stood up and went to the doorway of Kyo's room. She waited for a few seconds, craning her neck to see the drawing he was working on. He had his phone out, and was sketching an outline of Ayako feeding Coltrane from a photo he must have taken earlier. Ayako was impressed at how good it was – she instantly wanted the drawing of her and her favourite cat. But she didn't want to admit this.

'Come on,' she barked, enjoying making him jump. 'Let's go to the bathhouse.'

Kyo shut his sketchbook quickly and looked at the time on his phone. 'Oh, it's a bit earlier than usual.'

'Things change,' she said sharply, eyeing up the sketchbook. 'What are you writing in there?'

'Nothing.'

'Don't tell lies.' She narrowed her eyes. 'Must be something.'

'I'm not lying, Grandmother,' said Kyo. 'I just doodle.'

'Drawing, eh?' Ayako hesitated; her eyes travelled to the wall, and she began thinking deeply before she spoke as if she might regret what she was about to say. But she went ahead anyway, pointing to the hanging scroll on the wall. '*Kaeru no ko wa kaeru – The son of a frog is a frog.*'

Once again, she spoke in proverbs Kyo didn't quite follow. He looked at the hanging scroll of the Matsuo Basho poem which he'd seen many times before, but never taken any real notice of. 'Pardon?'

She huffed. 'Your father was a gifted calligrapher. Didn't you know?'

Kyo's eyes lit up at the mention of his father, and Ayako detected an unexpected intensity emanating from him. She'd not mentioned her dead son – his father – to the boy before and the effect it had was startling. His eyes shot to the scroll, studying it intently as though he were seeing it for the first time.

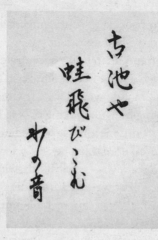

Ayako read aloud the script:

'*Furuike ya / kawazu tobikomu / mizu no oto*

An old pond and/ a frog jumps in / sound of water.'

She studied Kyo's face as he got up, walked to the scroll and began tracing his finger over the lines.

'You know who composed the haiku?' she asked.

'Basho. Everyone knows that.' Kyo rolled his eyes. Luckily, he was facing the wall so Ayako wouldn't see. He turned to look at her, his eyes burning. 'But . . . Father drew this scroll?' he continued, urgently pointing to the blank bottom corner. 'Why didn't he sign it?'

'Because it was one of many I rescued from the bin and hid away.' Ayako sighed. 'He wrote the poem out over and over again, and each one was never quite right for him. He'd throw each one away every single time, because they *weren't perfect,* as he used to say.'

'But it's so good,' said Kyo.

'I know that,' said Ayako. 'But he couldn't see it that way.'

'But—'

'Kyo,' said Ayako abruptly. 'Bath. Now.'

They walked in silence to the sento, and went their separate ways – Ayako to the female baths, Kyo to the male.

Kyo sat by himself in the large men's bath, no other customers to keep him company. His mind spun. He had so many questions about his father.

Why would no one tell him the stories he desperately wanted to hear?

Ayako regretted bringing up the subject of Kenji and the scroll. Was it right to dangle these stories in front of the boy and dredge up the past? It wouldn't do him any good to tell him these things. Secrets weren't lies, were they? And sometimes the truth can hurt. Which was the kinder path, which the crueller?

A deeper regret rose through her body – at her own failure. And a fear at failing again. How could she make things right this time?

How could she do better?

They both sat in their baths, lost in their minds.

The drip drip sound of a single tap releasing endless droplets into the still waters.

Ayako vs. The Mountain:

Part One

On Friday evenings, Ayako would occasionally go off to meet with her friends from the café, leaving Kyo in the house by himself. She left him supper to eat, and strict instructions to stay home and do something useful. He would take these solitary times to work on his art in peace and quiet. Coltrane would even come to visit, sitting on his lap while he drew, or rubbing up against him when he did not show him enough attention.

One particular Friday evening, he had been gently stroking Coltrane with his right hand, while inking a four-panel manga with his left. He was considering entering the piece in a competition run by one of his favourite weekly magazines, *Light & Shade*, when Coltrane had suddenly stirred.

'What's up, buddy?' he said to the cat.

The cat blinked in response, before turning around and walking out through the gap Kyo had left in the sliding screen doors. Kyo rubbed his tired eyes and followed the cat into the living room, and there he noticed the open window through which the cat had come in. On the floor was a large book, lying face down with the pages open, which had presumably been knocked from the shelf when the cat had jumped.

He picked up the book and flipped it over to see newspaper cuttings glued on to its pages.

Kyo knew immediately what they were – photographs taken by his father.

Torn metal; bleeding bodies; shattered concrete. All in black and white.

He took the book to the low table in the living room and opened it at the beginning, flipping through page by page and studying each photograph slowly, with a mixture of disgust and awe.

Harrowing scenes – bodies on the ground, soldiers staring through the lens, destroyed tanks, emaciated children, explosions, fire and flames, gutted buildings, the charred remnants of villages crumbling to ashes. It shocked Kyo – that Father had been to all of these places, with his camera. He'd seen those things with his own eyes. Kyo had to stop at one particular photo he had seen before – a pale-skinned child lying face down in the mud with a black dog hunched over him or her.

How had his father been able to look at those things? How had he not wanted to intervene?

To put a stop to the madness.

For Ayako, too, it must have been a difficult scrapbook to keep.

The cat was nuzzling up against him, and Kyo stroked his soft fur absent-mindedly, turning the pages with his other hand. Eventually he came to a news article about the death of his father. He turned the page quickly, not wanting to read about his father's suicide again. He'd read this exact article before. Kyo had discovered a book of his father's photographs in the local library in Tokyo when he was still in junior high school, and the book had reproduced this same article. Kyo knew it almost word for word. The book was hard to find these days, and had gone out of print many years ago, but Kyo had purchased a second-hand copy eventually, in one of the bookshops in the Jimbocho neighbourhood of Tokyo that specialized in photographic books. The owner of the shop had kindly helped Kyo lay his hands on it. His copy was currently hidden away in a box in his old room in Mother's apartment.

But he'd never had the chance to see how the photos appeared in the newspapers, and seeing them on the ever so slightly yellowing low-quality paper, they seemed punchier than they had done in the higher-quality photo book that Kyo owned. The blacks descended into solid blackness, the whites were more blown out, bleeding into the paper itself. There was more contrast in the roughness of the newspaper page. They seemed even harsher.

A loose leaf fluttered out of the book and on to the floor. Kyo bent over to pick it up, and noticed a lack of adhesive on either side. He did a double take as he was turning it over in his hand. There was a photo of his grandmother. Ayako. Not taken by his father, surely. She was standing in the snow, wearing a backpack, with an ice axe raised above her head.

She looked a little younger, but it was her, for sure.

Kyo stopped to read the article.

LOCAL WOMAN SURVIVES MOUNTAIN OF DEATH

TABATA AYAKO (pictured) of Onomichi is currently in a Tokyo hospital recovering from a broken leg and severe frostbite to her hands and feet after Mountain Rescue found her at the base of Mt Tanigawa, Gunma Prefecture, last Friday.

Tabata had attempted to climb the mountain solo, and had ill-advisedly not informed local authorities of the route she was going to take, nor the date on which she planned to summit the mountain.

Mt Tanigawa has become known colloquially as 'the Mountain of Death', due to the large numbers of lives it has claimed since it was first explored in the 1930s. In a similar period of time, Mt Tanigawa has claimed around 800 lives in comparison to Mt Everest's roughly 200.

In 1943, an entire climbing party disappeared from the face of the mountain, and still to this day, climbers are often lost to its cruel temperament. Avalanches and inclement weather are common on the terrifying peak.

This is not the first time Tabata has had ill fortune with this particular mountain. Several years ago, her husband, TABATA KENZO, lost his life there, as part of a larger climbing party.

Tabata Ayako declined to comment when we approached her, but it is speculated that she was climbing the mountain to pay her respects to her husband, whose name is commemorated on a plaque affixed to the face of the mountain, alongside those of other climbers from his team who lost their lives in the same incident.

Rescue workers who discovered Tabata at the base of the mountain say she was caught in a storm and an avalanche, but somehow survived two nights alone on the mountain, and managed to get herself down safely, despite her broken leg.

'That's one tough lady,' remarked a member of the Mountain Rescue team.

Kyo read the article over and over, and as he did so, his eyes flicked back and forth between the text and the black and white photo of his grandmother. It was hard to process. Grandmother had almost died climbing a mountain. How could he not have known anything about this?

But then the more he dwelt on it, the more obvious it seemed. Her café was called EVER REST. She had a daily obsession with walking to the top of the mountain in Onomichi. She was missing fingers and toes. It did add up, now he thought about it, but at the same time, there was something unreal in not having known such an important detail about her life.

Why hadn't Mother told him about Grandmother's brush with death?

He placed the loose leaf back inside and closed the book of newspaper cuttings, putting it away on the shelf. Kyo had no idea what to make of it, and found his brain was still processing the information. And even with the book back on the shelf, he spent the rest of the night occasionally stopping to scratch his head and shake it from time to time, wondering why Mother had never said a word.

Flo: Summer

Flo rubbed her eyes.

She placed the small, well-thumbed paperback of *Sound of Water* face down, spine broken, on the table in front of her, and let out a sigh. Staring at the strange rocky interior walls of the café, she took a sip of coffee from an elegant white china cup. The coffee was good, at least, but the hazy atmosphere of the underground café in Kichijoji was making her eyes sore. She'd only been there for thirty minutes, but with all of the chain-smokers in today, she was finding it difficult to concentrate.

She was currently grappling with a couple of puns in the book that she was struggling to translate. One was relating to the word 'kaeru', which was conveniently a homophone for three different words in Japanese, depending on how you wrote it:

蛙 – frog   変える – change   帰る – return home

It was impossible to retain this play on words, relating to Kyo's toy frog and his wanting to return home to Tokyo. Then there was a wry joke relating to Sato's name, and how he took his coffee. His surname was written as 佐藤 (Sato) but it was also a homophone for 'sugar' 砂糖 (sato). Flo was completely stuck on how she could render these two particular sentences into English, without losing the humour present in the original. Needless to say, it served as a distraction from other things in her life which she wanted to forget.

Flo had come to this specific café for a number of reasons. One was that it had no Wi-Fi connection. A few days ago, she'd impulsively sent a sample of the Spring section of the book to her editor in New York, and was already dreading his email response. Another reason for coming to this café was that it had excellent, strong coffee, albeit a little expensive at over 600 yen per cup. And she also wanted to take a stroll around Inokashira Park after lunch.

Despite it being a Thursday, and a break from the office, Flo was not making much progress with her translation work. She'd begun the day trying to start on the next seasonal section of *Sound of Water*, but had been unsuccessful, and found herself revisiting parts of the Spring section which she was still not happy with. She'd been cringing all morning, seeing all the errors she'd made in the document she'd emailed to her editor. What a mistake it'd been, sending him the sample. She'd done it recklessly, not even reading over the email she'd written him (*Thought you might be curious to see what I'm working on . . .*), and deeply regretted it.

It was the rainy season in Tokyo now, and her apartment felt stuffy without air con. When she'd first opened her eyes in bed that morning, it wasn't too bad, but gradually the air had begun to feel close in her little apartment, and even Lily had become unbearable, walking across Flo's keyboard, yowling and meowing constantly for attention. Eventually Flo had decided it was a bad idea to work at home. She often found herself distracted by emails, or browsing on the internet to find out more about some of the cultural and historical background of the town of Onomichi in Hiroshima Prefecture.

One of the dangers of literary translation work was falling down research rabbit holes. Whether it was googling a tonbi coat to see what kind of overcoat Ayako was wearing (she'd seen online that it looked a bit like Sherlock Holmes's coat), or working out how to weave into the text that Japanese of the older generations put cloth covers over their landline phones (she still felt she'd done that poorly), she'd keep falling down on a single sentence and it would suck an hour from her morning.

Nor had she ever been to Onomichi, and found herself insatiable, wanting to know more and more about the place. Her most recent wormhole was finding out about one of Onomichi's many festivals called Betcha Matsuri. In this festival, three of the townsfolk dressed up as ogres and patrolled the streets hitting children with sticks. A hit from one of the ogre's canes promised intelligence, while another promised good fortune. Flo had scrolled through countless photos of parents holding out their crying, petrified children, waiting to be tapped with the ogres' sticks. But when falling into the trap of looking at photos on the internet, understandably, progress on translating the book had slowed.

Another basic detail she was grappling with was whether she would visit Onomichi. She'd been toying with whether it would be better to visit the town while she was working on the translation, or perhaps after she'd finished. It seemed a shame not to go at all, but she worried that seeing the place might destroy the image she'd built in her mind from reading the book. Fiction vs. reality. Which was more important?

These and many other concerns plagued her.

And so she'd decided to get out of the apartment, take a trip to Kichijoji and find a nice café. All she needed was her annotated copy of the book and her laptop. The place in which she was now working had come highly recommended online, with reviews praising the first-rate coffee, and the curry they served for lunch. If she wasn't going to go to Onomichi, she should at least take a trip to a more traditional café in Tokyo, in order to get a sense she was actually sitting in the kind of coffee shop she imagined Ayako's to be.

Sort of like method translation.

Or at least, that's what she told herself.

▲▲

Flo stared at her open laptop screen now.

The flashing cursor blinked back at her, expectantly. She frowned, screwing up her eyes, and projected her anxieties on to the little cursor. It seemed to appear and reappear at a rhythm that offended her sensibilities. *Faster!* it said. *So slooooow! How could you not have finished this chapter yet?* it screamed.

Part of her mind asked questions like:	and another side of her brain said:
What's the point in translating the next section when you don't even know whether it will be published?	*I don't care!* *In any case, I need something to do.*
Isn't it a waste of energy?	*I want to translate this book,* *whether a publisher wants it or not.*
But maybe you'll fail again?	*Someone might want it.*
Failure . . .	*Failure . . .*
Failure . . .	*I am a failure . . .*

It was this mental struggle that was causing Flo to furrow her brow and stare at the flashing cursor on her laptop right now instead of doing something, anything, productive, like reading over the Summer section she was about to start on.

Every time she thought about working, her mind would hit upon the uneasy idea that she was only one quarter of the way through the book. What she'd done so far felt like only the tip of the iceberg, and there was still no guarantee that her work would ever see the light of day. There would be no one to read it, and what she had done would languish in a digital void on her hard drive, or as a spectral online document she shared only with her mentor, Ogawa.

But it was better to work than to allow her mind to drift on to the subject of her previous aborted translation venture. The one with Yuki. It had not gone well, to put it mildly.

Sitting in the café now, thinking about what had happened, Flo winced. A waitress noticed Flo's expression and came over to ask if everything was all right. Flo smiled amiably and told her everything was fine. Just fine.

You say all the time it's fine, I'm excited – but you never tell me what you're actually feeling. I'm constantly guessing.

Her concentration now officially broken, she reached for her phone and opened up Instagram.

She scrolled through Yuki's feed of her recent photos from New York: riding her bike, Brooklyn dive bars, museums, bagels, smiling in crowds of people. Picnics with friends. She looked happy. Yuki looked like she'd made good life decisions.

Flo was not so sure that she had.

▲▲

In their relationship, the first major mistake Flo had made was getting so invested in a project that meant more to her than it did to anyone else.

She'd been the one to encourage Yuki to write her memoir, *Kyushu Queer*, and had read each chapter as it came in. Yuki had begun the project as a piece of fun, writing about her experiences growing up gay in rural southern Kyushu within a traditional and conservative family. Flo had read the initial essay Yuki had written in Japanese, and had been gripped. She couldn't stop reading it. She had to have more.

And so Flo had encouraged (well, pressured) Yuki to write more essays. To keep going, perhaps even when Yuki had not wanted to. But each week, Flo had pestered Yuki for a new essay, calling each a 'chapter', and eventually Flo started to refer to it as a 'book'.

'Where is it?' she'd ask, on the Sunday evenings when she'd not received anything.

'Argh!' Yuki would groan and swear. 'Please. Give me a break! I don't want to.'

Flo had usually responded with passive aggression at this point, saying things like, 'Fine . . . if you don't want to, that's fine. I just think it's a shame . . .', causing Yuki to disappear to a late-night café for an hour before coming back with something hastily scribbled on the squared manuscript sheets the Japanese use to write compositions on by hand.

Flo had loved reading Yuki's particular script.

Part of her was jealous of the native effortlessness that went into composing essays on the magically squared composition sheets. Something that Yuki took for granted, and even seemed bored with, was Flo's everything. She wished she had grown up writing essays in kanji, hiragana and katakana on those wonderful genkoyoshi sheets.

She marvelled at the way Yuki wrote her kanji characters – there was something amazingly idiosyncratic about the shape and form. They were characters only Yuki could have produced, and seeing the essays in this imperfect human hand made Flo feel special. It made the bond between them feel stronger – girlfriend and girlfriend, writer and translator. She was privileged to read the rough, early drafts that no one else would see. The crossings out. The mistakes. The errors.

And she was going to translate it all into English.

Flo could see now, with hindsight, that it had all been an act of selfishness on her part.

Even months later, she still felt guilty about the whole palaver.

They'd performed this strained dynamic for several months, until Yuki had got something of a manuscript together. They'd worked hard on editing and getting it into shape. Yuki had then gone about submitting it for various prizes and to publications in Japan, but was each time met with personalized rejections, always saying the same kind of thing: *This is very interesting, and extremely well written. We sympathized with the plight of the narrator, too. However, we are not sure if it is suitable for today's climate in Japan, or for this particular house. We wish you the best of luck, and hope the project finds a home with the right publisher.*

And so despite Yuki's protests Flo had decided they would have to try to get it published abroad first. If they could just publish in the States, it might gain traction in Japan afterwards. She had written a proposal and translated sample chapters of the memoir. To begin with, everything had looked promising.

Her editor, Grant, had been positive at first about what he'd read, and both Flo and Yuki had been excited at the prospect of Yuki's work being translated into English. Flo had been quietly confident.

Even Grant had, too. He said it was exactly the kind of thing American readers were looking for in these times.

Yuki had been awkward about it all throughout, and slightly surprised by Flo's insistence upon choosing her work to translate and incorporate into her own professional life – something that Yuki had admired about Flo when they'd gone on a first date.

'You're different, Flo,' Yuki had said, smiling.

'How so?' asked Flo, raising an eyebrow. 'In a bad way?'

In that moment, she couldn't help but think about how the Japanese word for 'different' – chigau – also meant 'wrong'.

'You're not like most gaijin – sorry to use the word. You worked hard to learn Japanese. I can't believe you translated Nishi Furuni into English. I struggle to read him even in Japanese!'

'Oh come on, don't play around.'

'I'm serious, Flo. You're impressive.'

Flo had blushed, and she felt herself opening up to Yuki.

That was back when things still had promise. Before Flo had campaigned hard to translate and publish Yuki's memoir.

Before Yuki had fled to New York.

Flo had been far more nervous than Yuki when Grant finally and formally got back to her. It had been difficult for Flo to break the news to Yuki after she'd received the short email from Grant that day.

FROM: Grant Cassidy
TO: Flo Dunthorpe <flotranslates@gmail.com>
SUBJECT: Kyushu Queer

Dearest Flo,
I'm afraid it's bad news. Everyone here saw the potential for the piece, but we just couldn't justify publishing a memoir by an unknown in Japan. I'm truly sorry, but the house is passing on this. Chin up! Let me know what you're working on next, okay? And if you'd like to chat on the phone about this, I'm more than happy to (although the time difference is a bit awkward).
Yours,
G

Ironically, Yuki hadn't cared. Quite frankly, she'd seemed a little relieved. It had all mattered far more to Flo than it had to her. Flo wouldn't have said that this rejection was the reason that Yuki had decided to go to New York. Nor that this was the reason the relationship ended.

But it certainly hadn't helped things.

⁂

'Hello.' A voice. In English.

Flo was still staring at the flashing cursor. Her mind had drifted away from her body, reminiscing on past failures and shortcomings. The voice in English made her come back to herself, still sitting in the café in Kichijoji. She turned her head from her laptop to see an elderly gentleman sitting at the table next to her. He was wearing a casual shirt, but looked smart still. He was obviously retired. He had an intelligent thin face, and his eyes were inquisitive.

'Hello,' she replied politely, in English.

'Where from?' the man asked quickly, dropping the words *are you*, as a lot of Japanese people did, probably just literally translating from the Japanese *dochira kara?* which meant word for word *where from?* Here it was again: Flo's mind, racing away.

'America?' the man continued, bringing her back to the real world again.

Flo throbbed with anxiety. The number of times she'd been asked this question drove her crazy.

'Portland, Oregon,' she said slowly, smiling weakly.

'I lived in Dayton, Ohio,' he said, chomping on his curry.

'Lovely,' said Flo. 'Your English is so good.'

'You read Japanese?' he asked, pointing with his spoon at her copy of *Sound of Water*.

'Not really,' said Flo.

'Japanese is difficult,' he said, almost to console her.

She needed to get out of this situation. She wanted to sit and work on her translation in peace. She had to leave.

'I'm sorry,' she said, standing up quickly and putting her laptop and book in her bag. 'I have to go.' It was raining outside, so she grabbed a random umbrella from the communal stand at the doorway to the café.

The man looked slightly taken aback, but his face relaxed.

'Enjoy your time in Japan,' he said pleasantly, bowing his head respectfully and waving.

⁖

Out on the street, Flo opened her umbrella to discover the one she'd picked up had a hole in it. She laughed to herself, the droplets coming through and soaking her t-shirt. She felt awful for being so abrupt with the elderly man. He was just lonely and wanted to chat.

The truth was, life was not going the way she wanted it to, and so she had taken it out on him. Had she been in the right mood, she would've loved to stop and listen to tales of his time in Dayton, Ohio. It could've been one of those clichéd moments she read about in books by non-Japanese – young Western person in Japan lost in themselves meets wise old Japanese man who instils ancient Zen-like wisdom in their young protégé. Both learn from each other and grow as humans. Blah blah blah.

But this wasn't a heart-warming story. This was Tokyo. Real, cold, impersonal life, and she didn't have time to sit around and wait for words of wisdom.

There was something wrong with her. Why couldn't she connect with other humans? Yuki herself had said it – she was exhausting. She'd been a sad loser in Portland, and moving to Tokyo hadn't changed anything. She was still a useless person who couldn't relate to anyone real and living – only imaginary characters who existed on a page.

That bleak feeling of overwhelming darkness – here it was, returning.

Her mind was going round in circles as she made her way to Inokashira Park.

Flo liked coming to the park because she could switch her brain off and just walk without having to concentrate on where she was going. The act of gentle walking and observing her surroundings allowed Flo to meditate on the problems she was dealing with in life. The rain had finally stopped, and the sun came out from behind a cloud, drying her wet clothes. When in the sun, the heat was fierce, but as she followed the path that led round the shimmering lake, the trees provided welcome shade. She stared out across the lake at all the couples floating around in rowing boats or pedalos shaped like white swans. Her mind immediately moved to Yuki.

They had broken up, but were trying to maintain a friendship. Keeping painful contact on Instagram – Flo couldn't stop looking at Yuki's photos, which filled her with a terrible sinking regret. Why had she not gone with her? Why had she chosen to stay in Tokyo alone? What the hell was wrong with her? Flo had told Yuki about how hard she'd been working on translating *Sound of Water*, and Yuki's response had seemed sincere: *That's good, Flo. I'm glad you're happy.*

But Flo was not happy. It was true she'd thrown herself mindlessly into working on translating *Sound of Water*. She wasn't sure why, exactly. She had enjoyed the book more than she'd expected, and had found herself being sucked into its world. Spending time with Kyo and Ayako's problems was a pleasant distraction from her own life. Because if she stopped and thought about things too much (Yuki, her career, her stupid, stupid awkwardness as a person) – particularly when she was waiting for a train to the office – she couldn't help it. She'd start to think about jumping.

She'd heard all the urban myths about jumpers. The usual gaijin gossip.

It usually went something like this: a 'friend' had been on the platform waiting for the train. They'd been standing next to a vending machine when a guy had jumped in front of a high-speed train. The jumper had been hit by the train full force, bounced off the front, back on to the platform and collided with the vending machine. The body had whammed into the glass front. A smash. Cracked glass. The crunch of breaking bones. The hideous slap of flesh. The blood, mixed with the bubbles of leaking carbonated drinks.

What would that be like?

She knew it was messed up, but Flo had often done it: she'd thought about ending things. Like Kenji in *Sound of Water*. To die by her own hands. But she wouldn't choose water, she'd choose the train. Quick and painless, hopefully. This darkness crept over her often, mostly when she was exhausted. But work distracted her from these feelings. The heat today shimmered and swam, and the sound of the cicadas made her think about Ayako and Kyo in the Summer section of the book she was still working on. Reading about the pair of them took her away from the darkness she felt inside. She felt closer to Ayako and Kyo than she did to anyone in real life right now – they were always there for her, waiting on the page. Dependable.

She carried on walking along the path, lost in thought, past the shrine that sat on an island out in the lake. Doubling back, she entered the shrine and threw a five-yen coin into the collection box, rang the bell, clasped her hands together and prayed. She prayed that Grant would like the Spring section she'd sent him. And if not, that she'd find something else to translate soon.

Sweating from the afternoon sun, Flo left the shrine and carried on her way around the lake. She stopped at the Thai restaurant in the park for lunch, and it was while she was eating that she saw the email notification on her phone.

She opened it up and read.

FROM: Grant Cassidy
TO: Flo Dunthorpe <flotranslates@gmail.com>
SUBJECT: Sound of Water

Dear Flo,
I am interested – do you have any more to share?
G

Flo let out a whoop of excitement. Had the prayer actually worked? And that quickly? But then she put her hand over her open mouth almost immediately.

What an idiot she'd been, impulsively sending that sample to Grant. She didn't have more to share. She hadn't even contacted the Japanese publisher yet.

She didn't even know who the author was.

Summer

夏

五

Drops dripped. The sound of the rain was all that could be heard in the house.

'What are you drawing?'

Both Kyo and Ayako had been sitting in silence for some time, enjoying the peace and quiet of an idle Sunday.

Kyo was just outside the open screen doors, seated on the wooden veranda looking out into the small garden, sketching in his notebook. He leant against a wooden doorframe, sheltered from the rain by the eaves with Coltrane curled up on the floor, resting against his leg. Ayako was at the low table in the dining room, drinking a cup of green tea and looking out at the rain falling steadily. She had been studying the garden with its carefully clipped trees, watching the koi carp swimming together in the little pond beneath the Japanese maple tree – its green leaves slick with rain. But occasionally her eyes flicked to the boy, watching him working away on his drawing. Coltrane had taken to visiting the house more, ever since the boy had come. This both irked Ayako and pleased her. She was mildly jealous at the bond they'd formed, but also, it spoke highly of the boy – Coltrane was a good judge of character.

The rainy season was upon them, and now they were faced with its constant downpour, but also a muggy, sweaty feeling that clung to the skin. Temperatures were slowly rising as summer neared, but they didn't yet have the blue skies and sunny days. Instead, dark rain clouds mooched ominously over the town, and the days were sticky, grey and forlorn.

'Oh,' replied Kyo, looking up from his sketch in the direction of

Ayako, sitting not so far away. 'Nothing much, just this cartoon strip.'

'Let me see,' said Ayako, holding out her hand to receive the book.

Kyo passed her his sketch, bracing himself for Ayako's harsh criticism.

He'd drawn a four-panel manga: a pastiche of the Basho haiku hanging in his bedroom. He'd not been able to get its words from his head since finding out his father had drawn the calligraphic scroll, and his interest and interpretation of the haiku itself had been sparked. The cartoon he'd been working on had played around with the imagery of the poem. In the first frame, he'd drawn his signature cartoon Frog visiting the sento. In the second, Frog had entered the bathhouse, taken off his clothes and then gone into the bathing area. There were a few other customers in the large communal bath, and one frame showed their shock at a human-sized frog coming through the doorway. In the third, Frog was depicted leaping high into the air, bombing and splashing the other customers, all of whom left in disgust in the following panel. In the final panel of the cartoon, Frog was relaxing peacefully with a towel draped over his head, the entire bath to himself – the waters rippling smoothly around him.

Underneath the strip he had written the haiku out in full.

'Hmm,' said Ayako, studying the comic strip carefully, tapping her lip with her finger.

'What is it, Grandmother?' asked Kyo nervously.

'It's good,' said Ayako. 'Very good. I do like it, but . . .' She paused.

Kyo waited. 'But?'

'But it's missing something.'

Kyo sighed, pushing the air from his lungs through clenched teeth.

Ayako scowled at him. 'Hey, I'm just giving my opinion. Do you want to hear what I have to say or not?' She began to pass the notebook back to him. 'Because if you think you know everything already, then that's fine, just keep doing what you're doing and forget about the rest of the world. Enjoy yourself.'

Kyo shook his head.

'If you listen to other people now and again, you might learn something.'

'Yes, Grandmother.' He hid the irritation he was feeling from his voice. 'Please go on.'

She looked once again at the cartoon and continued. 'As I was saying, I like your style. The drawing is lovely. This Frog character is great – extremely good. But the only thing I think the strip is missing is, well, it's missing a sense of the artist. A sense of *you*.'

'Me?'

'Yes, you.' She scratched her nose. 'You've taken the Basho poem, and you've reinterpreted it, and that's fine and everything. But wouldn't it be better to base your work more on your own life? Because you don't want to be just retelling what Basho already told, do you? You want to tell something new.' She looked up at Kyo. 'You see what I mean?'

'I think so,' said Kyo.

'What do you mean, *you think so*?' she snapped. 'You either do or you don't.'

She passed the sketchbook back to Kyo. He studied it again, eyes downcast. Now that he looked at it again, it immediately felt wrong. A waste of time. Not good. Not worth it. Even the Frog caricature of his father sitting in the bath looked back at him mockingly. He shook his head angrily, and part of his mind urged him to tear out the page, screw it into a ball and throw it in the bin. Another failure. Better not to have drawn it at all.

But he resisted the strong impulse to be destructive.

Instead he muttered under his breath in the direction of the garden, 'I still don't understand that stupid poem.'

'What?' said Ayako, cupping her hand around her ear. 'Speak up. Can't hear you.'

Kyo, faced with a fresh opportunity to avoid the wrath of Ayako, made his words a little milder. He turned to face her, and spoke in a calmer voice. 'Oh, I just said I don't understand the poem.'

'What do you mean you don't understand it?'

'Well, I don't understand why it's so famous, you know?' He looked at Ayako sincerely. 'Why does everyone make such a big deal of it?'

'Well, I don't know much about these things, but,' Ayako raised an eyebrow, 'I suppose it's famous because it did something a bit different.'

'Different?'

'Yes. Different to everything that came before it.'

'How was it different?'

Ayako, despite her usual prickliness, now seemed calm and pensive. She looked out at the rain falling in steady vertical lines, listening to the drum of the water hitting the roof – gurgling and swirling in the gutters – streaming down the hillside in the storm drains. Coltrane stretched out fully, his long, sharp claws extending and retracting before he settled back into a snooze.

'Well, what's the seasonal word in the poem?' she asked patiently, looking back at Kyo.

'Frog.'

'Correct,' she said. 'And what season does that represent?'

'Spring.'

'Right again.'

'What makes Basho's frog so special? I still don't get it.'

'Well.' Ayako placed her chin in her hand, resting her elbow on the table. 'Before this poem, every haiku with a frog in it involved singing. Frogs make a racket every year in spring, and everyone knows that. So the frog got to have a reputation as a noisy fellow, who sings like a musician all the time in poetry and art. That's why you get those lovely old paintings of frogs playing musical instruments together, with their mouths open, singing.'

'I see,' said Kyo, breathing out gently.

'But Basho's frog doesn't sing, does he?'

'I suppose not.'

'So when we hear the frog in the poem in the second line, the audience is waiting for the frog to sing. But Basho doesn't let that happen – he subverts the expectations of the listener. Before you know it, the frog has leapt straight into the pond, and all we are left with is the quiet sound of the water. No frog song, just the cool ripples in the old pond.'

'So, Basho broke the rules?'

'You could say that. He did something different. Every other poet was making their frogs sing, but Basho made his silent. Sometimes, it's just as important what's left unsaid, as said.'

Kyo was silent for a minute. 'That is clever.'

'It is. And that final line, "sound of water", puts into your mind the ripples in the silent pond, and how even that sound, or that image, lasts only a few seconds. The ripples too will fade away gradually over time.'

They both looked out into the garden, the crackling sound of the rain enveloping them. The raindrops hit the small pond in multitudes. Coltrane yawned. Ayako sighed.

'As will we all.'

☯

'Come on. Let's go.'

Once again they were looking out at the rain, this time from inside the café.

Kyo packed up his backpack and looked outside uncertainly. 'Really?'

Ayako put down a stack of coffee cups. 'What do you mean, *really*?'

Kyo sucked in a deep breath. 'It's just . . .'

'Just what?'

'Well, I looked at the weather app on my phone,' he said, showing the screen of rain clouds to Ayako, 'and it says it's going to rain until midnight.'

'Pffft, app. Do you do everything that thing tells you to?'

'No, but . . .'

'So? What? You want us to stay here until midnight?'

'No, I'm not saying that,' said Kyo, putting his phone back in his pocket. 'But I thought it might be a good idea to skip the walk today? Perhaps we can go straight home?'

Ayako tittered, shook her head and carried on tidying away. 'Because of a little rain?'

'We'll be soaked in this.'

'Oooh, and Little Lord Kyo can't get his itsy bitsy feetsies wet, can he?' she said mockingly. 'What on earth will we do if the imperial socks get sodden?'

'Well, the walk won't be any fun if we're out in torrential rain, will it?'

'I don't know,' Ayako shot back. 'Won't it? You seem to have already made up your mind without having even been outside. And who says everything has to be *fun*, anyway?'

Ayako undid the strings of her apron, and hung it up on a hook behind the door, taking down an old-fashioned tonbi overcoat to cover her kimono. She also took two umbrellas from the stand at random.

Outside the shop, she rolled down the metal shutter and Kyo took out a plastic cagoule from his backpack and put it on. The rain was crashing down on the Perspex roof that covered the shopping street, and when Kyo looked up above, he saw the blasts of droplets exploding against it. He winced at the thought of being out in the open.

Once more, he pulled his phone from his pocket, fired up the weather app and looked in dismay at the endless row of rain icons. 'Hmmm.'

'Put that blasted thing away and walk,' said Ayako.

They turned left out of the café, and headed along the covered street in the direction of the train station, before turning right at the small opening which led to a bridge that passed over the railway tracks. Kyo had noticed that recently Ayako had changed the route. Instead of the winding alleyways that led through the mountainside, they now went straight up behind the station, up the steep path that took them directly to the top of the mountain, past the old castle on the left and the View Hotel just to its right. The steep pathway was cobbled, with steps, a sturdy handrail to hold on to, and antiquated iron gas lamps to light the way in the dark.

Umbrellas out, rain pounding down, they made their way up the path.

Kyo's muscles burnt as he pushed his way up the slope. The first few times she'd taken him this way they'd had to stop for a while, and he gripped the handrail as he got out of breath. Today, while he fared better in terms of physical fitness, keeping pace with Ayako, the water was streaming down the concrete, and his socks were already soaked. The view from under the umbrella was grey and miserable, and mostly he looked at the ground, not enjoying the walk at all.

They made it to the top of the mountain, and walked slowly along the path that cut through Senkoji Park, towards the observation point. All the food stalls from the hanami season were boarded up, or gone, along with the blossoms, and the park was completely empty. Only Ayako was mad enough to come up here in this awful weather.

At the top of the observation tower, they paused for a couple of minutes. Kyo bent over to catch his breath. His trainers and socks were soaked, and underneath the cagoule his t-shirt was drenched in sweat. What use had the umbrella been? At least it had kept half of his shorts dry.

'See,' came the voice of Ayako beside him. 'Look.'

He straightened himself up, and looked at Ayako. She was pointing out somewhere on the horizon.

The rain had eased, and Kyo followed the direction of her finger. In the distance, he saw a gap in the clouds and the sun peeking out. Beams of sunlight leaked from behind the dark rainclouds, and the rays shone down at patches of the sea, making them sparkle, swirl and glisten in the shimmering light.

'Without losing to the rain,' Ayako quoted the Miyazawa Kenji poem. 'Without losing to the wind.'

And as they both leant against the wet handrail, they began to see a double rainbow forming in the sky over the town. The rain had subsided completely now, and the wind was still. Kyo reached into his pocket for his phone to take a photo, but Ayako sensed his action, speaking to him without breaking her gaze at the scenery.

'No need for that, Kyo-kun,' said Ayako softly. 'It can't capture this feeling in here.'

She rapped a fist against her breast.

Kyo let the phone fall back into the damp pocket of his shorts, placed his hands on the wet handrail and studied the scenery intently, in the same manner as Ayako.

They stood there in silence for a few minutes, the gentle breeze blowing, and the soft golden light of the sunset brushing against their cheeks.

'Ah . . .' Ayako sighed.

Kyo watched the boats drifting slowly across the calm waters, lost in thought.

'Shall we go?'

☯

Back at the house that evening, after they'd taken their baths, Kyo had left his sketchbook open on a drawing he'd been working on since they'd taken their walk in the rain. While he was using the outdoor toilet Ayako snuck into his room to take a look.

She picked up the sketchbook and studied the single cartoon frame he'd drawn.

It depicted Frog sitting in a chair with his back to the window, a miserable expression on his face, studying his smartphone intently. On the screen of the phone was a weather application, telling him it was raining outside. But behind Frog, out of his line of sight, through the window there was a rainbow visible, which Kyo had depicted in colour. The scene was entirely black and white, apart from the rainbow, which made it stand out all the more.

Ayako smiled. It was perfect.

Kyo came back into the room. 'What are you doing?'

'I was looking at your drawing, Kyo-kun,' said Ayako sunnily. 'Oh, it's wonderful.'

'It's private.' Kyo took the book from her roughly. 'You shouldn't just go through my stuff like that.'

'Now then.' Ayako adjusted her stance for war. 'This is my house. Don't talk to me like that. Who do you think you are?'

'Am I not allowed my own private thoughts or property?'

Ayako wasn't sure what to do or say; this wasn't how she meant for the exchange to go. She was genuinely impressed with his drawing, and had wanted to tell him how much she liked it. But the boy was being insubordinate now. She had to make a choice: either hit hard or back down.

But she was not going to back down. That wasn't Ayako's style. No one spoke to her like that and got away with it. She had control, at all times.

She shook a finger at him. 'Insolence!'

Kyo was shocked: not only had a temper risen quickly through his body the moment he saw Ayako looking at his sketchbook, but also, what shocked him even more was the swiftness with which Ayako had transformed from good humour to rage. Her whole body shook. Her face was like stone. What had he done? He was no match for her. But now he was locked into the principle of the matter. She shouldn't have gone through his private belongings without asking him. But how could he get her to acknowledge that?

'Apologize, at once,' she said.

Kyo remained silent. He couldn't bring himself to speak, so he looked at the floor.

'No? You don't have anything to say for yourself?' Ayako lowered her finger, and placed her hand over her chest instead, eyes like ice axes. 'You miserable child. Your mother has spoiled you rotten, but we're having none of that nonsense here. This is my house, do you hear me? My house. My rules. No one talks to me like that. Anywhere.'

Ayako was shaking. Kyo let her torrent wash over him.

They were being swept away. Ayako continued, unable to stop.

'You and your selfishness. Your childishness. You expect everyone to bend over backwards for you, and what do you do? Nothing. You just idle your way through life like a dull loafer. Daydreaming your life away while others work themselves to the bone to support you. And what thanks or courtesy do you show them?'

Kyo saw her gaze fall on the toy frog carving sitting on his table; it enraged her further. Infantile boy! She had seen him holding the frog at night before bed. She continued.

'Childish. That's what you are. A child.' She paused, then shouted, 'Look at me when I'm talking to you! And answer me when I speak to you. Are you a coward? Grow up!' And then she said coolly, 'Be a man.'

She left the room, and no words passed between them for several days.

○

A few days later, Kyo was on his way to the café from cram school when he finally rang his mother. He stopped and sat down on a bench by a vending machine to make the call.

'Hello, Mother.'

'Hello! How are you? How is everything going?'

'Terribly.'

'What happened? Is it your studies?'

'No . . . it's not that . . . it's . . .'

Kyo sighed.

'Grandmother?' came Mother's knowing voice.

'Yes.'

'Ah.' His mother made a sharp intake of breath over the phone. 'Go on.'

'Well, we had a fight the other day, and now she's not talking to me at all.'

'A fight? What happened?'

'She was going through my sketchbook without asking . . . and well, I know I shouldn't have spoken to her so roughly, but I did, because I was upset that she went through my sketchbook without asking, and well . . . it all went downhill from there.'

'Oh, Kyo-kun . . .' Her sigh came over loudly on his phone. He had to dial down the volume so it wouldn't hurt his ear. 'What have you done?'

'What have I done? It's her! I tried to talk to her, to apologize, but she ignores me completely. She acts as if I'm not even here.'

'Yes, that sounds like your grandmother.' She paused. 'You're both so stubborn.'

'Stubborn? Me?! It's her, Mother!'

'See! There you go again.'

'I just don't know how much more of this I can take. I miss home. She's horrible.'

'Kyo, don't say that.'

'Well, it just upsets me, how she always thinks she's right, you know?'

Mother paused, leaving an awkward silence before she continued reluctantly.

'Well, it will be summer soon, won't it? You can maybe come home for a few days in summer during Obon. Perhaps that would give both of you a short break from one another?'

The thought of going home welled up inside Kyo, emotions pulling strongly at his heart. He could see his friends, who would be home from university, too. 'Yes, I want to come home.'

'I mean,' she began backtracking, 'I'll be on call at work all the time and there will be patients to see so you might be on your own, but—'

'Right.' The patients came first. Always.

'I'm thinking I'll visit you both in autumn, anyway, when work is a bit calmer.'

Kyo's spirits rose a little at the thought of his mother coming to visit. 'Only if you can take the time off work . . .'

'I'll come in autumn. We can all visit Miyajima together and see the red maple leaves. How does that sound?'

'That sounds amazing. Maybe she'll be kinder with you here.'

'Have things been all that bad between you two?'

'It was all right before we fought, but now she just looks through me like I'm a ghost. She doesn't even take me on walks or anything. Just ignores me.'

'Have you tried to apologize?'

'Even when I try to talk to her, she won't look at me.'

'Have you tried writing something to her?'

'Writing?'

'Yes, like a letter of apology or something.'

'But why do I have to apologize? Why should I be the one who has to be the adult? She called me childish, but sometimes she acts like a huge baby.'

'You know, Kyo-kun, your grandmother is not a bad person or anything. She has had much hardship in her life, did you ever think about that? You have to talk to her with respect. You can't just talk to her the way you talk to me. She's from another generation. They did things differently to how we do them nowadays.'

'Right.'

'Try to say sorry – even if you have to write it in a letter to her.'

'Okay.'

'Even if you think otherwise, in her world she's never going to see what she did as wrong. If you apologize and take full responsibility, I'm sure she'll forgive you. Lord knows, I had my clashes with her in the past. But she forgives and forgets. She's not a bad person, Kyo-kun. She's got a good heart.'

'Maybe.'

'Just give it a go. See what you can do.'

Kyo blew air out from his lips, thinking. 'Fine,' he said.

Mother tittered back at him. 'Blast. Look. I've got to go. My beeper is going off. Goodbye, darling. I miss you.'

He could hear the beeper in the background.

She hung up just before Kyo could say, 'I miss you, too.'

A solid lump had formed in his throat.

He could tell Mother wanted him to fix things. Her offer for him to return home wasn't genuine. It would inconvenience her. But the thought of her visiting in autumn buoyed him. In the meantime, he could make up with Grandmother, so Mother could focus on her job and her patients without any distractions. Since he'd failed his exams, he knew it was his job to make life easier for Mother. Even if it meant apologizing to Grandmother.

He walked slowly towards the café, not wanting to arrive.

●

Ayako had almost lapsed a few times.

She'd had to keep remembering she was punishing the boy for the way he'd spoken to her. But every now and again, she'd almost forget what had happened, and words would be on the tip of her tongue. Particularly when he was drawing – she wanted to ask him what he was working on, but she was too proud to break their silence. Instead she'd taken to sneaking glances at his work over his shoulder when he couldn't see she was looking. A couple of times she'd had to catch herself from commenting on the sketch he'd been working on. She'd stopped inviting the boy for walks with her, but she did miss him. It was lonely, being on her own again. Another thing that made her feel empty was Coltrane's absence. He hadn't visited in a week now, and it was starting to make her worry.

Sato and the other regulars had noticed the iciness between Ayako and Kyo, and it hadn't taken long for word to get around the town that the two weren't out walking together in the evenings as they had been before.

'So what's wrong with you and the boy, Aya-chan?' asked Sato one morning. 'You're giving him the cold shoulder?'

Sato was the only customer in the café, so Ayako had no reason to worry, but she instantly flinched at the question.

'Mind your own business,' she shot back at him.

Sato laughed off her coldness.

'But seriously, Aya-chan,' he persevered. 'Don't you think you're being too hard on the boy?'

'He needs it. He needs to learn some manners.'

'But I hear he's doing well at the cram school?'

Ayako raised an eyebrow. 'Oh?'

'That's what I heard from one of his teachers.' Ayako looked startled. 'A regular at the CD shop,' said Sato, holding his hands up as if he were in real danger from her glare.

She continued to bustle around the kitchen, nervously moving cups from one side of the kitchen to the other, then back again, for no good reason. Creating jobs where there weren't any. Usually she would've made a cup of coffee for herself and sat down next to Sato for a decent chinwag, but mention of the boy had put her on edge.

He leant back on his stool. 'Yes, I hear he's getting great scores. He's working hard.'

She paused. 'Well, that's right, he should be.'

'It is.'

'So, maybe I'm having some good influence on him.'

Sato chuckled again. 'I'm sure you are, when it comes to his studies.'

He sipped on the last bit of his coffee and gave a wide stretch.

'But there's more to life than studying,' he said quietly.

Ayako shook her head roughly, and frowned. 'Mind your own business, Sato. Manners and respect are timeless.'

He laughed again. 'Go easy on him, Aya-chan. Times are different now.'

After Sato left the café, Ayako sat on his empty stool and drank a cup of coffee by herself.

Perhaps she had been too hard on the boy. Perhaps she'd punished him enough.

She shook her head again.

She'd be damned if she was going to apologize.

●

The next morning, Ayako awoke early, as usual, only to find a note on the low table in the living room. She did a double take while walking by, before going over to have a look. The boy must've put it there after she'd turned out the lights and gone to sleep the night before. She picked up the top sheet, unfolded it and read.

Dear Grandmother,
Please accept my humble apologies for the way I acted. My behaviour was unforgivable. I shall never speak out of turn like that again. I am eternally grateful for the kindnesses you have shown me, and it was insolent and disrespectful to address you in the way I did. I apologize profusely from the bottom of my heart for my behaviour, and ask that you please forgive me.
Yours sincerely,
Kyo

P.S. Please accept this drawing as a gift.

She looked down at another thicker piece of paper, with its heavier ply, on the table that the letter had been resting on.

The rainbow Frog cartoon.

The boy had neatly cut the sketch from his notebook and signed it in the bottom right corner with the katakana: Hibiki. Hibiki must be the artist name he wanted to go by. Ayako smiled. Hibiki – as in 'echo' – the alternative reading of the kanji for his name. It sounded cool. She traced a finger over Frog's wonderful expression. She jumped as she heard the boy stirring in his room. She quickly hid the letter and drawing, tucking them inside her kimono under her obi sash, and went about her usual morning routine, preparing breakfast and readying herself for another day.

○

She had still not said anything to Kyo since he'd left the letter out for her the night before.

Kyo wondered if it'd had any effect whatsoever. She'd continued to ignore him that morning, saying nothing at all about the letter, or the drawing. He noticed both were gone when he came out for breakfast, which meant she must've seen and taken them. Unless a gust of wind had blown them off the table . . . No. That couldn't have happened.

Well, he'd done his best. He'd tried to apologize. It was her move – whether she wanted to accept the apology or not was up to her. He could do nothing more but go to cram school and study. But that day, he found it harder to focus on what the teacher was saying.

What would he do this summer? Would Mother allow him to return to Tokyo?

Would Grandmother talk to him ever again? Was he due to spend the rest of the year living in silence? These anxious questions bubbled inside his body, and he found it difficult to see a way forward.

A couple of days passed uneventfully after he gave the letter to his grandmother. Kyo was sitting at the usual table he worked at after finishing cram school when he noticed something different in the café. What was it? The interior had changed somehow. And then he saw it.

On the wall. Something new, framed, hanging there. His Frog drawing.

He blinked, and it was still there. Kyo couldn't help but smile, and settled back into his studies. He was so lost in studying he didn't notice the customers disappearing. He didn't notice his grandmother tidying away the kitchen either, and only jolted back into his body when she finally spoke to him. He looked up at her vacantly, having not caught what she said.

She stood still, looking at him in expectation.

'Pardon?' he said timidly.

'I said,' she spoke quietly, 'come on. Let's go for a walk.'

六

Kyo awoke from another nightmare, drenched in sweat, and clutching the little toy frog in his hand.

He looked at his phone screen – it was still only 4 a.m. His heart was beating fast, and he knew there was no chance he'd get back to sleep again. Mouth parched, he slid the door open stealthily and went to fill a glass of water at the sink, then came back to his room and lay on his futon once more.

But the nightmare kept cycling through his mind, and he could not fall asleep again. It was still very early, despite the dawning light outside. Ayako was not awake yet. He got up and went to the low desk, determined to get the nightmare down on paper this time. If he could just draw it, perhaps he could face it in the cold light of day, and it would cease to hold power over him.

He gripped his pencil, held his sketchbook open with a sweaty finger and thumb, and began to outline each panel roughly, as quickly as he could, while the vision was still fresh in his mind. The ripples in the water, as his father's body disappeared beneath the surface. And then a terrible stillness as silence swallowed everything. Then the ripples began to form a whirlpool, which sucked Kyo closer to the water. A close-up on Kyo's face as he fought the immense pull of the swirling waters, then a shot of his fingers, desperately trying to grab on to something solid, objects crumbling and snapping in his grip under the strain. Change of perspective, looking straight down from above: his body and arms wrenched to breaking as he was pulled under.

His feet touching the surface of the water, waking drenched in sweat, clutching his toy frog statuette in his hand, mouth parched with dehydration, desperate for water. It never ended.

He heard Ayako stirring in the next room.

'Kyo?' came her voice, as she began clinking around the kitchen. 'Are you awake?'

'Coming, Grandmother,' he replied.

He quickly tore out the rough drafts and hid them in the cupboard.

The heat of summer was only making these nightmares more frequent.

●

'But Ayako, all I'm saying is that you can't seriously keep him locked up in this café all the time.'

Ayako, ignoring Sato, pulled up the sleeves of her summer kimono, clattered the crockery into the sink and scrubbed at it furiously.

'But don't you think it's a shame?' he continued. 'He's come all this way from Tokyo, and here's an opportunity for him to learn about his roots – where one side of his ancestors came from. It's a chance for him to see what Onomichi has to offer. I mean, there's the whole of Hiroshima Prefecture out there for him to explore, and you've got him chained to his books every day. It just seems a bit,' Sato carried on blithely, despite Ayako's rising frown, 'well, a bit wasteful.'

'He's here to work. Not play.'

Sato shook his head, took a sip of his coffee and turned to the wall.

He studied it intently for a few seconds, cocking his head to one side. Putting down his cup, he stood up and walked over to the Frog illustration, newly framed and hanging on the wall.

'Well, hello. What do we have here?' he said quietly to himself. 'This one wasn't here before, was it?'

Ayako continued to scrub the cups and saucers clean, rinsing them off before placing them on a rack next to the sink to dry. She shook her head as she did so. Who did Sato think he was? Interfering in other people's business. What a busybody! What nerve!

'Hibiki,' came Sato's voice from behind her. 'Who is Hibiki? A local artist?'

'Huh?' Ayako turned her head an inch at mention of the name.

'Ayako, who drew this picture on the wall?' asked Sato, louder now. 'It says Hibiki down in the bottom right corner. Who is Hibiki?'

She turned off the tap, dried her hands on a towel, and came around the counter, smoothing her apron down as she went. She stood next to Sato, took her fan from her obi sash and wafted at her face furiously.

'What do you think of it?' she asked Sato tentatively, flicking the fan shut nimbly for a second so she could point at the picture with it. Her other hand rested on her hip.

'Hmmm . . .' Sato scratched his white beard. 'Well . . .'

Ayako opened the fan once again and continued flapping at herself nervously. Sato continued.

'I like it. I like it a lot.' He grinned. 'It's very good, don't you think? Is the artist from round here? I've never seen any of their work before.'

Ayako felt her chest swell with pride, and she cracked a smile. It was one thing that she herself thought the cartoon of Frog was good, but to hear it praised by someone outside the family was even more encouraging. Better still, Sato had not yet connected the sobriquet Hibiki with her grandson. Had Sato known Kyo drew the picture from the start, she wouldn't have received an honest opinion from him. But for him to praise the drawing without knowing who'd drawn it, well, that lent some veracity to what he was saying.

'Ayako? Who is this Hibiki?' he asked again, turning to look at her, studying her face. 'And why are you being so cagey? You aren't answering any of my questions.'

'Cagey?!' Ayako hid the smile on her face with her fan as quickly as possible. She huffed. 'Yes, Hibiki-san is a local artist. I'm surprised you've not seen his work before.'

'It's very good.' Sato studied the picture again, nodding. 'I like it a lot.'

He turned to look at Ayako, eyes widened. 'Could you give me his contact details?'

Ayako suddenly stopped fanning herself, hid all traces of shock from her face, yet still couldn't help but blurt out, 'Why do you want those?'

'Because I might have a job for him.'

'Of course.' She went back behind the counter, replacing the closed fan into her obi sash and turning her face from Sato as she spoke. 'Hibiki-san is a regular. I can arrange a meeting – today – if you'd like?'

'He's a regular?'

'Yup.'

He scratched his head. 'I'm surprised I've not run into him before.'

Once Sato had left, promising to swing by the café later that day to meet the elusive Hibiki, Ayako hummed to herself in time to the jazz CD she had playing. Her spirits were soaring from the inter-action. She shook her head – silly vanity! Why should she feel a sense of pride at hearing the boy's art praised? It was nothing to do with her, and only came from a passing comment made by Sato. But somehow, it made her happy and brightened the day. Her mood lifted much higher than usual.

Ayako looked forward to Kyo coming to the café later on. All the while, she thought about this and worked away cheerfully. Her regular customers couldn't fail to notice her high spirits, but they were nervous of destroying her good mood so none of them ventured to ask what had got into her.

If Ayako was genuinely happy, well, that was good enough as it was. It would be foolish to spoil such a rarity.

○

Kyo followed Sato dutifully through the streets, unsure where he was being taken.

When he'd arrived at the café that day after cram school, he didn't have time to say anything to his grandmother before she was introducing him as 'the local artist Hibiki' to Sato. At first, Sato looked incredibly shocked, while Grandmother tittered into her hand. Then they both began cackling away to themselves as if the funniest thing in the world had taken place.

Kyo was baffled.

'Kyo-kun, if you're free right now, and it's not interrupting your studies, I wonder if I might borrow you for a bit this afternoon,' said Sato, then, looking to Grandmother, he added, 'If that is okay with you, Aya-chan?'

'Of course.' She beamed. 'Just get him back here at closing time.'

And so Kyo found himself making his way through the long sho-tengai covered market away from the station, Ayako's rare smile still in his mind, as Sato walked by his side whistling 'You Really Got Me' by The Kinks as they went.

'Sato-san?' Kyo ventured.

'Yes, Kyo-kun?'

'I wonder if you wouldn't mind telling me what exactly is going on?'

'Yes, sorry, Kyo-kun!' Sato chuckled. 'We've been rotten to you. I'm afraid your grandmother played a little trick on me, and I do believe we've both got so carried away with ourselves that we've left you in the dark. My apologies!'

As they made their way through town, Sato, just like Grand-mother, attracted the attention of passers-by. Everyone would nod and greet him with a smile. But unlike Grandmother, Sato would return the greetings with an endless supply of joviality. He was friendly and approachable, in stark contrast to Grandmother's scary and formidable.

'Kyo-kun,' he carried on, 'I saw a drawing you did, on the wall of the coffee shop.' And here he turned his head to Kyo and winked. 'Or should I say, a drawing by *the local artist Hibiki-san*?'

'Ah.' Kyo nodded. 'The Frog and the Rainbow.'

'Yes, that's the one.' Sato tugged lightly on Kyo's elbow, and they dived down a back alley that led away from the main street in the direction of the seafront. But they did not walk as far as the sea. Sato stopped midway along the alley, outside a small shop on their left-hand side, and gestured with his hand.

'Here.'

Kyo studied a faded old black and white sign that read *SATO CD's* in English.

He was pretty sure the apostrophe was incorrect. But he kept quiet about it.

'So . . .' said Sato. 'This is my kingdom!'

He waved his arms around enthusiastically, clearly waiting for Kyo to react.

'Looks lovely,' said Kyo politely.

Sato raised an eyebrow and studied Kyo's face with suspicion before carrying on.

'It's not much, I'm afraid.' He sighed. 'But it's mine.'

Sato pulled the door open, a bell rang out, and he reached for a handwritten sign he'd tacked to the glass of the shop door that said 'BACK IN 5 MINUTES'.

Kyo realized, with a degree of shock, that the door had been unlocked the entire time Sato had been away. But squinting through the windows, Kyo wondered if a thief would actually bother to steal from such a dingy-looking place.

'Come in, come in,' said Sato, holding the door open for Kyo.

They stepped inside, immediately hit by a strong smell of intermingled cardboard, coffee and dust. Adjusting his eyes to the darker interior after the bright sunny day outside, Kyo marvelled at the hundreds (or perhaps thousands?) of CDs lining the walls, shelves, bookcases and racks in the centre of the room. There were fliers pasted on the walls promoting live music – usually for venues in Hiroshima and Fukuyama, but there were some older ones that advertised gigs in Onomichi and in Mihara, which Kyo had never visited but he knew was two stops on the train towards Hiroshima. On the walls there were also handwritten ads:

DRUMMER WANTED FOR BRITISH PUNK COVER BAND
GIBSON GUITAR FOR SALE
DO YOU LIKE ELECTRONIC MUSIC FROM ICELAND? COME
JOIN OUR CLUB!

'Like I said, it's nothing much, but this is my empire,' said Sato. 'Would you like something to drink?'

'I'm all right,' said Kyo. 'Thank you.'

'I'm sure I have a mug of coffee around here somewhere . . .' Sato scratched his head. 'Now, where did I put it . . . ?'

He went around to the other side of the counter, and hunted under empty CD jewel cases, receipts and letters, eventually finding a half-full mug of black coffee that had surely gone cold from its long abandonment. The mug had *I WANNA ROCK 'N ROLL ALL NIGHT!* printed on it, again in English. Kyo wondered again about the apostrophe, and its direction.

Sato sipped thoughtfully on the ancient coffee, before slipping on his reading glasses and pulling a single record from shelves of many he had stashed behind the counter in a tall bookcase. He deftly slipped the vinyl from its sleeve and put it on his turntable, dropping the stylus partway through the first track. The album cover was predominantly white, with a small photo of two men shaking hands on the front. One of the men was on fire.

'You like Pink Floyd?' he asked.

'I've not listened to them,' said Kyo.

'What?' Sato blinked through the thick black rims of his reading glasses. 'That's criminal. Listen to this.'

An atmospheric sound, not unlike that of a person drawing a wet finger across the rim of a wine glass, came through the huge speakers mounted on the walls. Sato readied himself with two pencils he'd picked up off the counter. The beat kicked in, and he began to drum enthusiastically in time with the pencils on his coffee mug.

'Good, right?' Sato threw down the pencils and began strumming an air guitar.

'Yes,' said Kyo politely. 'So, ummm . . . what did you want to talk to me about, Sato-san?'

'Oh, yes!' Sato blinked again, lowering the volume slightly. 'So basically, I was wondering if I could engage your, ah, how should I put it? Your *professional artistic services*.'

'Services?'

'Yes,' Sato continued quickly, gesturing with his hands around the room. 'As you can see, the shop is in need of a little updating. It's pretty dark inside, and, well, I want it to be easier for my customers to discover new music. To connect with it. I was wondering if you might be able to liven the place up a bit with some of your drawings? Nothing too elaborate, mind. Just something that adds character.'

'My drawings?'

'Yes! You know, some illustrations. Anything you like. For decoration.'

'Oh, Sato-san . . . I'm not sure . . .'

'Look, no pressure or anything.' Sato held out his arm; hand with palm facing Kyo, fingers spread wide. 'I'm not expecting much – just something a bit fun. A bit different. This dusty place needs something new.' He paused in thought for a moment, then walked over to a section of the shop. 'Here, you see I've got these handwritten signs.'

He pointed to the labels sticking out in various areas of the shop. They were all written in the same black marker, on fading old paper, and said things like:

ROCK   CLASSICAL   SALE – HALF PRICE!
ロック   クラッシック   セール・半額！

'Perhaps if you could just make some replacements for these?' He scratched his beard. 'You could maybe draw some cartoon characters on them, or even just make the writing a bit more stylish? I have no idea; I'd leave the technical stuff to you. What do you think?'

'I don't know, Sato-san.' Kyo paused. 'I'd have to check with Grandmother.'

'I think she's fine with it, Kyo-kun, but of course we can check.'

'Right . . .' said Kyo lamely.

'If you don't have the time or the inclination, that's quite all right, you know. But if you think you could do something, then I'd be very appreciative. I can pay you in CDs, or cassette tapes – as many as you like.' He grinned.

'Oh, Sato-san,' said Kyo, blushing. 'That's very kind of you, but I don't think my drawings would look . . . well . . . they're not good enough for your shop.'

'Nonsense! Don't say such silly things.' Sato halted, and studied Kyo's face intently. He blurted something out, as if speaking to himself. 'Gosh, you look and sound just like your father sometimes, you know?'

An awkward silence descended on them both, the music still playing in the background, and Kyo was filled with the sensation of a million questions bubbling up through his body. His mind was trying to assemble a sentence, any kind of question . . . *Did you know my . . . ? How did you know my . . . ? When did you know my . . . ? Were you friends . . . ?* But before he could string the words together, even just in his brain, he suddenly felt the familiar presence of somebody else in the shop.

They were no longer alone.

A soft meow came from the other side of the counter, down by Sato's feet. Sato looked down at the floor and his eyes brightened.

'Hullo, Mick!' he called out. 'How nice of you to join us.'

On to the counter hopped a one-eyed black cat with a round white patch on its chest. Sato gave the cat a stroke and smiled.

'Excuse me, Sato-san. But isn't that . . .' mumbled Kyo. 'Isn't that Coltrane?'

'Coltrane? Is that what you call him? I call him Mick, like Mick Jagger – because he's got a certain swagger. He moves like Jagger does on stage. He gets about town, too. Like a rolling stone.' Sato then spoke to the black cat. 'Comes here every day to listen to some records and have a stroke, don't you, Mick?'

Kyo reached out and gave the black tomcat a little scratch behind the ear. Coltrane/Mick Jagger blinked, yawned widely, and lay on his back with a look of bliss as Kyo stroked him under the chin and rubbed his belly.

'He definitely likes you,' said Sato. 'He doesn't usually let people do that.'

'We've met before,' said Kyo.

Kyo left Sato in the shop with the vague promise that he would have a think about anything he could do to help, but that he wasn't sure he would be able to. Sato was friendly and amiable as ever, and told him not to worry about it if it was too much trouble. Just if he had 'the urge or inclination', as he put it with an affable grin.

☯

A few days later in the evening, Kyo and Ayako were sitting in the living room at home, listening to Debussy at a low volume on the stereo. Despite the relaxing music, the constant sound of the cicadas could still be heard faintly outside in the background.

Kyo had taken to drawing in the living room, seated at the low kotatsu table in there, rather than the one in his bedroom. He liked listening to the music Ayako put on the stereo in the evenings. Ayako sat the other side of the table, reading a novel while enjoying the music, but sometimes she found herself peeking over her book at the sketches Kyo was drawing. She watched him now, inking over in pen a rough pencil sketch of a snowy owl wearing reading glasses and dressed as a samurai, slashing the word 'PRICES' in half with his sword. The owl was the spitting image of Sato. It made her chuckle.

'Something funny?' asked Kyo without raising his eyes from his work.

'Eh?' said Ayako, caught off guard.

Kyo looked up at her. 'In your book?' He pointed with his pen at the paperback she held in her hand.

Ayako glanced back down at the open novel. 'Oh, yes.'

They'd both been to the bathhouse, but Kyo was already sweating again. Ayako was at a perfect temperature, in the yukata she wore to and from the sento, and looked extremely comfortable. Now and then, she wiggled her remaining toes under the table in her white socks. Kyo, on the other hand, was hot and uncomfortable. He occasionally picked up a fan resting on the table next to him and flapped vehemently at himself. Ayako wondered if it wasn't in fact the vigorous act of fanning that was making him hot.

'What's wrong with you?' asked Ayako sternly.

'Nothing.' Kyo put down his pen and stared at the wall for a second, considering whether he should say anything.

'Come on, spit it out. It's obvious you've got something on your mind. Spluffing and splurping over there all evening. You can't sit still for a minute without fidgeting. How am I supposed to concentrate on my book with all that racket you're making?'

Kyo didn't know how to broach the issue. Ayako's house lacked air conditioning of any kind, and he found the nights unbearable. He would toss and turn on his futon, throwing the thin sheet he used to cover himself aside completely. He'd taken to lying on top of a towel because he sweated so profusely in the night. In the modern Tokyo apartment where he lived with his mother, each room had an air conditioning unit, and they'd turn them on during the summer.

But Ayako's house had no such luxury, and he found the muggy Onomichi nights intolerable and oppressive. When he did fall asleep, he had strange dreams, like the recurring one he'd attempted to draw, but also others in which he was chasing after Sato, trying to ask him questions about Father, but Sato would turn into an owl and fly away. And then he'd have to watch from afar as Coltrane began to stalk the old owl, who was completely oblivious to his impending doom, no matter how loudly Kyo called out to him.

All of this had put Kyo considerably on edge during the days, and he was even finding it difficult to concentrate on his studies. But here, now, faced with Ayako's stern gaze, he was unsure how to articulate any of these thoughts and feelings. How could he even begin to explain the root of his problem?

'It's just so hot in here, Grandmother.'

Ayako snorted. 'Of course it's hot. It's summer.'

'I know but—'

'What were you expecting?'

'I just, I'm not used to this heat. It's hotter here than in Tokyo.'

'Bah. Not by much.'

'It's really humid. And you don't have air conditioning.'

'Wasteful. Bad for the body.' Ayako shook her head.

'But I struggle to sleep, Grandmother.'

'Pffft. Rubbish, boy. You're just weak. You'll get used to it.'

'But I can't sleep, and I find it hard to concentrate at school.' Kyo looked down again.

Ayako raised an eyebrow. 'Is that so?' She put her book on the table, spine cracked wide open, studying the boy carefully. Kyo had gone back to his drawing, and was absorbed in the task.

'Are you doing those drawings for Sato-san?' asked Ayako.

'I'm trying out some rough sketches now.' Kyo frowned. 'But I hate them.'

'I think . . .' she began, but then thought better of it. 'Well, you don't care what I think.'

'That's not true.' Kyo looked up. 'I do.'

'Well, from what I've seen of the sketches,' continued Ayako. 'The ones where he's a snowy owl. I think they're brilliant. He'll love them.'

Kyo's chest filled with pride. But he didn't say anything.

Ayako thought to herself for a while before speaking.

'Kyo?' she said finally.

'Yes?'

'How are your studies going?'

'Pretty well.'

'Define "pretty well". I don't know what that means.'

'I mean, good.' He scratched his nose with his pen. 'Well, great, actually.'

Ayako scrutinized him. 'What do your teachers say?'

'They seem pleased.'

'How pleased?'

Kyo smiled and pulled his phone from his pocket. 'Hold on a sec.'

'What have you got in there? Always with that infernal thing.'

Kyo scrolled through his camera roll, finally coming to one in particular. 'Here.'

He tapped on the photo, and it filled the screen. He passed the device to Ayako.

She held it flat in her hand, worried that her touch might disrupt it, and studied the photo carefully. It was a list of names with scores next to them, printed on white pieces of paper, pinned to a cork-board on a wall.

'What am I looking at, Kyo?'

Kyo came around to sit next to Ayako and zoomed in on the photo while talking.

'It's the leader board they put up each week to show our scores at the cram school. So we can all see how we're doing. Anyway.'

He zoomed in on the list, tracking around the photo till it came to the top.

'There, that's me.' Kyo pointed to the second-highest name on the list.

'Wait.' Ayako's heart jumped. 'So this means you are in second place out of all the students at the cram school?'

'Yup.'

'Kyo!' She slapped him lightly on the arm. 'Why on earth did you not tell me about this? This is wonderful!'

'I dunno.' He shrugged, taking back the phone and putting it in his pocket, blushing.

He went around the table, and slumped down again in front of his sketchbook, continuing to work away on his drawing. Ayako gazed at him.

Second place. That was fantastic. Ayako must tell his mother.

'Still,' Ayako joked, jutting out her jaw. 'Second place?'

'Huh?' said Kyo, looking up from his sketch.

Ayako tilted her head in mock derision. 'Why not first?'

Kyo thought about it carefully, replying with a proverb in the manner of Ayako.

'*Saru mo ki kara ochiru – Even a monkey falls from a tree*, right, Grandmother?' he said gleefully. 'Isn't that what you'd say?'

'Watch your cheek.'

They both laughed.

Kyo continued to joke playfully. 'Maybe if you got me an air con-ditioner in my room, I'd be first.'

'Hah!' Ayako guffawed. 'No such luck.'

Kyo carried on. 'But seriously, why don't you have any electrical appliances in here? You don't even have a TV.'

'I've got my stereo, and the phone,' said Ayako, smiling now, enjoying the back and forth. 'And my books.'

'You should get a TV.'

'And watch the trash they show on there? No thank you very much.'

'You could hook it up to a PlayStation or a Nintendo Switch and play games.'

'PlayStation?!' Ayako spat out the words. 'Nintendo Switch?! Games?! You don't need a TV for games, my boy.'

'For good ones you do.'

Kyo continued to sketch away, bantering as he drew. 'And anyway, you'd just be scared of losing to me, Grandmother.'

Ayako studied the boy, a smile on her face, eyes moist. She brought her hand to her chin, lost in thought for a short time. Suddenly, she slapped a fist in her open palm.

'We'll see about that,' said Ayako, holding up a finger. She got up from the table and went to hunt around in a cupboard. Kyo looked up from his drawing, to watch her rummaging around deep inside. He shut his sketchbook, pushed it aside and rested his pen on top of it.

'Here it is,' came her voice from inside the cupboard. 'I knew it was in here somewhere.'

She came back holding a large playing board under her arm, and two pots, one in each hand – one white, one black.

'If you want a game,' she said, placing the pots on the table. She blew dust from the board, before unfolding it and placing it in between them on the kotatsu. 'You've got one.'

'Go?' asked Kyo with a smile, studying the board with its many square lines. 'All right, you're on. Which are you, white or black?'

'I'm black,' said Ayako, placing the black pot of stones in front of her, and handing him the white pot. 'You're white.'

'No fair,' said Kyo. 'Black has the advantage.'

Ayako flashed a wicked smile. 'Life's not fair.'

Kyo studied the board carefully, taking the lid off the pot and removing one of the single white stones within. He weighed it up thoughtfully in his hand. Then paused.

'What are the rules again?'
Ayako tittered.

●

When Hayashi-san, one of Ayako's regulars, walked into the café the next morning the idea popped into her head. Hayashi ran a second-hand electronics shop a few doors down on the shotengai. While she was making his coffee (cream and two sugars) she asked him if he might be able to deliver an item to her later that day. Hayashi was at first surprised at the request, but quickly nodded. And so, when Ayako and Kyo returned from their walk up the mountain, there was a parcel sitting just inside the front door in the genkan entranceway. Ayako left her front door unlocked, as did most of the inhabitants of the town.

'What's that?' asked Kyo, taking off his shoes and eyeing up the unusual box with HAYASHI ELECTRONICS stamped on the top.

'Ah, that's for you.'

'For me?'

'Yes, *you*.' She huffed. 'Who else? Now come on. Pick it up, take it inside and let's not stand around in the genkan for eternity and a day. I have things to do, you know.'

Kyo picked up the box and carried it to his room.

Ayako sat in the living room, pretending not to care about the sounds of ripping cardboard coming from the boy's room. Out of the corner of her eye she caught sight of him removing the shape of the electric fan from its box. She heard a sharp intake of breath, and busied herself in the kitchen, pretending to prepare their supper. She noticed his soft footsteps behind her, and then his voice, trembling with emotion.

'Thank you, Grandmother.'

Ayako ignored his thanks and continued rinsing vegetables under the tap, hiding her smile from him.

七

An eerie green light illuminated the desiccated corpse of the Atomic
Bomb Dome against the blackness of the night sky. The sun had set
on the city of Hiroshima, and now the streets were teeming with
people paying their respects to all those who had lost their lives
many years ago. The moon shone a dull light above, occasionally
hidden by passing clouds. Trams clanked by on rails that led across
bridges, and the lights from passing cars dotted the roads with slow
movement, like fireflies drifting through the city. The banks of the
river were bursting with people praying.

Ayako and Kyo stood on the bridge side by side, looking out
across the scene.

The Dome loomed above the dark waters of the river, on which
floated the paper lanterns lit by well-wishers. Hundreds and hundreds of coloured lanterns – reds, yellows, pinks, oranges and
blues – drifting gently along with the current, past the empty shell
of the hollowed-out grey building, whose jagged and exposed brick
walls were now lit up with green floodlights.

On August 6th, 1945, an atomic bomb detonated in mid-air, directly above the Dome, razing the city of Hiroshima to the ground,
destroying its inhabitants, taking life away from them completely in
a flash of flame, or for those lucky enough not to perish, scarring
them irrevocably, poisoning their bodies and leaving them in pain
for the remainder of their pitiful lives. Skin melting – peeling off –
constant raw reminders.

The Atomic Bomb Dome itself, formerly a public building, was
left standing but only as a skeletal husk of what it had been before.

While the debris of the dead city was cleared away over time, the Atomic Bomb Dome was reinforced with iron girders and left standing as a reminder of the atrocities that humans can commit towards one another, when they put their minds to it. The modern city of Hiroshima arose from the ashes of the old, a vibrant and youthful place, but the ghostly shell of the Atomic Bomb Dome was still there, standing silently, lest anyone should forget what had happened.

☯

But earlier that evening, back at the train station in Onomichi, Kyo had been griping.

'What are we going to Hiroshima for, anyway?'

'You'll see when we get there.'

For the past couple of days, the plan had been that Kyo's mother would be meeting up with them in Hiroshima, and then coming back with them to stay the night in Onomichi before returning to Tokyo the next day. However, she had got an emergency work call minutes before boarding the bullet train, and had cancelled her trip at the last minute. Ayako was understanding of her daughter-in-law, but felt a little bad for the boy – he'd been deflated after hearing the news. He was in a listless, angry mood because of it, and Ayako was cutting him a tiny bit of slack. Not too much, though. She wondered how she might take his mind off things. Lighten the atmosphere a bit.

'And why are we taking the slow train?' He continued protesting. 'It takes ages! An hour and twenty minutes! We could catch the bullet train from Shin-Onomichi Station and it would be much quicker.'

'Oh.' Ayako smirked. 'So now he wants to take the faster train? What happened to Mister *I'm going to take the local train all the way from Tokyo to Onomichi*? What happened to that young man I once knew?'

Kyo shook his head, but there was a slight smile tugging at the corners of his mouth. She had him there. He looked out of the train into the dwindling evening scene. Houses flicked across the window drowsily as they passed by small town after small town. Ayako was reading a book called *Black Rain*.

Kyo fidgeted, jigging his leg up and down repeatedly. His Walkman batteries had run out, and he'd not had time to buy any more before the train. He had nothing to read, and had experienced trouble drawing earlier that day, ever since he'd heard the news his mother was not coming. He'd been trying to work on a longer idea for a manga story, but was now too agitated to take out his sketchbook.

Ayako scowled at the offending, jittering leg now and again. She continued to read her book, but the leg was distracting her.

'Will you stop that?' she said eventually, her voice kind, eyes still on her book.

'Sorry.' Kyo stopped bouncing his leg for a minute, then began tapping his fingers on the windowsill absent-mindedly.

After a while she closed her book and put it back in her bag with a sigh.

'What's up with you today?' asked Ayako, knowing it was because of his mother.

Kyo shrugged, not wanting to admit the truth. 'Nothing.'

'Did you not bring anything to read?'

'Nope. Forgot.'

'Why don't you draw something?'

Kyo sighed. 'That's the problem.'

'What do you mean?'

Kyo screwed up his face in a frown. 'I tried drawing something earlier, and I couldn't.'

'You couldn't?'

'I just stared at the white page, and nothing came.'

Ayako paused a beat. 'Has that happened before?'

'Not really. But recently I've been trying to work on a longer comic. I started out okay, but tried to work on it some more today and it just wouldn't come. I didn't know how to continue the story.'

Ayako huffed. 'So what are you worried about?'

'What if I can't draw any more?'

Ayako couldn't help but laugh. 'So melodramatic.'

'You could be a bit more sympathetic,' said Kyo, wounded.

Ayako placed her hands in her lap.

'I'm sorry, it's just, well, it's only one day, isn't it?'

'What do you mean?'

'*I mean* that you tried to draw on one day, and you couldn't.'

'Right.'

'Maybe relax a little.'

Kyo rubbed his face in frustration.

'But how am I going to draw a whole comic if I'm struggling to even put my pen to the page?' He sighed. 'It all feels useless. I may as well just give up.'

Kyo looked out of the window again. What was really wrong? He couldn't even tell himself. It had never happened to him before. He'd always just sat down to draw and something had come without thinking. But that day he felt the page glaring back. It was the whiteness of the page that above all things appalled him. Its very blankness seemed to mock. He'd tried shading parts of the space, just to eliminate the terrible paleness of the thing, but each time his pen hovered over a corner, he would decide that section needed to be unshaded, and so he would move on to another, and the same thing would happen in his brain, over and over again. His pen continued to hover, and he felt his arm resist when he tried to put it to the paper. He felt a fear grip him. Turning to another page in his sketchbook, he tried again, and it was just the same. The blankness, mocking him.

He even turned back to old drawings in his notebook, to find sketches he'd already completed. He had an idea that perhaps he could copy some of his older sketches, line by line, and that way he would feel like he was doing something. But when he looked at his older sketches, they just disgusted him. They were crude and awful. How he hated them. It filled him with a sense of failure that pulled at his heart, gashed his stomach. Colossal, gut-punching failure.

Then he decided it wouldn't do to dwell on this too much, so he began to read manga by his favourite artists, and for a while that took his mind off the problem, but gradually, reading the works he loved and admired, the same sense of failure began to roll and throb through his body again. He would never be as good as these people.

Thoughts swirled and gnarled around his head, but he couldn't express himself to Ayako succinctly. He lacked the articulacy to formulate the feelings he was experiencing within his mind and body and put them neatly into words. His mode of expression was through drawing, and now that he couldn't draw he felt doubly frustrated. Doubly dumb now.

But he was also scared that whatever he said to Ayako, she would deride him for it.

A dark idea came to him: were these the kinds of thoughts his father had had before he'd died? They say a picture is worth a thousand words, so what happens to a visual person who loses faith in their medium? They lose thousands of words of expression. It seemed a dangerous thing, to want to create.

Better to be a mechanic of the body – a doctor – like his mother wanted him to be.

Then there'd be no disappointments.

Ayako looked at the boy.

She could tell from his drooped shoulders and downcast expression that something was up. He appeared to be carrying a deep sadness within himself. It made her think of Kenji, and old wounds reopened. She thought of all the times she'd seen him like that and wanted to do whatever she could to appease his pain and suffering. But she never knew what to do or say. Especially when neither Kenji nor Kyo ever expressed what was going on inside.

And she herself had other things on her mind. Today was a strange day for Ayako. Every year she went to Hiroshima to see the floating of the lanterns down the river next to the Atomic Bomb Dome. She'd done it with her mother ever since she was a child. Eventually her mother had passed away, but she'd continued the tradition with her husband, until she lost him, too. And then her son.

This was the first time she'd had company in many years, and it was a different experience for her. Inwardly, she tried to reconcile the thoughtful grief she carried with her to the ceremony. But today, Kyo was there, with his mind on other things, and she was finding it difficult to know what to think, what to say, or how to feel. His problems seemed small and insignificant, especially compared to the dropping of an atomic bomb. But they were still bothering him. They mattered, right now, to him. She silently considered what to say next. What did she know about drawing comics? She'd never done it herself. But there were things she did know. She knew a lot about failure. She knew about loss. She knew a good deal about hard work, and achievement. And she knew everything there was to know about not giving up. Perhaps there were things from her own life, her own experiences; perhaps some of these things she had learnt could help the boy right now. She just needed to translate it into a language he would understand.

Finally she spoke.

'Kyo?'

'Yes, Grandmother?'

'Don't overthink things. Relax. Tomorrow is a new day. Today, you might feel like you can't do anything, or you might be struggling, but this day will end, as all do. Tonight, the sun will set, the moon will rise. But tomorrow brings a new day. A fresh head, and a fresh outlook on life.'

Kyo listened quietly without moving, just staring at the floor.

'Some days you will pick up your pen and you will feel like a hero. You'll feel unstoppable and you'll achieve everything you set out to do – sometimes even more than you originally thought yourself capable of.' Ayako looked down, studying her remaining fingers, but her eyes were glazed over, as though she were still seeing even the fingers she'd lost. 'But there will be other days when you pick up the pen and it feels awkward in your hand. Everything will feel wrong, the light will be too bright, the shade will be too dark. Every brushstroke or pen flick you make will seem like a mistake or just wrong.'

She looked at Kyo again before continuing, and he raised his head to look at her.

'But that's life, Kyo. It goes up and down.' She smiled. *'Yama ari tani ari – there are mountains, there are valleys.'*

Kyo nodded. 'Mountains and valleys.'

'You won't draw an entire comic in a day. It'll take days, months, maybe even years. You might never even finish one in your whole life.'

'Right.'

'But the important thing is that you turn up, you get out your pen, and you draw one small thing, one line at a time. That's how you achieve something big. Not in one giant leap, but in ten thousand tiny steps.'

Ayako noticed her eyes misting. That wouldn't do. Silly to get emotional over something so trivial. Luckily for her, the train was pulling into Hiroshima Station; neither of them had noticed, they had been so absorbed in their conversation.

'We're here,' she said, pointing out of the window at the platform sign. 'Come on. Hurry up. Don't dally.'

They disembarked with the mass of other passengers. The streets were busy that evening due to the memorial ceremony, but Kyo was still none the wiser. Instead, his chest tightened at the crowds.

'Gosh,' he let slip as they were making their way to catch the tram from in front of the station. 'So many people.'

Ayako laughed. 'I never thought someone from Tokyo would have that to say about Hiroshima. It's not such a big city, is it? I thought you were a hot-shot city boy?'

Kyo blushed.

Over the time he had spent in the small town of Onomichi, Kyo had surprised himself by how quickly he'd become accustomed to its gentle pace. There was so much space, relative to the number of people. Even the other day, when Ayako and he had visited the Sumiyoshi Fireworks Festival in the town, he'd been surprised at the crowds of people who gathered by the water along the coast to watch the fireworks dancing and flashing in the skies above the sea. They'd bought yakitori from a yatai stall and watched the fireworks together. Kyo had even worn a blue jinbei to complement

Ayako wearing a yukata. But at the time, even Onomichi felt overcrowded.

He preferred the peace and quiet.

How was he ever going to get used to the sweat and crush of Tokyo again?

Was he becoming a country mouse? If he was, he could not admit it to himself yet.

They boarded a tram bound for the Peace Park, and it was then that Kyo realized where they were going and why. He looked at the date on his phone and immediately made the connection. Ayako noticed the boy take out his phone and somehow sensed a change in his demeanour. She wondered what was wrong. Perhaps he had received a message from his mother.

They didn't talk much on the tram, but neither did the other passengers. Kyo now picked up on a sombre sense of ceremony throughout the city. Getting off at the tram stop, they began to walk together slowly and in silence around the Peace Park as the sun was setting. They went to pray at the flame memorial, then to see the thousands of origami paper cranes folded in remembrance of Sasaki Sadako.

Ayako and Kyo stood on the bridge side by side, looking out across the scene.

Kyo had never seen the Atomic Bomb Dome before. He'd read about it in textbooks, and seen it on TV, and of course he knew about what had happened. But it was another thing to see the effects up close. There were questions bubbling up inside him. Things he wanted to ask Ayako, but wasn't sure he should.

He turned to look at her.

'Did you . . .' he began, but stopped.

'Yes,' said Ayako, knowing exactly what he was going to ask. 'My father. Your great-grandfather.'

'What happened?'

'I don't know exactly. Only what my mother told me. I was just a newborn.'

She paused, voice trembling, ever so slightly.

'Grandmother, you don't have to . . .'

'He worked in the city.' She sniffed, and continued. 'He commuted every day from Onomichi.'

Ayako looked down at the floor. 'That day, he never came home.'

They both stood still, and the music flowed softly around them.

'I'm sorry, Grandmother.'

'Nonsense.' She shook her head, speaking sharply. 'It's not for you to apologize.'

Kyo remained silent, unsure of what to say.

There came a cry to their left. A young man's voice, shouting something.

Ayako and Kyo turned their heads towards the voice, and the same shout came again, but this time nearer.

'Kyo! It *is* you!'

Passers-by were beginning to turn their heads and look as a young man running towards them came into view. Kyo recognized him.

'Who is this shouting fool?' asked Ayako quietly under her breath as he approached, not noticing that next to her Kyo had broken into a broad grin.

'One of my old classmates from Tokyo, Grandmother. His name is Takeshi. I don't know what he's doing here, but he's a nice guy. One of my best friends back home.'

'I'll take your word for it,' said Ayako just as Takeshi arrived, and she stopped herself from adding that he seemed like an ass.

He had a round, portly, honest face, and Ayako's iciness towards him quickly melted. He was smiling pleasantly at them both and catching his breath.

'I *knew* . . . it was . . . you!' said Takeshi between breaths. 'I thought I saw you earlier in the crowd, but it took me a while to be certain.'

'Yup, it's me,' said Kyo, smiling. 'Grandmother, this is Takeshi. Takeshi, this is my grandmother.'

Takeshi quickly straightened himself up, before bowing low to Ayako, and spoke in the politest register she'd heard in some time.

'It is an honour to make your acquaintance,' he said in a heartfelt tone.

Ayako returned the greeting and the bow. It was difficult to dislike such a simple soul.

'So what are you doing here?' asked Kyo.

'Me? I study at Hiroshima University,' said Takeshi, baring his teeth and tapping them with his nail. 'Dentistry.'

'Impressive,' said Ayako.

Kyo heard this word, and read its subtext.

He is impressive, Kyo. You are not. Why can't you be impressive?

Takeshi waved a hand in embarrassment, but continued speaking politely to Ayako. 'I'm still just a first-year.'

He turned to Kyo. 'But I didn't know you were in Hiroshima. What are you doing down here?'

'I'm staying in Onomichi with Grandmother,' Kyo mumbled. 'We're just visiting the city for the memorial.'

'Onomichi?' said Takeshi, beaming at both Kyo and Ayako, before asking Ayako directly, 'Isn't that the place from Ozu's *Tokyo Story*? I've been dying to visit!'

'Yes, that's right.' Ayako nodded and smiled, her civic pride now touched by this charming young man from Tokyo. 'You're well informed. You must come visit us.'

'I'd be honoured,' Takeshi said, nodding enthusiastically. He turned his head from Ayako to Kyo constantly, lest he should neglect either of them. 'Anyway, I'm here with some student friends from the university.' He pointed to a group of people in the distance.

'Oh, that sounds fun!' said Ayako.

'Yes,' said Takeshi. 'We're having a little get-together this evening. We're all part of the same social club at the university.'

He jolted, as if he'd been struck by lightning. 'But why don't you join us, Kyo?'

Kyo looked at Ayako, already knowing she wouldn't allow it.

'Oh . . . Takeshi, that's such a lovely invitation, but I don't think—'

'That sounds wonderful,' said Ayako before Kyo could finish. 'Kyo, don't be rude. Accept the invitation.'

'But Grandmother,' said Kyo, taken aback. 'We have to get the train back home together.'

'I'm perfectly capable of taking a train by myself, Kyo.' She looked at Takeshi, rolling her eyes at him. 'Are you sure you want *him* to join you?'

Takeshi laughed. 'Yes, come on, Kyo. Don't be a stick-in-the-mud. You're welcome to stay the night at mine – you can crash in my dorm – or you can catch the last train back to Onomichi. Whichever suits.'

'Stay with your friend, Kyo,' said Grandmother firmly. 'I'll be quite all right taking the train home by myself.' And then she continued quietly to Kyo, 'You deserve some fun.'

'Okay,' said Kyo, turning to Takeshi. 'Are you sure it's all right if I come along?'

'Yes!' chorused Ayako and Takeshi in unison.

●

Ayako watched the boy disappear into the crowd with his friend. He stopped to look back once, waving to her one last time before being swallowed up. She waved, and wasn't sure what to make of the final expression she saw on his face. What was the emotion behind that look? The downcast mouth; the eyes glistening in the low evening light. Sadness? But why? She thought he would be happy to spend some time with people his own age, to blow off a little steam. She was standing by herself in a massive crowd of people, overwhelmed. The boy was gone for now, and she was alone with her thoughts once again.

Perhaps she was projecting her own sadness on to the boy.

Sato's words had been playing on her mind recently, that the boy being in Onomichi gave him an opportunity to learn about his ancestors. She had thought bringing him to see the Peace Memorial was a start, but then this school friend had turned up serendipitously. Kyo must get bored, having only an old woman for company. The old and the young . . . How eternally different they were. But each could not exist without the other.

She took one last look at the frame of the Atomic Bomb Dome, bowed her head and clasped her hands in prayer, before turning and leaving the bridge, slowly making her way through the droves of people.

As she rode the tram in the direction of Hiroshima train station, she thought about everything that had happened since the boy had come to stay with her. She could see that he had changed – that was clear enough.

A few Sundays ago, she'd started a new routine of marching the boy over to Jun and Emi's townhouse, which they were renovating. Along with the project he was doing for Sato, Ayako was making attempts to integrate him into the town by getting him to help the young couple. On the way, he'd protested slightly.

'What? So I'm just going to work for them for free?'

Ayako had sighed. Such a Tokyo mindset.

Down here in the countryside, favours were a commodity with a strong exchange rate. But she didn't have time to explain this to him.

'You'll get some good exercise! Good for the mind.'

A couple of Sundays later, she'd been out on a walk. He had obviously finished his renovation work for the day, because she'd come across him sitting on a craggy boulder at the top of the mountain, staring out across the water, balancing a sketchpad on his crossed legs, shaded by trees.

She'd been startled, studying his appearance from afar. He wore a sleeveless shirt that day, and she could see the transformation that had taken place in his body. He looked fitter and healthier than he had done when he first came to the town back in spring. He'd developed muscles in his legs from all of the walks they'd gone on each day. His arms looked stronger – from helping Jun and Emi.

He was growing into a sturdy young man.

But, Ayako thought, his face still bore something. Some residual sadness that he'd brought with him from Tokyo.

He looked so much like his father. He really did.

And that was what worried Ayako.

The tram clacked along its tracks, and Ayako rocked back and forth gently in time to its movements. The same questions kept floating through her mind.

Was she doing it better, this time?

Would she fail again?

She tried to put these thoughts from her head, stepping on to the train bound for home.

She sat at a window seat, by herself, and took out her book, but her mind kept drifting on to other things. The words of the novel just flowed through her without registering.

Gradually, her eyes moved away from the page to the window, and she stared out into the blackness of the night, occasionally seeing a ghostly dark silhouette of herself.

An empty form staring back at her.

○

Kyo had already drunk three glasses of beer at the izakaya and was a little tipsy. The room spun gently around him, and he tried to focus on what the girl sitting next to him was saying.

'So you're like an illustrator, right?'

'Kind of . . . but not really . . .'

'His drawings are amazing,' Takeshi chimed in, leaning across. 'Show her your sketchbook, Kyo.'

'So cool,' said the girl.

A guy sitting across the table was smoking a cigarette and eyeing up Kyo suspiciously.

Kyo fumbled in his backpack for his sketchbook. He didn't want to show it to anyone, but Takeshi was doing his best to blow Kyo's trumpet, and he didn't want to let his friend down or seem ungrateful. His mood had slowly improved, and, even though it was at this point unfamiliar to him, he was getting into the party spirit, surrounded by a group of university students, eating and drinking. Laughing and having fun. He'd joined the group quietly, but Takeshi, being so gregarious, was doing his best to introduce everyone to Kyo as his 'Illustrator Friend From Tokyo'.

Kyo was feeling a little uneasy with this moniker.

The guy sitting across the table was also making him feel uneasy.

After he'd waved goodbye to his grandmother in the Peace Park, he'd felt a sadness grip him at the thought of leaving her alone by herself. When he'd turned back to look at her, he'd been shocked by the image: an elderly, weak woman, alone on a bridge. She did not seem her strong, fierce self. Grandmother had looked as though she'd aged ten years in those several paces he'd taken. When he'd seen her standing like that, hunched slightly in her kimono, waving to him, the ghastly green light of the Atomic Bomb Dome in the background, he'd been possessed with a strong urge to go back to her. He still could have made his excuses to Takeshi, and returned home with his grandmother, to make sure she was all right. But he'd heard Takeshi's gleeful shouts, telling him to hurry up, or they'd lose each other in the crowd, and so he'd dragged himself away from Grandmother, reluctantly. He fell into step with his old friend.

'Christ, how ya been, man?' Takeshi dropped the formal Japanese he'd been using in front of Grandmother. 'Had no idea you were down here!'

'Yeah, all right, you know,' mumbled Kyo.

'Kyo – you've lost weight! You're looking pretty ripped, mate.' And then he paused, as if unsure whether to continue or not. 'And you've, uhm, picked up the Hiroshima dialect a bit, haven't you?'

'Have I?' said Kyo, in shock. 'I hadn't noticed.'

'No worries, man.' Takeshi laughed. 'I actually think it's pretty cool. I wish I could speak like these guys do, but I worry they'd think I was taking the piss, ya know?'

They walked quickly in the direction of Takeshi's friends, who were all standing around in a circle.

'So, we're all in the same social club, and we're heading to an izakaya.'

'Great. Which social club?'

'I forget, I joined so many. Maybe badminton?' Takeshi laughed at Kyo's surprised face – they both knew he was not the athletic type. 'Anyway, there are lots of cute girls, so don't worry.'

'Oh . . .' said Kyo awkwardly.

Takeshi slapped his forehead as if remembering something. 'Ah, shit, are you still with Yuriko?'

Kyo shook his head. 'Nah, we split up.'

'Sorry to hear that, man.'

'It's all right. I'm kind of glad, to be honest. I'm happy if she's happy.'

'What happened with that? If you don't mind me asking.'

'It all fell apart when I failed the exams for medical school.' Kyo looked glum. 'I wasn't part of the life plan any more. I felt like I was holding her back, somehow. To be honest, I'm not sure it was the life plan I wanted, either.'

'Tough break, man.' Takeshi nodded his head sagely. 'I know you had a rough time in spring.' He punched Kyo on the arm softly. 'But you didn't reply to any of my texts!'

'I'm sorry . . .' said Kyo, trailing off. 'I . . .'

'Don't worry about it,' said Takeshi, rescuing the flailing Kyo. 'To be honest, since I started university, I haven't kept in touch with any of the guys from school. I feel bad about it, but I've been busy. I know how it goes. Friends are always friends though, right?'

Kyo nodded, but said nothing. He hadn't really been too busy to reply to texts from his friends. The truth was, he'd felt ashamed of his failure, and didn't want to drag them down with him. And so he'd hidden away from them all, until the texts stopped coming and he'd isolated himself completely. Recently, he'd been enjoying his life in Onomichi, that wasn't the problem, but he knew that he missed people his own age – the easy shared grammar of his peers.

'You going home for Obon?' asked Takeshi. 'Maybe we could all get together while everyone is back in Tokyo?'

'Ah, thanks, but I'm thinking of staying with Grandmother in Onomichi for Obon.'

Kyo hadn't broached this subject with either his mother or his grandmother yet. He wasn't even sure if this was what he wanted to do, or whether he was using it as a makeshift excuse to avoid meeting up with the old gang in Tokyo. He didn't want to be the millstone around their necks. They were all enjoying their new lives and happiness, and he was a constant downer – a ronin-sei with nothing to be happy about. This had made it impossible for him to join the group when they all got together after their exam results.

Takeshi paused, just a few metres away from the group.

'Okay, you ready?' he asked.

'Sure.'

'I'll try to introduce you to the cutest girl,' joked Takeshi. 'Just let me know which one you like.'

'Nah,' said Kyo, swatting at the air in embarrassment. 'Let's you and me catch up. It's just good to see you again.'

○

They'd all filed through the city along Hondori – the long, busy covered main shopping street of Hiroshima. It put Onomichi's tiny shotengai to shame. Here, in the big city, there were throngs of young people Kyo's age, all out and about enjoying the evening. It was such a strange disconnect for Kyo after the sombre atmosphere of the Peace Memorial to see all these people partying.

Bustling, vibrant Hiroshima was almost like being back in Tokyo again – surrounded by excitement. Taxis, trams, salarymen, office ladies, students, cafés, bars, restaurants, bookshops, game centres, manga cafés, cat cafés, maid cafés – Hiroshima had pretty much everything Tokyo had to offer. The infinite possibilities were opening up to him once again. In Onomichi, he had no choices – there was nothing to do, except draw, study, renovate with Jun and Emi, or chat with Grandmother while they played Go or went for walks. But here, in the big city once again, walking its streets with people his own age, he recognized the freedom rising through his body.

They'd all piled into a chain izakaya just off Hondori, and now Kyo found himself chatting to a girl who wanted to see his drawings. He was rustling in his backpack a little drunkenly, trying to get hold of the sketchbook. But the guy on the other side of the table was still smoking and looking at Kyo with an expression of contempt.

'Here it is,' said Kyo, producing his sketchbook.

The girl snatched it from his hands and began flicking through it quickly.

'Wow!' she said, as she leafed through the sketches. 'These are amazing!'

Kyo smiled and dismissed her praise politely. 'They're not great, just some doodles.'

'Kawaii. This frog character is so cute! And I love the owl and tanuki!'

The guy sitting across from them eyed up the sketchbook, and then Kyo.

'What are you studying?' he asked.

'Oh, I'm not at the university,' replied Kyo.

'So you're a professional illustrator?' He looked at Kyo directly in the eyes.

'Not exactly, no.'

'Do you have a website?'

'I don't.'

'So you have an Instagram account?'

'I do, but I don't really post anything there. I'm trying to spend less time looking at my phone.'

'Have you published anything?'

'I haven't.'

'So, forgive me for my rudeness.' The guy stubbed out his cigarette. 'But, how exactly do you call yourself an illustrator?'

Kyo wasn't sure how to respond to such a direct question.

He cast around for an answer.

The girl had stopped leafing through the sketchbook, and was now looking up expectantly at Kyo and the intense guy on the other side of the table. Takeshi was talking to someone else.

'I don't,' said Kyo. 'I don't call myself an illustrator.'

'So then what are you?' The guy crossed his arms. 'Do you have a job?'

'I'm a ronin-sei,' said Kyo.

The guy smirked.

'That must be tough,' said the girl to Kyo, handing him back his sketchbook and patting him on the wrist. 'But your drawings are really good.' She smiled sympathetically.

The guy leant back smugly and lit another cigarette.

'You need a web presence, if you're going to be an illustrator,' he continued, this time addressing the girl herself, as if Kyo no longer existed. 'I also dabble.'

Feeling like he was no longer in his own body, Kyo observed the guy taking out his phone and pulling up a social media account with several thousand followers. The images were highly stylized, awash with garish colour. Kyo swallowed.

'Cool!' said the girl, forgetting about Kyo. 'Wait, what's your handle? I'll follow you.'

The guy spelled out his handle to her, and Kyo watched silently as she searched for it on her own phone, and began scrolling through the images, cooing at his drawings. Kyo sipped on his beer, but it now tasted sour and warm in his mouth.

He felt an overwhelming urge to leave. To get out of here. Away from this group to which he didn't belong. He put some money down on the table to cover his drinks and food, stood up, grabbed his backpack, and was almost at the door before Takeshi bounded after him.

'Hey, man! Where are you going?'

Kyo placed a hand on Takeshi's shoulder, and tried to arrange his face into a relaxed expression. He really was grateful to his friend.

'Ah, I'm gonna grab the last train home,' said Kyo. 'Thanks, though.'

'Are you sure you'll make it?' Takeshi had his phone out and was looking up the times. 'It's getting late, man. Better you stay here with me. We don't have to stay long, but let me just check the train schedule. Hi-ro-shi-ma.' He tapped on his phone, speaking out loud phonetically as he typed. 'O-no-mi-chi.'

'It's okay, buddy.' Kyo took the opportunity to leave while Takeshi was distracted by his phone. 'Thanks for inviting me along, I had a blast.' He pulled his shoes from the locker at the entranceway and slipped them on quickly. 'I'll catch you soon, all right? I'd better get going, or I'll miss the last train.'

Kyo turned and moved swiftly out the door.

He could just about hear Takeshi calling after him.

'Wait! Kyo! You've already missed it!'

Kyo stepped out on to the streets, and hurried away from the izakaya as fast as he could.

The city swallowed him whole.

八

Ayako picked up the phone on the fourth ring.

She had been eating her breakfast the morning after the memorial ceremony when the phone started to trill, and at first she was a little surprised. She put down her chopsticks, swallowed the piece of fish she'd been chewing, and went to retrieve the disturber of her peace from under its embroidered cloth cover.

Who could be calling at this time in the morning?

'Moshi moshi?' she said a little hesitantly.

'Hello, am I speaking with Tabata Ayako-san?' came a crackly middle-aged male voice down the line.

'Yes, this is she,' said Ayako. 'Who is this?'

'My name is Officer Ide.' He paused, perhaps for dramatic effect. 'Hiroshima City Police.'

Ayako couldn't help but raise her hand to her open mouth.

She froze, unable to say anything.

'Are you the grandmother of Tabata Kyo-kun?'

'Is he all right?' she said through her fingers.

'Yes, yes.' The police officer's voice changed to a lighter tone. 'He's fine. Please don't panic. He seemed a bit lost this morning, so we picked him up and brought him into the koban. Could you come and collect him today?'

'Absolutely, Officer. I'll be there as soon as possible. Could you give me the address?'

'Certainly. Do you have a pen?'

Officer Ide told Ayako the address of the koban police box, and she wrote it down carefully on a pad she kept next to the phone.

They were about to hang up, but Ayako couldn't help herself from asking a further question.

'Officer Ide?'

'Yes?'

'Is he, is the boy in trouble? Did he do something wrong?' she asked nervously, pausing. Then finally, 'Is he safe?'

'All is well,' Officer Ide said amiably. 'Please don't worry, Tabata-san. He was a little, uh, shall we say *disoriented* when we picked him up this morning. He was in the Peace Park, near the bridge. A couple of our patrolmen went over and chatted to him, and he was pleasant and polite. But we were a bit concerned when he told us he was nineteen and worried he shouldn't have been as, uh, *disoriented* as he appeared at five in the morning. We just want to make sure he gets back home safely. But.'

There was a short pause over the line. Ayako could not stand the wait.

'Yes?'

'Uh, perhaps I'll tell you more when you get here, but he seemed a little, uh, shall we say, reluctant for us to contact you.'

'Really?'

'Yes.' Ide chuckled. 'Don't tell him I told you this, but I think he is far more scared of you than of us.'

Ayako's face flushed, half in anger, half in embarrassment.

'Thank you,' she said coldly. 'I shall see you both shortly, Officer Ide. And I shall have some words for the boy when I get there. He'll wish you'd locked him up and thrown away the key.'

Ide chuckled again, but nervously this time.

She hung up the phone, called for a taxi to Shin-Onomichi Station, then busied herself getting ready. After she was dressed, it suddenly dawned on her that she wouldn't be able to open the café today. She rang Sato on his mobile phone and asked if he might put a sign on the door, informing customers that there had been a personal emergency and it would be closed today.

'Absolutely, Aya-chan,' said Sato, before continuing in a concerned tone, 'but is everything okay?'

'That boy,' was all Ayako could say.

'What happened?' asked Sato.

'He's for the high jump.'

'Go easy on him,' said Sato.

'Mind your own business,' said Ayako. 'And put up that sign for me!'

She rang off and made her way down to the main street, where she'd asked the taxi to meet her. Shin-Onomichi Station, where the bullet train stopped, was too far from her house to walk, and the alleyways that led to Ayako's, while fine for a bicycle or moped, were too narrow for a car. She hurried out the door, racing through the alleys.

She would take the bullet train to the city today.

○

Kyo had drifted through Nagarekawa, the nightlife district.

He sat at the counter of each tiny drinking establishment, ordering only beer at first, then moving on to whisky, chatting despondently to various barmen about any old thing.

'You know where the word "whisky" comes from?' asked one barman after Kyo ordered it.

'Scotland?'

'Yeah, but you know what it means?'

'No,' he replied. 'What does it mean?'

'It's from the Gaelic words "uisge beatha", which mean "water of life".'

Kyo studied the amber liquid in his glass through drunken eyes. Water of life.

Water could often be life. But it could also be death.

He stumbled from place to place. Watching the happy revellers in Mac Bar dancing to Bob Marley and the Violent Femmes' song 'Blister in the Sun', the whole room singing in unison to the chorus of 'Let me go on!' Then he went to Barcos and saw a different crowd dancing to a different kind of music, more like hip hop and R&B than the indie crowd at Mac. He would go into a place, order a drink, stand and watch for a while, then leave and go to another.

Everywhere he went, he found himself watching, never participating; he did not belong. The coloured lights of the clubs flashed and shone, illuminating the glass of whatever drink he happened to be holding at that time. The bass from the speakers pummelled his ears, and he watched as young guys and girls his age danced with one another. They all looked happy and content. But Kyo's mind was occupied with the same thought, ricocheting in his skull: how did he fit into any of this?

He lurched out of the club and found himself in a small bar which served beer and gyoza. He ordered himself a plate of gyoza, and a beer, but only managed to drink half of it before falling asleep at the counter. The owner shook him awake to say he was closing up, and Kyo continued stumbling through the streets as the sun rose. He would have to take a train back to Onomichi soon, but he had no idea where he was, or which way to walk to the station.

Morning laundry services were dropping off clean towels at the soapland brothels he passed, and they were picking up huge bags of dirty towels to clean and launder for the next customers. He watched a man stagger out of one of the brothels and was gripped with sadness. Kyo's legs ached from walking. His feet were forming blisters, but he carried on past all of the seedy sex shops and escort services of the nightlife district, now awash with grey morning light, until eventually he made his way back to the edge of the Peace Park. He crossed the first bridge, and looked out over the still waters and moored boats, at the warm sun peeking through gaps between buildings that stretched out across the horizon. The city looked beautiful in the morning light. If his phone had any battery still, he would've taken a photo.

広島 – Hiro Shima – Wide Island.

That's what the characters meant, and now, seeing all the bridges that led across the various rivers that cut through the city and divided the land up into an island, he could see why it had been given that name. He carried on through the Peace Park, making his way to the same bridge he'd been standing on the night before with his grandmother.

Pausing in the middle of the bridge, he took in the Atomic Bomb

Dome. It looked different now, warmed by the orange glow of the sun.

But the more Kyo thought about it, the more he began to imagine the bomb falling on the city. Kyo imagined it falling again, last night, wiping out and killing all of those people who had been in the nightclubs dancing, all the people who had been on the riverbanks praying. It was hard to conceptualize; all those varied and vibrant lives met with instant death. How could the rest of humanity function when they knew human beings were capable of doing such dreadful things to one another? How could anyone go on living? He began to think of what his father must have witnessed in his life as a war photographer. No wonder he did what he did.

Kyo felt a darkness rising within himself as he looked down at the water.

It was peaceful. He wanted to feel what his father felt.

Apparently, death by drowning was a wonderful sensation.

Enchantingly inviting, its coolness in contrast to the heat of the day.

He put his backpack down on the ground.

Climbed on to the stone barrier of the bridge.

And leapt in.

Splash.

●

Ayako sat on the bullet train, willing it to move even quicker than it already was.

Faster still were the questions running through her mind. What was going on? Was she losing control of the situation? How had the boy ended up in police custody? Was she wrong to have let him go out with his friend the night before? What was the right thing to do?

She jostled her leg nervously, and when a salaryman sitting in her row looked at it in disdain, she stopped.

But then she began tapping her fingers on the window.

The salaryman gave the same disdainful scowl at Ayako's fingers, but when he saw that some were missing, he looked down at his newspaper in fear. She was used to the feeling of people assuming she was yakuza – at first it had irritated her, then she had begun to find it funny that men of all ages cowered when they saw her. This morning, though, she was too worried about the boy to even care.

Ayako disembarked at Hiroshima Station, this time leaving through the Shinkansen exit on the other side of the station to the night before. Outside there were plenty of taxis, and she jumped into the open door of the first available one, reading out the address of the koban police box that Officer Ide had told her over the phone to the driver.

In the taxi, she rehearsed the dressing down she was going to give the boy.

This was it. The final straw.

○

A couple of patrolmen had fished Kyo out of the water straight away, without much in the way of kindness.

'What the fuck are you doing?' the younger officer had shouted at Kyo, as they pulled him on to the bank of the river, coughing and spluttering. 'You fucking idiot. Why did you do that? Are you simple? Are you touched in the head?'

'You're in a lot of trouble, kid,' said the older officer, grimacing.

They'd hauled him into the back of the patrol car, thrown his bag next to him, and driven him to the nearest koban. He'd made the seat of the patrol car slick with water from his sodden clothes.

The two patrolmen had bodily shoved Kyo out of the car and into the small koban.

Behind the desk sat a large man with a kind face. His hair was cut short at the sides, slightly longer on top, and he had a habit of rubbing his face with his hand when he was thinking. His forearms were huge – like a couple of hams stuck to the bone and covered in stretchy skin.

'Sit down there, asshole,' said the younger patrolman to Kyo, pointing at a chair the other side of the desk from the senior officer. Kyo was sobering up rapidly but on balance was still in an extremely drunken and bedraggled state. He noticed the wince on the senior officer's face at the rough language being used by the younger patrolman.

'Found him swimming in the river by the Atomic Bomb Dome, Officer Ide,' said the older patrolman to his senior.

'I wasn't swimming,' said Kyo stubbornly.

'So what were you doing there, idiot?' asked the younger patrolman roughly. 'Sinking?'

Officer Ide was now staring intently at Kyo. 'Did you fall in?'

Kyo didn't know what to say, so he told the truth. 'No, I jumped in.'

'Why did you jump in?' asked Ide, leaning forward in his chair.

'I don't know.' Kyo looked down at his feet. He did know, but didn't want to say.

He was shivering now.

Ide paused, and studied the quivering Kyo, weighing up something in his mind.

'Yahata,' said Ide to the older patrolman, 'go fish in lost property for some dry clothes.'

'Yes, sir,' said Yahata.

Kyo and Ide sat in silence, while the younger patrolman muttered 'Idiot' under his breath from time to time.

'Fujikura,' said Ide abruptly to the younger policeman, 'give it a rest, will you?'

Yahata came back in with a grey tracksuit and a towel, handing them to Kyo politely. Kyo went into the next room to change his clothes and dry off, and when he came back into the main room with his wet clothes wrapped neatly in the damp towel, Ide spoke briskly to the two patrolmen, with an easy air of authority.

'You two, take these wet clothes and put them through the tumble drier at the launderette. Bring 'em back when they're done.'

'Both of us?' asked the younger patrolman, looking nonplussed.

'Yes, both of you,' said Ide. 'Off you trot.'

The two patrolmen left the koban, and now Ide and Kyo were alone, looking across the desk at one another. Kyo was embarrassed, and stared around the room. On one wall was a detailed map of the local area; on another were posters explaining that doing such and such a thing was a crime. On a different wall from these educational posters, there were WANTED posters with photos of hardened criminals, and the amounts of money on offer for information leading to their arrest. Kyo wondered whether, if he ran out the door now, his face would be up there soon. How much would they offer for someone who'd jumped in a river?

'So,' said Ide, folding his arms.

Kyo looked up, and saw that he was smiling amiably.

'What do you have to say for yourself?'

'I'm really sorry.'

Ide smiled broadly.

'That's a good start.'

Ide sat forward in his desk, readying a pen and a pad of paper.

'Now that we're alone, first of all, where do you live?'

'Onomichi. With my grandmother.'

'You are going to tell me your name, address and your grandmother's phone number. I'm going to ring her and tell her to come get you.'

'Yes, sir,' said Kyo, then wondered why he was calling the man sir.

'And then,' Ide continued, 'you are going to tell me exactly why you jumped into the river at 5 a.m.'

Kyo wriggled in his seat, and after some time, he sighed.

'I can tell you everything, Officer Ide,' he said, voice trembling. 'But please don't tell my grandmother I jumped in the river. She'll kill me.'

'I can't make any specific promises like that – I may well have to tell her we fished you out. That is, if she gets here before your clothes dry.' Ide laughed. 'But if you need to talk, I'll listen to your story, and I promise I won't tell another soul what you tell me. Unless it is about breaking the law. I'm a man of my word, so you can trust me.'

Kyo was still a bit drunk; he had nothing to lose.

'Officer Ide, I've never told anyone about this in my life, but I've always known that my father died by suicide in Osaka, when I was still just a baby. He was a war photographer, a fairly famous one, and I've always just assumed that he was scarred by all the things he saw and photographed. He took an overdose of medication on top of a lot of alcohol, and then jumped into the canal in Dotonbori and drowned. I know it's going to sound stupid, and you probably won't believe me, but I promise I wasn't trying to commit suicide this morning like him . . .'

'So what were you doing?'

'I don't know, maybe I was just trying to understand what he experienced before he died? I never knew him, and I thought by doing this one thing he did, I might somehow feel closer to him. But I don't want to die, I promise.'

The last sentence wasn't entirely true.

Kyo had, in fact, thought about ending his life before. Many times. He'd envisioned all the different ways he could do it. Slashing his wrists in the bath. Hanging himself. Gassing himself in a car. Jumping from a building. Stepping out in front of traffic. Taking an overdose of pills. But it was drowning himself that he always returned to with particular fascination. People said it was an easy way to go. But what if it went wrong, and he ended up living the rest of his life as a vegetable?

He was too much of a coward to do more than think about it. He was too scared of the pain. But life itself was pain, too. Therein lay a conundrum he could not solve. He had always kept these thoughts to himself, though. Even now.

But Kyo had begun to talk to Officer Ide in a way he'd never talked to anyone in his life, not even his school friends or his ex-girlfriend. Especially not his mother. Kyo kept thoughts of his father firmly locked away, deep inside himself. But for some reason, this random police officer seemed far more approachable and open than anyone in his family had ever been. All the things he'd wanted to talk about with his mother, with his grandmother, with his friends, all these things that he just couldn't talk about poured out of his mouth in a torrent.

'My father drowned himself. That much, I can live with, and I've come to accept that was the way he chose to end his life. But the thing that upsets me still is that no one in my family has ever talked to me about this. I've pieced together what I know now from snatches of information I've heard family members say over the years. But there's never been anyone who I can talk to about him. Never been anyone who would just sit down and tell me stories about my father, you know, what kind of person he was, what he liked to do.'

Once he had finished, he wiped the tears from his cheeks and finally looked up to meet Officer Ide's gaze. Ide had not interrupted him while he spoke, and he was still silent now. Kyo couldn't read his expression – was it fear? Or maybe compassion? Ide moved his weight in his chair, and Kyo saw that it was a look of worry behind his eyes. A colour in his irises that had not been there before.

But Kyo had not told him everything, not all of it. Not the darker, more painful thoughts about giving up on life altogether. Those stayed locked deep within himself. If he kept them hidden there, maybe he could convince himself that life was worth living.

●

Ayako arrived at the koban, and entered, heart pounding.

The boy was sitting the other side of the desk from a chubby officer, and they were both rolling around in their seats laughing, with cup ramen and chopsticks in their hands. They both fell silent instantly as Ayako stepped into the room, and set their noodles and chopsticks down on the desk. The boy's expression immediately fell into a look of shame, and he hung his head and looked at his feet. The officer behind the desk, upon noticing the boy's change in demeanour, quickly stood up and bowed formally to Ayako.

'You must be Tabata-san,' he said. 'My name is Ide. We spoke on the phone earlier, but it's a pleasure to meet you in person.'

'I'm terribly sorry for the trouble my grandson has caused you,' said Ayako, bowing as low as she could to indicate the shame of the situation.

'Please, no need to apologize.' Ide waved a hand. 'Everyone is safe.'

'You.' Ayako turned to the boy, speaking fiercely. 'How can you sit there laughing? Apologize at once to Officer Ide for causing all this trouble.'

'I'm sorry,' said Kyo.

'Ah, please,' said Ide. 'It's my job. And he's been excellent company this morning. We've had a good chat. Haven't we?' Then Ide turned to Kyo. 'Go on, like we discussed before.'

Kyo nodded and stood up, bowing low to Ayako.

'I'm terribly sorry for making you worry, Grandmother. I'll never do it again. It was thoughtless and irresponsible of me to behave this way. Please forgive me.'

Ide was smiling at both of them. White-hot rage boiled inside Ayako.

Why was this fat policeman not taking the matter seriously?

'You,' she said to Kyo. 'Outside, now. We're leaving.'

Kyo grabbed his backpack and left the koban.

Ayako followed behind, and was almost out the door, when she heard Ide's voice from behind.

'Uh, Tabata-san?'

'Yes?' She turned to face him. He was still standing up behind his desk.

'Can I just have a quick word?'

'Certainly.'

'I, uh, don't want to step on anyone's toes, so to speak.'

'Officer Ide.' Ayako felt very tired. 'Please say what you have to say.'

'It's just, well, the boy told me some things,' He scratched his chin nervously. 'Some things I promised not to tell anyone.'

'I apologize for the burden he has been.'

'No, no.' Ide shook his head. 'It's not like that. He's a good kid.'

'Having had to take two taxis and a bullet train from Onomichi to come collect him from a koban, I'm not seeing him in the best light right now, Officer.'

'Yes, no . . .' He stumbled on his words. 'Quite. But . . .'

'Apologies, I don't mean to be rude, but what is it you want to say, Officer?'

Ayako stood there, with her arms crossed, tapping her foot.

Ide backed away a step. 'I don't know, Tabata-san.'

'You don't know?'

Ide sighed. 'I suppose, what I'm trying to say is: please go easy on him. He's a good kid, not like some of the city punks we get in here. He's honest and decent – very polite – you and your family should be proud. He has many things he needs to say to you, and I've told him to say them. But I think there are also many things he'd like to hear from you about, you know, his dad, I mean, your son.'

Ayako's face flushed red, and her body shook.

'Is that all, Officer?'

'I'm sorry, Tabata-san,' said Ide, bowing. 'Perhaps I've over-stepped the mark.'

'Good day.'

She turned around and left, lest she say anything untoward to an officer of the law.

● ○

They sat on the slow train together in silence.

Ayako was relieved that Kyo was safe, and alive. When she'd got the call that morning, she'd been gripped with déjà vu. She'd had a similar call from the Osaka police all those years ago. She was also relieved he wasn't in any real trouble, so to speak. She had wasted a whole day on the stress of collecting him, and that irked her, but ultimately, she found her anger replaced by something different. The boy's bearing had changed – he appeared eager when he looked at her. Hungry. Perhaps that Officer Ide had said something to him which had altered his attitude. She still had not said a word to the boy; it was a rare occasion when she did not know what tack to take with him.

He seemed contrite, but wasn't talking much, other than a few words more of apology he'd said quietly to her as she was buying tickets for the local train home. Still, something annoyed her about that stupid policeman. Where did he get off, offering advice on family matters? What business did he have to talk of her Kenji like that? How did he know even a fraction of the suffering and grief she'd had to overcome in her life? And what made him think he had any right to tell her how to treat the boy now? Insolence! If she wanted to punish him, well, that was her business, not his!

Kyo also had a lot going through his mind. He ran over the conversation he'd had with Officer Ide, and thought through what they'd talked about. Some of the advice Ide had given scared him even now – *Talk to her. Ask her the questions you need to ask. Don't bottle these thoughts and feelings up inside. It won't help anyone.* It had all seemed simple when Ide was saying it in the koban and it was just the two of them. He'd felt inspired to change the relationship he had with his grandmother. To talk to her frankly about the father he'd never had, and also to find out more about her and her brush with death. How she'd felt out on the mountain, alone and cold. He wanted to hear what had possessed her to follow in Grandfather's footsteps up Death Mountain. Had it been the same emotions that gripped her that Kyo had experienced, jumping off a bridge into some water as his father had done? Perhaps there was something depressive and suicidal in the family that could not be fixed. But now, seated next to his real-life seething grandmother, all that talk seemed preposterous. How would he be able to broach anything with her? It was hard enough even apologizing to her for the trouble he'd caused, let alone asking her difficult questions about family history, which he knew she would never answer (and would probably enrage her even more). What to do? How to act?

They did not talk for the rest of the journey home.

● ○

Days passed. The two continued in an awkward silence.

It was not like the silent treatment Ayako had given Kyo before – they still spoke to each other about basic things. They communicated, but there was an unease between them, and Ayako was fearful that if she did talk to the boy about anything serious, she would lose control of herself. Ayako discovered that her rage dissipated quickly, but the words of Officer Ide plagued her. Kyo, equally, felt too timid to ask her the questions he wanted to ask, as Officer Ide had suggested. He found himself many times on the brink of saying something to her, but backed out of it. He really was a coward. A failure.

Kyo truly committed to the idea of staying with his grandmother over the period of Obon, rather than returning to Tokyo. He discussed his plans with his mother over the phone, and she was happy for him to stay. He wanted her to respond with feeling, but her simple 'Ah, is that so' made him worry that she was relieved.

Kyo drew a sketch of Coltrane the cat, and left it on the kotatsu table in the living room for Ayako.

He wrote the name Coltrane underneath it, but realized afterwards there was no need. It was obvious who the sketch was of. Ayako thanked him perfunctorily, and once more had the sketch framed and put up on the wall.

Kyo desperately wanted things to go back to normal.

But it felt like they were drifting apart.

● ○

On the morning of Obon, Ayako woke Kyo early.

They had breakfast together in silence, then she led him out of the house, and they began to walk along an alleyway he had not been down before. He wondered where she was taking him. Eventually they came to a small graveyard, packed tightly with little graves, surrounded by an old stone wall, and with a temple building behind. Kyo had seen this graveyard from time to time on his walks around the town, but he'd never been inside.

Ayako got a wooden bucket which had a long-handled cup, and she began to fill it with water. Kyo had of course seen this kind of bucket before, and he had been to a similar graveyard when visiting the graves of the other side of his family in Tokyo with his mother and her parents. But he had never been to this particular graveyard, and he had never done this ritual with Ayako.

She gave him the wooden bucket of water, and he followed behind her, carrying it to the grave. She had brought with her a bag filled with food and drink to lay out at the base of the stone in offering to the dead.

They came to the family grave, and Kyo saw the names of his ancestors written on the stone. There was his father's name: TABATA KENJI, carved into the gravestone. Ayako and Kyo first purified their hands with the water from the wooden bucket, before they began to wash and clean the grave using the long-handled wooden cup to scoop and trickle water on to the stone. It was still early morning, and not hot yet, but the cicadas were making their continuous overpowering sound.

A fizz of electricity passed through Kyo as he poured water over his father's grave.

They washed the grave in silence, and then laid out tiny cans of Asahi beer, mikan oranges and sweets for the dead.

'Well, aren't you going to talk to them?' asked Ayako.

Kyo paused and thought of what he might say to his father, to his grandfather, to all of these ancestors he had never known and never met. Having never spoken to any of them before, he didn't know what to say. He thought about it for a short while before speaking.

'I wish I'd known you,' he said quietly. 'I wish I'd known you all. And I wish I knew more about you.'

Ayako looked at Kyo, and was gripped with emotion.

How callous she had been, to never tell this poor boy about his father.

Kyo watched Ayako, who averted her gaze back to the grave and started speaking as though he were not there.

'You were such a talented photographer, you really were.' Her voice trembled. 'But oh how I pushed you. Oh how we fought, didn't we, Kenji?'

She hung her head, and Kyo moved away from the grave, not wanting to stop his grandmother from talking. She carried on.

'I still blame myself, Kenji. I should never have let you take your photographic talents to war. The violence. What terrible things you must have seen. I should've let you go to the mountains instead, like your father. I should have encouraged your early passion for nature. But it was only because I cared, Kenji. You know that, don't you? It was only because I was scared I'd lose you to the mountains, like I lost your father. And then of course you ran off somewhere even more dangerous, out of sheer defiance. But I should never have stopped talking to you like I did. I was trying to control things. I thought if I didn't talk to you any more, it would make you stop chasing bullets on the battlefield. I thought I was doing the right thing.'

Kyo watched a tear fall from Ayako's face.

'I'm sorry, Kenji. I failed you.'

Kyo moved towards his grandmother. He wanted to reach out, to touch her, to tell her everything was okay. But he could not bring his hand any closer to her.

She sighed. Kyo exhaled.

☯

They both clasped their hands in prayer.

And walked back to the house in silence.

Ayako vs. The Mountain:
Part Two

While Kyo was extremely curious about what had happened to his grandmother on the mountain, he lacked the confidence to just come out and ask her questions. A side of him was also worried that she would react badly to being questioned about her past, and in revealing that he knew about the scrapbook, it might make it look like he was snooping through her belongings, which he hadn't been. It had been Coltrane who knocked the scrapbook off the bookcase. But Ayako would never hear a bad word against Coltrane.

Kyo also felt awkward thinking about the fact that he might have to address the matter that he'd discovered his father's photographs, and this made him worry that she would clam up even more about his father, and that he would never hear any of the stories she had locked away inside herself.

And so he carried on attending cram school and sketching by himself, unsure how he should act with this knowledge in his head that he had secretly stumbled upon.

But sometimes fate intervenes.

Kyo had been helping out Jun and Emi with the renovation work for a month or so now.

The hostel was a beautiful old townhouse which was currently missing its windows and doors. The first time he'd been there, Ayako had marched him over on a Sunday, and he wasn't really sure what was going on, other than his grandmother wanted him to help the couple. Kyo had enjoyed being there once Ayako had left, and Jun and Emi had barraged him with questions about how he was getting on at cram school, whether he was enjoying living in Ono-michi, whether he'd had a chance to explore other parts of Hiroshima Prefecture. Kyo found them both easy to talk to. He hadn't had the opportunity to hang out with people his own age – or even close to his own age (other than his recent failed night out in Hiroshima) – and it was a welcome relief to speak openly and casually.

They'd walked into the hostel through the garden, in which there were power tools, a workbench and timber. They had explained to Kyo on the way over that they needed him for the heavy lifting that Emi, with her pregnancy showing now, could no longer carry out. So he and Jun set about their tasks of clearing out one of the rooms and sanding down floorboards, while Emi did some smaller carpentry jobs over at the bench, pausing occasionally to rest a hand on her bump or offer advice. Before they began work, Jun inserted a CD into a small portable player, and they listened to a hip-hop group called Tha Blue Herb, who, as it happened, Kyo was also a fan of. Meanwhile, Kyo enjoyed the physical exercise and the banter. As they worked, they chatted about the music they listened to, the TV shows they liked to watch and the video games they played.

One particular Sunday, they were sanding down the floorboards.

'So,' said Kyo. 'What games have you been playing?'

'Ah . . . I've not had time to play anything recently,' said Jun.

'He's too busy.' Emi narrowed her eyes at Jun as she said this. 'And he'll be even busier when he's a father. Bringing home the bacon.'

'But there's a soft spot in my heart for Mario Kart on the Super Famicon,' said Jun, winking at Kyo.

'I never played that one,' said Kyo. 'But I played the one on the Switch.'

'Bit before your time, right?' asked Jun.

'See, he's getting old,' mock whispered Emi to Kyo, laughing.

They sat down to rest, and drank hot green tea, which Emi poured from a Thermos flask into three polystyrene cups. She also produced three momiji manju cakes from her bag, which they ate with their tea.

'So,' said Jun, pausing to sip from his steaming cup. 'How are you getting on with your grandmother?'

Kyo paused. Perhaps for too long, which caused Emi to laugh.

'She's scary, isn't she?' said Kyo nervously.

Jun and Emi nodded, smiling.

'A little,' said Emi. 'But she has a very good heart. And that's what's important.'

'She's always been there for us,' said Jun, wiping his forehead with the back of his hand. 'Whenever we've needed help or advice, she's been there.'

Kyo fixed his eyes on his slippered feet.

'Hm . . .' he began, and then wondered whether he should continue.

'What's up?' asked Emi.

He shook his head, but couldn't stop himself from asking. 'Do you guys know anything about what happened to her up on the mountain?'

They both went silent, and exchanged uneasy glances.

Jun eventually spoke. 'We don't know much, Kyo. We're fairly new to Onomichi, and all we hear are the rumours.'

Emi nodded. 'Yes, I don't think we could exactly say what happened to your grandmother. Someone like Sato-san might know better.'

Kyo looked at the bare wooden floorboards.

'But why don't you just ask her?' suggested Emi. 'I'm sure she'd tell you everything. It's not like it's a secret or anything – the whole town knows she almost died on Mount Tanigawa. It's no secret.'

Jun nodded in assent, and then cocked his head slightly as if thinking deeply.

'And I suppose,' said Jun, almost to himself, 'the only person who truly knows what happened up there on that mountain is your grandmother.'

Emi went around, stacking the three cups they'd drunk their tea from, and taking the wrappers from the momiji manju in her hand. She went out the back to throw away the rubbish.

'So, Kyo,' said Jun, his voice noticeably lighter, 'how about you put on an art exhibition in this space?'

Kyo looked around, confused. 'In here?'

He studied the bare walls of the room, and imagined his artwork hanging there.

'Yes,' said Emi, coming back in. 'We were thinking – when we finally open the hostel, how about having some kind of exhibition of your artwork? We saw the two pieces hanging in your grandmother's café, and we thought they looked wonderful. How about exhibiting more of the stuff you've been working on recently? We can invite a load of friends and have a party to celebrate the grand opening of the hostel. It'll be fun!'

They both looked at Kyo expectantly.

'Ah . . .' he hesitated, '. . . that sounds great and everything, but I'm not sure I have anything I'd want to exhibit . . .'

'No pressure,' said Jun kindly. 'Just if it's something you'd be interested in.'

Kyo flashed them both a thin smile – inside, he felt nothing but doubt.

Flo: Autumn

'Are you sure you'll be all right without me?' asked Flo, running a hand through Lily's soft fur.

The cat, obviously, made no response.

Lily was lying on Flo's lap, snoozing away, entirely oblivious to the difficult emotions Flo was experiencing. The cat's little chest rose in and out slowly, in time with her snoring. Eyes shut tight, Lily's small head nuzzled into the crook of Flo's arm. As always, Flo marvelled at the softness of the cat's long fur as she gently stroked her fingers through it.

Doing her best not to disturb Lily's tranquil slumber, Flo raised her head and looked across at her packed rucksack on the other side of the apartment. She made a quick mental checklist of all the tasks she'd already done to get ready for this upcoming trip – the most important was providing clean linen, towels and bedding for Ogawa, who was coming to cat sit while Flo was away. Ogawa was Flo's former Japanese teacher, from her time living in Kanazawa, when she'd first moved to Japan on the JET Programme all those years ago. Ogawa had been coming to Tokyo anyway to see her friends, so the timing was perfect. Flo had written anxious instructions all over the apartment on Post-it notes, and a longer letter to Ogawa describing in detail how and when to feed Lily while she was away.

She moved her arm ever so slightly to look at her watch. Lily grumbled. Flo would have to leave soon if she were to catch her train. But now, with Lily's warm belly on her lap, the thought of leaving the cat and the apartment seemed foolish.

Was it crazy for her to be going all the way to Onomichi to find Hibiki? Was this really the best use of her time?

Lily readjusted her head on Flo's arm once again, getting more comfortable.

⁂

Over the past few months, Flo had feverishly sought to make contact with the author of *Sound of Water*, known only as Hibiki. She'd looked up the book online, and saw it had been published a few years ago. It had only a handful of online reviews – mostly positive, but some negative. The consensus was that this book was not mainstream at all in Japan.

Her next step had been to google the author's name. With a cryptic nom de plume like 'Hibiki', it was difficult to find information on the author. Most of the results were related to a famous Japanese whisky produced by Suntory with that same name. The word also meant 'echo', which only further confused the search results.

The best course of action would be to contact the publisher directly: Senkosha. The top result was a dodgy-looking web page listing an email address which Flo had written to immediately. Unfortunately, it had bounced straight back with a mailer-daemon error response. Address not found. Since her first visit, the site itself had expired, and was now showing a 404 domain error when Flo tried to revisit it. Luckily, she'd jotted down the postal address listed for the company Senkosha at the bottom of the website. She'd noted at the time that, just as in the book, it was an Onomichi address. Flo had now put two and two together with the name of the publisher – the Senko of Senkosha was a reference to Senkoji Temple in Onomichi – the Temple of One Thousand Lights. She wagered that the book must've been published by a small press in the town, or even self-published. She was practically convinced now that the author was a local. The novel itself was set in Onomichi; this all made sense to her.

But here, the trail went cold. She'd thought of giving up – going back to her editor and telling him she couldn't get in contact with the publisher or the author. The thought of that made her blood run cold. How unprofessional of her as a translator – to have begun translating a novel and sent it off to a publisher, without having secured permission first. Grant would be angry with her for wasting his time. She might never get another translation gig from him again.

It had been Kyoko and Makoto who suggested Flo go to Onomichi to chase down the publisher and find Hibiki.

'You've gotta go!' they'd both chorused in unison at the izakaya.

'You can't give up so easily!' said Kyoko.

'But I'm worried it'll spoil my translation,' she'd argued. 'Reality might clash with the work I've already done.'

'Nonsense!' said Kyoko. 'It'll only enrich the writing.'

They were the ones who'd paid for her bullet train ticket to Onomichi. Flo was overwhelmed by the gesture, and deeply embarrassed. The train ticket was not hugely expensive, but she felt uncomfortable taking it from the pair. She'd tried to refuse over and over again, but in the same way that she had attempted to get out of going for dinner at the izakaya in spring, she was no match for Kyoko's vice-like grip on her wrist, forcing the ticket into her hands. Flo was secretly grateful to them for getting the ball rolling, something she wouldn't have done by herself – she'd needed a shove. Makoto had even made up some posters for Flo, with a little QR code on them, and a big tagline that said:

'Go on, Flo-chan!' He pointed at it with his cigarette. 'Scan it with your phone!'

Flo had scanned the code reluctantly, and it had taken her to a web page Makoto had made up for her. A simple layout in English and Japanese, asking, 'Are you Hibiki?' and 'Please contact me.' He'd listed Flo's email address there too, and included a picture of a one-eyed black cat.

'That's Coltrane,' said Makoto bashfully. 'You told me about him before – I'm not sure if that's what he looks like, but I thought it might help the real Hibiki know it's in regard to his book.'

'Oh, Makoto,' said Flo, tearing up.

'It's really stupid, isn't it?' Kyoko snickered. 'He got a hundred of these dumb fliers printed up. And I've no idea why he wrote the website in English and Japanese.'

'I'm just trying to help!'

'You're a fool.' Kyoko shook her head. 'What's Flo going to do with one hundred fliers?'

Flo had laughed, then immediately burst into tears.

'What's wrong?' Kyoko's face fell.

'You don't need to take the fliers, Flo-chan,' said Makoto. 'I'm sorry if it creates extra work for you.'

'No.' Flo shook her head, trying to hide her embarrassment. The wall she kept around her had momentarily crumbled, and she now felt terribly exposed. But neither Kyoko nor Makoto seemed that bothered. 'Thank you. Both of you. You're the best.'

They'd beamed.

⁂

At Tokyo Station, Flo checked her phone. She had a message from Ogawa.

Flo-chan,
I've arrived at your apartment – Found the key no problem. Lily was mewing and meowing at me, so I gave her some treats. I hope that's okay.

Have a safe journey to Onomichi, and thank you for letting me stay
in your apartment with Lily. We'll take good care of each other.
Have a wonderful time, and we'll both see you when you get back.
Ogawa

Lily was clearly in good hands, which filled Flo with relief. Her
finger hovered over the Instagram logo on her phone. She and Yuki
had been messaging less and less these past few months, but Flo had
sent a message saying she was visiting Onomichi. It was still marked
as unread. Flo did mental calculations as to what time it was in New
York, and whether Yuki was awake or not. Recently, almost at the
same rate their conversation had decreased in frequency, Yuki had
been increasingly posting photos with the same girl. Flo did not
have the guts to ask if they were dating.

She looked up from her phone at the departure boards.

Her Shinkansen would be leaving soon.

She'd entertained the idea of taking the local train all the way to
Onomichi, staying the night in Osaka, as Kyo had done, but Kyoko
and Makoto's kind gesture had saved her the bother. Even just the
thought of all that time on the train made her tired. The money
she'd saved on her ticket would go towards paying for her
accommodation.

She shouldered her rucksack and made her way through the gates.

⠤

It had been a while since Flo had taken the bullet train.

She'd taken it more before she'd moved to Tokyo. While living in
Kanazawa, she'd spent a lot of her time travelling round the rest of
Japan. At first, there was arguably a side of her that felt resentful of
the fact she had to live in the provinces. On weekends and holidays
she would take the bullet train to bigger cities like Osaka, Fukuoka
and Tokyo, and feel jealous of her fellow JET friends living in these
vibrant communities. There were shops that sold American food.
There were restaurants that served other countries' cuisines. There
were parties. There were museums and art galleries. Libraries that

had English books. Bookshops that had English books. There were even English book clubs. Most importantly, these were communities that welcomed non-Japanese.

But it wasn't until she moved to Tokyo for work that she realized what she'd lost from the smaller community she'd had in Kanazawa. Being in rural Japan had afforded her more opportunities to immerse herself in Japanese language and culture – not many people spoke English out in the countryside. She had noticed her Japanese language ability progressing, while friends who lived in the bigger cities stalled, as they clung tightly to their English-speaking circles for a sense of belonging. While translating *Sound of Water*, Flo had often found herself nodding in agreement at Kyo's experiences of moving from the city to the countryside. They were worlds apart.

She looked out of the window at the grey clouds – far too cloudy to see Mount Fuji.

It was drizzling outside, and despite being autumn, her favourite season, the scenery was dour and dismal. She watched the raindrops falling down the windowpane, and thought of how she'd snuck a sentence from *War and Peace* into her translation of *Sound of Water* – 'Drops dripped.' She'd taken it from the Pevear and Volokhonsky translation she'd been reading over the summer.

Would anyone ever get to read it, though? Not if she couldn't get in touch with the author – that was for sure.

At this point in the journey, the metallic glass buildings of Tokyo had been replaced by windswept paddy fields, smattered with the houses of smaller satellite towns that thinned as the train went further and further from the city. She took out a copy of *A Dark Night's Passing* by Shiga Naoya, which she was really enjoying. Slowly, as she read, she found her excitement turning to exhaustion, eyes strained with tiredness. She set an alarm on her phone, and lay her head back in her seat, closing her eyes, relishing the sensation of the fast-moving train, accelerating like an aeroplane about to take off. She drifted away into a slumber and had a short but intense dream – chasing Coltrane through the winding alleyways of Onomichi, struggling up a mountain she never seemed to make progress on, always ten steps behind Coltrane, until she eventually turned a corner, only to come upon the cold, lifeless bodies of Ayako and Kyo lying on the ground. She tried to wake them, but they would not stir.

She awoke with a start to the sound of her alarm.

It was raining in Fukuyama, too.

▲

It was while she was changing to the local train at Fukuyama that Flo began to feel nervous. Doubts crept into her mind about the imminent reality of arriving in Onomichi. She wondered if it would've been better not to have come at all. Surely, seeing the place before she'd finished would disrupt her workflow. It could spoil her translation. But how else would she get permission to translate the novel, if she couldn't contact the publisher or the author?

Her mind drifted to Kyo's journey as she stepped on to the local JR West line, with its blue stripe on the side, which he'd noticed. The carriage rattled and clanked along on its tracks, and the closer she got to Onomichi, the more she started to think that she might be making a mistake. From the window of the train she could see the Seto Inland Sea, but it looked as dull as gunmetal today, as the louring skies cast shadows on the waters.

The greyness of it all – it was like that passage from Mishima Yukio's book, *The Temple of the Golden Pavilion*, which she'd read in college many years ago, before coming to Japan. The book was hazy, and her memory of it not perfect, but the sentiment still remained all these years later. Her professor at Reed College had set the book for a class on Twentieth-Century Japanese Literature, the only course the Literature department offered on Japan. There was a lot that she didn't like about Mishima: both about the book and what she'd read of the author. She'd watched a film about him directed by Paul Schrader, and it had confused her even more. Mishima committing seppuku from the top of a government building – none of it made sense. Why would a writer do that? Why would someone with so much talent and so much to live for throw away their life like that? It made her think of Kenji again, throwing away his life and talents as a photographer – why had he done what he did? Was there any sense to some people's actions? And, selfishly, she thought about her own darker moments when she'd considered similar ideas.

The author and his life aside, the part from *The Temple of the Golden Pavilion* that Flo was thinking about now was when the monk who narrates the book becomes obsessed with the temple building, and falls into a jealous love affair with the inanimate Golden Temple. It was all based on a real-life monk who really did set fire to the Temple of the Golden Pavilion in Kyoto. But the section that truly chimed with Flo was when the monk first comes to see the temple in actuality. Before this scene, he has only read about it and seen it in pictures, but never in real life. When it comes to seeing the building, he's already built up an image of it in his head: a perfect image. Then, when he sees the real temple for the first time, he's disappointed – the weather is grey and overcast, and the building looks leaden and lifeless. The monk is dismayed, and feels that he has misplaced his love.

But then, all of a sudden, a gap in the clouds appears, and the temple is illuminated by the sun. The gilt temple begins to sparkle and twinkle in the sunlight, and the phoenix on the roof appears to soar, wings outstretched. And just like that, the monk is smitten by the true glory of the temple he loves so dearly.

Right now, this scene was troubling Flo.

What if she, like the monk, had built up Onomichi in her mind to be something it was not? What if the reality did not live up to the image? And worse still, what if Flo fell in love with the town, as the monk had fallen in love with the temple? She would still have to return to her life in Tokyo again afterwards.

But the most dreadful thought of all:

What if, even if she found Hibiki (whoever he was) – he said no?

Right on cue, a gap in the clouds opened, revealing snatches of blue sky. The castle of Onomichi was now looming high above her on the mountainside. In an attempt to distract herself, she took a photo of the castle on her phone and uploaded it to Instagram.

尾道に着いたよ。Arrived in Onomichi!

Makoto instantly liked the post. '頑張れ! Good luck!' he posted back.

Yuki was online – Flo could tell when she checked her messages – but she hadn't liked the post. Flo sighed. She'd mostly uploaded the photo to get attention from Yuki, but it hadn't worked. Her heart was pounding in her chest.

'Onomichi. The next stop is Onomichi. Doors on the right side will open.'

⚞

The Seto Inland Sea. Grey and cloudy, windswept and rusty. She was really here.

It stretched out in front of her, and she inevitably thought about how Kyo felt, the first time he came. There was no Tanuki taking her ticket – there were automatic ticket barriers, which must've been installed recently. Her impression of the town was not the same as Kyo's – the town seemed alive. Obviously, quieter than Tokyo, but there were people milling around here and there.

There it was, just like in the book – the mountain, the train station, the old shopping arcade – the shotengai – a word she'd agonized over how to translate into English, finally settling on the lengthy and laborious 'shotengai covered market'. She spun around slowly on the stretch of grass, not knowing what to do with herself first.

She found the statue of the feminist writer Hayashi Fumiko, the one that Kyo called naff. Again, Flo didn't think the statue naff at all. She had never read Hayashi Fumiko before, but knew that Yuki was a fan of her writing.

So Flo took another photo and uploaded it, in an effort to snag Yuki's attention.

HAYASHI Fumiko (1903–1951). Feminist writer.
Attended Onomichi Higashi High School!

Everything was just how she thought it would be, but slightly stranger. She'd seen photos of the place online, but nothing compared to standing there in real life, with a soft sea breeze on her face, clouds hanging over the bay, and the quiet murmur of passers-by filling her ears.

The first thing she needed to do was check into her guesthouse and drop off her rucksack.

Then she could explore.

The guesthouse was an old converted townhouse by the sea, reno-
vated to accommodate visitors. The couple who ran the place were
friendly enough, and looked exactly as Flo imagined Jun and Emi to
be. Flo anxiously weighed up whether she should ask their names,
certain that they must be Jun and Emi, but also scared that they
might not. They obviously couldn't be – life and literature were
never that directly linked. Right? And there was something about
these two that didn't match with the characters from the book.
They seemed more sombre and serious. As she walked upstairs to
her room, she finally overheard them address each other with different names, and she couldn't help it; her heart sank a little.

Flo's room was a great deal for the modest price she'd paid. It
looked out over the coastal road, with a clear view of the Inland
Sea. She stood at the large window for a time, watching the water.

She was really here.

⁂

After a short rest, Flo grabbed a tote bag filled with the fliers Makoto
had made up for her, and began wandering around the town. First
things first: she had the address of Senkosha publishers written in
her notepad. She'd also tried dialling the phone number listed at the
time, after the email she sent had bounced back, but was met with
a *number does not exist* message. She was not expecting much today,
but struck out in the direction of the address she had, holding
tightly to a glimmer of hope. From time to time she would stop and
affix one of Makoto's fliers to a noticeboard or a pylon, but mostly
she took in as much of the town as she could.

As she wandered, she found herself wanting to go back to previous sections of the book and rework some of her prose. She
recognized aspects of the place that she had translated already, but
on seeing the real-life version of something, she became gripped
with a better word or phrase to describe the real thing. If nothing
else, the trip would certainly help with the precision of her

translation. But again, if she couldn't find Hibiki, no other reader than her would ever know.

After climbing up a surprisingly steep hill, she arrived at the address for Senkosha. Immediately, she felt confused. In the place where the Senkosha building should have been, there was a derelict office building with closed gates, and a notice saying it was soon to be demolished.

Flo stood still, her heart beating fast.

This couldn't be right. Perhaps she'd got the address wrong. She checked her phone again, and her maps app. No, all was correct. It was supposed to be here. But what was arguably here was nothing.

Fortunately, there was a koban police box over on the other side of the road, so she made her way there to ask directions. As she did, she thought of Kyo's mishap in Hiroshima, and how he ended up in a koban with Officer Ide. Translating the word 'koban' had proved difficult. If she got rid of the word and just wrote 'police box' it seemed to eliminate some of the Japanese culture involved. It also sounded a bit too *Doctor Who* to her mind. Koban were small buildings which housed a single policeman, and offered support for the community, rather than handling major crimes, which were dealt with by larger police stations. Most people went to the koban to report lost and found items, or ask for directions, just as she was doing now.

There she was, off in translation mode again! Flo shook her head to refocus herself and stepped into the koban. The policeman behind the desk instantly froze and looked uncomfortable.

'S-s-sorry,' he stammered in English, waving his hand. 'No English. Excuse me.'

'It's okay,' said Flo quickly in Japanese. 'Quite all right. I speak Japanese.'

The officer breathed a sigh of relief and smiled. 'Phew! You got me worried there. English was my worst subject at school. Failed every test, didn't I?' He laughed, before continuing. 'I must say – your Japanese is wonderful.'

'I just have a quick question,' she said, ignoring the compliment and taking out the notepad she'd written the address down on. 'I'm looking for this address, but I think I must've come the wrong way. All I found was this abandoned building that's about to be demolished.'

'Ah, yes, miss,' he said, nodding. 'I'm afraid you've not made an error. That is the correct address for the building across the street. It was an office building, until several months ago, but the last company renting a space in there must've left, and now the building has been condemned by the council and is due to be demolished. They'll be rebuilding soon enough – probably a convenience store, pachinko parlour, or some such.'

'I see.' Flo bit her lip. 'I suppose you don't know Senkosha publishers?'

'Senkosha?' he said, rubbing his chin. 'Sure you don't mean Senkoji? That's the temple up there.' He pointed in the direction of the mountain.

'Never mind,' said Flo. 'Thank you very much.'

'You're welcome, miss. Enjoy your visit!'

▲▲

She couldn't think of anyone else to call, and she needed to talk to someone to clear her head. Now, immediately. The bleakness was back, threatening to overwhelm her. She called Ogawa, who thankfully picked up promptly.

'Flo-chan? Are you okay?' said Ogawa. 'Lily and I were just having a cuddle. She is *adorable*. Did you know that she sucks on the purple blanket?'

'Ogawa-sensei . . .'

'Yes?' Then Ogawa spoke to the mewing cat. 'Lily! I can't stroke you right now, *and* talk to your mummy at the same time. Please be patient.' She addressed Flo again. 'Flo-chan, what happened?'

'I'm so sorry, Ogawa-sensei, but I didn't know who else to call.'

'What happened, Flo-chan?'

Flo studied the old shopfronts of the town as she stood by a vending machine. She thought of Kyo calling his mother, and wondered whether this was the same vending machine he'd been standing by when he'd phoned her. All those scenes she'd already translated. All those words . . . Flo sighed, and did her best not to get emotional.

'How's Lily?'

'She's good! We're both good, Flo-chan. Is something wrong?'

Flo didn't know where to begin. Her one lead had gone cold. Despite her initial desperation to connect with someone, it now felt much easier – less burdensome to others – to just put up a wall, and not let Ogawa know what was really going on. 'No,' said Flo. 'I'm fine. Just worried about the cat.'

'Oh, she's great! But make sure you take time out to have fun while you're down there,' said Ogawa kindly. 'It's not often you get a break.'

Flo didn't have the courage to tell her this was not a holiday. She'd come here to find Hibiki. That was the sole reason, and now that wasn't looking hopeful, she was filled with despair.

'Oh!' said Ogawa, as if remembering something important. 'I hope you don't mind, Flo-chan, but I went ahead and bought you a present online. It will be delivered to your apartment in Tokyo.'

'A present?'

'Yes,' said Ogawa hesitantly. 'I hope you won't think I'm meddling, but I noticed you had run out of bookcase space, so I bought you one of these fancy bookcases that everyone raves about. It's sort of shaped like a snake, and they interlock, so you can combine them to make a bigger bookcase. A Japanese designer came up with the idea, but they're popular all over the world.'

Flo couldn't help but feel ashamed of the piles of books she'd left lying around in her apartment. What a mess she'd left for her poor teacher. 'Oh, Ogawa-sensei. You really shouldn't have.'

'Please, Flo-chan. Indulge me.'

They said their goodbyes and hung up. The last thing Ogawa said was 'Are you sure you're all right, Flo?' And once again, Flo had insisted she was fine. Just fine.

I'm supposed to be the closed-off Japanese one. You're supposed to be the open and easy American who talks about her feelings. It's exhausting, Flo. You exhaust me. Yuki's voice echoed in her head.

Flo had no idea what to do now. So she wandered idly along the shotengai, eventually finding a coffee shop that she imagined looked a bit like Ayako's, in roughly the same spot she'd pictured. The shop was an old one, with inner décor that looked to be from the Taisho era. Wooden and polished. Fancy, and somewhat European. She sat down at a table, and was served by a slim middle-aged man wearing a collared white shirt with no tie and smart black trousers. When he brought her coffee over, he complimented Flo on her Japanese. She thanked him, and as she was doing so, she noticed a picture hanging on the wall. She got up and went over to study it up close.

There it was.

Frog.

Looking at the weather forecast on the TV, with a rainbow in the background. Just like the picture Kyo had drawn. And down in the bottom corner it was signed Hibiki in katakana.

The man was watching her studying the picture, and Flo looked up at him.

'Is this Ayako's coffee shop?' asked Flo bluntly.

The man scratched his chin. 'Ayako?'

'Yes, an old lady who is missing fingers. Did her grandson draw this?'

The man appeared confused. 'I'm afraid I don't understand.'

'Who is Hibiki?' asked Flo.

'I don't know, I'm afraid,' said the man, laughing uncomfortably. 'I'm just running the shop for a friend. She's owned this place for about five years now. I think she bought it from an elderly couple who wanted to retire.'

Flo backed down. 'Ah, I see.'

She returned to her table and continued drinking her coffee. But she couldn't take her eyes off the picture. The only difference was that in Kyo's version, the frog was looking at a smartphone, but in this picture, he was looking at a TV weather forecast. Her eyes searched for any signs of a portrait of Coltrane the cat, but there weren't any.

They must be here, she thought to herself. *They must be real.*

▲▲

Flo tried to put the Hibiki issue out of her mind, and did her best to enjoy her stay in Onomichi. Her return ticket wasn't until Sunday, so she had plenty of time. She had surprised herself with a good night's sleep to reset. The first day, she took a stroll around the town, searching high and low for Sato's CD shop, but couldn't find anything that looked remotely similar. She did find a shop that sold art supplies, with a cat on its sign – she took a photo and uploaded it to her Instagram.

猫画材屋さん – Cat Art Supply Shop

Again, Yuki didn't like it. But Flo realized that this stung less now. It was funny – for some reason, she was feeling more distant from Yuki, calmer about the whole thing. Perhaps it was the immersive feeling she had, exploring the town she'd spent so much time exploring in her mind. She was now uploading the photos to keep Kyoko, Makoto and Ogawa up to date with her trip, rather than in the hope that Yuki might give her a dose of dopamine by liking them.

In the evening she wandered the thin alleyways, getting lost in the streets that led hither and thither through the mountainside. She did not yet want to climb to the top of the mountain on which Senkoji – the Temple of One Thousand Lights – was located. She planned on doing that on the last day, as the weather forecast predicted an improvement.

For dinner, she went to a cosy izakaya, and let the waiter recommend her dishes, enjoying the cheaper prices and fresher local ingredients than anything Tokyo had to offer. Slowly, she began to enjoy her holiday, forgetting the stresses of her life waiting for her back in the city.

商店街にある居酒屋。美味しかった。
An izakaya in the shotengai. It was delicious.

The next day, she woke early and took a train into Hiroshima. She wandered the streets, ate okonomiyaki at a restaurant Kyoko and Makoto had recommended, saw the Atomic Bomb Dome, and said a prayer for those who had died. Then she headed for the island of Miyajima. She took photos of the otherworldly red autumn leaves on the island, fed crackers to the deer, and watched the sun set behind the famous torii gate floating in the water. While on the island, she made sure to buy four boxes of momiji manju – the same kind of cakes Kyo had eaten with Jun and Emi. She planned to give boxes to Kyoko, Makoto and Ogawa as omiyage souvenirs, and to keep one for herself. Viewing the Japanese maples, she thought about the similar opinions she shared with Ayako regarding the autumn leaves and sakura. But something nagged at the back of her mind.

She still desperately wanted to introduce Ayako and Kyo to English-speakers. She thought her work was good. She wanted to finish what she had started.

And she wanted to find Hibiki.

⬩⬩

On her final day in Onomichi, Flo headed for the top of the mountain, via the Temple of One Thousand Lights. As she was making her way, she kept stumbling on things that reminded her of Ayako and Kyo.

猫の細道！本当に存在してる！
Cat Alley! It really exists!

She spent a while in Cat Alley, stroking the cats and taking photos. She uploaded one, which Makoto, Kyoko and Ogawa instantly liked. When she checked again in thirty seconds, to her surprise she saw that Yuki had written a comment:

So glad to see you're having a good time!

Flo smiled wryly.

A sleeping cat. Neko fact: the Japanese word for 'cat' is 'neko',
which is thought to be derived from the words 'sleeping child'.

As she was making her way up some stone steps, she saw a black
cat. For a moment, her heart stopped. Could it be Coltrane? But she
noticed it had two eyes. It wasn't him. She took another photo and
uploaded it anyway.

黒猫 – black cat

Even stranger still was when she passed a graveyard. It must've been the graveyard Kyo and Ayako visited. Where Kenji was interred. Flo searched high and low for a TABATA grave, but couldn't find one.

She wandered Senkoji Park, imagining how stunning it must be in the cherry blossom season. Would it have been better if Yuki were here? Perhaps not, Flo thought to herself while strolling slowly. This was not what she was feeling now. She wanted to share the town, but not only with a partner, or even with just Kyoko, Makoto and Ogawa. How beautiful this place was! How much she wanted to share it with the world! But how much more terrible that she could not find Hibiki – that she couldn't get permission to introduce Onomichi to a world of English-speakers. Flo felt her responsibility even more strongly: as a translator, she was supposed to serve as a bridge between cultures – to connect those who couldn't communicate with one another. Knowing that an obstacle stood in her way, the bridge being walled off, frustrated and saddened her deeply.

When she came to the top of the mountain, she took a photo and was uploading it when she thought she heard a sound to her left.

She turned to see two people. A thin old lady wearing a kimono standing next to a boy of about nineteen or twenty dressed in casual clothing. She watched them gazing out across the Seto Inland Sea. They were deep in conversation. The old lady was talking, and the boy just listened.

They turned to face her.

Unmistakable.

But as she watched, they began to slowly fade away into nothingness. And she could now see right through them. She blinked, and they were there no longer. They had never been there, despite how much she wanted them to be.

It had been a trick of the mind.

Autumn

秋

九

Summer waned, and over time, the coolness of autumn began to set in.

The mornings and evenings gradually became milder, with steadily declining temperatures and humidity. Kyo and Ayako found it easier to sleep at night, but caught themselves shivering in the mornings as they got up from under the sheets of their futons. The leaves of the Japanese maple by the pond in Ayako's garden began to change to a glorious shade of red.

The convenience stores also moved in time with the seasons: warm foods slowly returning, which had all but disappeared from the shelves during summer. Steaming hot nikuman meat buns, oden and corndogs were now invitingly back on the counter, enticing the chilly customer with a warm snack to stave off the cold. Vending machines switched their labels from a wall of blue COLD signs and were now split fifty-fifty with red HOT signs.

While other schoolchildren and university students had enjoyed the excitement of the summer holidays – visiting the nearby beaches, going to festivals, taking trips with their families – Kyo had still been attending the strict and structured programme of the yobiko cram school in which he was enrolled. Lessons had carried on all throughout the summer, and now into autumn. University entrance exams were due to take place in winter, and Kyo and the other ronin-sei were expected to work as hard as possible in the precious remaining time they had left.

Because of this, the summer was a mostly uneventful time for him. He spent his days studying at the cram school, and his afternoons working on his drawings. Sundays he helped Jun and Emi in the mornings, then he was free to roam the town as he pleased in the afternoons.

Ayako found herself slightly busier than usual.

With the summer holidays came the tourists from all over the country and the world, to see the quaint town of Onomichi. Her tiny café would fill to bursting with sightseers and travellers, who spilled inside off the streets, hoping for a bite to eat or a drink in one of the more traditionally styled coffee houses. Because of this, Kyo had started to feel he was taking up valuable space in the café – occupying a table that could've been used by paying customers.

And so Ayako and Kyo came to a new understanding born out of this busy period and Kyo's continued dedication: he would go somewhere else to study in the afternoons. Ayako suggested the local library. Kyo agreed.

Over the time Kyo had spent with Ayako, she had begun to trust him with his own studies more. He was still achieving good grades. Letting him go to the library and be more in control of his own study time was also an opportunity for him to grow as an adult. If he wanted to study, he could. If he wanted to take some time off, he was welcome to.

She would no longer force him.

On particularly busy days over the summer, he'd even helped out working at the café, taking orders from the customers, acting as a waiter. Ayako hadn't let him anywhere near the coffee or the food preparation, but she'd been extremely grateful for his help during those demanding days. Kyo had enjoyed chatting to customers from all over Japan, asking them where they were from, and filling them in on some of the local knowledge he had quickly amassed from his time spent living in Onomichi.

Ayako was particularly grateful for his help when the gaijin customers came in. She could understand English, but she felt embarrassed to speak it. When she was at school, English had been studied like Latin – as if it were a dead language – sentences cut up and analysed for the sake of learning grammar alone. She'd had very few opportunities to practise speaking the language. Kyo, on the other hand, had benefitted from an entirely different approach to English education at school. He'd had an actual native speaker in his classes all through junior high and high school. He had no problems taking the food orders of the foreigners who came to the café. Ayako was extremely appreciative, even proud, to see him speaking fluently with the foreign customers – going as far as bantering and joking with them.

However, when the crowds died down, she would turn him away, stubbornly insisting that she didn't need any help today, and that he should be focusing on his studies, not messing around in the café with her.

In reality, Ayako had decided that the boy needed more freedom. She couldn't be there to badger him for the rest of his life, telling him what to do. He had to learn independence – to manage himself.

Kyo, ironically, felt no urge to slack off on his studies. He had settled into a pleasant routine, and preferred the thought of sitting inside the library quietly revising rather than kicking about on the streets with nothing to do – as he'd done last year. The library was a great place to study, and also quiet enough to work on his drawings in peace without anyone bothering him. Afterwards, he would go and meet Ayako for a walk up the mountain when she closed the café.

The first time Kyo entered the library, he had been surprised to see a familiar face working behind the issue desk.

Station Master Ono's wife, Michiko, looked up at him as he entered.

'Kyo-kun!'

'Ah, Michiko-san!'

She'd shown him how the library worked, guiding him through the small number of shelves of books they had, saying things like, 'Nothing like the library in Hiroshima, so small here, so small!'

She took him through all the shelves, pointing out the different sections: fiction, non-fiction, history, science, art history and, of course, manga – Kyo was excited to see they had copies of Tezuka

Osamu's *Ayako* and even the two-book edition of Yoshihiro Tatsumi's manga autobiography *A Drifting Life* – he checked those out immediately. Afterwards, Michiko showed Kyo the way to a reading room which had small desks with wooden partitions, where he could sit and work with no one to disturb him.

And so Ayako and Kyo's shared routine began to evolve little by little.

But always with each other in mind.

O

Kyo had been at the library one early autumn day, working away on his drawings, when he was jolted out of his intense concentration.

'What are you doing?' came a man's voice from a few tables over.

Kyo instinctively looked up, thinking the voice was directed at him.

What he saw was a middle-aged man addressing a girl of about Kyo's age, who was sitting by herself reading a book with her back to him.

The man had an unguent appearance. His hair was greasy. His face was greasy. His clothes looked greasy. Everything about him oozed. He had grey stubble, thinning hair and was of average build. He wore an old, filthy raincoat, despite the fact that it had not rained today (and would not later, either).

As for the girl, Kyo could only see the back of her head, but she was dressed in clothes that he deemed slightly too stylish for Onomichi – jeans and a smart patterned top, autumn colours. Over the back of her chair hung a thin green coat with a fur-lined hood. She sat still with her book open, silently studying the page as if she had not heard the man. Kyo could not see her face, but he could see her light brown hair kept up in a ponytail, and her long, attractive neck. Her posture implied she remained unfazed by the man.

Kyo alternated between focusing on his sketches and surreptitiously watching the pair.

'What are you reading?' the man asked the girl again.

She slowly took a decorated bookmark from the table, slid it into the book and closed it.

'A book,' she said. 'Well, I'm trying to read a book.'

There was something familiar about her voice, Kyo realized. Where did he know it from?

'What kind of book?' the man shot back, his voice rising to unacceptable levels for a library.

'Fiction,' she said quietly.

'Pffft. Waste of time,' he said. 'Why read fiction? It's all lies anyway.'

'Lies?'

'Yes, all fiction writers are liars.' The man seemed extremely pleased with this pronouncement, leaning back and crossing his arms.

'How do you mean, liars?' The girl had placed the book down on the table, and was patiently entertaining the conversation of this stranger. Kyo was sure he recognized her, but he couldn't place her.

'Well, they make up things that aren't true,' said the man loudly, waving his hand around the library in excitement. 'That's what liars do. Better you read a history book, or a book about science. Don't waste time on lies.'

The girl paused, considering something before speaking. 'I beg to differ.'

'Oh?'

'Well, I think you've fundamentally confused the concept of what lying is. A lie is an untruth that is told, intentionally by a speaker, to deceive a listener, usually to achieve some kind of bene-fit for the liar—'

'Fiction writers make money from writing, don't they? That's where they benefit.'

She ignored the statement from the man and continued with the line of thought she had been pursuing before he interrupted her. '—but fiction is something entirely different. Fiction is an unspoken contract made between the writer and the reader – the very word "fiction" implies that it *is all* made up, and both the writer and reader know this. There's no deception involved. But both the writer and reader suspend their disbelief so that—'

'Pffft. Rubbish.'

'What do you mean "rubbish"? You don't agree with what I'm saying?' Kyo was surprised that her tone was one of genuine interest, rather than exasperation.

'You're talking garbage. Non-fiction books, like history, science, all of those. They're written in search of truth and facts. Fiction is just lies. None of it is based on truth.'

'Well, how do you know what is true and false?' She cocked her head. 'Do you believe everything written in a reference book simply because you are told it is true? You don't think anyone has ever written an untruth in a non-fiction book?'

'Stupid,' said the man, shaking his head. 'Stupid girl.'

Kyo had been listening and watching the whole time. Thinking about what was being said. But part of him felt ashamed. He wanted to go over and tell this strange middle-aged man to stop harassing the poor girl who was trying to read. But then the more he listened to her calm and considered responses, the more he realized that she was fearless – completely in control of what she was saying, and not intimidated by the weird man in the slightest. If the man had been confronting Kyo about his illustrations, Kyo would've given in long ago and just agreed with whatever he said, in the hope that the man would leave him alone to get on with what he was doing, saying something like, *Yes, yes. Manga is a waste of time. Rubbish. Completely rubbish. I agree. I hate it!* But this poor girl. She'd been trying to read, and this man had taken over her time and energy. There was something fundamentally rude at play.

For Kyo to go over there and interfere, well, wouldn't that be patronizing to the girl, who obviously had the situation under control? Or was that just an excuse to stay out of it?

Still, the man was making a lot of noise, and this was a library.

Kyo's mind raced with arguments and contradictions, but all the time he did nothing. Just listened.

'So, have you got a boyfriend?' the man was asking now.

'I'm afraid that's none of your business, sir.'

'Rude. With that tone, it's not likely you have.'

Kyo was almost on his feet, going over to tell the man to leave her alone, but before he could, Michiko was bearing down on the pair.

She immediately rained down her full-scale librarian onslaught on the unguent man.

'Please, Tanaka-san,' she said politely. 'We've had talks about this before! You can't be coming in here and disturbing other readers. They are here to concentrate quietly. You can't just go up and start talking to anyone you please. This is a library, after all.'

'But . . . but . . .'

'No buts.' Michiko raised a finger. 'Sit down and read in silence, or get out. We don't want to have to call Officer Ando again now, do we?'

The girl who had been reading slid her book into her tote bag, which Kyo noticed had an illustration of a black and white tuxedo cat on it. She picked up the bag and stood.

'It's okay,' she said politely, bowing to both the middle-aged man and Michiko. 'I was just leaving anyway. I apologize for causing a disturbance.'

She made her way quickly to the exit and, before leaving, turned briefly to look back into the room. Her eyes caught Kyo's, and when they fell upon him, she smiled.

He was now absolutely certain he'd met her before. But where?

And what could that smile be conveying? Amusement at the strange old man? A mocking smile that taunted a cowardly Kyo for not rescuing her?

The smile burnt right through him.

As he saw her face properly for the first time, he felt his heart jump. His own face instantly turned red. It was the girl from the train. The one he'd abandoned in Osaka. Ayumi.

He stared back down at the page he was working on.

When he looked up again, she was gone.

Kyo started on a new drawing immediately, trying desperately to sketch her face before he forgot what she looked like.

But the lines and shades of black and white eluded his grasp.

'Can you tell me more about when you first met Grandfather?'

Ayako raised her eyes from the table and studied Kyo's

expression even more intently than she had been studying the Go board up until now. The current game they were playing was pretty evenly matched, and she'd had to start concentrating properly.

The boy was improving.

'When I first met Grandfather?' she replied, shortly, but not tersely. 'Why do you want to know that?'

'Am I not allowed to ask?'

'No, you can ask. I just might not tell.' She coughed, and shook her head. 'I told you before. We met at university. We were in the climbing club together.'

Kyo weighed up a white stone in his hand and finally placed it on the board.

Ayako sighed, reached out and turned the white stone he'd put down the other way up.

'Oh,' he said glumly. 'Wrong way up again?'

'Yes. Why else would I be turning it over?'

He looked at another stone. 'They kinda look the same on both sides,' he said under his breath. 'I can't see the difference.'

'Well, you would say that, wouldn't you?'

They were seated at the kotatsu in the living room. Kyo and Ayako had established an autumn evening routine: sitting with their legs under the heated low table to play Go. Since the mornings and evenings had become chillier, Ayako had taken out a thick quilt from the cupboard, lifted the top of the table, placed the quilt on the frame of the table and then fixed the tabletop over it.

Sato had brought around a huge bag of mikan oranges which he'd grown at his orchard, and there was a steady supply of them in a bowl on the table. Then Jun and Emi, her bump fully showing now, had turned up on the doorstep with a big bag of persimmons as well. Kyo noticed this free exchange of goods that happened in the town, and again he felt that it was a far cry from the cold isolation of Tokyo. Here in Onomichi, the townsfolk never seemed to stop giving and receiving gifts of seasonal produce they'd grown on their home farms – rice, potatoes, mikan oranges, lemons, persimmons. And then there were the hand-crafted goods people produced through their hobbies, like ceramics and carved wooden objects. They all looked after each other.

Kyo often hypothesized that you wouldn't be able to lie down in the gutter in one of these rural towns – even if you wanted to – without someone coming over and asking if you were okay within seconds. Kyo had seen Tokyoites walk straight past people bleeding on the streets. But that would never happen here, and Kyo had gradually found a sense of pride growing within himself towards the town. He respected the townsfolk, and privately now thought of himself as one of them.

Occasionally Kyo and Ayako would argue over some topic or other. Ayako generally liked to wind up Kyo and antagonize him when it was his turn during their games of Go. It took him a while to figure this out, but while he was deciding his next move, she would engage him in a difficult debate or argument in order to distract him. It was a mean and clever tactic Ayako had developed over the years – true gamesmanship. Distract the other player; win at all costs. Be downright devious, if that's what it takes.

A recent conversation had gone like this:

Ayako: Will you be voting tomorrow at the election?
Kyo: I don't vote.
A: What do you mean, you don't vote?
K: I mean I don't vote.
A: How on earth can you say that?
K: I don't believe in politics.
A: You don't *believe* in politics? What a stupid thing to say!
K: Why?
A: Well, whether you *believe* in it or not – it's there! It exists!
K: But nothing ever changes. Whichever way you vote. Politicians are all liars.
A: And that's why you have to vote!
K: That doesn't even make sense.
A: Yes, it does. You vote to keep the lying politicians on their toes.

K: But they still lie, don't they? So what's the point?

A: Selfish boy. People died for your right to vote! Women couldn't vote!

K: Well, I'm not a woman, but I'd die for my right to *not* vote.

A: Foolish boy. You shouldn't be allowed to ride a bus. You shouldn't be allowed to use a public park. You shouldn't be allowed to take part in society if you don't vote. And you've got no right to complain about anything!

K: Fine. I don't want to complain about anything. Just leave me alone, will you?

A: Brainless boy. Numbskull. Ninny.

K: Anyway, shouldn't I be the one who *is* allowed to complain? You were the ones who voted us into all this mess we're in. Isn't it *your* fault things ended up the way they are? The people who vote are *actually* the ones to blame.

A: Hurry up and make your move! You've been staring at this board for hours!

K: Well, I'd be a lot quicker if you weren't haranguing me about politics!

They'd argue and litigate like this for hours, never getting anywhere, mostly just taking up opposing points of view so that they could get worked up about something or other. It was a bit of fun they enjoyed, alongside the game of Go they were playing. Kyo gradually cottoned on to Ayako's dirty tactic, and he started to employ the same moves against her sometimes.

Now it was Ayako's turn to make a move.

'Can I ask you something, Grandmother?'

'What?'

'Well . . . How did you know that Grandfather was the one for you? You know, when you met him.'

Ayako paused with her black stone between her fingers and peered through her eyelids at him. What was the boy up to this time?

'What do you mean?' she asked, testing the water.

'I mean . . .' Kyo placed his chin in his hand, elbow resting on the table, and stared out of the window into the darkness. 'How did you know when you were in love with him?'

Ayako studied Kyo's face. He seemed genuine.

'Why?' she asked, looking at the board.

'I'm just interested.'

'Hmm . . .' Ayako eyed up one of Kyo's white stones that she wanted to capture. 'It's difficult to say. What did I admire about your grandfather . . . ? Well, I admired his passion. We had a shared interest, back then at university, and we were both incredibly driven by our love of mountaineering. I'd never met anyone before who felt as strongly about the mountains as I did – the feeling of being out there, at the grace and mercy of nature. Not a lot of people understand that feeling, why a climber would risk their life in order to feel that connection. But above all, he respected me. He was a good man.'

'But what if you had different interests? Does that mean you're incompatible?'

Ayako chewed her lip. She looked briefly at the photo of her husband resting on the Butsudan family altar. He smiled back at her in black and white. Kenji was smiling, next to him, as if they were both urging her on. She looked back at the boy.

'Not necessarily. I think it's the passion someone feels towards something that's important. Me and your grandfather . . .' Ayako hesitated, 'even your father, early on, before he got more into his photography . . . we were all passionate about the mountains. I see that passion in all of us.' Ayako coughed hard. 'Anyway, I'm getting off the point – it's not exactly the thing itself we've all been passionate about, but rather the very fact that we *feel* and *understand* passion. A lot of people out there have no dreams, no ambitions, they just want to go to work and go to sleep each night, and that makes them happy. And there's absolutely nothing wrong with that, you know, different people have different priorities. *Junin toiro* – as the old proverb says – *Ten people, ten colours*. But when you meet someone who cares deeply about something the same way as you do, I don't know, there's something attractive about that. Don't you think? Particularly when it happens to be the same passion you yourself have.'

'So it was his personality?'

'Yes. But he was good-looking, too, in a rugged way.' She pointed at the photo of her husband, and while Kyo was distracted, she cast her eyes around the board. The boy must have made some kind of mistake she could take advantage of. 'Why are you asking me these personal questions anyway?' Ayako suddenly saw it: an opening on the board. His white stone was there to be captured. It would take several moves, but . . . 'Have you met someone you like?'

Kyo visibly jolted when she turned the tables on him. It was obvious. She had him now.

Right where she wanted.

'I don't know . . .' Kyo wasn't sure he wanted to show his cards yet.

'You're being decidedly vague. You either met someone or you didn't.'

'I saw someone, and I felt something, but . . .'

'But what?'

'How can I be sure what those feelings are?'

'Well, what did you like about her? Her looks?' Ayako put her black stone down in the pot and waved her hand dismissively at Kyo. 'With you men it's always about looks. You're all so superficial.'

'No, it wasn't her looks . . .' Kyo shook his head indignantly. 'I mean, she is pretty, but that's not it. It's more what she said.'

'So what was it you liked about what she said? Her voice?'

'It wasn't *what* she said, but *how* she said it. Or maybe that's not true. Maybe it was what she said as well.'

Kyo paused before carrying on.

'Maybe it's the thing you were saying before about passion. The way she spoke about literature. I could just tell she was passionate about it, and didn't care if anyone else thought what she loved was stupid, or something. She seemed brave. Fearless.'

'Literature, eh?' Ayako smiled.

They both looked down at the board.

'When are you going to make a move, Grandmother? You've been taking ages.'

Ayako shook her head. She'd lost track of her plan to capture his stone.

He'd distracted her somehow.

'What a mean and dirty trick,' she muttered under her breath.

●

'So what's going on with the boy then?' asked Sato.

Ayako huffed and put down the jug she'd been using to fill Jun and Emi's water glasses.

All the time. All the time it was about the boy, recently. That was all they talked to her about. She missed the idle gossip of the days before he came. Now, it seemed like the whole town wanted to know what was happening with Kyo, and it meant that Ayako didn't get to listen quietly to the stories about Yamada-sensei, the head-teacher of Onomichi High School, getting caught arm-in-arm with his girlfriend by his very own wife in Hiroshima. Those were the kinds of stories Ayako used to like to overhear and snicker about – not that she was a gossip, of course! – but now it seemed as though people were more interested in asking her for stories about how Kyo was doing, rather than telling her the juicy news she so desperately wanted to hear.

'He's fine,' she said sharply.

'Well, as you know, I'm missing his company. I'm so pleased with the illustrations he did for the shop,' said Sato, nodding pleasantly and taking a sip of coffee then swallowing quickly. 'Very pleased. I'm thinking of getting old Terachi to print me out a new sign to put over the door using the logo Kyo drew for me. I'll get it blown up and printed on a big banner – get rid of that nasty old one. Apparently, the apostrophe on the old one was wrong. Who would've thought?'

'Can I see?' asked Jun.

'Here,' said Sato, taking out his phone and showing Jun photos of the finished drawings Kyo had given him. 'I took pictures of them all on here.'

He passed the phone to Jun, who swiped through them all with Emi peering over his shoulder.

'Hahaha! Look at that owl – it looks just like you, Sato-san. And are those CDs for eyes? That's clever,' said Emi, pointing at the screen in Jun's hand. 'Hey, these are good.' Then she tapped Jun on the shoulder and spoke in his ear. 'I wonder if he'll do that exhibition we suggested.'

'Yes,' said Jun, nodding. 'It'd be fun, by way of thanks for the help he's given us. Maybe after his coming-of-age ceremony? We could turn it into a party!'

Emi turned to Ayako. 'Do you think he'd be interested?'

'I don't know.' Ayako sighed. 'You'll have to ask him.'

Now she was seeing them all getting excited by Kyo's art, she felt her bad mood shifting. It was true that on occasion she wished they'd all stop hassling her about the boy, but at the same time, she also felt an immense pride at their admiration of her grandson.

But she still worried about what was best for Kyo. Life had taught Ayako a lot of hard lessons – specifically, she had seen the shift in Kenji when his photography turned from his passion into his career. She didn't want the same thing to happen to Kyo. He had a lot on his plate with his entrance exams, and Ayako had been entrusted to make sure that he behaved himself and did well in his studies. Getting sidetracked with all this illustration work might not be the best thing for his future. But she knew, deep down, the boy had a gift.

There were many routes to the top of the mountain, as Ayako knew well.

And time and experience had taught her that some routes were easier than others.

She had to help him get to the summit, and if she could do the walking for him and make the mistakes on his behalf, that would make everything easier. But that was impossible.

Ayako began to fill up the empty water glasses of the regulars seated at the counter, listening to them chatter excitedly about all the plans they had for the boy and his illustrations.

All the while, Ayako kept quiet, thoughts running endlessly through her head.

Ultimately, everyone in life has to make their own journey.

Alone.

As the train rolled into Saijo Station, there were already drunken old men lying curled up on the platform fast asleep. Kyo peered out through the window of the train at the men lying on benches, or on the tarmac, all of them oblivious to the other passengers politely stepping over their prostrate bodies. Most were smartly dressed, wearing collared shirts and trousers. Some even had hats, which had fallen off their heads on to the ground beside them.

Kyo looked at his watch – it was still only midday.

He'd had to keep this trip top secret from his grandmother.

She would not be pleased if she found out he was going to a saké festival.

○

Situated roughly midway between Onomichi and Hiroshima, Saijo was a small town, home to the main campus of Hiroshima University. Once a year in October it also hosted the Saijo saké festival, which was currently in full swing. The festival lasted just two days, but started each morning and went on well into the evening.

Kyo disembarked the train, stepping over a couple of drunkards, and made his way to the ticket gate. As he was feeding his ticket into the slit and passing through the barrier, he heard a familiar voice calling out to him, 'Kyo!'

He looked over to see an amiable but slightly red face.

'Takeshi,' he replied. 'How's it going?'

They embraced lightly.

'Still sober,' said Takeshi, wiping his sweaty forehead with a towel. 'Barely.'

It was a hot, autumnal day called a koharu – a small spring – the kind of Indian summer that dragged on into October, with clear blue skies and a yellow sun that smiled warmly down on them.

'Where are all your friends?' asked Kyo, looking about him.

'Ah, they're in the enclosure,' said Takeshi, gesturing over his shoulder with his thumb. 'Follow me.'

They beat their way through the crowds to the main site of the festival. When they came to the entranceway Kyo paid the fee, receiving a bag, and a wristband which allowed re-entry into the enclosed area. Takeshi waggled his wrist at the security guard and they walked into the enclosure. He felt a little nervous going through the entranceway – he was still technically too young to drink by law, but he was now not far from his twentieth birthday, and looked the part. But still, he feared getting into trouble with his grandmother again. He knew he would take it easy that day.

'Hey, Kyo!' Takeshi turned to Kyo, eyes wide in excitement, gesturing to the many stalls around them, while workers poured huge bottles of saké into visitors' cups. 'Let's see if we can try something from all forty-seven prefectures!'

'Not a chance.' Kyo shook his head. 'I don't want to end up like those poor bastards passed out on the platform.'

'No?' asked Takeshi, a look of surprise moving over his face. 'I thought I might try that today.'

They both laughed, and walked around the site, past the other small groups of people enjoying the festival. Most were seated on blue tarps laid out on the ground, just like a hanami viewing party in spring. There were stalls selling foods like yakisoba fried noodles, dried squid and other greasy, salty snacks that would line their stomachs for drinking. Whereas the outside of the enclosure had been thronged with people on the streets – wasted teenagers congregating outside convenience stores, live music playing in the parks, drunks sleeping shamelessly on the ground – the interior of the enclosed area seemed a little quieter and lower-key. Paper lanterns hung throughout the trees, but were not yet lit.

They came to a crowd of Takeshi's friends seated in a circle.

'Don't worry,' Takeshi had whispered in his ear as they'd neared the group. 'It's a different bunch from last time. These are good people, friends from my course. They're all doing dentistry. There are a couple of medics, too.'

Kyo took off his shoes and sat down quietly next to Takeshi on the blue tarp. Everyone introduced themselves to Kyo, and he noticed the group warming towards him immediately. It was a marked difference from the party he'd joined before in Hiroshima. This group seemed more adult, and so Kyo did the polite thing of formally introducing himself.

'Nice to meet you. My name is Kyo, and I'm a ronin-sei,' he began, bowing while he did so. 'I'm currently studying for my university entrance exams to do medicine. Please treat me kindly.'

'Nice to meet you, Kyo-san,' they all chorused, bowing back. 'Please treat us kindly.'

'Good luck with your retake exams,' said one skinny guy with round, wire-framed glasses, sitting at the other end of the tarp from Kyo.

'Yes, good luck!' they all chorused. 'You can do it!'

'I was a ronin-sei, too,' said a guy to his right, smiling sympathetically at Kyo.

'Were you, Fujiyama?' another joined in from across the way. 'I never knew that. Me too!'

Kyo smiled and settled into the party, relaxing this time, feeling comfortable in his own skin. He had felt nervous about introducing himself honestly as a ronin-sei this time, rather than hiding behind Takeshi's previous bungled attempt to pass him off as an illustrator.

Now, he listened politely to them all talking about the experiences they'd had, failing their exams and retaking them the next year, and from hearing their stories of failure and redemption he – for the first time in front of a group of his peers – felt less shame at his current position in life. From their nodding and encouragement, he was reassured that the situation he was in right now was not irredeemable. Other people had passed through similar experiences and come out the other end just fine. Slowly, some ideas began to dawn on him, and he heard silent words of positivity whispering throughout his body.

But the words lacked shape and form, and he could not discern them. He was still unsure what he really wanted in the future. For now, he was enjoying that refreshing sense of excitement felt upon meeting a new bunch of people for the first time. He sipped on all the different saké pointed out to him by Takeshi's friends.

Some tasted sweet. Some bitter. Some dry.

But all of them somehow tasted fresh and new.

○

Kyo and Takeshi sat next to each other, occasionally getting up to take a wander around the saké stalls together, sampling the various makers. They walked slowly and peacefully. Kyo felt the warmth of the saké spreading leisurely through his body, making him content.

As they were queueing up for yakisoba, Kyo broke the silence.

'Look, I'm sorry about the time before, you know . . .' he began, before trailing off.

'Please, don't mention it.' Takeshi shook his head.

'No,' said Kyo, raising his hand. 'I should apologize. I shouldn't have run off like that. Especially since you'd been so kind as to introduce me to your friends.'

'Well,' said Takeshi, 'I'm not going to lie – it did surprise me a little when you legged it out the door. But they weren't friend friends, you know. That was back in the early days when I was going to any social club I could think of to meet people. But that night, later on, I spoke to the girl you'd been chatting to, Fumiko or something, and she mentioned what that guy had said, and then I put the pieces together.'

Kyo nodded. 'Still, I shouldn't have run off like that without explaining myself.'

'You don't have to explain yourself.' Takeshi turned to face him. 'I'm just sorry I set you up in that way.'

'He was a bit much,' said Kyo. 'I wish I could set my grandmother on him.'

'They'd get on, would they?'

Kyo chuckled. 'It'd be a bloodbath.'

They both smirked.

They'd come to the front of the queue, ordered a couple of portions of yakisoba and began walking back in the direction of the group.

Before the others came into sight, Takeshi put his hand on Kyo's shoulder.

'Just a second,' he said, turning to face Kyo. 'Before we go back, I wanted to tell you something.'

'Yeah?'

Takeshi paused, and exhaled a heavy breath. Kyo tried to hold eye contact with him, but Takeshi's eyes flicked around the park without settling on one thing in particular, least of all Kyo. Finally he spoke.

'Look, don't tell any of the guys back home in Tokyo, but, well, I'm thinking of dropping out.'

'Dropping out?' Kyo did his best to hide his shock. 'Of university?'

Takeshi nodded.

'But why?'

Takeshi sighed. 'I just don't think I can do it.'

'Do what? The course? Is the workload too demanding?'

'No, it's not that.' Takeshi shook his head. 'Quite simply, well, I just don't think I can wake up each morning for the rest of my life and look into people's mouths. I can't do it.'

He paused for a moment before continuing.

'I don't know what I'm going to tell my parents. They're gonna kill me.'

'I'm sure they'll understand,' Kyo said, not even believing it himself.

'You think?' Takeshi looked Kyo in the eyes at last. 'I wonder. Dentistry. It's what my father did. It's what my father's father did – it's been in the family for generations. Dad already had it in mind that when I graduated I'd go to work for him in his practice in Ocha-nomizu. I don't know how I'll break this to him.'

'Is there any way you could just finish the degree and then do something else? Would that make your parents happy?'

'I've thought about that – work for some dental supply company or something. It crossed my mind. But whenever I think about fin-ishing the degree I think about the practical sessions, the clinics we have to do. And I think about the day I spent watching all these old fogies swilling that pink rinse around their mouths after their examin-ations. The way they'd mush it around their cheeks and then gob it out into that metal sink. Every time I saw it, I felt like I was going to gag. And even thinking about it now makes me want to throw up. That, or I just get gripped by this incredible sense of depression. That this is all there is to life, you know? That for the rest of my life I'll be watching people spit out mouth rinse, then wiping drool from their chins. That, repeated over and over again each day, until death.'

They stood there, the revellers around them cheering and sing-ing, drinking and laughing.

Kyo felt an inordinate pity for his friend, but didn't know what to say to make him feel better. Takeshi carried on.

'Worse still, one time we were watching an operation – they were cutting into this guy's gums, sawing away at his teeth. I watched the surgical instructor pulling on a cracked tooth with a pair of pliers. I hadn't had breakfast, and well, there was all this blood . . . and it sounded like his jaw was about to snap, blood and bone, mixed with saliva, all sucked up in a tube the nurse kept poking in his mouth.' Takeshi blushed. 'Next thing I knew, I was coming around on a bed in the hospital with a nurse telling me I'd fainted. Fallen back and whacked my head like a chump. Out cold.'

'Shit.'

'I just felt such shame.' He shook his head. 'Yeah. Imagine. A den-tist who can't stand the sight of blood. So that doesn't make me any good for surgery. Who knew I was squeamish?'

They paused and stood there, plastic containers of yakisoba in their hands. Takeshi necked his choko of saké in one and grimaced. Must've been a bad one.

'What are you going to do instead?' Kyo asked eventually, regretting the question as soon as it came from his lips.

'That . . .' Takeshi wiped his sweaty forehead with the back of his hand, still holding the plastic container of yakisoba. A stray noodle dragged across his face, but he didn't notice. 'That is the big question, Kyo. What am I going to do instead? I have no idea.'

'Is there another course you can transfer to?'

'I don't know.'

They both cast their eyes around the revellers seated on the ground in small groups enjoying the festive atmosphere of the day. Kyo felt cut off from it all now, unsure of what to say or do. They stood there awkwardly for some time, Takeshi furrowing his brow, weighing up his next words carefully. He scratched his nose with a finger.

Takeshi looked at Kyo. 'You know what?'

'What?'

'That's something I've always been jealous of you for.'

'Jealous?'

'Yeah. Jealous.' Takeshi smiled, but sadness lurked beneath the smile; like a silver penny peeping out from amongst the rocks in a deep pool of water, it flashed for a second but then was gone. 'You have something you're really good at. Something you're passionate about, and always have been. You are an artist. No matter what you do. You always have been, and you always will be.'

Kyo felt his face flush, and he shook his head. 'Nah . . .'

'It's true, Kyo.' Takeshi looked serious now. 'You're an artist, no matter what you choose to do in life. You have a talent with your drawings, and it's something you can do any time, if you feel like it. It doesn't matter what you end up studying – even if you graduate and go to work as a salaryman in a firm, even if you don't go to university and work in a convenience store or a construction site – you'll always have your art. And it's something that can never be taken away from you. That's something special, Kyo. A lot of people would kill for that kind of thing in their lives.'

'But I'm studying to go to medical school. I'm going to medical school,' Kyo said limply.

Kyo paused; he didn't know whether he'd finished speaking, or not. He kept his eyes down.

He waited, and after a while Takeshi spoke again.

'You don't have to, though,' his friend said, with a tilt of his head. 'You can do whatever you like, man. It's your life. Don't live it for other people.'

It was a simple statement, but it shocked Kyo.

They were about to go back to the party, but Takeshi stopped them one last time.

'Thanks for listening,' he said, placing a hand on Kyo's shoulder and looking squarely at him. 'You're probably the only person I know who I can talk to about this kind of stuff.'

'Any time,' said Kyo, patting his friend on the back. 'Any time.'

They returned to the group, and when Kyo looked across at Takeshi, it was barely visible on his face that he was going through such turmoil in his mind. He joked and laughed with the others as if he hadn't a care in the world.

Kyo looked down at his empty saké cup, Takeshi's words vibrating through his body.

You don't have to. It's your life.

○

Eventually, the party came to an end, and they all filed out of the enclosed area, making their way slowly along the road that led to the train station. The group chattered and buzzed, and most of them wanted to head back into the city and drink more. Especially Takeshi, who was now completely red-faced and excited at the prospect of further festivities.

But Kyo felt a rising calm inside.

He hadn't ended up drinking that much saké and did not feel drunk at all.

Takeshi tugged on his sleeve and begged him to come into the city with the rest of them, but Kyo refused. He didn't feel like it, and that was that. The party was over for Kyo. It was time to go home.

And so, he stood on the other platform alone, waiting for a train to take him in the opposite direction to the bustling hub of Hiroshima, back to Onomichi. He watched the boozy group fooling around and laughing, gesturing and calling out to Kyo, before the local train with its JR West insignia and blue stripe running along the side came and picked them up. He laughed as Takeshi and the others pressed up against the glass, waving to Kyo and pulling faces as the train departed slowly, taking them off into the cool blackness of the night, onwards to a night of drunken debauchery in the city.

And then he was alone.

○

The train was mostly empty, and the journey wouldn't be a long one.

Kyo got out his Walkman and pressed play on a cassette – Pink Floyd's *Wish You Were Here* – which he'd salvaged from the second-hand cassette section of Sato's shop. He put on his headphones, got out his sketchbook and began to draw, focusing on the emotions he'd had in the seat of his stomach since his conversation with Takeshi. They began to take shape, forming patterns and oscillations of black ink against white page.

He hadn't been drawing long when someone sat down in the seat in front of him.

He looked up.

It took only a fraction of a second for him to recognize who it was. The girl from the library. From the train journey. From Osaka.

Ayumi.

She smiled at him and waved.

Kyo froze, unsure of what to do. Shit.

'Hello,' she mouthed.

He took off his headphones. 'Uh, hi.'

'I still have that pencil you gave me,' she said. 'And I saw you in the library. I remember you. Do you remember me?'

'Ayumi,' he mumbled, bowing his head low to hide his blushing face. 'I'm sorry,' was all he could manage.

'Correct.' The girl giggled. 'It was Kyo, wasn't it?'

'That's right,' said Kyo, the blush spreading into a whole body sweat.

She studied his face. 'I should be angry with you for ditching me like that. That was a particularly cowardly thing to do. Although, I appreciate that you left money for the bill. I might even forgive you.'

Kyo couldn't hold her gaze for long, but now he saw her up close again, she seemed even more beautiful than she had before. He could tell from the slight redness in her cheeks that she'd been drinking. Her hair was not tied up in a ponytail today, as it had been at the library.

He didn't have a clue what to say to her. Part of him wanted to tell her why he had ditched her – that he'd gone to the place his father had committed suicide. He was still too ashamed to admit such a private matter to someone he didn't know well. And so he stared out of the window into the darkness. But the lights were bright in the interior of the train, and he could see absolutely nothing through the window, just the reflection of what was on the inside. Even when he tried to look away from them both, he just saw their reflections. Kyo spotted a discarded *Chugoku Shimbun* newspaper on the seat the other side of the aisle. He pretended to look at the headline. They sat there awkwardly like that for a while, the empty train carriage moving back and forth as it trundled slowly along the tracks. Stop by stop they gradually neared Onomichi.

They were running out of time.

But Kyo didn't know what to say.

Words. Words. Words.

She looked down at his sketchbook, which he now gripped in his sweaty hands. His fingers were smudging the drawing he'd just been working on, and his fingertips were stained an inky black.

'You're still drawing?' she asked, pointing at the notebook.

'Ah, yup.'

'That's good. And how is cram school? Still going to be a doctor?'

'I'm not sure . . .' Kyo trailed off.

'I'm telling you, you should be a manga artist. You're so talented.

You're an asshole who ditches a girl in a bar in Osaka, but a talented one.'

Kyo's blush was at his toes now.

She carried on innocently. 'Do you draw things you see with your eyes, or things you see in your head?' She gestured to each body part as she spoke.

Engaging with her in conversation made it easier for him to distract himself from the guilt about what he'd done. He carried on, losing himself in their dialogue.

'I think . . . maybe both?'

She nodded, eyes glistening, clearly expecting him to continue.

He did. 'I see things in my head, and sometimes they fuse with reality. I'm not sure what comes first – you know, whether I see an object and then something weird happens to that object, or whether the thought itself began in my brain.'

'When did you start drawing, or seeing things like that in your mind?' She pointed at the strange, spiralling shapes of emotion he'd just been working on. The black and white that danced together on the page. Kyo found her manner so light and easy, he began to open up to her again without even noticing it himself.

'I think it was when I was about five or so?'

'That early?'

'Yeah . . .' Kyo swallowed sheepishly, but kept talking despite himself. 'Mother used to have to take me to work with her, because she was my only parent. Father . . . well, he died when I was two. Anyway, she's a doctor, so she'd just take me to the hospital, and I'd sit in the reception with the nurses, and they'd take turns looking after me.'

The girl nodded, and her eyes were wide, hanging on to the story Kyo was telling as if it were the most interesting thing in the world. Kyo carried on, without recognizing the fact that he'd barely talked about these childhood experiences with anyone in his life before.

'I was too young to read, and there was no TV or anything in the hospital reception, and so I would sometimes just sit and stare at the wall. I didn't even have any pens, pencils or paper to draw with.'

'That sounds tough,' she said.

'It wasn't so bad.' Kyo shook his head gently. 'That was when I started to draw things in my head. I'd stare at the patterns in the wallpaper, and I'd start to move the things I saw around in my mind. It was like I was staring at my own TV. If I just let my mind wander, this small blob would sprout legs and become a giant spider, then this . . .' Kyo began to gesture with his hands as if he could still see the wallpaper he was describing, and that it currently hung in the air between the two of them, '. . . this long, thin, spindly shape here would become an elderly knight, like the ones they have in old stories from Europe. And the knight would have to kill the spider, who had now connected to some other blobs in the wallpaper and morphed into a dragon, but the knight was old, and this would surely be his final battle . . .'

Kyo faltered, looking at the girl now, wondering if he'd lost her or not.

What the hell was he saying? Waving his hands around in the air and talking about elderly knights battling dragons in the wallpaper. She would surely think he was a nutter now.

'I'm sorry.' He shook his head. 'This probably all sounds completely crazy to you, right?'

'Not at all.' She smiled. 'I find it fascinating. And, I know how you felt, you know?'

'Really?' asked Kyo, a little puzzled. 'How?'

'I know what it's like to lose a parent at a young age.' She stared at the floor. 'My mum died when I was three.'

She looked up sadly into Kyo's eyes, and he nodded. They didn't need words, because they both knew how each other felt.

The train juddered and came to a stop.

Onomichi.

○

They disembarked silently, and left through the ticket gates one after the other.

Coward. Failure.

The words chanted in Kyo's mind.

Coward. Failure.

'Oh look!' said Ayumi, pointing at the hundreds of coloured, decorated lanterns placed on the ground, everywhere the eye could see. 'I forgot,' she said quietly to herself. 'It's the Festival of Light in the town today. It's beautiful with all these lanterns.'

They looked at one another, and Kyo thought she appeared before him as a pale ghost, with the shimmering light from the lanterns illuminating the underside of her face, casting flickering shadows at the same time.

'I'd better get home,' said Kyo. 'My grandmother will be waiting.'

'Right,' she said. What was that tone Kyo detected?

'Goodbye,' he said.

'Goodbye,' she said, bowing her head.

They both turned and walked away from each other.

Kyo felt something burning inside him. He turned around to see her diminishing form disappearing through a path of darkness that cut through the lanterns.

'Wait,' he called out, unable to stop himself.

She turned in surprise. 'Yes?'

'Will I see you again?'

'Sure?' She shrugged. Was she smiling too? 'If you like. Come see me in Yamaneko café. I work there on Wednesdays. You know where it is, right?'

He nodded, despite having no idea. He would find out later.

'Bye for now.'

'Bye.'

She was about to go when she remembered something. 'Oh!'

Kyo looked her in the eyes. 'Yes?'

'You can only come,' she said, smiling properly this time, eyes twinkling in the light from the lanterns, 'if you promise not to just run off again, like before.'

Kyo felt his stomach lurch. She was only joking. 'I promise.'

'See you around.' She turned and left before his face went entirely scarlet.

He watched her disappear into the darkness, cursed himself, then headed home.

'Yamaneko café. Yamaneko café.'

Kyo repeated the words over and over again as he walked.

Yamaneko café.

Yamaneko café.

☯

When he got home his grandmother was still up, waiting for him, sitting at the kotatsu table reading a novel.

'Okaeri,' she said, turning a page in her book without looking up.

'Tadaima,' he replied, as he stepped out of his shoes into the house.

He sat down opposite her at the kotatsu and studied the Go board.

'It's your turn still,' said Ayako, still without looking up.

'Huh?' said Kyo, lost in a pleasant daydream.

Ayako lowered her book and narrowed her eyes at Kyo.

What was up with him this evening? Was he drunk?

'How was the saké festival?' she asked, knowing full well he'd been.

'It was good, yeah,' he replied absently.

Ayako raised an eyebrow. Something was up with the boy, if he wasn't even making an effort to hide the fact he'd been to the festival.

After some time, he suddenly broke the silence.

'Grandmother?'

'What is it?'

'Where is Yamaneko café? I feel like I've been there once, but I can't remember where it is.'

'Why do you want to know?' She attempted a joke. 'And why are you giving business to my competitors? What's wrong with my café? If you want a coffee, come to me.'

'No reason.'

'Well, if there's no reason, you probably don't want to know that badly. Do you?'

Kyo regretted his impatience; he could have searched on his phone when he got to his bedroom.

'Please.'

'Please what?'

'Please, just tell me where it is.'

Ayako sighed and put down her book.

'Pass me that pad and pen, and I'll draw you a map.'

'Thank you, Grandmother.'

Kyo listened to Ayako's explanations as she drew, but inside his chest he felt his heart beating. The café was down by the waterfront, and as soon as Ayako began drawing the map he knew exactly where it was, but he listened to the full explanation anyhow. Part of him wondered why he hadn't just searched for it on his phone, rather than go through the fuss of asking his grandmother. He knew deep down that it was because he wished he had someone to share his excitement with.

Ayako, on the other hand, thought nothing of being asked to draw directions and make a map – it was normal for her in her daily work. But at the same time, while she was explaining where the café was, she could sense that there was something different about the boy. But she couldn't quite put her finger on what it was. It was nothing bad. He was listening carefully and politely, but there was something else going on – she could see it in his glazed-over eyes.

He'd changed.

It did not take long for Ayako to hear the rumours.

Word travelled quickly in the town. If, say, Keiko, the girl who worked at the ticket desk of the small cinema by the station, saw a couple of people come into the theatre together one afternoon, it didn't take long for her to mention it in passing to Ota the Postman when he swung by to deliver the mail. And Ota the Postman was sure to say something over a cup of green tea to Tada the Priest when he stopped in at the temple for a natter. It was only natural for Tada the Priest to chat about it to Miyuki, the young girl who came to help clean the temple on Tuesdays, and she was sure to tell her mother everything she'd talked about with the priest that day. It was perfectly ordinary for Miyuki's mother to bend the ear of Michiko the Librarian when she stopped by the library to pick up some books. And then, well, it was only a matter of time before Michiko said something to her husband, Station Master Ono, on his lunch-break, who was sure to tell Sato over evening drinks at Ittoku, the izakaya behind the station. And Sato, who, as we can all imagine, wouldn't hesitate for a second to bring this up the next day over his morning coffee at Ayako's café.

'I hear young Kyo's got himself a girlfriend,' he said with a smirk.

'What?' Ayako turned her head suddenly, like a cat who'd heard a loud noise.

Sato's smirk became slightly smug when he saw clearly that Ayako had no idea.

'Apparently he went to the cinema with a young lady the other day,' said Sato breezily. 'They watched *Tokyo Story*.'

'Wonder why he's going to see an old black and white film like that.' Ayako scratched her chin with her remaining forefinger.

'Perhaps the girl has good taste?' Sato tilted his head.

Ayako narrowed her eyes at him. 'Who is this girl, anyway?'

'Name's Ayumi.' Sato picked up his hot coffee and blew at the rising steam. 'Works at Yamaneko café.'

'Ayumi?' It fell into place.

'Think so.' Sato took a sip of coffee and his smug expression melted into one of distress as he burnt his tongue. He put the cup down on the saucer and drank water from the glass Ayako had put next to his coffee, swilling it around his mouth, eyes bulging.

Ayako looked out of the window across the sea. 'I knew something was up with him.'

'Luviz in th'air,' said Sato, slurring his speech through a mouth of ice cubes.

'Who is the girl?' Ayako asked again, then she shot out questions rapid fire. 'Is she local? What's her family name? What's her background? Do we know anyone who knows her well?'

Sato shook his head and swallowed. 'She's not local, as far as I'm aware.' He paused, and raised his hand to Ayako in a *stop!* gesture. 'But, Aya-chan, don't go steaming in and ruining things, please.'

Ayako looked hurt. 'I'm just interested. He's my grandson after all.'

'Yes, but you don't want to go rushing in and scaring her off.'

'I just want to know a bit about her.' Ayako jutted out her bottom jaw. 'Is that a crime? To be interested in who my grandson is going about town with?'

Sato shifted in his seat.

'Well . . . what I do know about her is that she's a university student.'

'What's she studying? Which university?'

'Hiroshima University. She's only working part time at the café, lives in Onomichi, and commutes to her lectures on the train. Station Master Ono told me that much.'

'Interesting.' Ayako tapped her lips with her finger. 'Why didn't she choose to live in the city, or Saijo, like all the other students, I wonder?'

'Like I said, maybe she's a girl of taste,' said Sato, the smugness in his expression having slowly returned as the burnt tongue was forgotten.

'That, or she's a weirdo,' said Ayako, staring at the wall, lost in thought. 'Interesting.'

'Now,' said Sato. 'Please don't go in heavy-handed – you'll scare the poor girl off.'

'Pffft. I won't,' said Ayako, coming back to herself.

She began making herself a cup of coffee, thinking all the while about how she was going to approach this.

The first thing she needed to do was meet the girl. That much was obvious.

Ayako needed to find out exactly what was going on.

She'd noticed several changes in the boy of late – the most recent being the most alarming. Ayako had been pleased to see him getting into the swing of things in the town – he was doing well at cram school, which was all to the good, but the thing that especially delighted Ayako was to see his artwork blossoming. She could tell the boy had talent, and she also saw this as a fresh opportunity. To right the wrongs of her past failure with Kenji. She'd discouraged her son from pursuing mountaineering, and now she had to admit it to herself, she'd actively manipulated him in order to prevent him going to the mountains like his father. She saw clearly now what she should have done: let Kenji pursue his own passions!

But the boy didn't need a girl coming along and ruining everything for him. Young love was all very well, but there was a time and a place for it. If the girl was just stringing him along, or didn't have serious feelings in return, that could knock his mental state. It could get in the way of his passion. There had to be a way she could meet the girl and find out what her intentions were. Kyo didn't need more drama in his life right now, he needed less of that sort of nonsense. He needed a clear headspace, to either focus on his studies and pass his entrance exams, or – and this is what Ayako sensed he wanted most – to become a manga artist. Ayako had been entrusted with this one job by his mother – to look after the boy – and she didn't plan on letting it all go to pot at the last minute, just because he had a crush on someone.

His safety and security were all that mattered to her now.

If this girl was an obstacle to the boy's happiness in life . . .

. . . well, she had to go. And that was that.

Ayako would do better this time.

○

Kyo had been trembling the first time he'd gone to Yamaneko café.

He'd walked slowly along the coastal road that led there, past the open café, trying to peer in through its windows, but without much luck. The brightness of the day reflected off the glass and all he saw was the outside world reflected back at him. His lanky form and his confused eyes. He circled back around, passing the café once again, studying its painted white wooden sign, with the logo of a cartoon wildcat on it. Kyo had never seen a yamaneko in his life, and had no idea if the cartoon did the species justice. It looked pretty much like a normal cat, with an arrogant smirk on its face.

'Kyo, are you coming in or not?' came Ayumi's voice from the doorway. She poked her head out. 'Or are you just going to walk past a few more times?'

'Ah, sorry,' said Kyo.

'Or . . .' She tittered. 'Were you going to run off again without saying anything?'

'Ah . . .' Kyo froze – he still felt he owed her a proper apology for abandoning her in Osaka. Shame seeped into his stomach.

'Don't worry.' She waved a hand. 'I won't keep dragging it up, I promise . . . maybe.'

He followed her inside.

The interior was brighter than it had appeared from outside. The café was decorated with ageing signs and memorabilia, all from the Showa era. Faded adverts for tobacco, Coca-Cola, sweets, Ramune and a host of other products decorated the walls. The tables and chairs were random items with little relationship to each other, thrown together from flea markets and antique stores, no doubt.

Kyo wondered what his grandmother would think about the décor. It most likely would not sit with her traditional views on aesthetics. Kyo liked it, however.

It reminded him of the places he frequented back home, which could be found all along the different stops of the Chuo Line in Tokyo – places like Nakano, Koenji, Nishi-Ogikubo, Asagaya and Kichijoji. There were even chain cafés in central Tokyo now, in places like Shibuya and Shinjuku, where they tried to replicate this aesthetic, but it always came off as a bit manufactured. Yamaneko felt authentic.

Ayumi sat him down at the wooden counter, and he looked around while she busied herself with other customers. On the walls were photographs of the local area – all taken by local photographers, with their names and contact details listed below. It looked like they were having some kind of exhibition.

Kyo was wary of these sorts of things. He'd had friends approach him back in Tokyo with the idea of exhibiting some of his artwork in these kinds of spaces, but he'd never liked the idea much. Inevitably there'd come mention of the fact that he would have to pay money to exhibit his work, and there was no guarantee anyone would buy it. Since Jun and Emi had invited him to show his work at their hostel, he'd partly been curating a little exhibition in his mind, and partly worrying they were going to hit him with a fee. He hadn't brought it up again, for fear that they did indeed want to charge him. But then again, they'd sounded genuine, so perhaps there were no strings attached.

Ayumi came back to see him with a glass of water, and Kyo smiled and bowed his head to her.

'So,' she said, putting the glass on the counter next to him and filling it from her jug. The ice clinked against the sides as she poured. A few cubes fell expertly from the jug with the water into his glass. 'What can I get you?'

Kyo jolted. He hadn't even looked at the menu.

'Uh . . .'

'Hungry?' she asked.

'A little.'

'Okay. You like pasta?'

'Yup. Love it.'

'Coffee?'

'Sure.'

'Leave it to me.'

She bustled off in the direction of the kitchen. Kyo could just about see a young lad in there wearing a white chef's uniform. He caught sight of her giving him some kind of instruction, before she was back out again behind the counter, busying herself with the espresso machine.

'So,' she said, taking out some milk from the fridge and pouring it into a metal jug before frothing it with the steam wand, 'how are you?'

'I'm fine, thanks. And you?'

'Good, yes.'

Kyo paused, and then ventured a question.

'This is awfully rude of me, at this stage, but . . .' Kyo paused again, as he watched her freeze with the metal jug in her hands. '. . . but . . . I'm really sorry about how I behaved in Osaka. It was inexcusable.' He bowed low.

'Please forget it.' She bowed a little stiffly before turning her back on him to carry on making his coffee.

Kyo shrank down inside himself. Maybe he shouldn't have said anything.

He took out a Tanikawa Sakutaro comic book about two masters of Go he was reading and tried to act nonchalant, but his eyes barely focused on the page; instead he watched Ayumi as she deftly made a café latte. She wore the same blue and white striped dress shirt that all of the other staff were wearing. He watched as her hands worked away pouring the milk into the coffee cup with deft flicks of her wrist, then taking a long thin implement to stir about in the foam. Kyo leant forward to get a better look. She was doing some kind of artwork with the foam, but he could not quite see what she was drawing. As she came over to him with his coffee, he sat back down in his seat and threw his gaze at the manga again, pretending to read.

'Here you are.' She placed a coffee cup on a saucer neatly in front of him.

She'd drawn a cat in the foam. Its face stared smugly back up at Kyo.

'Wow,' said Kyo, genuinely impressed. 'How did you learn to do that?'

'I practised at home.' She smiled. 'It took a long time, let me tell you.'

'Cool!' Kyo took out his phone and snapped a picture of it. 'I could never do something like that.'

'Sure you could,' she said sunnily. 'Anyone can, if they practise. After seeing your drawings, I bet you'd be a natural.'

'I almost don't want to drink it,' said Kyo, picking up and studying the white china mug from different angles. There was the café's cat logo printed on the side. 'I don't want to spoil the perfect picture you made.'

'You know what they say . . . *bijin hakumei – beautiful thing, short life.*'

So she liked proverbs, just like Grandmother.

'Anyway,' she carried on, 'I'd rather you tasted it, and enjoyed the coffee I made especially for you, while it's hot. Don't let it get cold.'

Kyo sipped quickly, and she laughed at his comical expressions.

There was a shout from the kitchen, and she came back with a piping hot plate of spaghetti covered in an aubergine and meat sauce. It was about two o'clock and Kyo realized he was now the only customer. Ayumi sat down next to him and they chatted while he ate his spaghetti and drank his coffee.

They talked about books and manga. Ayumi recommended her favourite writers to Kyo, and he in turn recommended some of his favourite manga artists. Before long two hours had passed.

'Oh shit,' he said, catching sight of the time on an old clock. 'It's already 4 p.m.'

He was going to be late to meet Grandmother before she closed her own café and they went on their evening walk together. Kyo took out his wallet and tried to pay, but she wouldn't let him. And so he had asked for her number, promising that they would get together again, so that he might take her out and return the favour.

Kyo left the café with a jubilant swagger to his walk. He'd had a girlfriend before, sure, but there was something different about Ayumi. She was intelligent, a gifted speaker and a great listener. She was so knowledgeable about literature, and he knew he could learn a lot from her. He felt that she respected him, despite his slightly younger age. Kyo didn't want to get ahead of himself, but he was excited.

○

Over the next few weeks, Kyo and Ayumi began to meet up frequently.

On her days off, they would go for a walk and chat, and on days when she worked at the café, Kyo would sit at the counter and nurse a coffee while he worked on his sketches and talked with her when she had a minute. Needless to say, he preferred the days when he had her undivided attention, and he got the impression she did too. He found it incredibly easy to talk to her, about anything, and she was relaxed and open with him. She was studying at Hiroshima University, but wouldn't tell him which subject, and made him guess. At first, he'd guessed literature, because of the encounter he'd witnessed in the library before.

'No,' she'd said, shaking her head. 'I love literature too much to study it. I never wanted to turn the thing I love into my work. I worried it would spoil reading for me.'

Then Kyo had guessed medicine.

'Absolutely no chance – I'm terrible with that kind of thing. Also I'm a massive hypochondriac.' She laughed, and her eyes sparkled. 'If I had to study all those diseases and conditions, I'd start to think I had every single one of them.'

In the end, Kyo had given up guessing, and she'd told him she was studying law.

'Law?' he said, somewhat defeated. 'I would never have guessed that.'

'I suppose it's because I love stories,' she said thoughtfully. 'And

247

arguing. It was the one thing I reckoned resembled literature without being literature. Court cases are just hearing people's life stories.' She paused, thoughtful for a moment, then laughed. 'And I actually want a job at the end of my studies.'

Kyo nodded glumly. Since his chat with Takeshi, he'd been thinking a lot about what he wanted.

'And you're hoping to study medicine?' she asked in return.

Kyo sighed. 'Yup.'

'You don't sound too enthusiastic about that,' she said with concern.

'I don't know . . .'

'Well,' she said, in slow consideration, 'I don't know much, but I would say if you're going to spend the rest of your life doing something, you should probably be sure it's something you *want* to do. Otherwise you'll just make yourself miserable, no?'

Kyo nodded.

The thought of Takeshi watching people rinsing and spitting each day came to his mind.

Rinse and spit.

Rinse and spit.

●

It was the last straw for Ayako.

She'd heard rumours that Kyo's grades were slipping slightly at the cram school, but that wasn't what bothered her. What really bothered her was something she'd noticed when she'd been photocopying the boy's sketchbook.

She'd figured out, long ago, that she could sneak the book out when they both went for their evening baths together. It had been a tricksy move for Ayako to pull off, and one she took delight in.

Ayako had justified what she was doing in her mind – she was making photocopies of the boy's work, partly for her to keep, but it was also a huge 'just in case'. She'd learnt her lesson with Kenji, when he'd set fire to some of his photographs unexpectedly years ago. Kenji had done it seemingly at random, and Ayako had been bemused, and then vicariously experienced her son's painful regret, days later. Kenji had holed up in his room and refused to speak to her. It had been a terrible time for Ayako, and she hadn't known how to communicate with her son. That was the worst part – not knowing what to say.

But, by photocopying his work, if Kyo did anything similar, she would be able to step in and save the day. She would have saved his sketches. Yes, she was doing something slightly devious, but it was for the boy's own good!

Kyo always left his sketchbook when he went to the bath – and it was easy for her to take the book once in a while, hiding it in her yukata. She pretended to go into the women's bath, and once he was safely inside the men's, she'd sneak off to the convenience store near the bathhouse, and photocopy the new sketches he'd drawn. Sakakibara-san, the man who ran the store, would kindly keep the photocopied sheets behind the counter for her to collect the next day when she photocopied her handwritten menu for the café.

She would steal back to the bathhouse, take a quick dip, then smuggle the sketchbook back home and return it to the exact place she'd got it from, while making the boy dry and put away the dishes from their evening meal as a form of distraction.

But one evening, while photocopying the book in the convenience store, she noticed that Kyo had barely drawn anything over the past week. And when she went through her collections of his drawings the next day in the café, she noticed a glaring trend – his output had drastically decreased since he'd met this Ayumi girl.

This would not do.

She'd humoured Sato's advice when they'd last spoken about the girl, but this had all gone too far. She had to find out what was going on – if this girl was distracting him from his studies, that was one thing, but if she was obstructing his dream of being a manga artist, well, that wouldn't do at all. She nodded her head resolutely, hand-wrote a sign, and put it up on the door of the café.

BACK IN TEN MINUTES
AYAKO

She walked down the shotengai a way, then turned off the covered street, diving down a small alleyway, hurrying past Sato's CD shop, hoping he wouldn't see her, in the direction of the coastal road. She continued along the pavement that ran alongside the sea for a way, until she came to the place she was looking for. She studied the sign.

YAMANEKO CAFÉ

She shook her head, and went inside.

Seating herself at the counter, she waited for someone to come over. She picked up a paper menu with the Yamaneko logo on and studied it. What a fussy place, Ayako thought, looking through the items listed there. She began to fold the menu to pass the time, shaping it into a fan. But glancing down the counter, she was taken aback by the pretty girl who approached, smiling politely, impeccably dressed. She hastily stashed the menu into her sleeve and looked firm.

'Irasshaimase. Will you be eating today, or may I bring you a drink?' asked the waitress.

Her appearance, demeanour and manner of speaking were all extremely polite.

Assured and confident.

'I won't be having anything today,' said Ayako sternly. 'I came to talk to a girl who I'm told works here – named Ayumi.'

The serving girl visibly jumped, but stood her ground.

'I'm Ayumi,' she said, smiling and revealing dimples on her cheeks. 'How may I help you?'

'For a start, you can tell me what intentions you have regarding my grandson.'

'Intentions?'

'Yes, what do you want with him?'

'What do I want with Kyo?' The girl steepled her fingers, the student lawyer emerging. 'I suppose I don't want anything in particular. We enjoy each other's company. We're getting to know one another. He's an interesting guy. You have a lovely grandson. You must be proud.'

Ayako ignored the flattery and cut to the chase. 'So you're not serious about him?'

'I'm very serious. I like him a lot. We enjoy spending time together.' She paused. 'But, and I don't mean to be rude, is this really any of your business?'

Ayako's jaw dropped. The question was not entirely aggressive, but it was a clear challenge. She studied the girl's face for a crack or weakness. 'He's my grandson. Of course it's my business.'

'But it's his life, he can make friends with whomsoever he wishes, surely?'

'So you just want to be friends? You're not interested in him romantically? Have you told him that?'

'I'm not sure what I want our relationship to be. Like I said, we're still getting to know one another. No disrespect, but times have changed. This is not an omiai arranged marriage we're discussing, is it? We're talking about your grandson, and with whom he chooses to spend time, of his own volition. It's his life, after all.'

Ayako was incensed. How dare this young lady. How dare she.

'Who do you think you are? Talking to a customer like that,' Ayako hissed. 'Have you absolutely no respect?' She raised her voice a pitch higher as she spoke these last five words. People in the café were turning their heads to the scene now.

Ayako saw a shift in the girl's mien, as if she had remembered she was working – she was not a lawyer in a courtroom yet – she was a girl in an apron working in a café. She blushed. Despite Ayako having not bought anything, she was still technically a customer right now and *kyakusama wa kamisama – the customer is a god*.

'I apologize,' she said, bowing low. 'I spoke out of turn.'

'Too right,' said Ayako, lowering her voice again. 'You're lucky I don't fetch the manager on you. Now you listen here, young lady.'

Ayako pointed a finger at the girl, and she also took pleasure when Ayumi's eyes widened as she noticed some of Ayako's fingers were missing. This would send a message.

'This boy has been through a lot in his life, and he's going through a lot right now. I won't have him distracted or heartbroken by someone who isn't taking him seriously. I'm not asking for much – just that you leave him be during this difficult time.' Ayako looked the girl up and down from head to toe. 'Even then, I'm not keen on you

251

seeing him, unless you know what it is you want from him, and you learn a little bit of respect. Take some time to think what it is you want. Don't mess him about. I won't have you interfering with his life.'

Ayumi nodded like a scolded child while Ayako frothed and foamed.

'I understand,' said Ayumi gently. 'I'm sorry I caused you distress, it was extremely rude of me. I will tell Kyo that I can't see him until after his exams are over. I'll tell him to focus on his studies, and that we can't see each other until his exams are behind him.'

'That's all I ask,' said Ayako. 'Was that so difficult?'

'I'll do exactly what you ask, if you think it's best for Kyo.' And then she added sadly, 'I only want him to be happy.'

Ayako rose from her seat and left abruptly without saying anything further to the girl. She hurried back to her own café as quickly as she could, and the closer she got to it, the more she allowed herself to breathe.

But still, the words she had just spoken echoed in her mind.

I won't have you interfering with his life.

They continued to come back and haunt her throughout the day, and it wasn't until she saw Kyo walking towards her as she pulled down the shutter of the café that she began to forget exactly what she'd said to the girl.

As they walked to the top of the mountain together, pausing on the way back down to feed and stroke Coltrane, Ayako let the resolution grow inside her.

She had done the right thing.

This was the right thing to do, in the long run.

Kyo hung up the phone.

Ayako could guess from his responses what his mother had said to him.

'We don't have to go today, you know?' said Ayako. 'We can wait and go another time, when she can make it too?'

'No,' said Kyo resolutely. 'The leaves will fall if we don't go today.'

Kyo's mother had once again cancelled the trip she'd been planning – to see the autumn leaves on the island of Miyajima. And so Ayako and Kyo boarded the local train to visit Miyajima, just the two of them. The mood was slightly fraught – Ayako could tell that the boy was again disheartened, because his mother had reneged on her promise. Equally, Kyo could sense in Ayako some desire to placate him, and that was also making him feel uncomfortable. He had a right to be upset.

Kyo had mentioned in passing some months ago that he still had not been to see the red torii gate out in the water at Miyajima, and Ayako had looked surprised.

'You've still not seen it?'

'Nope.'

'But it's one of Japan's three great views!' said Ayako, in shock. 'How can you not have seen it?'

'If you didn't keep me on such a short leash, I might have made it out there.'

'Watch it, young man!' said Ayako, wagging a finger.

As they walked through the station to catch their train to Miyajima, they said good morning to Station Master Ono, who rushed round to greet them.

'Kyo!' he called out in excitement. 'You just missed Ayumi! She took the train to Saijo.'

'Ah,' said Kyo, trying to indicate to Tanuki with his eyes that the timing was awkward – Kyo still hadn't told Ayako about anything; he'd also not heard from Ayumi in a few days. Kyo looked over at Ayako, but luckily she seemed distracted by a train timetable.

'Where are you two off to?' asked Ono, picking up on Kyo's distress and changing the subject.

'Miyajima,' said Kyo.

'Ugh,' said Ono, 'I'm jealous! Take some photos of the leaves for me.'

The train arrived, and they said their goodbyes to Ono, who waved from the platform as they pulled away.

The mountains and villages ambled slowly past the train window.

The leaves of the trees covering the mountains were reds, yellows, ambers, golds and oranges. Kyo swigged on a hot black coffee he'd bought from the vending machine on the platform. Ayako sipped from a tiny flask of green tea she'd brought with her from home.

Kyo had brought a book to read that Ayumi had given him when they'd last met.

It was called *Desolate Shores* by Nishi Furuni. She'd raved about the author, saying he was her favourite, and that he must read this one book in particular. Kyo didn't like reading novels that much, he preferred manga, but he persevered because he wanted to please Ayumi. She'd also pointed out astutely that if he wanted to be a manga artist, he had to understand the art of storytelling, and there was no better way to do that than by reading novels. He was gradually beginning to enjoy the book a lot, but today on the train he found himself distractedly scrolling through his phone.

'What are you doing with that thing?' asked Ayako. 'Always with that thing.'

'Nothing . . .' He put his phone away and sighed.

In truth, Kyo was waiting for a message from Ayumi, but he didn't want to talk about her with Ayako.

'You're sad your mother couldn't make it?' asked Ayako.

'Yes,' said Kyo.

'Don't be too hard on her,' said Ayako. 'She's doing her best.'

'I know.'

'It's hard work being a single mother.'

Kyo nodded. 'But it's strange, when you think about it.'

'What is?' asked Ayako.

Kyo looked up at her. 'We both grew up with only our mothers to look after us.'

'Yes,' said Ayako, the wind knocked from her stomach. 'That's true.'

An awkwardness descended, their minds obviously moving on to the two large elephants in the corner of the train carriage. They'd both lost their fathers at young ages. They had a lot in common. As a child, Ayako had sworn to herself she would try to create a stable and secure family for her child, having grown up watching her own mother struggling as a single parent. But fate had intervened, and she'd lost her husband too soon. And it had happened to her grandson, too. Kyo had experienced almost identical heartbreak. If only they could broach the matter. But they did not have the words.

'What are you reading?' asked Ayako, changing the subject.

'Just some book,' said Kyo despondently.

'What book?' Ayako persisted.

He showed her the cover. '*Desolate Shores*.'

'Oh wow,' said Ayako, in surprise. 'That's a classic. One of my favourites. Since when did you read Nishi Furuni? Did Michiko at the library recommend it?'

'No. My friend gave it to me.'

'Which friend?'

'No one you know,' said Kyo, clamming up.

Ayako stared out the window. So the girl had given him this book. The girl had great taste in books, at least.

They arrived at Miyajima-guchi Station around lunchtime, and Kyo had been begging to eat some ramen, but Ayako wouldn't relent. She knew exactly where she was going to take them for lunch, and they had a bit of time to eat before they caught the ferry across to the island. She dragged him into a rickety wooden restaurant by the port. Kyo studied the menu.

'Eel on rice?' he asked.

'Yes.' She smiled. 'The best. Wait and see.'

They ordered two boxes of eel on rice, and Ayako was pleased when Kyo's eyes lit up as his appeared in front of him. Neither left a grain in their bowl.

When they'd finished their lunch, they boarded the ferry which took them across to the island of Miyajima. The weather was perfect, blue skies and low-hanging clouds. The sun was partially hidden from sight, casting rays of shimmering light upon the water. The trees of the island radiated their autumnal colours in the sunlight.

Everyone on the ferry moved to the side of the boat to look at the famous red torii gate, which, at high tide, appeared to be floating in the water.

They landed, and the pair strolled slowly along the old stone path that led to a viewing point on the coastline opposite the shrine. As they went, the wild deer of the island milled around under the red maple trees. Some of the deer approached the pair to beg for food.

'Back, you little bastard,' said Ayako fiercely.

'But they're so cute!' said Kyo, shocked. 'How can you say that?'

'Just you wait till you've been bitten on the behind by one of them,' said Ayako, chuckling. 'Or headbutted! Then we'll see whether you still think they're *cute.*'

As they neared the shrine, Ayako tugged on Kyo's sleeve.

'Not yet,' she said, shaking her head. 'Let's go for a walk.'

She led them in the opposite direction to everyone else, and they made their way steadily to the top of the mountain. They were alone on the path – the majority of visitors simply strolled along the coastline to view the torii gate, then maybe spent some money in the shops and restaurants along the street, before taking the ferry back to the mainland. Of course, Ayako preferred a more strenuous challenge.

They made it to the top, and Kyo was grateful for the view, surrounded by the autumn leaves. Looking out across the bay, he could now appreciate why they had put in the effort. He'd seen endless photographs of the floating shrine on the internet, but he had never once seen it from this angle. Once again, his grandmother was showing him a new way of looking at life.

He snapped a photo of the scene on his phone, hoping to sketch it later.

Ayako tutted as he did so. 'Always with that thing.'

As he was putting his phone away, he got a text from Ayumi on LINE.

Hi Kyo,
I need to talk to you. Can we meet tomorrow?
Ayumi x

Kyo studied the text, alarm bells ringing.

I need to talk to you.

Ayako was already heading back down the path. Kyo put his phone away in his pocket and made after her. But he was worried about Ayumi's message.

When they finally made it back down to the viewing point, they stood and watched the sun set behind the shrine. The sky turned a glorious pink and purple as the sun slowly slid away from view. Kyo took as many photos on his phone as he could. Ayako watched him, feeling strangely moved. His face, his eyes, his expression. His whole demeanour changed when he was composing photos. He looked more like Kenji than ever when he was concentrating on a creative task. That was what Ayako enjoyed about Kyo's expression when he was drawing – it took her back in time to when Kenji would sit hunched over brush and ink while he composed the intricate flowing characters of his calligraphic scrolls, or when he was crouched over negatives picking out photos for enlargement and printing. Ayako wondered if this was why she encouraged Kyo to draw – to bring back a version of Kenji that she had lost long ago, even before his death.

They were standing side by side, at the water's edge. Kyo, anxious to reply to Ayumi, took out his phone and began typing.

'You know,' said Ayako, then stopped, not wanting to interrupt his texting.

Kyo looked up from his phone and put it away in his pocket, sensing something there.

'Yes?' he asked.

'Never mind,' said Ayako, waving her hand dismissively.

'Go on, Grandmother,' said Kyo. 'Please say what you were going to say.'

She shook her head, but thought better of it.

'You look just like him,' said Ayako, still staring straight out at the sun slowly slipping down behind the red torii gate. 'Especially when you take photos, or draw. You are the spitting image of your father when he was your age. You have his eye for beauty, too.'

Kyo studied his grandmother's face in the warm sunlight.

His heart pounding harder in his chest, and a warmth spreading through his body, Kyo turned his eyes to the sunset. They stood side by side in silence for some time, until the evening shrouded them both in grey. They walked back to the ferry, towards home.

He hadn't even asked. And she'd talked about him.

Ayako vs. The Mountain:
Part Three

They were sitting at the kotatsu table playing Go one evening, when Kyo finally summoned the courage to broach the matter of the newspaper article with her. Even though it had been months since he'd found out, he knew she would never believe how he'd made the discovery and so he'd kept quiet.

'Grandmother,' he said cautiously. 'Will you tell me about what happened on Mount Tanigawa, please?'

Ayako moved her gaze slowly upwards.

Kyo's whole body tensed up, readying itself for the storm that might come.

But no storm came.

Ayako chuckled. Her expression relaxed. She actually laughed.

'Oh! That debacle.' She shook her head. 'Who told you about that? Was it Sato? That old blabbermouth.'

'I just heard rumours. A few people mentioned it.' Kyo hoped she didn't realize he was lying.

She placed her black stone on the board. 'Your move.'

Kyo hesitated again. The clock on the wall ticked.

'But Grandmother,' he reached for a white stone, 'aren't you going to tell me what happened?'

'What happened when?'

'On the mountain.'

'Of course, I can tell you everything. It might require some background, though.'

Kyo nodded. Ayako took a deep breath, and began her story.

'I discovered the mountains when I was a teenager. My mother spent so much of my childhood in grief that I'd find whatever excuse I could to take off to the mountains, to disappear into nature. It was the only activity that calmed me down, a thing that made me feel like there was something bigger in the world than my own anger and my mother's sadness. I was an angry person growing up. I still am. I think having my father taken from me at such a young age made me question the universe – why had I been dealt such a bad hand from the start?'

Kyo felt himself being sucked into her story, closer to her than he had ever been before. They had so much in common. He sat very still, not wanting to miss another word.

'But, when I went out walking, being out there in the wild with the elements around me, I found the lack of control liberating. My tiny problems were just that, and I found the scale of the mountains reassuring. It calmed me. Some years later, I also discovered the writing of Tabei-san.'

'Who?' asked Kyo.

'You've not heard of Tabei Junko-san?' asked Ayako, mouth opening in amazement.

Kyo shook his head.

'Well, you should have. She was the first woman in the world to summit Everest. And she was Japanese, of course. When I read her essays, that lit a fire under me. I realized that even a small Japanese lady like myself could achieve great things. That the physical world doesn't place limits on a person in the way that society does.

'All my life I'd been told what I can and can't do, as a woman, but here was a woman who had ignored all of that rubbish and just gone ahead and shown everyone what she could do with her actions, not just her words. Anyway, hearing more about Tabei-san inspired me. I read everything of hers I could get my hands on.

'It was when I was a university student that I met your grandfather. We were both members of the climbing club, and I soon fell head over heels in love with him. There was just something about him. He was good-looking, of course, and the other girls chased him. But it was like he was different – he was obsessed with the mountains. And so was I. A lot of the other men joined the club as a social thing – to make friends, or even meet girls. But I never sensed that from your grandfather. The mountains were the thing we valued most in life.

'We'd go on expeditions each weekend, and I think we both tried to drop back to speak with each other while we walked. But the day I fell for him – no, it's silly.'

Kyo motioned for her to continue.

'Well, I still remember how he gave me his onigiri one day, when I'd forgotten to pack my own lunch. He told me he had two in his bag, so I ate it all up. That must've been the best onigiri I'd ever eaten. Then I noticed he wasn't eating his. From his smile, I realized he'd only ever had one, and I had eaten it. He told me he got more pleasure from watching me eat it than he would've from eating it himself. That was it for me. I fell for him hook, line and sinker. I know it must sound strange, but each time I give away my onigiri at the café, it is in his memory.'

She paused, and straightened her posture before continuing.

'But the thing with your grandfather was that he respected my own climbing above any societal expectations placed upon me. He told me we were a team. And we were. We opened the café in town together, using some money he'd inherited from his parents after they'd passed away. We named the café EVER REST because we liked the pun. The idea was that we would take it in turns to go out on expeditions, but that one of us would be there to run the café while the other was out climbing. It would be the place where we rested.

'But when your father, Kenji, was born, there was a change. I'd been unable to be as physically active while I was pregnant, and if I'm honest, I already resented little Kenji – your father – for obstructing my biggest passion in life. But your grandfather, surprisingly, remained true to his word, and rather than telling me to stay at home and look after Kenji, he offered me freedoms that most women my age would have to fight for. Ah, we spent several years in perfect bliss. But all good things come to an end.'

Ayako sighed.

Kyo placed his hand on the table, but didn't quite reach for Ayako. Her eyes were starting to water.

'Then Mount Tanigawa happened.'

'Grandfather died up on the mountain?'

Ayako sniffed and nodded.

She put the black stone she'd been holding back in the pot, and became lost in thought, staring at the Go board. Then she spoke, eyes downcast.

'It was your grandfather's first expedition in a long while. I'd been the one encouraging him to get out on the mountains again, and some friends of his from his climbing club had managed to raise enough money from sponsors to cover the climb. I told him to go, and that I would manage by myself with your father. It was his turn to enjoy himself. But I didn't know he would never come back.'

Ayako looked at the Go board with a wry smile.

'And that was the beginning of my life as a single mother. I gave up mountaineering during that time, and I threw myself into looking after your father. I tried to live vicariously through his successes, encourage his photography. But he wanted to follow in his father's footsteps, and, well, I tried my best to keep him away from the mountains. But that, well, we both know how that turned out . . . I don't know . . . I was too hard on him. Part of me resented having to look after this child by myself – and having the mountains taken away from me. It terrified me when he took such an interest in mountaineering, and I did my best to keep him away. I know that my first reaction is often anger, and I wasn't the kindest mother. I know that now. That was my biggest failure in life.'

She wiped a tear from her cheek.

Kyo bit his lip. 'You don't have to talk about this, Grandmother, if it's upsetting.'

Ayako shook her head. 'No, I want to tell you my story. It's important.'

She continued.

'After your father took his own life, I thought about taking my own. I'd lost everything dear to me, and I didn't understand what I'd done wrong. It felt almost as if there was something out there punishing me – a great force in the universe – mocking me. It took pleasure from toying with me, my life and my loved ones. Everything I'd loved had been taken away from me at different times in my life. I had nothing to live for any more, and I struggled to even get out of bed in the mornings. I drank too much. I fought with people. I lost the will to live. I distanced myself from you and your mother. I came close to losing myself.'

'I never knew this,' said Kyo, shaking his head. 'Mother never said anything.'

'Ah, she didn't know the full story. She was busy with her own grief, and her job, and raising you.'

'So, what happened?'

'Climbing found me again,' said Ayako, smiling. 'I threw my life into the mountains. My fitness returned. I'd gone beyond caring about life, and so I took increasingly bigger risks. I pushed my body to its absolute limits. I didn't care about pain any more. I'd already lost everything. When making the pitch on a rock or ice wall, I would be reckless. I'd take the most insane routes that everyone else was scared to climb. And it seemed to pay off. My skill was undeniable. I felt like I'd been born again. I'd become the mountaineer I'd always dreamt I would be, and I still didn't care whether I lived or died. I wanted one thing, and one thing alone: to climb.'

She stopped, and looked at the clock.

'Not long till bath time.'

Kyo was dumbfounded. 'Grandmother! Please! Finish the story!'

Ayako frowned. 'Well, it didn't last for long. In my selfishness, I did something unforgivable. I decided I would summit Mount Tanigawa alone – with a portion of your father's ashes. I wanted to take a part of your father up the mountain, to leave his ashes at the plaque that commemorates your grandfather. I became obsessed with the idea. I ignored safety precautions, and went alone in the depths of winter, around the anniversary of your grandfather's death. All I wanted was to reunite your father's ashes with your grandfather's spirit. His body had never been recovered, and I was plagued with the idea of him haunting the mountain, lost and alone. This way, he would have your father for company.

'I pushed on ahead by myself, knowing that if I left early in the dead of night, it would give me more time to get to the top and back. I didn't know at the time, but no one else would be out on the mountain that day. If I'd checked, I would've heard the radio reports of the storm that was fast approaching, and if I'd told anyone of my plans, they would not have allowed me to climb. But I was determined to reach the top, at whatever costs.

'And so I stole away. Alone, I made my way up the mountain. Disregarding the risks, I went out into the darkness by myself, in the middle of the night.

'At first it was fine. I made a good pace, and pushed my body through the numbness. I kept going, and had a feeling deep within my bones that I could endure this climb. I could survive any pain my body had to offer. As the sun rose, I kept my pace – making good time. I could see what I knew to be the rock with your grandfather's commemorative plaque in the distance, and could also feel a sense of excitement rising through my soul. I was going to do this.

'I made it to the plaque, wedged the small urn with your father's ashes securely in a gap in the rock, and offered a prayer to them both, and to the mountain.

'Turning back, I noticed the dark storm clouds on the horizon. I knew what they signalled but I was filled with hubris. And also, I had given up caring if I lived or died. I should have begun my descent at that point, but I decided against it. The summit was in sight, and I wanted to reach the top – only for myself. I pushed on until I suddenly realized the storm was coming in fast. The winds whipped around at incredible speeds, kicking up icy snow that beat against me. My pace slowed throughout the morning, and it was as if I were walking through treacle. My crampons were heavy on my feet, as I made one slow laborious step after another. I'd barely made any progress.'

Kyo had his hands to his face in horror. 'Why did you keep going?'

'Summit fever, they call it.' Ayako laughed. 'Mountaineers get so obsessed with reaching the top that they can't stop themselves. Can't turn around and give up.'

'So what happened?'

'I carried on for a bit, until I saw how dangerous it was getting. When the wind blows so hard that you fall over, you begin to understand that this is not a joke. That nature is far stronger than you could ever have imagined. I began to feel how fragile my body was against the elements. I was scared. You probably won't believe this, but I heard your grandfather's voice in my head at that point. "Turn back, Aya-chan," he seemed to say.

'And so I did turn back. I came to the realization that I had made a mistake, and that what I was doing *was* suicide. Instead of welcome bliss, I felt pure fear. Deep down, I wanted to live. But when I turned to go back down the mountain, the severity of the situation hit me. I couldn't see a thing. The winds had blasted the snow up into a thick white mist that roiled around me viciously, and now I had no idea where I was. In panic, I stumbled on a rock, falling to the ground, and a sharp stab shot through my ankle. I tried to stand, but an agonizing pain coursed through my leg and ankle. I'd broken it.'

Her story was interrupted by Kyo's phone buzzing. It was his mother.

Kyo stood up. 'One second, Grandmother. I am so sorry!'

He ran out of the room and she heard him frantically but kindly telling his mother that yes all was well but that he couldn't talk right now.

Ayako sat back and looked out of the window at the stars. What to tell the boy? What was this story really about? Maybe she should tell him about how she'd spent the night tucked under an overhang as the winds beat around her, trying her best to stay awake, not letting herself fall into unconsciousness – afraid that she'd slip away in the night – another frozen dead body sacrificed to the Mountain of Death, along with the others. All that time she'd been up there alone, she'd known that she had to keep moving. She knew the dangers all too well, but the storm had forced her to stop.

Her husband and son had come to visit her on the side of the mountain. They'd told her to keep going. To live. And that's what had given her the strength to drag herself down the mountain on her hands and knees. But she'd never told another living soul about that. She knew that if she told people she'd seen ghosts on the mountainside, they would just chalk it up to hallucinations from her condition, but Ayako knew they were real. She knew there was something more to the visions. It meant something to her – that they were still out there. She'd seen them, and they had told her not to give up. They'd both urged her to fight for her life.

Kyo came back, his face bashful, and she continued.

'I'm not going to spin the story out, because you know how it ends – I'm here now talking to you, aren't I? So you know I got down off the mountain. But there are some things that stay crystal clear in my mind. I remember when I was tucked under an overhang, trying to stay awake. I remember the storm passed, and all of a sudden, the stillness of the night was around me. I remember looking out into that dark night sky, and I remember feeling something I hadn't in a long time – *I want to live.* Having found myself that close to death, I suddenly knew that I wasn't ready to die. I experienced awe and wonder at this world we live in. How incredible existence is. The probability of our being here, of having survived as a species on this tiny speck of a planet. I was gripped with a desire to keep going – to experience more of this thing we call existence. It dawned on me how precious life is.

'And so I fought with my own body. My body told me to lie down and sleep, but I knew that if I did that, I'd never wake. And so I set myself tiny goals. I knew I must get down off the mountain, and that it was an incredibly long way. But if I just told myself, look, all you have to do is get on your hands and knees. Just that, that's all. And then I'd battle to move into that position. But once I'd done it, then I told myself, right, now get to that rock, over there. Just as far as that rock. You can do it. Then I'd crawl my way there. And once I got to that rock, I cast around for the next tiny goal.

'And so I carried on, in the stillness of the starlight, crawling my way down the mountain, a little bit at a time by the light of the moon, never allowing myself to rest. I knew I had to get as far down the mountain as possible if I wanted to get home alive, and that I couldn't rely on anyone coming up to rescue me. The sun rose the next day, and that made things even worse. It roasted me. I'd exhausted my water supply, abandoned my backpack, and had no stove to melt ice to drink. I'd lost my gloves earlier, and my hands were exposed to the cold. My body felt hot and roasted, but I knew this was just a symptom of the extreme conditions. I'd strongly fought back the urges to strip off my clothes coming from within me, knowing full well that if I took my jacket off, I'd be dead. All I needed was to get down the mountain as fast as I could. I was running out of time. Every second I wasted took me closer to death.

'But as I crawled, I also started to become acutely aware of how thirsty I was. All I could think about was water. I laughed like a crazy person as I thought about the irony of my situation – surrounded by all that water, frozen as ice, but unable to drink any of it. My tongue lolled fat and dry in my mouth, and all I could hear in my ears was the trickling sound of water. In my mind, all I could picture was a pool of water. I thought of the pond in my garden, beneath the Japanese maple tree out there, with water running down a piece of bamboo into the pool. And the *drip drip drip* sound of the water, ripples cascading out from the droplets. It was driving me crazy. Water. A simple thing we take for granted in our daily lives. And I had none of it.

'But I kept going. I was frustrated even further when I made it down to one of the emergency huts on the mountain. It was empty, and there was no one there. I stopped a while to cry, thinking this was it, I was going to die. I still had far to go, and I would die of thirst. But after twenty minutes, I realized this was getting me nowhere. And so I kept going, crawling bit by bit, determined to get off the mountain. Determined to live.

'I came close to giving up, but I never did. And that's how I knew my life would be different if I ever got home safely.'

'What happened?'

'I kept going. I never gave up. I made it to the bottom of the mountain, and I was discovered by some Mountain Rescue guys, who whisked me off to the hospital. The days I spent recovering were strange. Some people seemed embarrassed for me, as if I'd failed.

'But I knew the truth, Kyo. I hadn't failed, at all. I had triumphed! It was a turning point in my life. One that I'll never forget. A resounding success, and something I'll never feel ashamed of. I learnt from my failure, that life is sacred.'

She looked at the clock. 'Bath time.'

○

Kyo could not sleep that night.

When he shut his eyes, he kept picturing Ayako – alone on the mountain, staring up at the stars. He cringed about the selfish thoughts he'd had in the past, of ending his own life. He remembered the stupid 'swim' he'd gone for in the river in Hiroshima back in the summer. Thinking about it now, he was ashamed. He really hadn't considered how it would make her feel – doing the exact same thing her son had done. How thoughtless he had been.

But he'd learnt a lot from her story, and slowly the guilt and shame subsided, and was replaced by a fierce respect for his grandmother. She'd lived through worse than he had, and she'd kept it together. She was inspiring.

The next morning, he began work on a series of paintings he planned on exhibiting at Jun and Emi's hostel in January. He worked on them in secret, without showing them to his grandmother, afraid of what she might say.

Flo: Winter

Flo slid further down inside the kotatsu with the book in her hand, trying to stay warm. She ran a hand through her hair, shocked at the grease. All this time, she hadn't showered or bathed.

Lily had disappeared two weeks ago. It had happened so quickly: Flo had come home from the coffee shop, and immediately noticed how chilly the apartment felt. She'd left the window open as usual – it was probably foolish, given that winter was upon them. But she liked leaving it open for Lily to come in and out. Lily didn't roam much, but enjoyed sitting out on the balcony of the apartment and just watching the world go by.

So it had alarmed Flo when she called Lily for her supper, and she didn't come. She was nowhere within the apartment, and even when Flo called outside, the cat did not come in.

Flo had not been outside the apartment since, terrified to leave lest Lily returned.

She'd been ignoring her phone and her computer. Just reading over sections of her dog-eared copy of *Sound of Water*, jotting things down in the margins or in a notebook she kept to hand. Her copy was almost falling apart now – spine creased to bursting, underlined throughout, pages turned over in the corners, different coloured adhesive tabs acting as bookmarks. Flo had long forgotten her own colour-coding scheme. It didn't seem to matter much any more. She just focused on the words, wanting to spend more time with Ayako and Kyo each day. If nothing else, it was a world she at least had some control over.

Outside, the weather was dire. Inside, it didn't feel much better.

Flo opened her laptop to make a LOST CAT poster for Lily. She planned on printing it out at a nearby convenience store and pasting it around town. What else could she do? It made her positively sick to think of Lily out there in the cold. Yes, Lily had been a street cat when she and Yuki had first taken her in. Flo clearly remembered finding her – an adorable white long-haired kitten with a single black spot on her chest, green eyes and a big bushy tail. They'd found her crying down an alleyway in the cold when they'd been out for a walk together. But what if all this time living with Flo had made Lily forget how to survive? What if she was hungry out there, or scared, or hurt?

She *had* to find her.

It was when she opened her laptop that she got a call from Kyoko. She let it ring off, ignoring the call, as she had done with so many over the past two weeks. Emails were surely piling up in her inbox, as were the messages on her phone. But Flo had ignored them all.

The ringing stopped, and seconds later a message came through from Kyoko.

PICK UP. NOW. OR I'M COMING OVER TO YOUR APARTMENT.

Flo's stomach lurched. She didn't want to talk to anyone. She didn't want to deal with real human beings. She just wanted to be left alone with Kyo and Ayako, or for Lily to come home.

Kyoko was calling again. This time, Flo's hand hovered over REJECT before she eventually picked up.

'Hello?'

'Flo. Are you okay?'

'Sure, I'm okay.' Even Flo could hear how robotic her own voice sounded as she spoke. 'What's up?'

'What's . . . what's up?' Kyoko's voice was choked. 'What's up is that you haven't been answering your phone or emails for two weeks. Flo – what the hell is going on? I've been so worried about you. Are you all right?'

Flo tensed up. The wall was growing higher. Before she could answer (*I'm fine, just busy with the translation*), Kyoko kept talking. 'And don't tell me you're fine or busy. Flo . . .'

Flo closed her eyes. This time when she spoke, her voice shook a bit.

'Lily ran away,' she whispered.

'She did?'

'Yeah.'

'Oh, Flo. I'm so sorry . . . I . . . But why didn't you tell us? We can come help you look for her. Do you want me and Makoto to come round after work today?'

Flo exhaled deeply. 'It's not just that, Kyoko.'

'What's wrong, Flo?'

Flo steeled herself. Struggling to translate her thoughts into words. To sum up everything that had been going on with her in this past year – in a sentence. She could list to herself all the things that had happened: losing Yuki, losing Lily, losing Ayako, losing Kyo, and, of course, never even finding Hibiki. But how did she translate these very untranslatable feelings that coursed through her body and mind? How could she put this pain into words that other people could understand and relate to? Was it even possible?

'Kyoko . . .' Flo began.

'Yes?'

'Look . . .' Flo battled on, trying her best. But she'd built the wall too high. 'I'm fine, honestly.'

'Haaaaaa!' Kyoko almost screamed in frustration.

'What's wrong?'

'You keep everything to yourself.' Kyoko sighed. 'It's exhausting.'

Exhausting. There it was again.

'But I can change,' said Flo, her eyes tearing up.

'People don't change,' said Kyoko, sounding tired. 'They are what they do.'

Flo could hear office noise in the background of the call.

She fought back the rising pain in her throat. There must be a word that perfectly encapsulated everything she was experiencing – if she could only strike upon it.

'I have to go, Flo,' said Kyoko. 'I'm sorry about Lily, but I'm so busy right now. If you need me, I'm here. But I'm not sure you do. Goodbye, Flo.'

'Kyoko, I . . .'

But Kyoko had already hung up.

Flo sobbed wretchedly into the quilt. She cried until she fell asleep, awaking in the dark.

Exhausting. Flo, herself, was exhausted. Of course she was exhausting.

But Kyoko's other words echoed in her head.

People don't change. They are what they do.

She could do something. She could do something about Lily, right now.

She went back to her laptop, determined to make a poster to find Lily. First, she needed a good photo of the cat – she remembered sending one to Ogawa recently, and it was in her Gmail somewhere. It was when she opened her inbox she saw it, nestling at the top of her inbox, above scores from other people, most worryingly one from Grant with the subject: ANY UPDATES?

But she opened this most recent one, because of the subject line:

FROM: Henrik Olafson
TO: Flo Dunthorpe <flotranslates@gmail.com>
SUBJECT: I know Hibiki
Dear Flo,

I came across a strange flier with a QR code in Onomichi – where I live now. You can probably tell from my name (Henrik Olafson) that I am neither a) Hibiki nor b) Japanese. But I do know 'Hibiki' very well, and he is dear to me. May I ask what this is in relation to, and why you would like to contact him? Is it about his novel SOUND OF WATER?
I presumed the one-eyed cat was Coltrane.
Kind regards from Onomichi,
Henrik

274

Flo couldn't breathe. Could this be a hoax? A scam? Why was a Scandinavian-sounding person living in Onomichi, and why were they emailing her about a Japanese writer? Could it be a tourist, messing with her? She dashed off an email in reply, explaining the situation, and begging Henrik to put her in contact with Hibiki as soon as possible. She attached a Word document to the email, containing her draft translations of the Spring, Summer and Autumn sections.

Afterwards, she continued to work on her LOST CAT poster for Lily in the dark, compulsively refreshing her inbox every minute.

Eventually, a response came.

▲▲

Settling into her Shinkansen seat, she got out her laptop, notebook and, once more, her battered copy of the novel. The train had left the station and was racing smoothly along, leaving Tokyo far behind. She took out a pen, and began to write out the rough translation of the final section, taking sips from the hot can of coffee she'd bought from a vending machine on the platform. After writing rough versions in a notebook by hand, she would type them up on to her laptop, editing herself slightly as she went.

It was snowing when she'd left her apartment, and as she stared out of the train window now she could see myriad snowflakes dancing in the air, falling slowly towards a sea of white covering the landscape that disappeared in the surrounding mists. She looked at the tray table in front of her, her laptop and notebook. It was time to finish the final section of *Sound of Water* – Winter.

Ever since autumn, Flo had been grappling with this last part, deftly avoiding questions from her editor about whether she'd got permission from the author and publisher yet. She'd kept him at bay with obfuscations: she was still trying to make contact, she had several promising leads, etc., etc. To appease him, she'd sent the three completed sections of the book, and was now drawing out the Winter section, sending it to him piece by piece in a Scheherazadic gambit, which had worked for a bit, but was now losing its charm.

I love this, Flo. But have you got permission? If not, there's not much we can do. She had left that most recent email unanswered.

It had been hard to maintain momentum on the project with the idea that she might only be translating the book for herself. But it was something to do, it kept her busy, and – most importantly – she simply enjoyed the process. She had only the final few pages left to translate, and was sure she'd finish soon. The idea of completing the work now made her nervous. What would she do without Kyo and Ayako in her life any more? Writing the final sentence of the novel into her notebook, and then typing it up on to her laptop, she was gripped with an intense fear. Was this it? Was she done with the project? What now?

She stared out of the window for a short time at the winter landscape, not sure how to feel. Part of her wanted to cry, part of her wanted to laugh.

She took out her phone, and saw a message from Kyoko.

I'm sorry, Flo. I was too hard on you when we spoke last. It's partly stress from work. But I'm sorry, I shouldn't have taken it out on you.

Flo tapped out a reply.

It's okay. You were right. I've been too closed off recently.

She hesitated for a second, but kept typing.

I had a bad break-up this year. Can we meet for coffee soon? I'll tell you everything – I promise. I'm sorry, Kyoko. You are a good friend, and I don't want to lose you. Please don't give up on me just yet. I'll do better. I promise.

Her eyes teared up as she hit send. It seemed like everything made her cry these days, since Lily's disappearance. She tapped nervously on the window and thought of Ayako performing the same nervous action on her way to get Kyo from the police box in

Hiroshima. It was still a way to Fukuyama, where she had to change trains. She took one more look at the email she'd received from Henrik last night.

FROM: Henrik Olafson
TO: Flo Dunthorpe <flotranslates@gmail.com>
SUBJECT: Re: Re: I know Hibiki
Dear Flo,

Thank you so much for your email. I have spoken to Hibiki about this, and while he is still slightly uncomfortable about having his novel translated into English, I have persuaded him to meet with you to discuss the matter. Just between us, I think he is a little ashamed, and feels the book was a failure. He can't understand why, if no one read it in Japanese, anyone would want to in English. I did, however, read over some of your translation myself, and I think you've done a fantastic job. Can you come to our house in Onomichi? I'm not sure if we can convince him, but I think it'd be good for him to meet you. He's an old man now, and quite set in his ways.
I can't make any guarantees, but please do let me know if you will come and visit us. It will be nice to meet you, whatever his decision regarding the translation.
Yours,
Henrik

Her fingers were so clammy with sweat she left marks on her phone screen as she scrolled up and down the email, reading every line carefully.

They were passing Osaka now. Still a fair way to go.

She had to kill some time. She still wanted to see if she could work out who Hibiki was – whether there were photos of him online with Henrik. Could Henrik himself be Hibiki? Was that possible?

She googled the name Henrik Olafson on her phone, just in case it threw up some more information. The top hit was a Wikipedia page for a bookcase.

The photo of the bookcase was disconcertingly familiar. She stared at it for a while, zooming in close. The shape of the shelves – like a backwards 'S', almost like a slithering snake.

The moment she realized it, she almost dropped her phone.

It was the same type of bookcase Ogawa had ordered for her online. It was sitting back in her apartment right now, and had been since autumn. Flo had unpacked and assembled it herself when it arrived. She'd marvelled at the distinct design, and its pleasing shape. It had been so cleverly thought through, everything just in the right place to allow the bookcase to be shipped easily as a flat-pack. She'd promptly tidied away her overflowing stacks of books on to the case, and thought nothing more of it.

That shape. She'd seen it somewhere else before, too. She picked up her copy of *Sound of Water*, and studied the Senkosha logo on the spine.

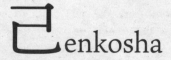

己enkosha

She looked from the kanji to the photo of the bookcase, and back again.

The kanji and the bookcase – they were the exact same shape!

She read through the rest of the Wikipedia page as fast she could: apparently, these bookcases were massively popular across the world. As of 2013, 30 million had been produced worldwide, and about one and a half million were sold annually.

Flo stopped reading. Her heart was fluttering. She scrolled back up to the top of the page, where she'd seen a Japanese name. 'Kentaro Tanikawa' – it had a link, too. Its own Wikipedia entry. The surname was also familiar – a common enough name, but there was a character in *Sound of Water* who shared it – the manga artist, Tanikawa Sakutaro, who wrote the comic about the game of Go. Flo clicked the link, and the page loaded.

She gasped audibly when she saw his place of birth: Onomichi.

Other people on the train turned around to frown at her, but she was far past caring.

Hibiki and Tanikawa Kentaro – it *had* to be him. The publisher's logo on the book was a bookcase! Not the kanji for 'onore'! There were no photos of Tanikawa online, and information was scant, but over the next hour she devoured everything she could find.

Tanikawa Kentaro, born in Onomichi in 1950, no death date listed. Attended Onomichi Kita High School, before moving to Tokyo in the late sixties to attend design school. Tanikawa had then left Japan in the early seventies for twenty years to work as the first ever Japanese designer for an extremely famous and ubiquitous Scandinavian furniture manufacturer and supplier that dealt predominantly with wood. He'd formed a close bond with product manager Henrik Olafson and the pair had collaborated on the design and manufacturing process for the Onore bookcase. Quotes from an interview lifted in 2005 had Tanikawa saying that the idea had come to him when looking at the kanji for 'onore', an archaic word for the pronoun 'you'. He'd designed the bookcase to mimic the kanji character in shape, and the concept of the kanji's meaning – being able to suit 'you', and your needs as a reader. The bookcase could be used by itself, or in a variety of configurations with other Onore units, to create larger bookcases. 'It all hinges around you, the reader,' the article quoted him as saying.

There was no clear information about what had happened to Tanikawa, and nothing about *Sound of Water*. The most recent article mentioned that he still regularly gave visiting guest lectures at design colleges throughout Japan. This article also said he resided in Onomichi.

Flo's mind whirred as she read. Tanikawa Kentaro was Hibiki – she finally had a name.

How close she was now.

She closed her eyes. Still a few stops to go.

▲▲

Arriving at Onomichi Station, Flo immediately made her way towards the address Henrik had sent her.

The town in winter was an entirely different kind of beautiful to autumn: the alleyways were blanketed in soft white snow, which crunched beneath her heels. She wandered the pathways that led to the top of the mountain, deciding impulsively she would swing by Cat Alley first. Since Lily had disappeared, she'd been fraught. Had Lily been hit by a car? Had she found another home? Or perhaps she'd just become another one of the many alley cats that roamed the streets of Tokyo, making good lives for themselves.

The not knowing what had happened to her – that was what troubled her the most. And another thought haunted her – what if Lily came back to her apartment while she was away? What if Lily had just got lost, and finally found her way home?

So many unanswered questions.

Flo crouched down, stroking a tabby cat eating from a can of tuna. These poor strays – out in the cold with no one to look after them. All these things she was powerless over. If only she had the same kind of control over life as she did with her translation work – the words she put on the page, one at a time.

It was when she looked up that she saw him.

An elderly black cat. One-eyed, slightly greying. With a little white tuft on his chest.

Surely not?

He was perched on a wall, blinking at her slowly. She blinked back, heart pounding.

Coltrane.

He leapt down from the wall clumsily, and she followed him through the narrow streets, keeping her distance. He would occasionally stop, looking back at her with his one green eye, appearing to wait briefly before moving on again. Flo followed for some time, and eventually they came to a stop in front of a door in a wall. She looked at the nameplate listing the surname of the occupant:

谷川 – Tanikawa

Coltrane sat on the street and watched her, blinking his one eye slowly. She took out her phone and checked the address, to confirm. This was it.

She'd done it. She'd found Hibiki.

Coltrane looked at the wall, then stared back at her. But instead of opening the door and walking through to the other side, Flo just stood there. It was like she'd become frozen to the spot. Her toes were growing numb inside her trainers.

Are you going inside, or not? Coltrane seemed to say.

But Coltrane couldn't see the million thoughts now whizzing through her mind. Overwhelming her, threatening to suck her down and drown her. She was just a translator. She'd become a translator because she didn't want to be seen, didn't want the spotlight – didn't want to deal with real people and real emotions. All her life she'd hidden behind fictional characters, and kept them as her friends. They never disappointed her, or let her down. They were always there for her. How would she ever convince this man that he should let her translate and publish his book? What if he said no? What if he was offended at her already having worked on the book without his permission? What if he told her to get out of his house? She'd never had to deal with a living, breathing author before – Nishi Furuni had died long before she'd even read his work. His sons had given her permission to work on his collected sci-fi stories by sheer chance. She'd never had to negotiate or sell herself as a translator before.

It would be far easier to slip away now. Avoid any possible confrontation and disappear.

The cat was still watching her. Coltrane yawned and then leapt up on to the top of the wall. He paused, looking down at her from on high. *Can't you do it? Just this once? It's easy.*

'I can't.' It was only when she said it aloud that Flo realized how true it was. She shook her head, but the thought didn't leave. 'I'm scared,' she whispered.

Coltrane looked away and jumped. She heard a soft thump the other side of the wall, the sound of paws landing nimbly on crisp snow. Flo was now alone, standing outside Hibiki's house and shivering.

She was so close to achieving something real. But the thought of yet another failure suddenly felt unbearable.

What if he doesn't want to publish this book in English? What if all your hard work so far has been for nothing?

She tried to lift her leg towards the door, but it was as if she were walking through treacle. Her trainers were heavy on her feet as she made one slow laborious step after another. She'd not made any progress.

What if you're doing the same thing you did to Yuki – pressuring someone to do something they don't want to?

She tried to lift her arm, but could feel how fragile her body was against the elements.

You're exhausting. You're a failure. A coward.

She swallowed hard. Her hand grasped the handle, fumbling with trembling fingers. Tiny goals – that's what she could do. Like Ayako on the mountain: one thing at a time. She pulled down hard on the handle, turning it with a rusty creak. The next tiny goal: bracing herself against the heavy door, she shoved with all her strength. The ancient hinges squealed as they came to life.

You can do it, said Ayako's voice in her head. *You can.*

Winter

十二

Winter descended on the town, icy and bereft.

The slow death of autumn had brought with it a burst of colour. But all of this colour was gone now. Stripped away to sparse bleakness. The branches of the Japanese maple tree by the pond in Ayako's garden were bare. The koi had been taken out and housed elsewhere.

Worse still was the iciness that had descended on Ayako's house.

And this time, the icy feeling came from Kyo, not Ayako.

○

It had been sudden. Kyo and Ayumi had arranged to meet after her cryptic text. He went to Yamaneko one day as she was closing up. It was then that he'd begun to sense his grandmother's looming presence at play in his life.

When Kyo had arrived at the café, Ayumi had seemed stressed and Kyo realized what was coming.

'I just don't think we should see each other until your exams are over,' said Ayumi.

'Why not?'

'Because.' She bit her lip. 'You have to focus on your studies.'

'I *am* focusing on my studies.'

'I know that, but . . .' She sighed, looking out over the sea at some spot on the horizon Kyo couldn't make out. 'I don't want to distract you, or take you away from the important things going on in your life right now.'

'You don't distract me, Ayumi,' said Kyo, trying his best to hide the waver in his voice. 'You help me.'

'I promise,' she continued, eyes downcast. 'We'll go away on a daytrip somewhere together. But only when your exams are done, okay?'

'Okay.'

'Anywhere you want to go, just tell me,' she carried on sunnily. 'I can borrow a friend's car.'

'All right,' said Kyo.

Both of their smiles felt forced.

There was much that Kyo wanted to say and ask. They hadn't even been dating, really. Just hanging out. And Ayumi had been the one who most encouraged him to consider his art rather than his studies. He didn't understand.

And if it had all ended like that, everything would've been fine. Of course, Kyo was filled with sadness that he wouldn't be able to hang out with Ayumi for the next few months. He'd grown used to their regular chats and time spent together. He'd felt a racing excitement every time he was en route to see her. His heart would beat faster, and his palms would sweat. But strangely, all of that nervous excitement evaporated when they were together, laughing and talking. He'd grown accustomed to this feature in his life. It had become part of his daily routine, and with it gone, there was a gaping emptiness in his schedule.

There was also a fear that he'd done something wrong – that he'd messed things up with Ayumi, and that she didn't like him any more. Slowly, as the days passed, he threw himself once again into his studies and tried his best to forget about what had happened. Things would be fine once he got his exams out of the way. There wasn't long left now, and then he could relax and go on a trip somewhere with Ayumi.

Things would all be fine.

Well, they would've been just fine, if only his grandmother hadn't made her mistake.

One evening, he'd been working on a four-panel manga which he was planning on entering into a competition. He was pleased with it, but he was restless. Ayako, noticing this, had asked him to help her with tidying the house. Kyo had dutifully undertaken the chores he was assigned, sweeping the entranceway and taking out the rubbish. But when he did this last part, he saw something that made his heart jump from his chest into his throat.

At the base of the paper basket in his grandmother's room, there was a crumpled menu for Yamaneko café.

And that is how he knew.

Kyo kept to the new agreed situation. He saw no point in confronting Ayumi about what had happened – that would only make her more uncomfortable. But he also found it difficult to spend time with his grandmother now, knowing full well that she had butted into his personal affairs. She'd gone too far this time. She'd interfered, and now he could not trust her. It was difficult to even be in the same room with someone who could be so deceitful and conniving. He'd had enough of her.

●

Ayako sensed that something was up with the boy. One day he was completely normal, and the next he wasn't. He was moping around. Being sullen. He wouldn't say more than a syllable to her in response to her questions. He'd stopped coming for their walks after she shut the café, and he was reluctant to play Go with her. He just roamed the streets by himself, and then when he finally got home, stayed in his room, as he'd done when he first came, working on his drawings and listening to music on his personal stereo. The girl must've said something. She must have blabbed about their meeting at the café. It had to be that. She'd told him everything. Well, that was just further proof that this girl was up to no good. If she couldn't even do the decent thing and keep her mouth shut about the private conversation they'd had, then she was obviously untrustworthy.

But the way the boy had responded to this distressed her.

It upset her to be abruptly excluded from his life.

What was this strange sensation Ayako felt creeping over herself? Loneliness?

● ○

'What's up with you this evening?'

'Nothing.'

'So why is your face like a bulldog chewing a wasp?'

'Don't feel well.'

'Are you sick?'

'No.'

'You have a fever?'

'No.'

'What's wrong?'

'Can you just leave me alone, please. I'm working on this drawing.'

'Suit yourself.'

● ○ ●

'Why don't you come for a walk with me tomorrow? Coltrane misses you.'

'I don't feel like it.'

'What's got into you?'

'Nothing. I'm just focusing on my studies. Isn't that what you want me to do?'

'Of course, but you know . . . *all work and no play*, as they say in English.'

'I'm working on a manga strip.'

'Can I see it?'

'It's not finished.'

'You can't show me what you've done so far?'

'I don't want to show it to anyone until it's finished.'

'I see . . . Do you want to hear more of my climbing stories?'

'Maybe some other time. I'm kind of busy now.'

'Suit yourself.'

'Kyo?'

'Yes?'

'Why don't we finish up the game of Go we're playing?'

'I don't feel like it.'

'But I want to clear away the board. It's taking up space on the table.'

'Clear it away then.'

'But the game's not finished.'

'Let's just say you won.'

'But . . . looking at it now, it looks like you're winning.'

'I'm sure you would've won in the end.'

'Kyo.'

'What?'

'Please.'

'I don't want to.'

'Please. Let's just finish the game.'

'I don't want to play with you any more, Grandmother. I've had enough.'

Ayako brushed the tear away from her cheek as soon as it rolled down. She stood in the doorway, looking into her son's old room at her grandson with his back to her. She shook her head roughly. All of this nonsense had got to her. It was surprising. What had caused this mix of emotions? Regret rose and played inside her mind; it was keeping her up late into the night, worrying about whether the boy would forgive her. What had happened to her defences, which she'd said no one would ever break through? She hadn't felt this way in a long time. Her words weren't getting through to the boy – his walls were up too high. So, Ayako knew the best thing to do.

The next day, she went again to Yamaneko café.

This time, she called Ayumi outside to talk to her. She noticed the girl's happy expression fall as soon as she caught sight of Ayako. It made her feel good, to be feared.

Ayako launched at her.

'I don't know what you said to Kyo, but I hope you're happy with yourself.'

Ayumi paused. 'I'm sorry, but, what do you mean?'

'He's angry with me, and that means you must've told him what we talked about. You had to open your mouth, didn't you? Had to!'

'I'm sorry, Tabata-san, but I didn't say anything to him about the conversation we had,' the girl said gently. 'I promise. I wouldn't do that.'

Ayako turned and studied the girl's face.

Had she miscalculated?

'You must've said something to him about me,' insisted Ayako.

'I promise you, I didn't,' said Ayumi, shaking her head. 'I told him what you told me to say – that I wanted him to focus on his studies. I said we could meet up with each other once his exams were over. I promised to take him somewhere on a daytrip to celebrate.'

Ayako scrutinized the girl's expression.

It seemed honest. It seemed true.

'Then why won't he talk to me any more?' said Ayako, voice wavering. 'What have you done?'

'I can tell him it wasn't anything to do with you?' suggested Ayumi kindly. 'Honestly, Tabata-san, I don't want to cause any problems, for either of you.'

'Stupid girl.' Ayako shook her head. 'What have you done?'

Her expression cracked slowly, lips quivering, as though an earthquake were coming.

'What have I done?'

And then finally after a long struggle, her fierce frown broke.

Ayumi went inside for a glass of water and a box of tissues, brought it out to her and gently patted her on the back while Ayako blew her nose.

'I'm sorry,' said Ayako. 'I'm sorry.'

Kyo was extremely surprised when he saw he'd received a LINE message from Ayumi. He'd been sitting at the low table in his bedroom, stroking Coltrane idly, and adding final touches to the four-panel manga strip for the competition. But his phone flashed out a notification, breaking his concentration. When he saw the name AYUMI he tapped the notification immediately.

> Hey, I'm playing the koto and the shamisen at a concert on Saturday morning, and I'd like you to come. Are you free?

He scratched his head. Concert? She was a musician? And weren't they supposed to not be talking or meeting until after his exams? He wrote out several replies asking for more information, deleting each one in turn without sending it. Too many questions floating around in his head. He finally settled on this:

> Sure!

and tapped send. Ayumi responded promptly.

> Great. We can go up on the train together. Meet at the station at 9 a.m.?

Kyo replied again:

> OK!

Then another response from Ayumi.

> Oh, and please bring your grandmother! That's important. I won't let you come without her.

Kyo turned his phone face down on the low table in his room. Grandmother? Why? Did he have to? He didn't want to.

Kyo spent the rest of the evening checking over his manga entry, before sealing the envelope. It was finally finished.

He would post it out the next day.

●

The next morning, Ayako heard the boy stirring in his room.

Breakfasts had become silent affairs. Ayako had given up trying to make conversation, and so they usually sat there simply munching away on their rice and miso soup. The boy had even taken to occasionally leaving the house without eating breakfast. She presumed he would grab an onigiri at the convenience store on the way to cram school, and then she found the wrappers – that hurt. It felt like an almost deliberate dig, after she'd told him about how much it meant to her to make and give away onigiri. It upset her greatly. She was filled with a deep sense of sadness having to throw his miso soup down the drain. She'd also made too much rice, and this had to be wrapped in clingfilm and put away in the fridge. She'd even stopped making him grilled fish in the morning, because there was no guarantee Kyo would eat it.

But, she was happy to see that he took breakfast at home that morning.

They chewed on their food, and Ayako could tell something was going on inside the boy's head. Eventually Kyo managed to speak.

'You're probably busy,' he began. 'And you're probably not interested, but . . .'

'Yes?'

Kyo huffed. 'This Saturday, my friend is doing a traditional music recital in Saijo. She's invited us both to attend the performance. I said I'd ask if you'd come, but you're probably busy.'

'This Saturday?' asked Ayako, feigning surprise. She leant her cheek against the hand holding her chopsticks and looked thoughtful. 'Oh yes, I'm free.'

'You're free?'

'Yes, I'd love to come.'

'But what about the café?'

'Oh, I'll leave it closed for the day, or I'll get Jun and Emi to run it.'

'Really?' Kyo couldn't hide the disappointment from his face. 'Don't feel obliged or anything.'

'I don't,' said Ayako, continuing to eat her rice. 'I want to come.'

'Okay,' said Kyo tersely. 'I'll tell her.'

Ayako cleaned away the breakfast bowls and rinsed them in the sink.

'See you,' said Kyo.

'Have a nice day,' replied Ayako.

She smiled. The girl's plan might just work.

○ ●

That chilly morning, Ayako in kimono, Kyo wearing his suit.

They made their way to the train station together. Kyo ambled awkwardly wearing his formal black suit and tie, and a crisp white shirt he hadn't put on since he'd been in Onomichi. He shoved his hands in his pockets, certain that Ayako would tell him off for it. But instead, she linked her arm in his and leant against him as they walked. Kyo had not seen her wear this white kimono before, and he was surprised at how striking it appeared. She wore a black obi sash over it. The obi and the kimono had a subtle design which matched: small snowflakes drifting around the material, as though blown in a strong wind.

When they arrived at the station, Ayumi was waiting for them.

She carried a shamisen case in one hand, had a backpack slung over her other shoulder, and she was also dressed in a beautiful kimono. It was more modern and colourful than Ayako's – a light shade of blue with a floral pattern at the edges – but it suited her perfectly.

Kyo couldn't hide his surprise at her appearance.

Ayako and Ayumi smiled at each other, both bowing low and politely in greeting.

'Nice to meet you,' said Ayumi.

'Nice to meet you, too,' replied Ayako.

'Please treat me kindly,' they both chorused to one another in unison.

Kyo was not stupid. He could sense something forced or artificial about the interaction. They hadn't even given each other their names. Something was up, but he was beyond caring now. He was just happy to see Ayumi again.

'Kyo! Don't be rude!' barked Ayako. 'Take her backpack and shamisen case!'

While they were waiting for the train, the Tanuki, Station Master Ono, came over to make small talk. He mostly complimented the women on how good they looked. Occasionally he looked at Kyo and shook his head.

'And you're quite the dashing figure in that suit,' he said, beaming from ear to ear. 'Eh?'

Tanuki chuckled to himself as if he'd just thought of an amazing joke.

'*A flower in both hands*, as they say, eh?' He elbowed Kyo in the ribs and waggled his eyebrows.

'One of those flowers is much fresher than the other,' said Ayako gleefully.

'Don't be harsh on the young lady,' joked Tanuki. 'We can't all be as young and radiant as you, Ayako. I should watch my step, Sato-san might get jealous.'

Ayako hit Tanuki playfully on the arm, and Ayumi laughed behind her hand.

The three of them rode the train together to Saijo.

Ayako and Ayumi chattered on the train about this and that – talking about their favourite restaurants in Onomichi. Both of them said they loved the Thai restaurant in the View Hotel, next to Onomichi Castle. When Kyo said he hadn't been there, they berated him, as if he'd made some kind of massive error in his life. They mostly talked with each other during the journey, and when they did talk to Kyo, it was to make fun of him in a mild, but also mildly irritating, mocking way. Sometimes, Ayumi spoke to Ayako in a low voice behind her hand while looking at Kyo, and then they would whisper and giggle.

Kyo ignored them both and looked out of the window.

The concert was in a fairly large auditorium.

There was a printed paper programme with all of the recitals listed, and Ayako and Kyo sat down in their seats, waiting for it to begin. Kyo studied the programme carefully, noting all the perform-ances Ayumi was involved in.

The concert dragged a little. There were too many pieces, and some musicians were better than others. It was a long time to sit, and while Ayako sat stock still for the entire concert, Kyo fidgeted uncomfortably from time to time. Ayako noticed Kyo lean forward whenever Ayumi took the stage. Even for her ensemble shamisen performances, he would move from a relaxed slouch, to being perched on the end of his seat, focusing on the stage as though he didn't want to miss even the tiniest of details. Ayako smiled to her-self when she saw this.

Near the end of the concert, Ayumi took the stage by herself to perform a solo koto performance. She moved slowly across the wooden floor and bowed to the audience, before making her way to the centre. She placed her hand neatly under her kimono as she sat down on a cushion. Poised in the traditional seiza position in front of the instrument, she closed her eyes in concentration before her slim fingers began to pluck away at the strings, breaking the rapt silence in the room.

Kyo was enchanted, watching her play, lost in the music that reverberated around the hall. He held his breath, worrying that if he should make a sound it would destroy the spell she was casting with her music. Ayako studied the boy's expression surreptitiously. He was smitten, that much was plain to see. But she understood now. She could see for herself.

The more she thought about it, the more this made sense.

Ayako felt extremely foolish for having interfered now, but she had done it out of love. She'd done exactly the same thing with Kyo's father and mother all those years ago. Strange that she hadn't caught herself making the same mistake all over again. But this time it could be different. She didn't have to push Kyo away. She must stop trying to control things. That was the root cause of her problems. She needed to let go.

She knew that now, for certain.

She could hear it, in the vibrations that pulsated in the air around them.

The sound of the koto.

☯

Ayumi changed out of her kimono after the concert into a pair of jeans and a t-shirt.

The concert had lasted a long time, and the audience had been given a box lunch midway through. They took the one-hour train journey back to Onomichi together, and when they arrived at around 5 p.m., the younger pair stood around awkwardly, unsure of what to do or say. Kyo and Ayumi looked at each other shyly, while Ayako studied the pair of them, enjoying their youthful awkwardness.

'So,' said Ayako, finally breaking the silence. 'Congratulations on your concert today, Ayumi-san.'

'Thank you for coming,' said Ayumi, bowing to both of them.

Kyo was turning crimson, unsure what to do with himself.

'Ayumi-san?' Ayako continued speaking, turning to face Ayumi. 'I wonder if you might join us for dinner?'

'Dinner?' asked Kyo, shocked. 'What?'

Ayako turned a stern gaze upon Kyo. 'I am talking to Ayumi-san, not you.' She shook her head and turned back to Ayumi. 'What do you say?'

'I'd love to.' Ayumi smiled and bowed. 'As long as it's not an imposition.'

They stowed Ayumi's belongings at a coin locker in the station, then Ayako led the way. They crossed over the train tracks to the mountainside, the opposite side of the sea. Kyo wondered where

Ayako might be taking them. Perhaps to Ittoku, the izakaya behind the station. But they kept walking, along the narrow path that led up to the top of the mountain.

Kyo noticed as they made their way up the steep path with its ancient cobblestones and steel handrails that they were heading in the direction of Onomichi Castle. He knew where they were going, but kept quiet.

They walked up the steps, beneath the old iron lampposts that cast pools of light on to the path. Cat-like shapes darted around in the shadows. And then they were at the top of the mountain, walking past the angular outline of Onomichi Castle. The castle had long been shut to the public.

'You used to be able to go inside,' said Ayako to Ayumi.

'Even if you weren't a feudal lord?' Ayumi laughed.

'Yes,' said Ayako, nodding. 'It was open to the general public for years. But for whatever reason, they closed it up. You can still see that spooky model of a man standing there. Can you see him?'

'Creepy! Gives me the chills when I walk past, Ayako-san.'

'Wait a minute,' said Kyo, joining in with their conversation slyly. 'How did you know Grandmother's name was Ayako? She never said her name earlier, and I thought you two were meeting for the first time?'

Ayako's face froze.

'Oh, Kyo!' Ayumi jumped in seamlessly. 'Don't be silly! Everyone in Onomichi knows Ayako-san! She's famous!'

Ayako smiled and nodded at Ayumi, then scowled at Kyo playfully. 'Don't be so rude!'

When they walked into the restaurant, Ayako went over to talk to the waitress, who led them to a table by the window.

There was a RESERVED sign on it; Kyo laughed to himself. It was the last piece of confirmation he needed to know for sure that the day had been a set-up. Ayako had made the reservation earlier, and she must've done so before they'd left the house, because she didn't have a mobile phone.

He wasn't sure how they'd done it, but Ayako and Ayumi had planned this all along.

But Kyo didn't feel angry.

Quite the opposite – he was touched.

For his grandmother to go to such lengths, it was uncharacteristic. It was almost as if she was apologizing. She'd never actually say the words directly to him, but this act of kindness was good enough.

They sat down and ordered appetizers and main courses for sharing: tom yum kun soup, green curry with chicken, massaman curry with beef, and pad thai with tofu. Kyo tipped himself back in his chair, admiring the view from the window. Down below, he could see the entire town by night – the warm orange glow of the streetlights, the tiny specks of yellow light coming from the windows of houses, shops and office buildings; then there was the blackness of the water which extended out into the night sky, the dark outline of mountains and islands barely visible. Here and there, stars were twinkling dimly above, but the blue, orange, yellow and green lights illuminating the cranes of the Mukaishima Dockyard were at the centre of the view, drawing the eye. Red rear lights and white headlights of cars drifted slowly along the roads that snaked through the town. It was something else at night.

They ate and drank cheerfully, and Ayako settled the bill discreetly, completely out of sight, with neither Ayumi nor Kyo noticing. Their bellies full, they made their way down the mountain in the darkness, back to the station to retrieve Ayumi's belongings from the coin locker.

Kyo walked Ayumi to the taxi rank in front of the station. He helped her carry her things, while Ayako waited tactfully at the station for him to return. Before Ayumi got in a taxi, she turned to Kyo and spoke to him quickly.

'I like your grandmother a lot, Kyo.' The lights shone and reflected in her eyes.

Kyo scratched his head and shifted his feet.

'It's not long now, and your exams will be over soon,' Ayumi continued. 'When you're done, we can celebrate, I promise. I've decided on where I'm going to take you.'

Kyo raised an eyebrow. 'Where?'

'To Dogo Onsen in Matsuyama.'

'The one from the book *Botchan*?'

'Yup.' Ayumi nodded. 'That's the one.'

'Awesome.' Kyo smiled.

Ayumi ducked inside the open door of the taxi. 'Tell your grandmother thank you very much for the food this evening. It was delicious.'

'I will.'

'And be kind to her, Kyo. She's a good person. She cares about you a lot, even if she isn't good at showing it.'

'I know. I will. I promise.'

'Goodnight.'

'Goodnight.'

Kyo watched as the taxi pulled away; Ayumi waved from the window, and he waved back.

The taxi disappeared around a corner, and he rejoined his grandmother.

They walked slowly back to the house together in the dark night.

'Kyo?' said Ayako, breaking the silence.

'Yes?'

'I like her,' she said softly. 'I like her a lot.'

It was only a few weeks later that Coltrane disappeared.

The first few days he hadn't been at the usual place they fed the cats, and neither Ayako nor Kyo had thought anything much of it. True to his roaming nature, Coltrane would sometimes come and go like that – he was a free spirit. But the most he'd miss a feeding was only for a day or two, and after a whole week without seeing him, Ayako had grown noticeably more anxious each day on their walks. She held a sense of anticipation each time they neared the spot where he usually waited to be fed.

Kyo could sense Ayako's distress, and experienced his own – Coltrane was not beside him while he drew. And there was nothing much either of them could do about this; it was outside of their control. Coltrane's departure affected both of them more than they let each other know. They didn't talk about his absence, but there was a heaviness in the air. Kyo had been to visit Sato in his shop to see if he'd seen any sign of 'Mick Jagger'.

'I haven't,' said Sato glumly. 'He hasn't visited in days . . . maybe a week or so?'

Christmas came and went, and then New Year arrived. Kyo had originally planned to return to Tokyo for oshogatsu, but with the disappearance of Coltrane and Ayako's low mood, he decided against doing so, even for just the three days of the national holiday.

'You should see your mother,' said Ayako when he'd told her his change of plans.

'I'd rather keep you company.'

'Bah!' She waved her hand. 'I'll be fine by myself. Go back to Tokyo. Your mother must miss you.'

'She said she'll be here for my coming-of-age day.'

'That will be nice,' said Ayako, although deep down inside she harboured fears that his mother would again not appear.

They spent the three days of oshogatsu holed up under the kotatsu table together, eating traditional osechi ryori which Ayako had ordered in from a nearby shop.

'I can't be bothered to cook all that stuff,' she said grumpily. 'It's too fussy!'

They ate their New Year's mochi rice cakes and soba noodles, and went to watch the sunrise from the top of the mountain to bring in the New Year. Then they walked to the Temple of One Thousand Lights for the hatsumode first prayer visit.

It was the day before Kyo's coming-of-age ceremony that he spotted that his carved frog was missing from his bedroom.

'Grandmother?' he said, approaching her in the living room.

She was seated at the table reading a book. 'Yes?'

'Have you seen Frog?'

Ayako looked up from her book. 'That old toy you kept by your bed?'

'Yes, that one.' Kyo stood the other side of the table from where she was sitting. 'Have you seen it? It's missing from my room.'

Ayako nodded. 'Yes, I gave it to Jun and Emi.'

Kyo's mouth dropped in shock. 'Why?'

Ayako looked surprised. 'For little Misaki – their baby, of course.'

A cold sweat formed over his body. He tried his best to remain calm.

'But, Grandmother . . . why would you give it away without asking me?'

'Pfft!' Ayako frowned. 'What need does a grown man like you have of a toy? I thought you wouldn't mind. I thought you'd be fine to give it away to baby Misaki. It'll make her happy.'

'But . . . you could've asked me first.'

'Perhaps.' Ayako jutted out her jaw. 'But what does it matter? You're an adult!'

'Because,' Kyo sat down, folding his arms over his knees. 'Well, it's just, Father carved that frog, from a piece of Japanese maple. That's all.'

Ayako's stern expression fell and her eyes glistened. 'Oh, Kyo. I didn't know. I'll go over there right now and get it back for you.' She stood with determination, and went to the genkan entranceway to put her shoes on.

'No.' Kyo shook his head and raised his chin. 'Don't worry about it.'

'But it's . . .' She looked back at him, studying his face with a new compassionate expression Kyo had never seen before. 'I didn't think . . .'

'It's okay.' Kyo shrugged. 'I don't need it any more. I'd rather Misaki-chan had it.'

'Are you sure?' Ayako reached for her overcoat. 'Because I can go and get it right now.'

'It's fine,' said Kyo quietly. 'I'm glad you gave it to her. Frog found a new home.'

Ayako sat back down. She placed a hand on the table.

'I'm sorry.'

'It's okay, honestly.'

Kyo looked up and smiled reassuringly.

Before Ayako could respond, Ota the Postman was calling out with his characteristic early-morning cheer. Kyo and Ayako greeted him as he handed over a small envelope, addressed to 'Hibiki'. Ayako studied the envelope before passing it to Kyo, who opened and read it immediately.

Dear Hibiki-san (if I may),
I hope you don't mind, but I noticed your work when I was judging
a manga competition which you entered recently. I thoroughly

*enjoyed your four-panel Frog Detective manga, and while not
perfect, it left a lasting impression on me. I'm afraid, despite my
protestations to the other judges, you were not successful in winning
a prize. I am extremely sorry about that.*

*However, I know potential when I see it, and if possible, I'd like
to meet with you. I can't promise anything, but I am perhaps
looking for an assistant – someone to work with me in my studio. I
do not offer much by way of fame and riches, but I can perhaps
show you the ropes of the manga industry. I myself got into the
profession this way, and it is common practice for established artists
to take on disciples and help them with their careers. You would
start out mostly inking and outlining my work, but it would be a
useful insight into the process of making manga.*

*I know nothing about you, but I saw something in your drawings.
You don't have to give me an answer either way, and I think in the
first instance it would be best if you came to my studio in Kokubunji,
Tokyo, so that we could meet and get to know one another. If you
have a portfolio of work, please do bring that to show me, and if you
have any ideas for longer form stories, I'd love to hear them.*

*If this is something of interest, please do let me know. You can
write to me at the address on the card I have enclosed.*

Yours,

Tanikawa Sakutaro

Kyo could not take it in. He handed the sheet of paper to Ayako,
who read it while he studied the business card with the address of a
studio in Kokubunji on it. The logo on the card was the black silhouette of a cat.

'Who is this Tanikawa-sensei?' she asked, looking up.

'He's a great artist!' said Kyo, eyes wide open. 'You remember the
manga series I was reading about the game of Go? The one where
the two masters are fighting to be crowned the best in Japan?'

'Vaguely . . .'

'He drew that! And he wrote the story, too! It's called *Go! Go! GO!*'

Ayako beamed. 'This is fantastic news.'

'It is.'

'What are you going to do?'

It was only then that Kyo remembered: medical school, the exams, the life mapped out for him.

'Well, first things first,' said Ayako, looking at the clock. 'Let's have breakfast, get dressed and get to the station to meet your mother. Plenty of time to think about all of this later.'

Kyo dashed off to his room with the letter.

'I'm proud of you,' said Ayako.

But she said it too quietly, and he did not hear her.

They met Kyo's mother at the station; she was dressed in a classy kimono – the colour and design perfectly muted and understated. Mother, ever the professional. Around her milled an assortment of young adults wearing formal dress for the ceremony, accompanied by friends and family who would attend as guests.

Setsuko was standing in front of the station, tapping away on her smartphone, waiting for the two of them, and as they approached, she put away her phone in a small handbag. And waved.

'Kyo!' Her face lit up.

'Hello, Mother.'

'You've lost weight! You're looking in great shape!'

They hugged briefly. It was not something they did normally, but today felt special.

She stepped back to look at him, her eyes running head to toe and taking in his formal kimono. 'You look so much like him today. Like your father,' she said.

Kyo blushed.

She looked at Ayako, and bowed formally.

'Mother.'

'Setchan.' Ayako returned the bow.

'It's been so long. I can't thank you enough for looking after Kyo this past year. I hope he hasn't been too much trouble.'

'He's had his moments.' Ayako grinned, and then shook her head. 'No, it's been a pleasure to have him. A real pleasure.'

Kyo scratched the elbow of his kimono awkwardly.

'Shall we?' said Ayako, indicating that they move off with the other droves of people to the Town Hall, where the coming-of-age ceremony was due to take place.

☯

After the ceremony, everyone hung around outside. Some of the young men were wearing suits, a few, like Kyo, wore formal kimono instead. All of the girls wore elaborate, bright and extravagantly coloured kimono, with fur lining on the collars, and long furisode sleeves. The scene became a large number of small photoshoots. Poses were struck. Cameras flashed. 'One more! One more!' groups called out here and there.

Kyo's mother and grandmother took turns snapping photographs with him. Sato even turned up and took photos of Kyo, Ayako and Setsuko on his old Canon SLR. Then the four of them got into Sato's beaten-up car and he drove them across the bridge to Innoshima island, where they had lunch at a fancy new Japanese restaurant run by one of Sato's cronies.

They ate their bento set lunches, chatting and laughing in response to Sato's stories of his own coming-of-age ceremony, with the backdrop of the Inland Sea visible from the huge windows of the modern restaurant. The sea stretched out into the distance, swallowed by the horizon.

●

That evening, Ayako had organized for Jun and Emi to hold a celebration for Kyo at their newly refurbished hostel.

But what Ayako didn't know was Kyo's surprise for her.

Kyo had helped Jun hang his paintings on the wall a few days beforehand.

Ayako was slightly taken aback to see the title of the series: *Ayako vs. The Mountain*.

Inspired by his grandmother's story of climbing and surviving

Mount Tanigawa, Kyo had drawn and painted a series depicting her struggles. Kyo had used the white space of the canvas to represent the snowstorm she had been caught in, and the paintings showed Ayako reaching the summit, battling the elements, leaving a small urn of his father's ashes and praying at the commemorative plaque for his grandfather, then a scene of her breaking her leg, hiding from the storm, crawling down the mountain.

At first, when she'd seen them, she was a little upset. It seemed crass to exhibit what had been such a personal experience to the public. But the more she studied each painting, one by one, the more she grew to love and understand them. Particularly the final one: Ayako lying on her back in the snow, seemingly broken, but for the triumphant smile on her face.

He gets it, she thought to herself. *He understands what I went through.*

And then she'd felt a rapid succession of guilt, shame, sadness and failure rising up inside herself. She shook her head. No, these feelings were real, but they weren't everything. They had no place in her life right now. She let them wash over her. These feelings would pass, and surely enough, within seconds, they did. She allowed herself to feel the joy that followed. Joy that she was still alive, which burst forth in her stomach into a sense of pride. Pride at everything she'd overcome, despite herself. Pride at the boy, and how he'd grown. She had to cover her face with her handkerchief, pretending that she had a runny nose.

○

Kyo was feeling a little light-headed from the beers he'd been drinking. He hadn't drunk much since that awful night in Hiroshima, but today, things seemed better. It seemed like there was hope in the air. He was opening another can of Asahi beer for himself and pouring it into a glass when he saw Ayumi at the door. She wore her hair up in a ponytail, and was looking around the small crowd of people. She spotted Kyo, smiled and waved to him. Kyo pointed at an empty glass, and she nodded in response. He poured a second beer and went over to pass it to her.

'Hello,' she said, taking the glass from him with a nod. 'Congratulations.'

'For what?'

'This!' Ayumi held her arms outstretched, beer sloshing around in the glass she was holding. 'Your paintings! Your work!'

Kyo blushed again.

'And . . .' She bit her lip. 'Congratulations on becoming an adult. You are finally allowed to drink beer legally.' She tapped the glass.

Kyo laughed. 'I'll drink to that.'

'Ayako told me about the letter, by the way, from Tanikawa-sensei. The manga artist.'

'Oh that.' Kyo looked down at the floor.

'Why are you looking so sullen?' she asked. 'It's incredible news, Kyo! These chances don't happen often in life. You are going to Tokyo, right? To talk to him.'

'I don't know . . .'

'What do you mean?'

'I kind of like it here, you know, in Onomichi. And . . .' He trailed off. 'I'd miss Grandmother . . . and you . . .'

'Kyo.' She shoved him lightly in the chest, and spoke sternly. 'If I see you moping around this small town in a month, I am seriously gonna be angry. Hell, I'll get Ayako involved; she and I will tag-team wrestle some sense into you. We'll beat your ass. Go to Tokyo. Follow your dreams.'

'Maybe,' he said, nodding. 'But—'

'Not maybe. It's your life, Kyo. It's important.'

He smiled crookedly. 'I suppose you're right.'

'I know I am. I always am.' She grinned. 'Anyway, let's chat more about this in the car to Dogo Onsen—'

She was interrupted by a clinking sound on a glass, and everyone looked at Sato, who was tapping an empty bottle of Kirin beer with a chopstick.

'Everyone,' he began his short speech, 'I'd just like to take this opportunity to congratulate young Kyo today on becoming an adult. Age is just a number, and we all know Kyo was already a young Tokyo gentleman when he arrived in our tiny little backwater town.' And here he looked directly at Kyo and spoke to him. 'But we were lucky to spend this time with you this past year. You've become a part of the community here in Onomichi. You've helped me with my shop, you've helped Jun and Emi with this wonderful hostel.' He paused, and looked around the room. 'And, most importantly, you've given us all something special – a wonderful new nickname for Station Master Ono – the Tanuki!'

Everyone cheered and laughed.

Tanuki blinked through his glasses at Kyo, who grinned back awkwardly. Tanuki winked and smiled. Sato continued.

'And you've even helped your grandmother, not just in her café.' Sato coughed and smirked a little. 'But you may have even made her a little softer around the edges.'

Sato chuckled to himself. The whole room guffawed, and Ayako shook her head.

'Not on your life!' she called out, eyes twinkling from the few glasses of umeshu plum wine she'd drunk earlier. 'Watch it, Sato!'

'But seriously,' Sato continued, gesturing at the paintings on the walls. Everyone looked around at the wonderful canvasses hanging about them. 'You came to Onomichi as a man, Kyo. But we, we all hope that our small town has helped you become an artist. Because, Kyo, today we can safely say, you are an artist, and always will be.'

Kyo's face flushed hotly.

'And we hope that wherever life takes you – and you are destined for bigger and better things than this little town – we all hope that whatever path you choose in life, you will forever take Onomichi with you, wherever you go, in your heart.' He tapped his chest, a little drunkenly. His eyes were misting over.

Tanuki jumped in. 'Here's to Kyo! Kanpai!'

They all raised their glasses and called out, 'Kanpai!'

Kyo caught Ayumi's eyes, and she covered her mouth to laugh.

Kyo took a sip of his beer, and looked about for his mother. She was nowhere to be seen in the room, but finally he saw her outside, talking on her phone.

She had missed the speech.

***

It was a cold, still morning and Kyo awoke to the smell of breakfast. He got up from his futon and padded barefoot into the living room. His grandmother and mother were preparing the food together silently. He took a seat at the low table and waited for them to notice he was awake. He shivered slightly in the morning cold, but the kotatsu was on, and he slipped under its blankets to keep warm.

'Good morning,' said his mother, finally noticing him.

'Morning,' said Kyo, yawning.

Ayako and Setsuko brought over the food, and they all sat around the table chomping thoughtfully.

Setsuko's phone vibrated on the table, and she picked it up and read a message.

'Ugh.' She put the phone back down. 'I'm sorry to do this to you both . . .'

Ayako nodded.

Kyo sighed.

'But I'm going to have to go back to Tokyo today. I'm sorry, Kyo. I know you wanted to take me to Hiroshima, to see the Atomic Bomb Dome, and eat okonomiyaki. And I really did want to see the floating torii gate at Miyajima, but I just have to get back to work.' She swallowed the last of her miso soup. 'I'm so sorry.'

'It's fine,' said Kyo. 'We'll be all right, won't we, Grandmother?'

'Of course,' said Ayako cheerfully, then she looked as if she had remembered something. 'Kyo, did you show that letter to your mother?'

Kyo made eyes at his grandmother and shook his head. 'No.'

'What letter?' asked Mother.

'Show it to her!'

Kyo went to get the letter, and passed it to his mother. She read it extremely quickly.

'That's nice, Kyo.' She smiled. 'It's good that an artist complimented your work like that. And I was touched at how your paintings went down at the exhibition last night. But . . .' She paused, screwing up her face slightly. 'I just hope all of this isn't distracting you from your exams. You need to pass those to get into medical school. You don't have time right now for daydreaming or drawing. You can do that in your spare time. It's just a hobby.'

Kyo's face fell, and he glanced across at his grandmother, who was also looking slightly disappointed.

'But what if I wanted to go and be a disciple of Tanikawa-sensei's?' asked Kyo, speaking quickly. 'What if that's what I want to do? What if I don't want to go to medical school? What if I don't want to be a doctor?'

Kyo's mother laughed. 'Don't be silly, Kyo! There's no stability in art. That's why they're called "starving artists". Take your exams. Become a doctor – and then you'll have a stable and steady life. You can do your drawings for fun in your own time.'

Kyo scoffed slightly. 'Own time?'

'Yes,' said his mother. 'In your spare time. As a hobby. We've been over this.'

'You have no time of your own,' said Kyo. He was shaking slightly, not meeting her gaze. 'You could barely even make it to my coming-of-age ceremony. This is the first time you've even come to visit me all year. You've never had any time for me. You've never cared about me. How am I going to be an artist in my spare time if you can't even handle being a mother in your spare time—'

'Kyo!' shouted Ayako, putting her bowl of miso soup down. 'Do NOT speak to your mother like that.'

Kyo looked at his grandmother, mouth wide open.

Her eyes were cold. Her expression one of anger.

How could she have betrayed him like that?

Why wasn't she sticking up for him?

Kyo stood up quietly. 'Thank you for breakfast.'

He turned around and walked straight to the genkan and put on his shoes. He grabbed the bag containing his sketchbook and pens from where it was hanging on a coat peg.

'Kyo, darling,' said Mother. 'Where are you going? You're still in your pyjamas, love. You can't go out like that.'

Kyo reached for an overcoat, turned wordlessly and walked out of the door.

'Kyo!' Setsuko made to stand. 'Wait!'

Ayako put a firm hand on her wrist. 'I'll go. It'll be okay. Don't fret.'

She put on her tonbi overcoat and burst out of the door.

She knew where she would find him.

○

Kyo sat on a rock, high above the town. Shivering.

This was his favourite spot to sketch the town. He knew now what he wanted.

He didn't want to leave. He wanted to stay here, in Onomichi. He didn't want to take his exams; he didn't want to study medicine. He didn't want to go back to Tokyo. He wanted to stay. This was home.

If only he could freeze time, to not have to make any decisions about his life and future.

He knew, deep down, that his grandmother had not betrayed him. The anger and indignation had fallen away from his mind as he'd made his way to the top of the mountain. When he got home, he would say sorry to her straight away. He would say sorry to his mother, too. But what he wouldn't apologize for is for how he felt in his heart.

What was so wrong about following one's dreams?

What was this life but his own, to do with as he saw fit?

He put his head in his hands and closed his eyes as a million lives unfurled and drifted through his mind, and he found it unbearable thinking of the myriad possibilities that awaited. Some of them appeared to him – married with children. Divorced. Drunk without a job. Earning lots of money. A happy family. A struggling artist. Bad reviews. Pain. Joy. A great task ahead of him, looming like a craggy, mountainous peak. Here it was, the definition of failure or success. Judgement from his peers. Praise from his idols. Thrown out on the scrapheap. Dying in anonymity. Acclaim. A doctor. A lifesaver. A member of society. A street bum. A loser, living in Okinawa, teaching people to surf. Cars. Kids. Cot death. Motorbikes. Trying to hold on to lost youth. Death in the family. Parents outliving their children. The loss of a partner. Grief. Cancer. Disgust. Affairs. Adultery. Theft. Murder. Assault. War. Famine. Inequity. Impotence. Failure. Overwhelming failure. Resounding failure. Frog. Suicide.

The more he thought, the more his mind spun.

What was he doing with his life? Where was he headed?

All he wanted to do was draw. To be an artist.

To be an artist. To live with his grandmother. To know more about her and his father.

It was then that he saw the whole story of his life; it floated into his head, from the first panel to the last. A glorious epiphany, born of conflict and pain. The peak of the mountain suddenly appeared, crystalline, harsh and icy in the distance, the sun kissing its windswept summit. He sighed, half in pleasure, half in resignation. The road ahead was going to be a long one, but he was certain he knew the way. All he had to do was just work on one pen line at a time, panel by panel. Just like his grandmother making her way down the mountain, he would set himself mini tasks each day, little goals done bit by bit that would add up to an entirety. And he would keep going and never give up. Sitting there alone on the mountain, all he had was the present. The past and the future didn't matter. The work was all he had – and therein lay the joy of being.

It all seemed simple now. The answer had been staring him in the face.

He saw the first few panels in his head: an outline of the shape of a woman wearing a kimono walking up a mountain, then staring out across the water. The town of Onomichi below her. She was a hard-faced, strong woman, with a grim expression. She walked with a limp and was missing fingers. But there was pain, knowledge and wisdom in her eyes. She'd lived a long life of hardship, the ripples of which she overcame each and every day. She had many things to say; not all of them were good, and some were even bad.

But she was an important person; she was real, and worth knowing. People should know her story. And Kyo could tell it.

In his mind he saw in the top left corner of the first panel a dialogue box that said:

Ayako had a strict daily routine from which she did not like to deviate.

He took out a fresh notebook.
I Ie opened it at thc first page and began to draw.

Ayako vs. The Mountain:
The Final Push for the Summit

Ayako pulled her overcoat tightly around her.

She pushed her way up the mountain, legs burning. She had to move quickly.

She knew exactly what she had to do now.

The wind blew a slight chill, and she felt it deep in her joints. She was getting old.

As she pushed her way up the mountain, she thought of the life she'd led, the mistakes she'd made, the joys, the despair, the peaks, the troughs. The mountains and valleys.

The town flowed around her, but she did not notice anyone or anything. Her mind was set on the summit. She knew exactly where the boy would be, sitting on the rock he loved to sit on. The exact same spot her son had gone to.

Her son. Her beautiful, charming son, she'd lost to this cruel life.

Her husband. Her darling, kind and generous husband, she'd lost to the elements.

Her father. The father she'd never known. Lost to the bomb.

There'd been woes, there'd been mistakes, there'd been hardships. But now she was old. She was wise. She knew what to do.

She pushed on. Feeling the burn inside. Nothing would stop her. Nothing could stop her.

People climbed mountains every day.

Some big, some small.

But they all got up, and there were those who never gave up. And then there were those who did . . .

Ayako pushed these thoughts from her mind, and focused on the boy.

She knew exactly what she was going to say to him when she found him.

She was going to tell him she loved him. She was going to tell him she was proud of him.

And she would go on to tell him everything he wanted to know about his father. About how much she'd loved him, too. And how proud she'd been of him. And about how cruel life can be, in taking the things from us that we love so dearly. But that it was no one's fault.

Life was tough, sometimes.

But the most important thing she wanted to tell her grandson was that his life was his own, to do with as he saw fit. That she would support him, she would love him, she would be proud of him, no matter what choices he made.

She would be his safety rope.

She could help him with the climb.

Her breathing was faster than normal. She pushed herself harder, chasing him up the mountain. She was almost running now, gasping for breath, panting.

And then he came into view, seated on top of the large boulder. She saw him clearly now. In one hand, he had a pen, drawing in a sketchbook on his lap.

His other hand stroked a black cat.

Ayako readied herself. What was this feeling, tugging at her, making it harder for her to go towards him? She felt a heaviness in her limbs; she was exhausted. Her muscles ached. She could see the boy, and her darling beloved Coltrane, but her body would not move fast enough. She couldn't move her legs any more.

Faster. She wanted to go faster.

*

She made herself a small goal. Steadied herself, and the soft, steady sound of words echoed in her head.

Get to that lamppost. Get to that lamppost.

You can do it. You can make it. Just a little further.

Keep going.

You can do it.

Translator's Afterword

The first time I meet Hibiki is at his house in Onomichi. His lifelong partner, Henrik, is there to welcome me, as well as their faithful one-eyed black cat, Coltrane. 'This house was my mother's,' Hibiki tells me as I follow him inside, slipping my shoes off at the entrance-way. 'She left it to me in her will.' Hibiki and Henrik spent most of their adult lives abroad in Scandinavia, but relocated to Onomichi when Hibiki's mother fell seriously ill. They threw themselves into doing up the old house, and now provide renovation services for other households in the town – fusing traditional Japanese carpentry with Scandinavian methods in an effort to revitalize the town's ageing properties.

The house is clean and well loved. Vinyl records, books and CDs fill a wall in the sitting room, all nestling neatly on a series of distinctive interlocking bookshelves. Henrik brings us coffee in a French press before retiring to another room. Classical music plays at low volume on a turntable, and I ask Hibiki questions while he strokes Coltrane pensively. It's snowing outside, and from the living room, we can see a beautifully tended Japanese garden, with a maple tree, bare branches covered in snow, next to an old pond. For the first time in months – it's been a long and difficult year – I feel something release inside me, like a muscle finally relaxing. Around Hibiki, I feel at peace.

Hibiki is an elderly man – well dressed in a collared shirt, blazer and slacks, with a shock of white hair and a neatly trimmed white beard. He has a deep, infectious laugh. His demeanour brings to mind the character of Sato from his book, and when I point this out, he chuckles and smiles, saying, 'Oh, so you noticed that, did you?'

He is polite and humble. He tells me he never expected *Sound of Water* to be read in Japan, let alone translated into English. Early on in our conversation, he remarks that he is still slightly confused as to why I want to translate his work.

This is what strikes me most about our conversation: he never wants to talk about the novel he has written, nor about the translation I have made. Naturally, I came prepared to ask and answer questions about the novel. There is a side of me that is extremely nervous – I need his permission for publication, and I'm certain he'll ask me a question about a difficult word or sentence which will stump me, and show my ignorance, my incompetence. But instead I get the impression he hasn't even read the sections I sent. He has somehow flipped the interview, and it's Hibiki who's asking questions about me – he seems genuinely interested in my life. 'What made you want to become a translator?' 'What made you want to learn Japanese?' 'How do you find living in Japan?' 'What originally brought you to the country?' 'Do you find it difficult living abroad?' 'Was it always your dream to translate fiction?' He fires off question after question, all the while stroking Coltrane and sipping at his coffee, nodding thoughtfully at my hesitant responses. Strangely, I find his inquisitive presence calming, and my nervous and stumbling Japanese begins to relax and become fluid again.

He tells me about leaving Japan: 'I spent most of my adult life abroad, mostly because I never felt like I belonged here in the first place. It was hard growing up in rural Japan as a gay man. My father wanted me to become a doctor, but I was always more drawn towards art, and design. In an ideal world I would've become a manga artist, but my father would never have allowed it.'

'So you drew manga? Like Kyo?'

He laughs. 'I was never as good as him. I suffered from the same problem: I struggled to finish whatever I started. My mother did her best to support my dreams, but it was hard for her. She fought with my father to allow me to go to design school in Tokyo – I suppose this was the beginning of my journey away from Japan and my father. I kept in touch with Mother by letter, but there's a side of me that feels extremely guilty for abandoning her.'

He takes a long sip of coffee before continuing.

'I never gave up on my desire to tell stories, though. Oh, how I wanted to make something! Anything! Something complete, something finished. But every time I worked I'd fall into a terrible panic about how much there was left to do – what other people would think of it – and become paralysed. My other career took off abroad, and it became harder and harder to produce any personal projects. Then Mother got sick, and I came back to Onomichi to be with her. I spent a lot of time by her bedside in the hospital, hoping and praying that she would recover. I'd long ago fallen out of practice with my illustrations at that point, but I began writing snippets of Kyo and Ayako's stories. I'd read them to her while she lay in bed. I wrote the stories for her, mainly. She'd always been a great reader, and found it difficult to concentrate on a book towards the end.'

Coltrane lets out a surprisingly loud meow, perhaps spotting something behind the window that's caught his interest. Hibiki gives him a good long scratch behind the ear.

'I never planned to publish, but Henrik pushed me to send the manuscript to an old school friend of mine who had worked for a large publisher in Tokyo. He'd retired back here and wanted to start a small press, Senkosha, mostly to keep himself busy, I think. *Sound of Water* was their first and only book. He sadly passed away recently.'

I ask him about the writing process, and how it felt to finally finish a novel, after years of dreaming of completing something. He answers, 'It's not about getting to the end – about completion. That's what I needed to learn. It's about the journey, the process itself. The cycle of work and art is like the seasons, flowing from one into another, round and round, over and over.'

We talk for what seems like hours, and it's only when Henrik re-enters the room that the conversation begins to come to an end. A familiar panic is starting to arise in me – I still technically haven't got his permission to translate the book. But as if he can read my thoughts, he speaks again.

'Please, Flo-san,' he says, 'by all means, translate the book into

English. You have my blessing. I myself have no interest in what happens to it, but I can see that it's important to you. That's what really matters – who am I to stand in the way of your dreams?'

I bow, and thank him profusely. We say our farewells, and just as he is about to leave the room, he pauses, as though something important has occurred to him. 'But if you do translate this book, Flo, you must promise me one thing.'

'What's that?'

'You must promise to make it your own.' He looks me straight in the eyes. 'Put something of yourself into it. So the readers get a sense of *you*.'

'I promise,' I say, bowing.

He turns to look at Coltrane, curled up on the floor of the tatami. His feet are twitching as he dreams. 'Oh, to be a cat,' he says. 'They dream, but they don't let their dreams consume them. That's the thing about humans – we feel like we have to make our dreams real. And that's what causes us such joy and discontent.'

▲▲

Translation is never an exact science. For those who see the glaring errors, the omissions, the awkwardness of language, these are entirely of my own doing, and I apologize for the loss of beauty that happened during the translation process. I do hope, however, that I have preserved the *spirit* of the original novel – that the characters of Kyo and Ayako live on as their true selves, in English.

I have made decisions in the text which I must explain here. By and large, I have not used italics for Japanese words, and have removed diacritics from the text. I have, however, italicized Ayako's beloved proverbs. A list of these with their kanji, short explanations and English equivalents is provided below. I have avoided the use of footnotes in order to preserve the fluency of the text. Instead, I've used the convention of defining Japanese words immediately after their occurrence in most places (e.g. umeshu plum wine). I trust this makes it easier for readers who are unfamiliar with Japan, while preserving a sense of the culture from which this story was born.

Names are listed as Japanese convention dictates: surname first, followed by first name (e.g. Tabata Ayako).

In spite of having met him in person, and spent even longer with his words and characters, I still know only a little about the author, Hibiki. He is an extremely private man and wishes to remain anonymous. He has refused any press interviews in tandem with the North American release of *Sound of Water*, has chosen to keep his identity secret, and certain names have been changed. I implore the reading public to respect his wishes. I myself can't help but pay thanks to him here, for allowing me to translate his words from Japanese into English. He also, very kindly, allowed me to write about our brief first encounter for this afterword, and following a few suggestions and revisions here and there to preserve his anonymity, he gave the go-ahead.

Thank you, Hibiki-sensei, Henrik and Coltrane. My fondest thanks also to: Kyoko, Makoto and Ogawa-sensei. And Lily, too, wherever you may be.

Flo Dunthorpe
Tokyo, 2023

Proverbs

gō ni haitte wa gō ni shitagae（郷に入っては郷に従え）
Literal translation: When entering the village, abide by the village
  rules.
English equivalent: When in Rome, do as the Romans do.

kaeru no ko wa kaeru（蛙の子は蛙）
Literal translation: The son of a frog is a frog.
English equivalents: Like father like son. A chip off the old block.

saru mo ki kara ochiru（猿も木から落ちる）
Literal translation: Even a monkey falls from a tree.
English equivalent: Even Homer sometimes nods (not so common).
  Essentially: Everyone makes mistakes.

yama ari tani ari（山あり谷あり）
Literal translation: There are mountains, there are valleys.
English equivalent: Life is full of ups and downs.

jūnin tōiro（十人十色）
Literal translation: Ten people, ten colours.
English equivalents: Everyone is different. Different strokes for
  different folks, etc.

bijin hakumei（美人薄命）
Literal translation: Beautiful person, short life.
English equivalent: Beauty is short lived.

kyakusama wa kamisama（客様は神様）
Literal translation: The customer is a god.
English equivalent: The customer is always right.

Acknowledgements

Eternal thanks: Bobby Mostyn-Owen, Ed Wilson, Hélène Butler, Anna Dawson, Tom Watson, Theresa Wang, Jacob Rollinson, Mike Allen, Hiroko Asago, Tamsin Shelton, Ryoko Matsuba.

All who supported my first book: David Mitchell, Rowan Hisayo Buchanan, David Peace, Elizabeth Macneal, Ashley Hickson-Lovence, Andrew Cowan, Amit Chaudhuri, Eleanor Wasserberg, Kirsty Doole, Gemma Davis, Sophie Walker, Carmen Balit, and all the talented translators who worked on the book.

All at Doubleday: Milly Reid, Hana Sparkes, Sara Roberts, Kate Samano.

Chie Izumi for the wonderful calligraphy.

Rohan Daniel Eason for the incredible illustrations.

Irene Martínez Costa for the beautiful cover.

Bradleys, Pachicos and Ashbys for always being there.

Rosie, Weasel & Julie, for the endless love and support.

Nick Bradley holds a PhD from UEA focussing on the figure of the cat in Japanese literature. He lived in Japan for many years, where he worked as a translator, and currently teaches on the Creative Writing master's programme at the University of Cambridge. His debut novel, *The Cat and The City*, was published in 2020.